W9-BFJ-611

DISCARD

03/02

CAPTAIN
SATURDAY

CAPTAIN
A NOVEL
SATURDAY

Robert Inman

LITTLE, BROWN AND COMPANY
Boston New York London

First Edition

The characters and events in this book are fictitious. Any similarity to real persons,
living or dead, is coincidental and not intended by the author.

Library of Congress Cataloging-in-Publication Data

Inman, Robert.
    Captain Saturday : a novel / Robert Inman.—1st ed.
        p. cm.
    ISBN 0-316-41502-2
        1. Television weathercasters—Fiction.   2. Cape Fear River Valley (N.C.)—Fiction.
    3. Raleigh (N.C.)—Fiction.   4. Midlife crisis—Fiction.   5. Unemployment—Fiction.
    I. Title.

PS3559.N449 C36 2001
813'.54— dc21   2001023529

10 9 8 7 6 5 4 3 2

Q-FF

Book design by Oksana Kushnir

Printed in the United States of America

FOR PAULETTE,

the girl I couldn't do without

The difference between the man who just cuts lawns
and a real gardener is in the touching. . . . The lawn cutter
might just as well not have been there at all. The gardener
will be there a lifetime.
　　　—Ray Bradbury, *Fahrenheit 451*

We shall never be content until each man makes his own
weather and keeps it to himself.
　　　—Jerome K. Jerome

BOOK
1

1 | WHEN WILL BAGGETT DROVE his automobile in Raleigh, North Carolina, a lot of people honked at him. Of course, the personalized licensed plate — ZATUWILL? — had a lot to do with it. Personalized licensed plates are popular in North Carolina, available for an extra twenty-five dollars if you're vain, cute, or just want to be recognized. In Will Baggett's case, it was the latter. Being recognized was part of Will's business. He was, arguably, the most recognizable man in Raleigh because he was Raleigh's most popular TV weatherman. Twice a night on Channel Seven, Will would tell you if it would rain or shine or anything in between, and do it with wit and charm. The folks who owned and ran Channel Seven were delighted with Will's recognizability and popularity. In fact, they reimbursed him the twenty-five dollars extra it cost for a personalized license plate. Will was good for business.

As Will left his home on LeGrand Avenue and drove through Raleigh early on a Friday afternoon in April, he got lots of honks and waves. It was a lovely spring day, the air clear and cleansed by a thunderstorm the night before, warm but not too warm in the embrace of a high pressure system that had established itself along the coast between Wilmington and Myrtle Beach. Other motorists had their windows rolled down, and they honked and called out to Will as they recognized his face or caught a glimpse of the license plate.

"Yo, Will! What's the weather?"

"Tune in tonight and see," he called back, his spirits buoyed by the lovely day and the good cheer of the good people of Raleigh who had made him their favorite TV weatherman. *Yo, Will! What's the weather?* It was a catchphrase in Raleigh, thanks to a series of promotional spots on Channel Seven in which local citizens were filmed leaning from car and house windows, poking their heads out of manholes, riding bicycles, standing on street corners—all of them calling out, "Yo, Will!"

It was impossible to escape Will Baggett in Raleigh, even if you were one of those odd people who never watched television. His face was on billboards and in newspaper ads and on brochures which Channel Seven distributed at the counters of a string of fast food restaurants throughout the city. There was a whole series of brochures—tips for saving on your utility bills in the winter, safety advice for tornado season, hurricane plotting charts, lawn care do's and don'ts—all of them written by Will from his own research and personal experience. He had never been in a tornado, but as any Channel Seven viewer knew, he enjoyed his lawn almost as much as he enjoyed doing the weather on TV.

Will's face was everywhere, and so was his voice. Just now, on the radio in his car, Will could hear himself giving a brief forecast for the Triangle area. *Hey, it's Friday! Get your barbecue grill ready, because it's a glorious start to the weekend, folks. Saturday, clear and pleasant with a high of seventy-eight, just a hint of a breeze from the northwest. Now Saturday night and Sunday, that's a different story, but you won't know the whole picture unless you tune in tonight at six.*

Just about any time of the day or night, you could hear Will on the radio. He tape-recorded a morning drive-time forecast before he left Channel Seven each midnight, and he updated it from home in the late morning. If you listened to the radio, you would think Will Baggett worked all the time. And that was the idea: a man who loved his job and was always standing by to help you through your day.

Will encouraged his celebrity. He was thoroughly at home with it. He did a lot of ribbon-cutting and contest-judging and banquet-emceeing. He spoke to garden clubs about soil moisture content and to classes of schoolchildren about the dangers of lightning. He was on billboards and brochures and the radio, and he had the personalized license plate, and when people waved and called out, he considered it a payoff, evidence that they thought him a good fellow, and useful to boot.

The billboards were Channel Seven's idea, but the brochures and the around-the-clock radio forecast were Will's. It was all part of the packaging, and Will instinctively understood packaging as well as he understood weather. When you got down to it, the details of the weather were pretty routine stuff—pressure gradients on a map, temperatures and precipitation and computer models. What you had to do was personalize the weather: relate it to how people lived, whether they needed an umbrella or sunscreen; and make an unbreakable connection in their minds between the weather and the weatherman. Will Baggett *was* the weather in Raleigh. He told people, only half-jokingly, that he worked for God. If you didn't believe it, ask the minister who phoned and asked him to be sure they had good weather for the Vacation Bible School picnic.

Will's first stop on this spectacular April Friday afternoon was a police roadblock on a busy street not far from his LeGrand Avenue home. Will glanced at his watch and drummed his fingers on the steering wheel as his car crept along in a line toward a young officer who was checking driver's licenses. Will was wearing sunshades, but he took them off as he pulled up. The shiny silver name tag above the officer's shirt pocket said his name was Grimes.

"What's the problem?" Will asked.

"Routine license che . . ." He peered in the window. "Hey! I mean, yo, Will!"

"Hi, Officer Grimes. How are Raleigh's Finest today?"

Grimes turned to another officer who was a few feet away, handling the opposite lane. "Charlie, look. Will Baggett." The other officer turned, grinned, popped off a little salute. "Yo, Will!"

"Heard you speak at the Police Athletic League banquet last month," Grimes said.

"Enjoyed it. Great crowd. Good kids. Laughed at my jokes."

"And the way you stayed around for an hour after, signing autographs . . ."

"Part of the job," Will said.

"Say, could I get your autograph?"

"I'll do better than that." Will reached into the glove compartment for the stack of five-by-seven glossy photos he kept there. Traffic was backing up behind. Several cars to the rear, somebody honked his horn. "I been watching you since I was a kid," Officer Grimes said, ignoring the honk. "Grew up in Smithfield. Channel Seven was about all we watched. My granddaddy said the knob was rusted onto Channel Seven."

"What's your first name, Officer Grimes?"

"Cleo. That's short for Cleotus, not Cleopatra."

Will wrote across the bottom of the photograph, *To my friend Cleo Grimes. With admiration and warmest good wishes, Will Baggett.* He handed the photo out the window.

"Could I have one for my girlfriend?"

Will autographed another photo for one Samantha Dugan. *Thanks for watching!* He shook Officer Grimes's hand. "Cleo, you have a nice day. Tune in at six."

As he pulled away, it occurred to him that Cleo Grimes had never asked for his driver's license.

An hour later, Will peeked out from behind the stage curtain of the multipurpose room at an elementary school in the bedroom suburb of Cary. The floor was filled with a seething, chattering mass of children — wide-eyed kindergartners and first-graders cross-legged on the front row, sullen sixth-graders along the back wall, and everything in between. Teachers were scattered among the crowd, islands of adult battle fatigue in a sea of squirming arms, legs, tennis shoes, giggles, whines, near fistfights. The air was thick with the heat of massed bodies in the unair-conditioned April afternoon, and the aroma of meat loaf and cauliflower still lingered from lunch hour in the adjacent cafeteria.

The principal—a stout woman, gray hair gathered in a ponytail and tied with a bright red ribbon—beamed at the crowd from in front of the stage, seemingly oblivious to the chaos. "Children . . ." It took a minute or so for the disorder to quieten to a dull roar. "Children, we have a special treat this afternoon. Is there anyone here who watches television?"

Hands shot skyward, the noise level mushroomed. *The Simpsons! Barney!*

". . . and you all watch the local news . . ."

Naaaahhhh. Booorrrrring.

". . . well, a local television celebrity is here with us today. Let's give a big welcome to the Weather Wizard!"

Will entertained them for forty-five minutes, dressed in a long, black velvet cape and a tall, pointed hat decorated with glittering stars, half-moons and lightning bolts. He did magic tricks, enlisting volunteers to help and keeping up a running chatter with the audience. He made a stuffed rabbit appear and disappear with the tap of a wand and had the place in hysterics while he pulled several yards of silk scarf from a teacher's ear. And when he had them eating out of his hand, even the sixth-graders, he talked about the dangers of lightning, about scooting for home at the first rumble of thunder, about lying down in a ditch (never, ever under a tree) if you were caught in an open area when a storm hit. He told them about hunkering in a bathroom on the ground floor of your house in case there was a tornado warning. And he reminded them to drink plenty of water while they were playing outside during the hot summer months coming up. Finally, he told them to go home and share all they had learned with their parents and be sure and watch the news and weather on Channel Seven every evening without fail, especially tonight, because they would be the stars of the show. Charlie, the Channel Seven news photographer who had slipped in a side door midway through the performance and reeled off several minutes of videotape, would make sure of that.

*   *   *

There was a small crowd of parents and school staff waiting for him out front, and he chatted and signed autographs for several minutes before heading back to Raleigh and the Channel Seven studios on Wade Avenue. The Weather Wizard costume was stowed away in the trunk of the car until next Tuesday, when he would make another appearance.

He only did elementary schools. Junior high students had lost the last of their innocence and thought a guy dressed up in a goofy cape and hat and talking about lightning safety was geeky. And junior high teachers, he had once said to a group of them, should get combat pay.

Will had done the Weather Wizard bit just once at a junior high. The show had bombed and his son, Palmer, one of the seventh-graders, had thrown up midway through the performance. After it was over, the principal took Will to the school nurse's office where Palmer was scrunched in a tight, miserable ball on a cot, face against the wall. Will sat on the edge of the cot and put his hand on Palmer's thin shoulder. Palmer flinched and pulled away. "Son, are you okay?"

A muffled "No."

"Do you want me to stay with you until Mom gets here?"

"No."

He called home at midafternoon to check on Palmer's condition and Clarice, his wife, could barely contain her anger. "That was a terrible thing to do."

"What?"

"You embarrassed him."

"How? My costume?"

"Just being there. It's hard enough on Palmer, having a father who's on television every night."

"For God's sake, Clarice, it's what I do. Other kids have fathers who fix cars and sell stocks and drive trucks . . ."

"But they don't do it in *front* of everybody. You don't realize what you *do* to people, Wilbur." (She never called him Wilbur unless she was angry or sexually aroused.)

"Yes I do," he shot back. "I do it on purpose because it's part of my job."

"Well, don't do it to Palmer."

He had never done it to Palmer again. And even though Palmer was grown now and in medical school at Chapel Hill, Will still stayed away from junior high schools. But since the day he had embarrassed his son, he had performed for several thousand elementary school kids in the Raleigh area. They gazed upon him with wonder on their upturned faces, their mouths making small "o's" of dazzlement and fascination, warming him with a glow that lasted for a long time afterward. Kids, bless their hearts, loved the Weather Wizard. Channel Seven loved the Weather Wizard because all the kids went home and made sure their families watched Channel Seven. And Will Baggett loved being the Weather Wizard because he loved his job.

Will worked at his computer in the Weather Center, a spacious room just off the station's newsroom. Putting together a weathercast was part meteorology, part graphic design. Will was not a meteorologist, not in the academic sense of the word, but he had studied and taken correspondence courses and earned the Seal of Approval of the American Meteorological Association. The best thing he had going, though, was experience. Twenty years on the air in Raleigh, watching the peculiarities of the local weather, the way systems would sweep in from the Midwest and hit the mountains over by the Tennessee line and do strange things. Will didn't always agree with what the meteorologists at the Weather Service said. Usually, he was right.

"Yo, Wiz." Charlie the photographer. "Whatcha want from the school?"

"Forty-five seconds, one magic trick, a quick sound bite where I talk about scooting for home when you hear thunder. And lots of cutaways of the kids. Lots of kids and teachers."

"My kid's selling Girl Scout cookies," Charlie said.

"Sure." Will fished in his billfold for a ten and a five. "Whatever that'll buy. You pick 'em."

Charlie consulted an order form. "How about thin mints and the butter stuff?"

"Fine. When you get 'em, just put 'em out in the newsroom. Don't you dare bring 'em in here." Will patted his belly, which was beginning to strain against the waistband of his trousers these days. "Urban sprawl."

They were good kids, Charlie and the rest of them in the newsroom. Kids, he thought of them, because he was the oldest person there except for ancient Bettie Fink, the newsroom secretary, who—as one fellow conjectured—might have been on the receiving end of Marconi's first wireless transmission. They were bright, eager kids, the young reporters and photographers and editors and desk assistants, the ones who pushed the studio cameras and swept the floor, reminding Will of himself years ago in New Bern, hoping for the big break. When things were slow, they congregated around the Weather Center because Will was good about listening to what was going on in their lives—a news scoop, a child with homework problems, a bit of gossip, a dead battery.

"Kids doing okay?" Will asked.

Charlie made a face. "Little one's got a cold. Susan had to stay home with her again today."

"Lots of chicken soup."

"Thanks, Uncle Will."

Fifteen minutes before airtime, his weathercast prepared and firmly set in his mind, Will applied makeup—a bit of pancake stuff to cover even the merest hint of beard stubble, powder to cut down on glare, and a dash of eyebrow pencil. The station's makeup consultant had told him he had weak eyebrows.

He put on his tie, a nice burgundy silk with fleur-de-lis design, and the jacket to his navy pinstripe suit. At home, he had a closet full of nice ties and suits and dress shirts, bought over the years with the generous clothing allowance that was part of his compensation at Channel Seven. The station provided the services of a clothing consultant who numbered all of his suits, shirts, and ties and gave him a chart he used to coordinate them into ensembles. When he got ready for work each day, he selected one from each category — tie twenty-three, suit five, shirt fourteen. It was idiot-proof. And it was part of the packaging. If people thought you knew what you were doing when you got dressed, they would assume you knew what you were doing when you forecast the weather.

By 6:15, the Channel Seven newscast had proceeded through a drive-by shooting, a huge traffic tieup on the Beltline caused by a wrecked cattle truck (two rednecks and a State Trooper chasing cows while motorists howled from their cars), and a state senator from the mountains haranguing the legislature over Harry Potter books in school libraries (he was opposed), all delivered with good cheer by Jim and Binky, the news anchors.

"Wow, what a day, Will," Binky chortled.

"Put this one in your scrapbook, Binky."

"Gonna put in that swimming pool at your house this year?" Jim asked. Folks in the newsroom were well aware that Clarice had long wanted a swimming pool in the Baggett back yard, but that Will had been resisting.

"Yessir, this is the year," Will said. "Soon as I get it from Wal-Mart and blow it up."

Will moved from his chair at the long, curving anchor desk to the nearby weather set — to amazed studio visitors, only a large flat blue panel. In the control room, the director electronically wiped out all the blue and substituted the maps and graphics Will had prepared on his computer in the Weather Center an hour before. Will could see the composite picture — himself and the maps — on monitors just off-camera. Another piece of weather wizardry, he told the visitors.

High pressure down here along the coastline, just dawdling along, taking its sweet time. Give this guy credit for the terrific weather today, folks. High of seventy-seven, just missed it a degree, so gimme an "e" for effort, huh? You know about a high, right? Winds go clockwise, just like this. And what's down here in the Gulf? Water. And what's the high gonna start pumping up our way? Bingo. Enjoy your Saturday, because the combination of the higher humidity and this cold front slipping all the way down from up here . . . well, we've got the makings for thunderstorms Saturday night. Could be strong ones, too. Lightning, high wind, maybe even some hail. And speaking of lightning . . .

Roll the tape. Forty-five seconds of the Weather Wizard at the elementary school. One magic trick, then the sound clip. Lots of good cutaway shots of the little kids on the front row, eyes big, mouths going "o." And a final shot of the Wizard posing with the principal and teachers.

. . . and remember, you can pick up this handy brochure on lightning safety from any Burger Barn in the Raleigh area. Kids, make sure Mom and Dad get one.

Wind up with the five-day forecast.

Couple of days of wet weather. Then clearing by Tuesday and cooler temperatures, maybe even down in the low fifties at night. We'll update you at eleven. If I don't see you then, have a great weekend.

Jim: "Coming up . . . can you really trust tanning beds to be sanitary?"

Binky: "Stay tuned for an exclusive Channel Seven investigative report."

Will called home and got, as he expected, the answering machine. He didn't leave a message. He was faithful about calling home as soon as the early newscast was over, and if Clarice was there, he would go home for dinner. She rarely was anymore, not since her real estate business had really taken off. With newcomers pouring into the Raleigh area and her firm, Snively and Ellis, one of the hottest sellers in town, she was up and gone early and out late. They were, Will sometimes thought, like ships passing in the night.

He grabbed a hamburger, fries, and chocolate shake—at Burger Barn, of course, where he autographed Lightning Safety brochures for several of the customers while he waited for his order. And then he went to the mall.

He had started doing the mall thing in the mid-eighties, five years after he joined the staff at Channel Seven. When the Nielsen rating service sampled Raleigh's viewing habits one November, it found that Channel Seven's popularity had taken a rather sharp and unexplained dip. Old Man Simpson, who owned Channel Seven, called the staff together and issued a call to arms. "We've got to go out and meet the folks," he said. "We've got to prove that we're real people. Their neighbors and friends."

The staff was galvanized to action. They loved Old Man Simpson, who was generous and fatherly. And they loved their jobs, which seemed a little precarious. The on-air personalities assaulted Raleigh with eager, outstretched hands and smiling faces. The station sponsored a contest: win a dinner with Hal and Hollee, then the news anchors. Promotional announcements showed Howard, the sportscaster, playing church softball. Will started working the malls during the evenings between shows, shaking hands and chatting up the shoppers. He spoke to civic and garden clubs and appeared at church picnics and Little League games.

Within months, Channel Seven was again Raleigh's most-watched station and had remained so ever since. A grateful Old Man Simpson told the staff, "You did it. You went out there and invited 'em in. Whatever you've been doing, keep doing it." The station adopted a new advertising and promotional slogan: "Your Friend Seven." Even the switchboard operator used it.

Since then, Hal and Hollee had moved on to Boston and Portland respectively and Howard the sportscaster left to operate a fishing pier at Myrtle Beach. Will remained. He became a fixture—a durable, dependable guy who made even bad weather seem palatable. It was, as one newspaper reporter had written of Will in recent years, "like having your uncle Harry sit down at your kitchen table over a cup of coffee and tell you not to worry about the tornado bearing down on the house. Will Baggett can make wind chill seem downright friendly." Channel Seven's ratings had remained solid.

This evening, he stayed at Crabtree Valley Mall until closing time. He drew crowds. He signed autographs and posed for pictures. He met a family of seven from Creedmoor who had driven over for the evening to buy a new television set, a teacher who remembered the Weather Wizard's appearance at her school two years before, and a widow who told him he looked like her brother who had been lost at sea in World War Two.

Five minutes into the late evening newscast, Will delivered a thirty-second capsule of the weather from the remote camera in his Weather Center office. He had insisted on having something about the weather soon after the beginning of the late show. "What are the three things people want to know at eleven o'clock?" he asked the News Director. "They want to know if the world's gonna be there when they wake up in the morning. Is it gonna rain? And did the Braves win? Not necessarily in that order." The News Director had balked at putting weather so high in the newscast. Old Man Simpson had settled the argument.

At 11:15 he did a complete weathercast.

Back in the newsroom he took a call from a man in Zebulon inviting him to speak to the Rotary Club in mid-May and accepted.

Then he drove home to his house on LeGrand, dark and quiet except for the gurgling of the fountain in the back yard. Clarice, as usual, was asleep. "If you think I'm going to stay up 'til you get home every night," she had said early on in their marriage, "you've got another think coming." She was bright, vivacious, sexy, witty in the mornings. But after eleven o'clock at night, she slept pro-foundly. From almost the beginning, he had worked the night shift—leaving the house in the early afternoon and returning after midnight—and she had never once, to his knowledge, awakened when he came to bed.

"You could have a woman somewhere," she had once said.

"But I cling only to you, my love."

"Not in the middle of the night, you don't."

"I do, but you just don't know it."

He sat now on the rear deck, unwinding from the day, thinking of all he had done and been since he had arisen at eight o'clock this morning, all the hats he had worn—weatherman, wizard, Channel Seven ambassador to the community at large, civic servant. He worked hard at it, and the people he worked for appreciated him and rewarded him handsomely.

He just wished Clarice thought more of it.

At the beginning, when they were first married and he was working at a small station in New Bern, he took her with him one evening and showed her the cubbyhole where he prepared his weathercasts. She pulled up a chair and watched while he read the Associated Press wire and roughed out his maps with pencil. "Why all those warm fronts and stuff?" she asked, peering over his shoulder. "Just tell me if it's going to rain or not." He tried to explain that folks at home wanted more. It was a show, a performance. "Smoke and mirrors," she said. Well, yes.

"Why," she had asked him once several years later, "do you keep talking about the Youpee of Michigan. Is it an Indian tribe?"

"No. It's the Upper Peninsula. U.P." He showed her on a map how Michigan was divided by Lakes Michigan and Huron, with Sault Sainte Marie stuck off up there by itself.

"Well, why would anybody in Raleigh, North Carolina, be the least interested in what happens on the Youpee of Michigan?"

"Because," he explained, "sometimes the weather that happens up there today comes here tomorrow. Especially in the winter, when you have these polar air masses . . ." His voice trailed off. He might as well have been speaking in Farsi.

These days, since she was up to her eyeballs in the real estate business, she rarely watched television at all. She usually got home after the early newscast was over and was asleep by the time the late news came on. She listened to the radio in the morning for the forecast.

"TV news," she said with a pained look. "You just scare people with all those stories about murders and convenience store holdups. It's not good for the real estate business. One of our agents was in Tillery the other day, and a man actually asked him if it's safe to go to Raleigh."

"But I don't do stories about murders and robberies. I do the weather."

"Then they should let you do the weather first so people who don't want to watch all that other mess can turn it off."

"I can't argue with that."

But then, she hadn't said anything about the TV news or the TV weather for a good while now. She was busy with her own thing. She was happy and productive. Their relationship had changed, sure, but maybe even for the better. They remained ardent lovers. There was still a lot of the old, good stuff left — probably as much as you could count on having in any marriage of twenty-five years.

The rest of it — well, it was pretty close to perfect. He sat in the quiet of his back yard on this soft April night and let the pretty-close-to-perfectness of it envelop him like cashmere. He was a mighty lucky man. A lot of people thought well of him. He had a job and a life that made him vibrate like the finely tuned strings of a bass fiddle, deep and resonant, in harmony with the world.

As he rose finally and headed for bed, he thought to himself, *I can't believe they pay me to do this.*

2 | CLARICE WAS AWAY EARLY on Saturday morning, on duty for the day at a model home in one of the new subdivisions that were mushrooming across the fringes of Raleigh and spilling like lava flow into the adjacent counties. New people moving in all the time

for jobs at Research Triangle Park, people who had sold homes in places like White Plains and Kansas City and had a pocketful of money they needed to plunk down on something new. They clogged the roads and the schools and the shopping centers, hundreds of arrivals every month. The audience, Channel Seven's consultants told them, was turning over constantly. Always somebody new to woo and win. Rest on your laurels, and all of a sudden you're yesterday's story.

But Channel Seven was far from Will's mind this Saturday morning. It was, if anything, even more spectacular than yesterday—temperature in the low seventies and not a cloud in the sky as he rolled his Honda mower out of the garage, dressed in jeans, T-shirt, jogging shoes, and his favorite baseball cap, the one with CAPTAIN SATURDAY lettered across the front.

"Yo, Will!" Chuck Durkin, his neighbor, washing his Blazer in the driveway next door, the fine spray from his hose dancing in the early sun. Chuck looked skyward. "Gonna rain?"

"Yeah, and it'll be your fault."

"How's that?"

"Washing your car."

Chuck laughed. He was a nice fellow, a chubby redhead who had a computer job at Glaxo-Wellcome, the big pharmaceutical firm in Research Triangle Park. When Palmer was in the fifth grade, Will had bought him a computer and Chuck had helped set it up. His wife, Phyllis, had been, at one time, the unofficial neighborhood social chairman. When Palmer and the Durkin kids were small, she organized playgroups and sidewalk picnics and Fourth of July parades. She and Clarice had been the instigators of a book club that made a quite extensive study of southern fiction. But that was all in the past. The kids were grown. The Durkins and the Baggetts were old-timers on LeGrand, which was being repopulated these days by younger families. Phyllis Durkin had found religion and was busy teaching Bible study courses. And Clarice, of course, was up to her ears in real estate. Years past, they had gotten together for dinner at one house or the other every few months. Will had arranged for

Chuck's Boy Scout troop to tour Channel Seven and sit awestruck in a corner of the studio during the six o'clock newscast. Palmer was a member of the troop, but he didn't make the trip. Clarice said he had an upset stomach that night. It had been, God, how many years ago?

"How's Rex?" he asked.

"Did Clarice tell you the big news? He got engaged last week." Rex was a year older than Palmer, graduated a couple of years before from North Carolina State with an engineering degree.

"Hadn't heard, Chuck. That's great. Local girl?"

"He met her in Guatemala while he was down there on business. Good family. They're in palm oil or something like that."

"Dang, Chuck. You'll be a granddaddy before you know it."

Chuck fingered his thinning hair. "Already look like it. And look at you, Will. Still pouring on that Grecian Formula."

"Nah, just good genes."

"Come on."

"I swear. Listen, tell Rex I said congratulations. Can't wait to meet her."

"Palmer doing okay?" Chuck asked.

"Up to his fanny in alligators, so he says. We don't see much of him. Hoped he'd be home this weekend, but he called last night and said he's studying for an exam."

"Yeah, but one of these days he'll be a rich doc and he can keep you in the style to which you'd like to become accustomed."

"Maybe."

"Or maybe you'll just stay over there and do the weather until they carry you out of Channel Seven feet first."

"That sounds more like it."

Will reached for the starter cord of the Honda and gave it a vigorous pull. It caught on the first try and settled into a smooth, deep-throated hum as he eased the control from Choke to Run.

"Really like your new anchor gal," Chuck called out over the engine noise.

"Binky? Yeah, we think she's gonna work out okay. Came from Toledo."

"She does a good . . . presentation."

Like most people, Chuck Durkin didn't know exactly why he liked or didn't like somebody on television. There might be something obviously negative, like a mannerism or a hairdo or jewelry that called attention to itself. (Viewers tended to be harder on female personalities than male, maybe because women watched TV more than men.) But the positives seemed mostly intangible and undefinable. You either liked somebody on TV or you didn't. Binky didn't wear oversized jewelry or have irritating mannerisms or a goofy hairdo. As Chuck said, she did a good presentation. Binky would stay in Raleigh for three or four years and then be off to a big-market job in Boston or Cleveland or maybe even something with a network. And Will Baggett would stay right here in Raleigh because he had found his niche and he was in a groove and things were pretty darn right with his world.

He gave Chuck a wave and turned the Honda toward the lawn.

————

WILL BAGGETT WAS NOT a gardener. A gardener planted things, fussed over what he planted, dug it up and replanted, and engaged in endless conversation with other gardeners over the relative merits of various perennials and ground covers. That didn't interest Will. A garden was blooming chaos. Give him a little green shrubbery and a healthy stand of fescue grass any day — things that could be mowed and clipped and then left alone until they needed mowing or clipping again. A well-tended lawn said that nice people lived there, the kind of people who voted, paid taxes, went to PTA meetings, recycled. And a TV weatherman who tended his lawn must be a regular kind of guy, right? The kind you'd invite into your home every night.

Every so often, Clarice would bring up the idea of hiring a lawn service. There seemed to be hundreds of them in Raleigh, rumbling across town in their pickup trucks, towing trailers loaded with power equipment: huge mowers, trimmers, edgers, leaf blowers. They would guarantee a well-manicured lawn—neatly mowed and edged, fertilized and aerated. No muss, no fuss. Many of Will's neighbors, including Chuck Durkin, employed lawn services. Will resisted. Clarice called him mule-headed. She and Palmer had presented him one Father's Day with the CAPTAIN SATURDAY baseball cap. He had laughed about the cap. They hadn't. But that had been years ago, when Palmer was still at home and Clarice wasn't off selling real estate night and day. Nowadays, he could be Captain Saturday without feeling guilty about it.

Will liked the muss and fuss that went with a well-tended lawn—grass neatly clipped, the shrubbery marching in a soldierly row across the front of the house. The work produced immediate, visible results—even more so than doing the weather on television. The weather changed by the millisecond. Mow a lawn and, by God, it stayed mowed. For a few days, anyway.

It was also something of an escape. It wasn't like woodworking, where you had to pay close attention or you'd cut your fingers off. Just follow the self-propelled mower, remember to turn around at the other end of the lawn. And don't get the cord caught in the electric hedge clipper. You could let your mind wander across the other things in your life, or you could just let it idle. And after a hectic week of dashing about, being Raleigh's most popular TV weatherman, you could use some idling.

Not that he was complaining. It was, hands down, Raleigh's best job. He made a fine salary and provided well for Clarice and Palmer. They had a nice house and drove nice cars and had a little stashed away for emergencies. There were intangibles, too—the hundreds of perks, large and small, that went with being recognized and thought well of. The woman behind the meat counter at Winn-Dixie made sure you got a choice cut she'd been saving for a special customer. The guy at the Amoco station dashed out to clean your windshield, even though you were filling up at the self-serve pump. People wrote nice letters and stopped you on the street and complimented your work, even if they complained good-naturedly about bad weather. All in all, it made a fellow feel like he was okay. As long as he worked hard at it and kept the customers coming, he could keep all that for as long as he wanted—until, as Chuck Durkin said, they carried him out feet first.

————

HE WAS SITTING on the back deck about five-thirty, sipping a scotch and water, when he heard Clarice's car pull into the driveway out front. After a moment she appeared at the back door, opened it, peered out. "Salud," he said, raising his glass. "Fix you a drink?"

"Stiff." She was wearing black slacks and a red blouse, a strong, rich color, almost burgundy. Despite a long day at the real estate wars, she looked smashing—trim, long of leg, hair the shade of honey framing her angular face. The color was high in her cheekbones.

"How was your day?"

"Great. Just fine."

"Tell me."

"Five minutes," she said, and disappeared back into the house. By the time she returned he had her vodka tonic ready. "Ummmm," she said, taking a long sip and then leaning back in the lounge chair, stretching her legs, cradling the drink in both hands.

"Well?"

"What?"

"Your day."

"Greylyn. New development out Six Forks Road. Past where they're building the Outerbelt."

North Raleigh. A creeping sprawl of subdivisions, apartment complexes, shopping centers, parking lots, and four-lane roads where there had been, not too many years ago, pine and hardwood forest. North Raleigh just kept oozing north, devouring land. The state was building a new circumferential highway out on what had been the fringes of the city. By the time it was finished, the fringes would have long since moved on. North Raleigh, Will had joked on the air not long ago, might someday take in the state of Virginia.

"Nice? The development?"

"Four hundred thousand and up. Golf course, water, clubhouse. The place was run over with people today. We could have sold the model a couple of times."

"Why didn't you?"

"Because it's a model. People want to see what a four-hundred-thousand-dollar home in Greylyn looks like. A month from now, after most of the lots are sold and several homes are up, we'll sell the model."

"And what happens after Greylyn is sold out?"

"Fincher's negotiating to get us an exclusive on a two-hundred-acre development about five miles on past."

That would be Fincher Snively, co-owner of Snively and Ellis, which had grown from a two-man boutique realty firm into one of Raleigh's largest. They had actively courted Clarice a year ago, hiring her away from the small firm where she had gotten her start. Already, she was Snively and Ellis's second-best producer. Only Fincher sold more. He was a man of abundant energy and almost-too-good-to-be-true cheerfulness. *Will! Damn good to see you, buddy!* Will thought he wore too much cologne.

"I can't imagine why people want to live so far out," Will said.

"A lot of them come from places where they've had to commute an hour to work each way. Or more. They're used to it. Not everybody has to live right in the middle of town."

"It's good for the real estate business that they don't," he said.

It was a sore point, and he was careful. They had been in the house here on LeGrand since they moved to Raleigh twenty years before. They had loved the location—a tree-lined street of older, mostly two-story homes not far from the Channel Seven studios. It was inside the Beltline, the perimeter road that was then taking shape around the city. Will loved LeGrand, and especially his particular house on LeGrand, because it looked like it had some history and some permanence to it. It was a solid, well-built house with real plaster walls and a slate roof on a quiet street of well-kept houses and lawns and people who were neighborly but not intrusive. LeGrand was Old Raleigh—not the oldest, but old enough. And that's what he wanted to be: Old Raleigh. So essentially connected to the heart and soul of the place that people thought of him as a fixture. Old Raleigh people stayed put. They weren't likely to move off to Poughkeepsie or Houston next week. Once you wooed and won Old Raleigh people, they stayed won. They were the core of his audience.

They had been in the house for about ten years when Clarice began to speak wistfully of something newer, with more closet space and a real den and a modern kitchen and a central vacuum system and maybe a back-yard pool. A couple of times, it had gotten to the point of heated argument. Will dug in his heels. It wasn't just the matter of being ten minutes from Channel Seven. It was the house itself. He could not imagine giving it up. It was Clarice who eventually surrendered. She resigned herself to LeGrand and began to do some refurbishing, using the generous checks that her parents, the Greensboro Palmers, sent each Christmas. She started with paint, wallpaper and curtains and moved on to ripping up carpet and refinishing the hardwood floors underneath. And then four years ago, just after Palmer had started college at Duke, she had sprung the big one on him.

They were in bed on a Sunday afternoon following an especially vigorous hour of sex. She rose, naked and magnificent, and went to the closet, wiggling her butt at him. *My God, what a woman—passionate, uninhibited, multiorgasmic. I am blessed among men.* She came back to bed with a cardboard box from which she withdrew architectural drawings, contractors' estimates, even samples of tile for the bathroom and paneling for the den. Will was taken aback. She had assembled it in meticulous detail, all quite without a hint to him. She went through the plans, showing him how the addition would be tied into the present structure, how the plumbing and electricity and heating and air-conditioning would be upgraded, how the den would be arranged with a sweeping curve of leather sofas and armchairs that would give them a simultaneous view of both the new fireplace and a massive entertainment center flanked by bookcases. Upstairs, the bath would be almost as big as the adjacent bedroom, complete with bidet and separate potty room. And a two-person Jacuzzi.

Will kept quiet while she flipped through the pages until she reached the last. His eyes went to the bottom: GRAND TOTAL: $87,265.94.

"Holy shit," he said softly. "I mean, gee."

"It's very reasonable," Clarice said. "I got multiple estimates on everything." She tapped the page. "These are the low bidders."

"It's almost as much as we paid for the house," Will said.

"That was sixteen years ago, Will. With all of the improvements we've made, the house is worth triple that. At least."

Will stared. He shook his head. "Eighty-seven thousand dollars? We can't afford that, honey. And if you're thinking . . ."

"No," she said firmly, "I'm not. I know how you are about that. You know, Will, I wish you'd just be honest and say you don't like my parents."

He could feel a nibbling at the back of his skull, an old familiar thing. He sighed. "Clarice, let's don't go through this again. I don't dislike your parents."

"You think they're snobs."

"I just," he said, trying to keep his voice from rising, "want to take care of my own family. I can. I do. That's important to me."

"You've never turned down one of their Christmas checks . . ."

"I think they're great, honey. And you've used the money just the way you wanted."

". . . or them paying Palmer's tuition."

"Duke? Med school? It would have strapped us."

"But you get this *look*, Will."

"I'm sorry. I'll try not to get any more looks."

She turned away from him. He picked up the papers and looked through them again—the architect's plans, the detailed description of materials, the estimate sheet. He studied the row of figures tumbling down the page like a snowball, gathering size and momentum until they came to a crashing stop at the final verdict. But then, it wasn't really final, was it. "Honey, where does it say 'Furniture'?"

She didn't answer. She was studying something on the wall, somewhere between the closet and the bathroom door.

"How much?"

"Another twenty-five. Or so."

"Thousand."

She nodded.

"It's really a great idea," he said gently. "You've done a terrific job. But it's . . . we just can't do it. Not now. Maybe later. Let's think it through. We'll start saving. Maybe after I sign a new contract . . ."

Clarice turned back to him then and looked at him for a long moment and he could see the muscles along her temples tightening. "I'm not going to argue with you. I never get anywhere arguing. You're too glib for me." She took the set of plans from him, rolled them up, climbed out of bed and stood there, her magnificent breasts, still lusciously firm at forty-four, rising and falling as she took deep breaths, clutching the plans like a family heirloom she had just saved from a fire. "You're on an entirely different wavelength, Will."

"What do you mean?"

"Did you hear what you just said? 'Let's think it through.' *Think.* That's the problem, Will. I tell you how I *feel* and you tell me what you *think.*"

"Well, what am I supposed to do?"

"Sometimes, you're supposed to do things simply because you *feel* something."

"Maybe," he offered, "you could feel something a little less expensive. Say, a bay window?"

"I don't want a bay window. I want this. I *feel* this. I feel *strongly* about this."

"Clarice, you're really an incredibly handsome woman."

"Don't *do* that."

"Please . . . come back to bed. Let's talk about this later."

"No." She glared at him for a while longer and then she said, quite calmly, "I'm getting a job."

"You're what?" He regretted immediately the way it sounded, so patently incredulous. But the notion of Clarice with a job just didn't compute. She had a degree in elementary education, and she had taught for a year in New Bern when they were first married, but once Palmer had come along she had stayed home. It was what they both wanted. They scraped by at first, and then they moved to Raleigh and the paychecks from Channel Seven kept getting larger and he was able to support them comfortably. Now, here she was in middle age, with no work experience to speak of, contemplating the job market. And what? Some menial clerk's position, selling greeting cards from behind the counter at a gift shop? He felt chauvinistically disloyal for even thinking it. It wasn't that Clarice wasn't capable. She was smart and clever, even if she was a bit disorganized. But there were plenty of smart, clever women who didn't really know how to do anything practical.

Clarice read him. "You think I can't."

"It's just that . . . you haven't."

"Well, I am. I've enrolled in a real estate course. I'm going to get my license and sell real estate."

Will was dumbfounded — both at what she had decided and what she had done about it, quietly and entirely on her own. It was the first time in their marriage she had done anything so momentous without a word to him. Of course, she had never done anything remotely resembling momentous before, not since the very first when she had chosen him and married him despite everything.

"Real estate is hard work, Clarice. Long hours, odd hours . . ."

"Oh." She made a wry face. "I know all about odd hours."

"Yeah, I guess you do. Look, honey, this happens to a lot of women. The kids grow up, the nest is empty, you have a lot of time on your hands . . ."

"What do you know about women, Will? I mean, really?"

Will smiled. "My experience is limited to one."

She didn't return the smile. "Men work, retire and die," she said. "I read the other day in the *News and Observer* that there are a hundred and eighty-five thousand widows in North Carolina."

"I don't believe widowhood is an imminent danger for you," he said drily. "And I don't believe you've given this business of real estate enough thought," he added, trying to move things back on track. "Is it you? I mean, if you want to try something new, why don't you think about . . ." he searched . . . "law school. Did you read the story in the paper about the woman judge in Charlotte? She got into law school at Chapel Hill after her kids got grown, practiced for a couple of years, and then won a district court judge-ship. The paper said she's pretty darn good at it."

He tried to imagine Clarice as a judge. She had the kind of no-nonsense manner that would keep good order in a courtroom. She would look smashing in black.

Clarice started to say something, held back, then started gather-ing all of her plans and estimates and tile and paneling samples and stashing them neatly back in the cardboard box. She placed the lid on the box and looked up at him. "I'm not going to debate this with you, Wilbur. I've made up my mind. I'm going to sell real estate. I'm going to sell enough to pay for the addition on the house. I'm going to do it exactly the way I want. And when that's done, I may sell enough to pay for a swimming pool."

"Well," he said, "you don't have to get mad about it."

"I'm not mad. I'm just determined."

And, he thought, as they sat here on the deck on this lovely April Saturday evening, sipping their scotch and vodka, that she had been impressively successful at it. She had her own checking and savings accounts, into which she put everything she made from the real estate business. He insisted on that. What she did with the money was her business. And he imagined that she was well on the way toward her goal of enough money to remake the house in exactly the way she wanted. They had not talked about the project for a good while. And Will wasn't about to tread again into that mine-field, not right now. She would reveal things in her own good time. And he would be happy for her.

So instead he said, "Let's go out."

"Dinner?"

"Sure. We'll celebrate."

"What?"

"Oh, I don't know. A successful day at Greylyn. A successful day in the yard. Your good health and ravishing beauty. My good health and . . . well, my health. Calvin Coolidge's birthday."

She sipped on her drink for a moment and looked at him over the top of the glass. "Yes," she said finally. "I'd like that a lot."

———

THE RESTAURANT WAS in the City Market area downtown, a couple of blocks from the state capitol—an old farmers' market that had been saved from demolition and brought back to life with shops and eating establishments. This particular one was a favorite watering hole for lobbyists who wanted to ply state officials, legislators, and hangers-on with food and drink while they conducted business in a manner so subtle and convivial that it seemed to transpire without transpiring at all. Will spoke briefly to several he knew, introducing Clarice and pausing for just a moment as they made their way to the quiet table in the rear that the manager had reserved for them. *Ah, Will. We're pretty full up tonight, but for you . . .*

They had another round of drinks. Will felt the warm glow of scotch, good talk. Clarice was animated, luminous in the soft light from the small brass-and-mahogany lamp set to one side of the table. She told a funny story about a new agent at Snively and Ellis who kept setting off burglar alarms at the houses she showed. He reached for her hand across the table. "I love you," he said. "I'm very proud of you."

"Yo, Will! What's the weather?" It startled them both. An elderly man, leaning precariously on a cane, was bearing down on their table. He had a raspy, cackling laugh. "Bet you don't get many people asking you that, huh?" He stopped abruptly, just in the nick of time. Another step and he would have toppled onto the table. He stood there swaying back and forth, then stuck out a trembling hand. Will took it.

"Will Baggett," Will said.

"Oh hell yeah, I know who you are."

"And you are . . ."

"Gordon Flxmstrmmblz . . ." The last name collapsed into mush.

"My wife. Clarice."

Gordon Flxmstrmmblz never even looked at her. Instead, he reached behind him and grabbed a chair from another table and, with surprising agility, scooted it up next to Will and Clarice's table and collapsed into it. "Got this problem," he said.

"Mister, ah . . ."

"Just call me Gordon. Last name's a booger to pronounce. Anyhow, I got slugs in the garden. Nasty things. Hundreds of 'em."

"Well," Will said with a smile, "that's kinda out of my realm of expertise, Gordon. I can give you chapter and verse on cold fronts, but I'm not much on slugs."

The old man leaned across the table toward Will, tapping a bony finger on the linen. "The point is, the weather affects 'em. Or maybe it's the slugs affecting the weather."

From the corner of his eye, Will could tell they were attracting the attention of the other diners. Their waiter scurried over. "Ah, um . . . sir, I believe Mister and Mizzus Baggett . . ."

The old man waved him off and Will gave the waiter a wink. *Just give me a minute and I'll humor the old geezer.*

"You see, Baggett, when it's about to rain, these little bastards start appearing in droves. Like they *knew* it was gonna rain. Eat every damn thing in sight, then the rain comes and they wash down what they ate with rainwater. Cucumber vines, parsley, flowering plants, you name it. Then they"—he gave a flip of his hand—"just disappear."

Will laughed. "Stealth slugs, huh?"

"I'm retired, you know."

"That's nice, Gordon. Enjoying your retirement?"

"Thirty-seven years at the bank. Got a helluva retirement package—cash, stock, pension—and a little pissant party where all the young guys I taught the banking business to got up and lied about how much they'd miss me." He cackled, enjoying his joke on the younger guys. "Bought Mama"—he turned and pointed across the room to a table where a tiny white-haired woman gave them a little finger-roll wave—"bought Mama a house at Linville Falls. Spend about half our time up there, except when the snow's up to your ass. I like to have run Mama nuts the first few months until she got me to gardening. You see?"

Will put a conspiratorial hand on Gordon's arm. "I enjoy a day in the yard myself, Gordon."

"Then these goddamn slugs showed up."

Clarice stood abruptly, rising above them to her full five-eight. Will looked up at her. She was staring at him with a look of disbelief and horror. Not at Gordon, at him. She dropped her napkin on the table. "I want to go home, Will," she said. And she walked away.

Will caught up with her across the street where the car was parked. She was pulling furiously on the door handle. It was locked, but she kept pulling on it. She was crying.

"Clarice, I'm sorry."

He really was sorry. She looked so terribly wretched. He wanted to put his arms around her, but she was a world apart from him, shoulders hunched, pulling again and again on the door handle. He had tried hard over the years to shelter Clarice and Palmer from the limelight, to protect them from the curious, from the downside of celebrity status, so that they could lead normal lives, even if he couldn't. He hadn't been altogether successful in his sheltering, but he had tried. And now, just when they were having a great evening and things seemed to be as comfortable between them as they had been in a good while . . .

She turned on him. She looked gaunt in the harsh whiteness of the street lamps—much older, weary and despairing. Her mascara was running. Will reached for the handkerchief in his back pocket, offered it to her. She ignored it.

"Look, come on back in, honey. Our dinner will be there in a minute."

"You know," she sobbed, "I thought I was marrying Will

Baggett. Instead, I got the Weather Wizard. Do you ever just tell anybody to go fuck off?"

"Clarice, honey, don't you think you're overreacting?"

"You should see yourself, Will. You get this look like an overeager child trying to please. Or like you're hungry for something you can't ever get enough of."

"I just try to be nice to people," he said defensively.

"And what about me? When I'm with you, I'm just an appendage."

"No you're not."

"Unlock the car. I'm going home. You can stay here and talk about slugs all night if you want to."

He took her straightaway home in deadly silence. He stayed downstairs for a long time, letting her have the bedroom to herself. He called the restaurant and offered to pay the tab. The manager wouldn't hear of it. *So sorry we let that guy disrupt your dinner, Will. Come back as our guest.* When he finally went upstairs and slipped into bed beside her and put a gentle hand on her shoulder, she was like concrete. "I'm sorry," he said again. She shivered. But that was all.

3 | HE WAS PUTTERING ABOUT the house at midmorning on Monday when the phone rang. Gretchen, Old Man Simpson's secretary. Could he come in early? Mr. Simpson wanted to see him. Will volunteered that he was available for lunch. No, Mr. Simpson already had lunch plans. Would one o'clock be okay? Fine.

It would be about his contract, of course. He thought about it as he showered and dressed. Old Man Simpson had been away from Channel Seven for two months. Back surgery to correct an old disk problem, he had told the staff before he left, and then some time in the Bahamas to recuperate. In the meantime, Will's contract had run out.

It was no big deal. It had been a fairly casual matter between them from the beginning. Old Man Simpson would call Will to his office, say kind things about his work and his value to Channel Seven and offer him a contract for another three years with a nice boost in his salary. Will would occasionally propose a perk or two— a clothing allowance, an increase in the Weather Center budget for a new piece of equipment—and Old Man Simpson would usually agree. The contract would be drawn up and they would go to lunch and Will would sign it. He never even had Morris deLesseps, his lawyer, look over the documents. Old Man Simpson treated him splendidly, and there was no sense in getting lawyers involved in what was a relationship of mutual respect and trust. Channel Seven needed Will Baggett. Will Baggett loved his work. What was there to quibble about? He damn sure wasn't going anywhere else.

———

OLD MAN SIMPSON OCCUPIED a corner of the second floor of the Channel Seven studio building. There was an outer office and reception area where Gretchen presided, one wall of which was occupied by a huge glass-enclosed case filled with plaques, citations and other memorabilia attesting to Channel Seven's service to the community and its civic causes, ranging from the Telephone Pioneers to the Association of Fishing Lure Collectors. Will could take credit for a good number of them, including a trophy he had been awarded after being selected—for ten years in a row—as "Favorite TV Weathercaster" by *Best of Raleigh* magazine.

Will waited in the outer office, trying to make small talk with Gretchen and not having much success. She was normally chatty, but today she seemed distracted and out of sorts. She spilled paper clips, mumbled darkly to her computer, and failed to make the usual offer of a cup of coffee. So Will sat comfortably in a leather armchair, thumbing through the latest issue of *Broadcasting*. Gretchen's phone rang. She answered it, listened for a moment, hung up. "They're running a little late," she said. "Mister Simpson said you could wait in his office if you don't mind."

Simpson's inner sanctum was both spacious and intimate, paneled in dark walnut, furnished with burgundy leather and mahogany, the walls adorned with specially commissioned oil paintings: the state capitol building, the Channel Seven headquarters nestled in acres of azaleas and dogwoods in full blossom, the chapel on the Duke campus, the eighteenth hole at Pinehurst Number Two, and a portrait of Confederate-era governor Zebulon Baird Vance, a remotely connected ancestor of Old Man Simpson's wife. Simpson's immense antique desk was at one end of the room, a cozy sitting area at the other, and in the middle, a sweeping oval conference table. The painting of the studio building was the only hint that the room belonged to a television executive. There was no TV set in sight, though Will knew that one was hidden away in one of the cabinets that flanked the tall windows on the exterior wall. Instead, the room brought to mind what Will thought might be the atmosphere of a London gentleman's club, or at least the office of a college president. A room where gentlemen did business.

Will took a seat on the sofa. He smiled, remembering the time he had sat in this very spot twelve years before and made the decision to become a fixture in Raleigh.

It had started with a job offer at another station, the only one he ever seriously considered. The manager of a station in Buffalo, New York, called the Weather Center one evening and asked Will to send a videotape of his weathercast. A week later, the Buffalo man was back on the phone offering Will a job at a considerably higher salary than he was making in Raleigh. Will was both flattered and intrigued. Buffalo, New York — a much larger TV market with weather that was spectacular in its extremes.

Will put off the Buffalo station manager for a few days while he thought about it. He kept it to himself, beginning to imagine being on the air in Buffalo, shepherding the city through the grip of a blizzard the way he guided Raleigh through its infrequent but paralyzing snows and occasional tornadoes and hurricane-induced floods. Until now, he had never aspired to anything beyond Raleigh. But now, Buffalo. Not the big time, but close to it. And what beyond? Chicago or Los Angeles. CNN or the Weather Channel. And maybe more. *Jeopardy?*

He mulled it over for several days, leaning more and more toward taking the Buffalo job. Finally, he went to see Old Man Simpson, who listened intently while Will explained his situation. Then Old Man Simpson got up from his desk and sat down beside Will on the sofa. He put his hand on Will's knee in fatherly fashion.

"Will," he said, "there are three reasons why you're not going to Buffalo. Firstly, North Carolina is your home and you are not the kind of person who would do well in exile, even if it is self-imposed. Secondly, you are beholden to this city, and it to you. Raleigh folks decide right off the bat whether they like someone who appears on TV. If they don't like you right off, they won't ever like you. But if they *do* like you right off, they like you more the longer you stay. And they like you a good bit already. You are not the handsomest or wittiest weatherman on American TV, but you have a quality that transcends beauty and wit. People trust you because you are trustworthy. They depend on you because you are dependable. You have earned that, and it makes no sense to chuck it and run off to Buffalo."

Old Man Simpson sat back on the sofa and hiked one long leg over the other.

"And what's the third reason?" Will asked.

"I'm gonna double your pay."

He told Clarice the next morning as they drank coffee on the deck. "I got a job offer from Buffalo, New York."

Clarice stared at him for a good little while. It was impossible to tell what she was thinking. Finally she said, "I thought you had a girlfriend."

"What?"

"You've been acting strange. All week."

"I've been struggling with this thing."

"You've known for a week and you haven't said a word to me about Buffalo, New York?"

"Well, I turned them down," Will said. "We're not going to Buffalo."

"But what if I *wanted* to go to Buffalo?"

"Do you?" He doubted that. Clarice's family, the Greensboro Palmers, were a notoriously thick lot, three generations living perilously close to each other, all of them up to their eyeballs in each other's business. He thought they had never quite forgiven him for keeping Clarice in New Bern—190 miles to the east of Greensboro—for four years before he brought her to Raleigh, which was only 80 miles away.

"It doesn't matter," Clarice said. "The point is, you didn't tell me. You didn't ask me. You decided without me."

Will reached for her hand, but she wouldn't give it over. "Clarice, I'm sorry. I just didn't want to worry you with it. I didn't decide anything without you. It . . . well, it was kind of decided *for* me."

Then he told her about his salary.

"That's nice," she said, and got up and went into the house.

Will heard voices in the outer office and started toward the door as it opened. Then he stopped in his tracks as Old Man Simpson appeared in the doorway, leaning on a cane, bent and frail, face creased with lines that Will had never seen there before. Two months ago, he had been a robust specimen—lean, erect, immaculately groomed, a scratch golfer who played at least thirty-six holes every week regardless of the season. Now, he was aged and fragile. His clothes hung loosely on his shrunken frame. He looked unkempt—badly shaven, hair akimbo. Will stared, unable to speak. Old Man Simpson held out a hand and Will took it gingerly, afraid of breaking something. "Will, good to see you," he rasped.

Will stepped back and gave him room to shuffle in. Simpson and the man just behind him.

Will closed the door and managed to say, "Good to have you back."

Old Man Simpson barked a short, mirthless laugh. Then he cut a quick glance at the other man, who had brushed past them and was striding toward the far side of the conference table. "Will, this is Arthur Krupp."

Krupp was short and stocky, dressed in a dark blue pinstripe suit, white shirt, and muted red tie, matching hankie peeking out of the suit pocket. Tanned, almost swarthy features—narrow brow and jutting chin, longish, wavy hair. He was carrying an expensive leather briefcase, which he opened on the table, giving as he did so a flash of Rolex watch and diamond ring.

"Pleased to meet you," Will said. They shook hands across the table. Krupp nodded but didn't speak. There was an awkward moment and then Old Man Simpson gestured Will into a chair and eased himself into another at the end of the table, hooking the cane over the chair arm. Krupp busied himself for a moment with the briefcase. He was out of place here—a bit too slick, too smooth, too obvious with his Rolex and diamond. He might be a manufacturer's representative, come to sell Channel Seven the state-of-the-art Doppler weather radar Will coveted. Or a lawyer for the mob. But the kind of fellow who might feel at home in this gentleman's sanctuary, sitting now beneath the painting of the eighteenth hole at Pinehurst Number Two? No.

Will glanced at Old Man Simpson for a clue, but Simpson was intently studying a large brown age spot on the back of his hand. Finally he looked up and said, "Mr. Krupp is with Spectrum Broadcasting, Will."

"Ah. Yes," Will said agreeably.

"Spectrum Broadcasting has bought Channel Seven."

Will stared, struck momentarily dumb. It registered, but it didn't. Then it did. Finally he managed to croak, "You've sold the station?"

"Yes." Old Man Simpson slumped in his chair, a look of exquisite, pained weariness on his face. His voice was barely above a whisper. "I've sold the station."

Another long silence, broken only by the faint rumble of traffic out on nearby Wade Avenue, the drone of a mower manicuring the sweep of lawn between Wade and the building. Old Man Simpson liked things neat and orderly. Or had. This had the smell and feel of rank mess. Chaos.

Krupp fished a sheaf of papers out of the briefcase. Old Man Simpson turned his head away and stared out the window. Will felt a wrenching pang of sympathy. Channel Seven had been Simpson's life. He had put the station on the air, had nurtured it for almost fifty years. And now this. Why?

Will started to speak, to ask, to offer some sort of lame condolence. But Krupp interrupted. "Mr. Baggett," he said, "Spectrum Broadcasting will be making some changes."

"I'll do this!" Old Man Simpson commanded, suddenly rousing himself with a flash of his old spunk and fixing Krupp with a no-nonsense look.

Krupp shrugged and let the papers fall to the table. He sat back, crossing his legs, gesturing to Simpson and then folding his hands in his lap. "Okay. You do this."

Simpson turned to Will. He took quite a long time to gather himself, and when he finally spoke his voice was gently mournful. "The new owners will not be picking up your contract."

"There *is* no contract," Krupp said.

"Shut up," Simpson barked. Krupp shrugged again. It seemed to be his best gesture.

Will felt light-headed. He gripped the arms of the chair to keep from sliding out onto the floor, or perhaps floating off toward the ceiling. He looked from Simpson to Krupp and back to Simpson. He tried his voice. Nothing there. Finally, "What . . ."

The strain was mighty on the old man's face, palpable and awful. He spoke slowly, deliberately, measuring out the words like bitter pills. "Will, you've been working without a contract . . ."

"Waiting for you . . ."

"I know. My fault. But even if we had one, it would just delay the"—a bleak glance at Krupp—"inevitable. As you know, all of our contracts include a clause that says if a new owner comes in, they don't have to assume existing contracts."

Will's mind pinwheeled. He had a vague notion of some wording about the eventuality of a sale. "Legalese. Standard boilerplate," Old Man Simpson had called it. But not something to be taken seriously. It was unthinkable—by Will, the old man or anybody else—that the Simpson family would ever entertain the thought of selling Channel Seven. They had given birth to it and loved it like a child. And it wasn't as if Old Man Simpson was the last of the line. There was a son, Roger, toiling now in the sales department toward the day when he would inevitably take over. A pleasant fellow—not particularly bright, but adequate. It didn't take a genius.

"We at Spectrum have our own ideas about how to run a TV station," Krupp interjected, and this time Old Man Simpson let him. He slumped again, defeated, dismissing it all with a weak wave of his hand.

Krupp sat perfectly still, perfectly at ease, only his mouth moving. "We're looking at every aspect of the operation with an eye toward cutting expenses and improving profit margins. Our initial impression is that certain aspects of the salary structure here are out of line. A condition of our purchase is that they be brought into line by the time the sale is approved by the FCC. Since you are working without a contract, Mister Baggett, we have decided that your services will be terminated." It sounded rehearsed. How many times and in how many TV stations had Arthur Krupp done this recitation?

Will gasped for breath. His bowels lurched. He felt nauseated. "You can't do that," he said.

"Yes we can." Krupp looked at Old Man Simpson, who looked at Will for a long moment and then closed his eyes and gave the barest of nods.

"We will be making an announcement to the local media," Krupp said, "about our purchase and your departure."

It dawned on Will that he meant *right now*. No grace period, no weeks to prepare his audience and himself for a rupture, to make arrangements, to alter his life from the straight, sure track it had been on. It was sudden, swift derailment. And Old Man Simpson was sitting there letting them do it.

Will found himself suddenly on his feet, spewing anger, arm thrust, finger pointing like a lightning bolt at Krupp. "You'll regret this," he cried. "I'll go to the competition and we'll whip your ass."

"No you won't," Krupp said mildly, impervious to lightning. "Your contract"—he picked up the papers from the table—"has a non-compete clause, Mister Baggett." He flipped to a back page and read:

> "For a period of one year following the expiration or other termination of this agreement, contractee shall not be employed by or appear on the airwaves of any other television or radio station within one hundred miles of Raleigh, North Carolina, nor shall in any way endorse, assist, or otherwise be associated with any other radio or television station in said area in any way that would bring material damage to Channel Seven in its competitive operations."

He looked up at Will. "Spectrum will enforce that clause to the fullest extent of the law."

"You sonofabitch," Will said softly.

Krupp blinked, but that was all. "We are prepared to make a generous severance offer." He reached into the briefcase for two more pieces of paper. One of them was a check. "Fifty thousand dollars. In return for which"—he held up the other paper—"you will sign a statement in which you acknowledge your long and happy tenure here and look with enthusiasm to exploring new opportunities."

Will spun toward the door, and as he walked through it he heard Krupp call out, "The offer's good for twenty-four hours, Mister Baggett. After that, you can kiss our ass."

Old Man Simpson caught him in the hallway, limping along on the cane. "Will. Will!"

Will turned on him—numb with shock, hurt, betrayal. Just as Simpson reached him, a secretary emerged from the Program Director's office nearby, started to speak, then saw the looks on their faces and ducked back into the office.

"Will, I'm sorry. If there was anything I could have done . . ."

"I need this job," Will gasped. He realized that there was a naked pleading in his voice—both in what he said and in the way he said it—and that it might be the most honest thing he had ever said.

Old Man Simpson put a trembling hand on Will's arm. "I know you do," he whispered. "I know that as well as anybody, and I know what you mean when you say that." Will saw tears, threatening to spill. "I wish there were some other way, but there's not. They made an incredible offer, and I have no choice but to take it. I'm old and worn out and sick, Will. I just want to go home and be quiet."

"What about Roger?"

"He just wants the money."

"Do these idiots realize what they're doing? Do they realize how stupid this is? What the public reaction will be?"

Old Man Simpson shook his head. "I think they are of a mind to get the unpleasantness out of the way and then go on about their business. The sad thing is, it'll probably work. People have short memories."

"They won't get away with it!"

Old Man Simpson looked away from Will's fury. "Will," he said, "I want you to calm down and think rationally. There is nothing either of us can do. Go home now. And then come back tomorrow and accept their offer."

"Home?" His voice sounded far away, as if he had indeed floated off, well past the hallway ceiling, perhaps a good distance above the studio building, up where the wind sang through the guy wires that fastened the transmission tower to earth, up where he could see his work, his life, toppling like an old Stalin statue in a Moscow square. Home, the man said? *This* was home.

"Straight home," Old Man Simpson said. "Don't go through the newsroom."

"Do they know?"

"No. I'll tell them."

"When?"

"Before the early newscast goes on the air. Before the announcement goes out. I want them to hear it from me. At least I can do that . . ." His voice trailed off for a moment. Then, gently, "You wouldn't want to be here. Not the way it's going to be. These new people will do business a lot differently. All bottom line, Will."

"You always managed to turn a profit without shitting on people," Will said bitterly, then instantly regretted the profanity. Old Man Simpson never used it and didn't allow it on his station. He had been known to yank entertainment programs that used foul language and had once risen at an affiliates' meeting to denounce the network's entertainment division as "smut merchants."

"Excuse me," Will said.

Old Man Simpson flinched, looked away for a moment, then back at Will. There was a distance between them now. When he spoke, there was some of the old firmness in his voice. The boss, explaining. "Will, this television station has no debt. My family owns it down to the last paper clip. When a bunch like Spectrum buys a station like this, they borrow every red cent they can get their hands on. Load it up with debt. And then they have to soak every last bit of profit out of the operation to pay back what they've borrowed. That means cutting costs. And in a TV station, that's mainly people. So at this TV station, a lot of good people are going to get hurt."

"This station has always been number one in Raleigh," Will said. "They'll destroy that."

Simpson shook his head. "If they can make more money being number two, or three, by cutting costs, they'll gladly do it. It's just business, Will."

Just business. Will thought of the kids in the newsroom. Most of them lived from one paycheck to the next. It would be an ugly, scary, demoralizing thing for them. At least he had twenty years of success under his belt—a reputation, a bank account. But they were all victims and there were all kinds of loss, some that you couldn't put a price tag on.

The hardness went out of Old Man Simpson's face and he grasped Will's shoulder. Will could feel the frailty there, the tremble of flesh—part emotion perhaps, but part physical ruin. "Will, there's no way I can tell you how much you've meant to this place. When Sidney Palmer called me twenty years ago and asked me to take a look at you, it was the best thing that ever happened to the station. You've put so much of yourself into it. Nobody could have done more. I'm grateful, Will." He gave Will's shoulder a squeeze. "And you'll be fine. You've got the talent and the drive. Stay calm, be gracious. Move on."

Will should have hugged him. He owed him that. The man had been almost like a father to him. But he couldn't quite bring himself to do it. If he hugged Old Man Simpson, they would both cry, and neither needed to do that just now.

He turned and felt Old Man Simpson's hand fall away, and he walked off down the hall and down the stairs and through the lobby and into the afternoon sunlight. It took all of his concentration to keep his eyes focused on the next step, the next door, to shut out the familiar sights and sounds and smells that had become so essential a part of who he was, why he existed. It was only when he reached his car that he let go a bit. He reached in his pocket for his keys and dropped them on the asphalt and stared at them for a long moment, and when he bent to pick them up he saw that his hand was shaking uncontrollably. He leaned against the car, bracing himself with both of his hands against the driver-side door like a man about to be frisked by the police.

"Mister Baggett? You all right?"

It was Dinkins, the security guard. Stooped, white-haired. His rumpled khaki uniform hung like a shroud from his frail frame.

Old Man Simpson had kept him on all these years, long after he should have been put out to pasture. He puttered about the halls, straightened pictures on the walls, conducted an occasional tour. He had been at Channel Seven since it went on the air in the early 1950s, and he was proud to say they had had only one "untoward incident" in all the years hence. A woman visitor had entered a rest room off the lobby, taken off all her clothes, and presented herself at the receptionist's desk. Dinkins calmly pulled down a drapery, covered the woman, and called the police. He had never carried a gun and had only reluctantly in recent years accepted a pager. The newsroom kids called him Barney Fyffe and made jokes: *If terrorists attack, Dinkins will divert them by dying.* But Will liked old Dinkins. There was a certain tenacity to him, defying gravity and time. They exchanged pleasantries and inquired about each other's families. Dinkins had a daughter in Zambia, a foreign aid worker. He returned from a visit full of stories and bearing a gift for Will, a small stone carving of an elephant. When Dinkins's tiny wife had died five years ago, Will had gone to the house with a basket of fruit. Dinkins had been speechless with gratitude. He was back at work the day after the funeral. Like Will, he depended on Channel Seven. They called each other Mister Dinkins and Mister Baggett in cheerful mock-formality.

"Mister Baggett?" Dinkins said again.

Will managed to stand. "I'm feeling a little ill, Mister Dinkins. I think I'll take the rest of the day off."

"Is there anything I can do?"

Will stared at the pavement. "My keys. I can't seem to get down there."

It took Dinkins a little while, too. But finally he retrieved the keys and handed them to Will. "Are you sure you can drive, Mister Baggett?"

"I am," Will said, straightening a bit more, "determined to drive."

"Not like you, getting sick. Never known you to miss a day of work because of being sick."

Will fumbled ineptly with the keys for a moment, found the right one, unlocked the car. "How's your family, Mister Dinkins?"

Dinkins broke into a smile. "Got a letter from my daughter. She's thinking about coming home. "

"Well, congratulations."

Will opened the door and eased himself under the steering wheel. His head swam and he sat there for a moment until the reeling subsided. "You sure you're okay?" Dinkins asked. "I can get somebody to drive you home."

"No. I'll make it."

Dinkins closed the door for him. Will rolled down the window and cranked the car. "Thanks, Mister Dinkins."

"What for? Ain't done nothing."

"Well, for everything. Over the years." Will realized he was again on the verge of tears. He put the car into reverse and started backing out of the parking place. He could feel Dinkins's eyes on him.

"See you tomorrow, Mister Baggett."

Will rolled up the window and drove away.

———

HE WATCHED the six o'clock news. Brent was doing the weather. Brent, the weekend weatherman and—until now—Will's understudy and substitute. A handsome young fellow, full of ambition. He had good teeth and hair and was working hard on his charm quotient. Tonight he was nervous and overeager, talking too fast and stumbling over words, calling Michigan Minnesota as he pointed to it on the weather map. Jim and Binky weren't at the top of their game, either. They misspoke, treaded on each other's lines, looked thoroughly spooked. The banter was forced, almost panicked, as if someone had told them they had damned well better be cheerful or they'd be out on their butts at 6:30. Their contracts, Will imagined, were written just like his. Watching it, he felt sick.

They didn't say anything about him until the very end of

the newscast, and it was brief. Will Baggett was leaving Channel Seven for "other opportunities." Brent had been appointed as the station's "chief meteorologist." *Hell, the kid doesn't know Michigan from Minnesota.* And that was all. *Not a thank you, not a kiss-my-ass.* Oh, and by the way, they said, Channel Seven has been sold. That was Arthur Krupp's doing, he thought. Old Man Simpson would never have done it that way. He hoped Old Man Simpson was at home now with the TV off and a big drink of bourbon in hand.

As soon as he switched off the TV, the kitchen phone rang. A reporter from the *News and Observer.* Will felt blood rush to his head. He came close to an outburst, then thought about Simpson's advice: stay calm, be gracious. Well, shit on being gracious. Calm would have to do. "No comment," he said, and hung up.

Immediately, his minister at First Presbyterian: "God works in strange and mysterious ways, Will," Reverend Curtis said. "Shall I come over?"

"No," Will said, "I'm fine. Really."

He had no sooner hung up than it rang again. A woman who identified herself as a loyal viewer from Franklinton, twenty miles north of Raleigh. "What the hell's going on down there?" she demanded. He started to ask how she had obtained his unlisted phone number, but instead he placed the phone gently on the counter and retreated to the living room just as the doorbell rang. It was Phyllis Durkin from next door. With a casserole.

"I just heard," Phyllis said, offering up the dish.

"A death in the family," Will said wryly.

"I was raised a good southern girl. When there's trouble, you take food. Are you okay, Will?"

"Frankly, Phyllis, I'm just sort of numb." He raised the lid on the casserole. "What is this?"

"Chicken and rice."

He looked at his watch. It was 6:37. "Did you just make it?"

"A good southern girl always has something in the fridge. Do you need somebody to stay with you until Clarice gets home?"

"No. I'm okay. I just need to be quiet, Phyllis. Thanks. You're terrific."

She turned to go.

"Chuck told me about Rex. Congratulations. A daughter-in-law now. That's wonderful. Let us know what we can do to help. With the wedding stuff, I mean."

Phyllis waved over her shoulder as she headed down the walk. "Take off your coat and tie, Will. Get drunk. Be a private citizen for a few hours. I won't tell anybody."

He put the casserole in the refrigerator and then went upstairs and took off his coat and tie. He hadn't realized, until Phyllis said it, that he was still dressed for work. Work? *My God, I've been fired. Out on my ass.* It happened to ordinary people, but not to Will Baggett, Raleigh's most popular TV weatherman. He felt a rush of pure, unadulterated rage. "Sonofabitch!" he bellowed into the silence of the house. But then the anger was replaced by something else. Dread, lying like a coiled snake at the pit of his stomach. Where just hours before he had been so dead certain about where his life was headed, now there was just a yawning nothing. This thing they had done to him had cut him loose from his moorings. He was adrift, rudderless, at the mercy of wind and current, out of sight of all the old familiar landmarks and beacons. It was enough to fill you with dread, pure and simple.

He went back downstairs. The woman from Franklinton had given up. The phone was bleating in off-the-hook protest. It finally fell silent, leaving the house empty and still and sucked dry. He fixed an enormous scotch and water and settled himself on a corner of the living room sofa to wait.

The evening purpled into night. He fixed another drink and was halfway through that one when he heard Clarice's car pull into the driveway. He glanced at his watch. Almost eight o'clock.

After a moment she came noisily through the back door, dropping keys and briefcase on the counter, placing the telephone back in its cradle, flipping on lights. The phone rang almost immediately.

She picked it up. The conversation was a mumble. Then she hung it up again. "Will?"

"In here," he called.

She stood for a moment in the doorway, framed by the rectangle of light from the hall.

"You're late," he said.

Clarice ran her fingers through her hair, a nervous habit he had noticed lately without knowing just when she had picked it up. She was forever mussing her hair and then searching frantically for a mirror to repair it. "Sales meeting," she said, "about the new development. Fincher got the exclusive."

"That's good," he said. "I've been fired."

"It's on the radio. But they didn't say you were fired."

"What did they say?"

"That you're leaving Channel Seven. Something about new owners." She stood there for a moment longer, her face in shadow. Then she crossed the room and sat down beside him on the couch and took his hand, her long, slender fingers cool against his fevered skin. "What happened?"

He told her about Spectrum, Old Man Simpson, the contract. The words tumbled out and stumbled over each other, tight and strangled, as he said it all for the first time out loud—putting voice to the mad welter that had been boiling in him since he had driven out of the parking lot at Channel Seven. She listened, perfectly still. When he finally fell silent, she said, "Channel Seven's not the only TV station in Raleigh."

"It might as well be." He told her about the non-compete clause.

She waited for a moment and then said, "I see."

"You see?"

"Well, I just don't know what to say." She let go of his hand and spread her own in a gesture of helplessness.

Will shook his head. A long silence. "The bastards will rape the place. I'm just the first."

"Will, I'm sorry." Her voice floated in the semi-dark. There was just enough light filtering in from the hallway that he could see her lovely form there on the sofa, but not enough that he could tell what she was doing with her face. She was, for the most part, an open book. Her face revealed everything. But he couldn't see that now. He could only hear her voice. Sympathetic, yes. But not what you would call agonized. He wanted her to be agonized.

She touched his cheek with her cool hand. "I know you're upset. Take a few days to get over this, figure out what you want to do. Money's not a problem."

"No. They offered me fifty thousand dollars to go quietly." But, he realized, she was talking about herself, about her own career, her own money-generating machine. Homes and land. Multiple listings. Émigrés from Cincinnati and Newark.

"Then you should go quietly," she said.

"They took my job!" he burst out.

She withdrew her hand, leaving the cool imprint. "Well, that's all they *could* take," she said.

No. She didn't understand. How could she?

"I can't believe I've been so goddamned naïve."

"Naïve?"

"It's just business. That's all it is. Just business."

"Well, what did you think it was, Will?"

"It's my . . ."

"Life?"

"Well, not all of it, of course. But some. You have your work, that has a lot to do with who you are. I worked like a sonofabitch for that station. I earned what I got—not just the money, the *place*. And quicker than you can blink your eye, it's gone. Twenty years. What's it worth? Fifty thousand dollars and get-the-hell-out-of-our-TV-station. Go away and vegetate for a year while everybody forgets there ever was a Will Baggett."

"You feel betrayed."

"Betrayed, stupid, maybe a little scared."

"Why? Will, you're a smart, attractive, personable man. There are all sorts of things you can do."

"Such as?"

She thought for a moment, her hand in her hair again. "Radio? The newspaper? Public relations. Run for office. You'd make a good politician."

"I'm a TV weatherman, Clarice."

They sat for a long while in silence and then the telephone rang back in the kitchen again. Clarice started to rise.

"Let it ring," he said. "I don't want to talk to anybody."

"It might be for me," she said. But she sat back on the sofa and they listened while the answering machine took the call after four rings, the message and the caller only a rattle of garbled sound. Whoever it was went on for a long time and then finally hung up.

Silence again. And finally Clarice said, "You know what I thought when I heard it on the radio, Will? I thought, well maybe he just got tired of it and left. Maybe he got worn out with the celebrity and people honking their horns and pulling and tugging on him. Maybe he got up this morning and looked in the mirror and said to himself, 'What's going on here? Why am I doing this? What does it matter?' Maybe he just said, 'I want to be somebody else for a while.' And you know, Will, I felt a great sense of relief when I thought that. I felt happier than I have in a long time. For you, for me. For us."

"Well, sorry, but I don't want to be somebody else."

"What if you don't have any choice?"

He shook his head. That wasn't what he wanted to talk about, to think about. No, what he had to talk about was what he had been thinking since he sat down here on the sofa. "We might . . . have to move."

"Move?"

"Charlotte, maybe. Atlanta. Denver. Wherever there's an opening."

She waited for a long time before she spoke, and before the first word came out there was a loud exhaling of the breath she had been holding. "Will, I've got a business here. You don't rush into real estate and become an overnight success. You have to work at it. Build up contacts. Referrals. I'm just now getting good at it."

Will felt a sudden emptying, everything in his body from just below his hairline on down rushing to his lower extremities, as it dawned on him how utterly things had changed between them, how the delicate balance of action and reaction and transaction they had constructed over twenty-five years of marriage no longer held true. They spoke now in different languages, untranslatable, across a gulf of time and space.

More than that, he realized, what had transpired in Old Man Simpson's office in the space of a few minutes this afternoon had altered geography. He and Clarice had changed places. She was no longer his appendage. He was hers.

———

SHE WAS IN BED, reading, when he came up about nine. She looked up from her book. "Have you talked to Palmer?"

He hadn't thought of Palmer, not for a moment. It caught him off guard, this mention now of his son's name, surprised him with a rush of guilt.

"Don't you think you should?"

"I don't want to bother him tonight. He's got that exam tomorrow. I'll call then, after he's done."

She gave him a long look, then she picked up the phone on her bedside table and dialed. She waited. "Palmer, call home."

It was almost ten when the phone rang. Will was in the bathroom brushing his teeth. He heard the mutter of Clarice's voice. Then, "Will . . ."

He rinsed his mouth and went to the bedside and took the receiver from her.

"Dad?"

"Hi, son."

"A friend heard it on TV and told me. I tried to call earlier, but the line was busy."

"Yeah," Will said. "A lot of calls. Then I took it off the hook."

"Is it really like they said on TV? You quit?"

"No. That's not the way it is at all."

"Oh." Then, "That's really rotten."

"Ah well, anybody can do the weather. It's not the end of the world."

Palmer didn't say anything for a moment, and beyond his silence Will could hear music, voices, the clink of glass, laughter. Finally he said, "Dad, don't shit me."

"What?"

"I know how much it means to you. So don't shit me by telling me it doesn't matter."

Will was taken aback. Palmer's voice was raw, almost angry. "Son . . ."

"Just be honest, huh?"

"Okay."

"It hurts."

"Yeah. It hurts."

"Okay."

"Where are you?" Will asked.

"In a bar."

"Don't you have an exam tomorrow?"

Another silence. "I can handle it," Palmer said.

"Palmer, are you okay?"

"Sure."

"Don't shit me."

Palmer laughed — a short explosion of sound with no mirth in it. "Yeah," he said. "We have to be up-front with each other, don't we. Just the guys, speaking plain truth and so forth."

Then he hung up.

Will handed the phone back to Clarice.

"So?"

"He told me not to shit him."

There was a tiny trace of a smile at the edges of her mouth. "He told you that?"

"Yes."

"Why didn't you want to talk to Palmer?"

"It's not that."

"Don't shit me," she said. The smile was gone.

"I guess," he said, "I just didn't know what to say. You want your son to think you're pretty special."

"People get fired all the time, Will. Some of them have sons. They deal with it. Don't you think yours is capable of that?"

He shrugged.

"You've always presented a moving target, Will. Maybe now you'll have to stand still long enough for somebody to get a shot at you."

4 | WILL WAS BLASTED from sleep the next morning by an explosion of splintering wood. He jerked upright in bed. "Aaaaghhh!"

He thought at first of the teenager down the street with the new Camaro. Had he failed to make the curve and crashed into Will's house, ripping up the lawn in the process? But no, this commotion was at the back of the house. And it continued. He glanced at the bedside clock radio: 8:43.

He struggled out of bed, wrapped himself in a robe, and stumbled into the hallway. "Clarice," he called from the top of the stairs. No answer except for the screeching protest of nails being pried from wood. He struggled down the stairs, wild-eyed with shock. The front doorbell was ringing, barely audible over the deafening racket coming from somewhere beyond the kitchen. "Just a minute!" he yelled toward the front door, and kept moving toward the smashing sound, fixing it at the kitchen's exterior wall. He bolted for the back door and flung it open to see a trio of rough-hewn men, armed with crowbars and sledgehammers, ripping the back off his home. Two of them were on ladders and another was working at ground level, prying off boards and tossing them into a growing heap on the ground. They seemed to be having a grand time of it. At the bottom of the steps, a boom box was blasting a Willie Nelson song. *I gotta get drunk and I sure do dread it.* Will stared in horror. "What in the hell are you doing?"

The workmen stopped momentarily and the one at ground level, a wiry man with bad teeth and a Durham Bulls baseball cap, gave Will a close look and said, "Hey, you're the guy on TV."

"Yeah. No."

"Sports on Channel Four. Right?"

Forgotten already. "Yeah. What's going on here?"

"Lady said take out the wall. We're taking out the wall."

"What for?"

"The addition."

They went back to work, ripping and crowbarring and smashing. Willie Nelson went on getting reluctantly drunk on the radio. Will spotted a makeshift table in the yard, a sheet of plywood laid across two sawhorses. He clambered down the back steps, sidestepping the boom box, and crossed to the table where some kind of drawing had been unrolled and was being held down at each end by bricks. He studied it, recognizing it as Clarice's plans for the addition, the ones she had shown him four years ago. "You can't do this!" he cried, waving his arms.

The man in the Bulls cap gave him an arch look, then tossed his crowbar on the ground and joined Will at the table. The two on the ladder went on with their demolition, paying them no attention. Will lifted the bricks off the plans, rolled them up and handed them to the man. "You can't do this," he repeated.

"Why not?" the man asked.

"We're not ready. Not now."

The man placed the rolled-up plans back on the table, reached into his rear jeans pocket and pulled out a pouch of chewing tobacco. He pinched off a wad and jammed it in the corner of his mouth between cheek and gum. "Look," he said to Will, "the lady done paid half the money. Your wife, I take it."

"Yes. My wife."

"Well, we got orders to take off that"—he pointed at the back of the house—"and put on that." He tapped the plans with a bony finger. "I reckon you'll have to take it up with the lady."

"Good God," Will groaned, and retreated to the house, slamming the back door just as a sledgehammer smashed a hole in the plaster above the breakfast room table. Will fled down the hallway, heading for the stairs. The doorbell rang again.

Dinkins was standing on the front stoop. He was wearing his security guard uniform and cap. Both looked slept-in. He was holding a copy of the *News and Observer.* "Morning, Mister Baggett."

"Mister Dinkins."

Will looked past Dinkins at the panel truck in the driveway:

CHRISTIAN CONSTRUCTION AND RENOVATORS
SPRUCING UP RALEIGH ONE JOB AT A TIME
JESUS SAVES

Dinkins's ancient, rusting Ford was parked at the curb. From the rear of the house, the smashing and rending went on.

"You and the missus doing some work?" Dinkins asked.

"The missus," Will said with a grimace.

Dinkins held up the newspaper. "I 'speck you've seen this."

"No. I just got up. I'd ask you to come in, but . . ." He gestured helplessly toward the noise.

"No bother," Dinkins said, and sat down on the steps. Will joined him and took the paper. The headline was at the bottom right corner of the front page:

CHANNEL SEVEN SELLS, BAGS BAGGETT

In a move that stunned the Raleigh broadcasting community, television station Channel Seven was sold Monday to Spectrum Broadcasting of Chicago. An immediate casualty was veteran weathercaster Will Baggett, who left to "pursue other business ventures," according to a statement by the new owners.

Spectrum Communications spokesman Arthur Krupp said his company would employ a college-trained meteorologist to forecast weather on the station. "It's a nationwide trend," said Krupp. "Meteorologists have more credibility with viewers."

Krupp's statement said that since Baggett's contract with the present owner of Channel Seven had expired last month, Spectrum decided to release him immediately. "We wish Mr. Baggett every success," said Krupp. "Spectrum Communications looks forward to further operational changes to better serve viewers in the Raleigh area."

Channel Seven president Barfield Simpson declined comment on the sale and Baggett's release. Baggett, reached at his Raleigh home, also had no comment.

Sources in the Channel Seven newsroom told the *News and Observer* that Baggett's dismissal was Spectrum's decision and apparently took Baggett by surprise. Baggett had been the station's chief weathercaster for more than 20 years and is credited by station insiders with helping Channel Seven maintain top newscast ratings in the Raleigh market.

Both parties to the sale declined to disclose the price Spectrum paid for Channel Seven, which has been privately held by the Simpson family since its founding . . .

There were two photographs: one of Will at his desk in the Weather Center, another of Old Man Simpson standing in front of the studio building.

Will handed the paper back to Dinkins, who folded it neatly and placed it on the steps at his side. "They shouldn'ta done that," Dinkins said.

"Well, it's their station now, or soon will be. I guess they can do anything they want."

They sat quietly for a while. It was a lovely spring morning, warm and budding. Showers expected by late afternoon, possibly even some heavier stuff. A cold front had moved through from the northwest, then turned stationary over Georgia and was drifting back north toward the Carolinas. A late-April day like so many that had passed across his weather maps over the years. Only this one was somebody else's. Brent's. He had a degree in meteorology. He was just two years out of college, and he would be cheap. They would give him a piddling raise and responsibility for the weekday weathercasts and he would think he had died and gone to heaven. His face on billboards. His voice on the radio. But he wouldn't stay around long enough to become a fixture. Not that that counted for anything, Will thought. Being a fixture and being bulletproof— well, it turns out they're two entirely different things.

"Brent the meteorologist," Will said. "I watched him at six. Not at eleven. I didn't watch the eleven."

"Neither did I." Dinkins said. "I got drunk."

"Because of me?"

"No, Mister Baggett. Because of Barfield Simpson."

Will could feel his face flush. He started to speak, thought better of it.

"He's dying, you know," Dinkins said.

Will stared. "He said he was sick. I didn't know it was that bad."

"Bladder cancer. A couple of months, maybe less. He told his doctor he's just gonna let nature take its course."

Old Man Simpson's face flashed in Will's mind—the sallow, sagging skin, the tiny fractures around his eyes that Will recognized now as the fault lines of fear.

"I didn't know," he said again, softly. He felt ashamed.

Dinkins took off his cap and rubbed his hand through his thin straggle of gray hair. It was the first time Will had ever seen him hatless. He wore the hat as he would have an armored helmet, indoors and out. He looked especially old now, and vulnerable and incredibly sad.

"You've known him a long time," Will said.

Dinkins settled the cap back on his head. "We went to high school together. Barfield's family had money, mine were mill people. But we were pretty good friends. When both of us came back out of the war, Barfield bought a radio station and he offered me a job. Then he put the TV station on the air. I stayed on all these years."

"I'm sorry," Will said. It sounded incredibly lame. "When did you find out?"

"Right after I saw you yestiddy afternoon. After that Krupp fellow left, I went up to Barfield's office and I said, 'Barfield, what in the hell's going on here?' And that's when he told me. All of it."

"What are you going to do, Mister Dinkins?"

Dinkins got slowly, painfully, to his feet. "Oh, I already quit. Went by this morning and turned in my keys. Now I'm gonna go home and think about what I'll do with the rest of my life. I'm considering Alaska."

"Alaska?"

"Always wondered what it would be like up there. When I came back out of the Navy in 'forty-five, I was all set to go to Alaska. Had a little money saved up. You could get a homestead up there pretty cheap in them days. But then I met this little girl and we got married and had a baby and Barfield Simpson offered me a job. So it just never quite worked out."

"Until now."

"I reckon I'm free to go. I'll have a little retirement money, Social Security. I imagine I can make it okay."

He started off down the walk toward his car, then stopped and turned back to Will. "Some of the kids in the newsroom want to come over. They're real torn up over this."

Will hesitated.

"If you'd rather not . . ."

"Not just yet," Will said. "Tell 'em to give me a couple of days. Get my legs under me."

"They think a lot of you."

Will felt the sting of tears and fought to hold them back. He raised a hand. It was all he could do for the moment. Dinkins turned away again.

"Mister Dinkins . . ."

Dinkins stopped and looked back at him.

"Do you feel betrayed?" Will asked.

"Oh, I guess I could if I wanted to," Dinkins answered. "So could Barfield Simpson. You talk about betrayal now, Barfield's body has plumb let him down. But I don't have time to feel betrayed, Will. And Barfield ain't got no time at all."

Dinkins turned around again and kept walking. It was, Will thought, the first time Dinkins had ever called him by his first name. He would have reciprocated, but he couldn't for the life of him think what Dinkins's first name was. They had just never been on a first-name basis.

"They offered me fifty thousand dollars to keep my mouth shut," Will called out as Dinkins opened the door of his old Ford.

"Take it, Will," Dinkins said with a grin. "Want to go to Alaska with me? We could have some good times."

"No," Will said. "You go ahead."

Dinkins gave him a wave and got into the car and drove off, leaving Will on the steps in his bathrobe. He looked again at the Christian Construction and Renovators panel truck in the driveway. It was blocking his own car. But then, Will thought, he didn't have anywhere to go. After a while he got up and went back in the house to call Clarice.

———

"SOME CHRISTIANS ARE over here destroying our house," he said when he finally reached her on her flip phone at midmorning. "Listen." He walked from the living room back toward the kitchen, holding up the cordless so she could hear the banging and smashing. The back wall was nothing but two-by-four studs now, and the Christians were inside the house, ripping away plaster and the lath work underneath, exposing the house to the fine spring day. Through the studs he could see the growing pile of debris in the back yard, ruining his grass.

"Will . . . Will!" he could hear her shouting through the phone. He put it to his ear. "All right. I hear it. That's enough."

"Well?"

"I didn't know they were coming this morning." He could hear the impatience in her voice as he retreated again to the living room. She was probably with clients. From Darien or Salt Lake City. *And look at all this cabinet space!*

"I didn't know they were coming at all," he said. "I had no earthly idea that people would be destroying my home this morning or any other morning. A natural disaster, I could handle that. Shit happens. But this . . ."

"I told you about the addition."

"But that was four years ago."

"Nothing's changed."

"Everything's changed."

He could hear voices in the background, then a muffled scratching as she cupped her hand over the mouthpiece of the flip phone. After a moment she took her hand away and he heard her say, ". . . a really terrific deck. I'll be on out in a moment." Then she spoke into the phone again. "Will, the world can't stop just because you've lost your job."

"How the hell do you think we're gonna pay for this?"

"I told you I would save up the money. I did."

"We may need that to live on."

"For God's sake," she said, exasperated. "You'll find another job."

"I don't want another job."

"You're sounding peevish."

"Yes, I suppose I am."

"What about the fifty thousand dollars they offered?"

"To hell with them."

"That's easy for you to say. Go get the money, Wilbur. Stop acting like a spoiled child." There was a long, pained silence and when she finally spoke again her voice was calm and soothing. "I'm sorry. I know how upset you are. I'm upset too. But life goes on. Take their money. It'll be okay, Will. It'll work out. Have you talked to Morris?"

"No."

"Call him. I'll see you for dinner."

———

SHORTLY BEFORE TWO O'CLOCK he was in Morris deLesseps's office, sunk deep in a leather armchair while Morris, feet hiked on his huge mahogany desk, flipped through the pages of Will's contract.

Morris had been his friend at Chapel Hill, then later on, best man at his wedding. He was from an old Charleston family, French Huguenot stock—impoverished gentility, to hear Morris tell of them.

Will thought Morris really should have been an actor. He was constantly reinventing himself—two wives before he was thirty and two more since, a series of legal personas. He had at one point favored buckskin jackets and cowboy boots in the fashion of a flamboyant lawyer who was frequently on television. At another, he had draped himself in sleek, dark double-breasted pinstripes accented by paisley pocket handkerchiefs and had slicked back his longish hair with an *Esquire*-style wet look. He had spent a year in ponytail and denim, another in leather and cigars. He was now in a tweed-pipe-penny-loafer-half-rim-glasses phase, drove a Saab with reckless abandon, and had taken up skeet shooting. He affected a cheerful breeziness, alternated with somber introspection. He read John Grisham and the existentialist philosophers. In his pinstripe-and-Gucci existence, he had been a master of quip and one-liner, delivered in Bronx staccato. Now, he had become an accomplished raconteur, charming dinner guests with rambling, bitingly witty

curved stem. He took a long time packing it carefully with tobacco from a leather-encased humidor, tamping it with a small silver device, lighting it finally with a brass lighter that he held sideways over the bowl. He sucked, exhaled a brief, short burst of smoke. He smiled across the pipe at Will.

"Restraint of trade. The non-compete clause," Will reminded him.

Morris held the pipe about ear level with one hand, picked up the contract with the other. "Question is, is a non-compete clause a restraint of trade? When you tell a fellow he can't go work for somebody else, are you depriving him of his right to make a living?" Morris put down the contract and stuck the pipe back in his mouth.

"So? Are you?"

Morris puffed a couple of puffs, cogitating. "Well, it depends. Case law is all over the map on it. Sometimes it's restraint of trade, sometimes it's a company's right to protect itself from unfair competition."

"And in my case?"

"You could go to court and find out."

"Could I win?"

"Maybe. With a judge, or a judge and a jury, you never know."

Will could feel exasperation creeping like hives up the back of his neck. "All right, Morris. Tell me what the hell I should do. I've lost my job and I want it back. Can I get it?"

"Not the one you had. They've got you dead to rights on that one. You signed a contract that said if somebody else buys the place, they don't have to keep you on, even if you had a contract. Which you don't."

"Can they keep me from working at another station?"

"Maybe. Maybe even probably."

Will jumped to his feet. "Goddamn, Morris! Will you speak common English instead of that Justice Brandeis bullshit?"

Morris gazed calmly, benignly, up at him and made a little gesture with his pipe, waving Will back to the chair. "Whoa, son. Easy there."

Will sat back down—hot, flushed, throat constricted.

"Justice Brandeis." Morris smiled. "Yeah. Nice thought, Will."

"Common English," Will repeated.

"Okay." Morris parked the pipe in a brass-and-glass ashtray, leaned back and made a little tent of his hands beneath his chin. "We could sue, alleging restraint of trade, and ask for an injunction declaring the non-compete clause unenforceable. We might win. We might lose. Might depend on whether the judge's underwear is too tight on any given day. At any rate, I would charge you a shit-pot full of money to handle the case and it could take, oh"—a wave of his hand—"eighteen months to wend its deliberate way through the judicial system of Wake County."

"Hell, the non-compete is only a year," Will said.

"Yes, it is."

"So win or lose, it's a moot point."

"We both deduce that it is."

Will stared at his hands, his mind blank for a long moment. He studied the lines and angles of his hands and wrists, the ridges in his fingernails. Nothing in particular occurred to him except that his fingers were beginning to look pudgy. He looked back at Morris, who was studying him, waiting.

Will spread his hands in resignation. "So . . ."

"Right. Take the money, lie low, wait it out."

"You know about the money?"

"I talked to Arthur Krupp right after you called this morning. Also, to one of the legions of learned attorneys that Spectrum Broadcasting has on retainer. This particular fellow combines the best of Harvard and Attica." Morris lifted a single sheet of paper from the desktop. "We agreed on the wording of a statement you might make to the media."

"Hey, wait just a damned minute!"

"I said 'might.' "

He handed it across to Will. Morris had written it out in long-hand, black ink on yellow legal pad, a flowing, elegant script. *My God, the man has even changed his handwriting.* His college class notes had been a primitive scrawl — virtually verbatim, but almost illegible. Will read:

> After twenty rewarding and enjoyable years at Channel Seven, it is time for me to move on to other opportunities and challenges. I thank the loyal viewers who have allowed me to visit in their homes, and I wish the new owners of Channel Seven every success in the future.

Will crumpled the sheet and tossed it onto Morris's desk. Morris picked it up, uncrumpled it, smoothed it out with the palm of his hand. "I'll have my secretary type it up and fax it to the media," he said. "Fifty thousand dollars is a nice sum of money, Will. You can sit on the verandah and sip mint juleps and play in the yard for a year. Then go to one of the other stations. A couple have expressed some interest."

"They have?"

"Yes. I've had calls this morning. Very discreet, you understand. Nobody wants to get in a legal pissing match with Spectrum Broadcasting over a non-compete clause. And, they've got non-competes in their own employee contracts. But when the year is up . . . Hell, son, you're Raleigh's most popular TV weatherman."

Will grunted.

Morris lifted a telephone receiver, held it halfway to his ear. "Meantime, you might find something else you like more. Lots of people in this town would love to have Will Baggett on their payroll. I'll keep my ears open."

"Clarice suggested politics," Will said drily.

"Bingo. City council, maybe even mayor. With fifty thousand dollars and your name, you could probably get elected."

"Not that I know anything about politics."

"Hell, Wilbur, this is a citizen democracy we've got here. Any half-wit with a filing fee can get on the ballot. Now, *that* would give Spectrum Broadcasting a case of heartburn. The guy they showed the door deciding all manner of public policy that might affect a broadcasting station. Whooo-doggies."

Morris punched the intercom button and put the receiver to his ear. "Gladys, I have something here . . ." He looked up at Will, held up the wrinkled piece of yellow paper, winked, waited.

Will felt suddenly drained, all the fight and anger gone out of him, even the coiled dread-snake in his belly gone to slumber. He remembered what some politician of the past had said: *Your balls are always in somebody's pocket.* Well, his were in Spectrum Broadcasting's pocket, and he might as well admit that and take their money and go on about his business. Bide his time. Serve in city government? Of course he could be elected. Just his name on yard signs . . . And then he might give Spectrum Broadcasting a little heartburn. Maybe a tax on television advertising. He shrugged, nodded.

". . . something for you to get out to the news folk."

While Gladys came to fetch the piece of paper, Morris launched into a story, rearing back in the chair and slinging his feet onto the desk again. He had been to Fayetteville the week before, had defended a businessman accused of laundering money for some nefarious people through the operation of a used car lot, had defended the man and lost. When the jury returned and the foreman read the guilty verdict, the judge asked the defendant (Morris pronounced the word *dee-FEN-dant* in the southern country lawyer way) if he had anything to say. The *dee-FEN-dant* had risen and addressed the various court participants in turn. Morris mimicked him—a perfect Fayetteville used car dealer dialect: "Your Honor, I just want to say that I been given a shitty deal. Now I don't blame you because you was just doing your job, and the same goes for the prosecutor. It's just bidness with him. And my attorney here, Mister *DEE-Lesseps,* he ain't worth a damn, but I guess he done the best he could under the circumstances. But I'll tell you folks up there in the jury box, you have done ripped yo ass wit' me."

Morris chuckled heartily, enjoying himself, peering over the tops of the half-rim glasses and inviting Will to join him in comradely merriment. Will stared. "What's the point?" he asked.

"Just a story," Morris said happily, rising behind the desk, raising his arms toward the ceiling as if he held a finely crafted walnut-stock twelve-gauge. "Boom!" He got off a shot at an imaginary skeet rocketing somewhere up near the chandelier. "Just a story, boy." He lowered his arms, then glanced at his wristwatch. "I 'speck you better get moving, Wilbur. You got twenty minutes."

"What?"

"The offer's good until two o'clock. After that, to quote Mister Arthur Krupp, you can kiss their ass."

———

HE DIDN'T NOTICE the police car until he pulled into the parking lot at Channel Seven. It was perhaps a hundred yards behind him, blue lights flashing. He was out of his own car and heading toward the front door of the station when the squad car pulled up behind him and an officer scrambled out. "Hey," he called to Will. "Hey!" Will stopped and turned back. "You just ran a red light."

Will glanced at his watch. Two minutes before two. "I'll be right back," he said, and kept walking.

"Hey!" the officer called, more insistent this time. "Stop right there."

Will spun. "Do you know me?"

"Yeah. You're the guy that just ran a red light."

Will pointed toward the second floor of the Channel Seven building. "Look, if I'm not up there in two minutes, I'm gonna lose fifty thousand dollars. You can wait in the lobby. I'll be right back. I didn't run a red light, but we'll get it straightened out."

Will was at the front door now, and as he opened it, he could see the reflection of the police officer in the glass, reaching for something on the dashboard of the squad car. He wondered fleetingly if the man was about to shotgun him in the back. Then he was through the door, crossing the lobby, glancing quickly at the desk where Dinkins usually sat. Empty. The whole station, open to terrorist attack.

He punched the button for the elevator, saw that it was holding on the second floor, then took the stairs two at a time. He burst into the upstairs hallway, breathing hard, and almost ran into Grace Hibbert, one of the secretaries in the sales department. Grace was a large woman—massive hips and linebacker shoulders. She filled up the hallway, blocking his progress. "Will!" she cried, reaching for him. "Will, how awful!"

Will sidestepped, trying to edge by. "Hello, Grace. I'm just—"

She grabbed him in a smothering hug, mashing him to her bosom. She smelled lilac water, the stale afterbreath of cigarette smoke. Grace was one of what the staff referred to as the "Marlboro Irregulars," the small, defiant band of smokers who huddled periodically through the day in the station's rear loading dock and puffed away, banished from the interior premises by Old Man Simpson's edict. "Grace, I've gotta . . . ," he mumbled into her nubby-weave jacket.

She thrust him suddenly at arm's length, holding vise-like to his elbows. "What are we gonna DO?"

"Just stand there," Will cried. Grace's eyes widened. "I mean"— he pointed down the hallway toward Old Man Simpson's office— "I've gotta see Old Man . . ." He glanced at his watch, the second hand sweeping toward two o'clock, twenty seconds away. "Shit!" he blurted and broke free from Grace's grasp. "Wait right there, Grace. I'll be back in a second. I love you, Grace."

He sprinted down the hallway, planted his right foot and made a hard left into the alcove in front of Old Man Simpson's door, felt his knee give way with a searing blast of pain. "Aaaaghhh!" He went down in an undignified heap in front of the door, rolled once, looked up frantically at the doorknob a couple of feet above him. He clawed for it, struggling to balance himself on his left knee, grasped the doorknob, pushed mightily, and sprawled into Old Man Simpson's outer office with a thump. Gretchen peered over the edge of her desk at him. "Hello, Will," she said pleasantly.

"Gretchen."

"Looking for this?" She held up an envelope just as the door to

Old Man Simpson's inner office opened and Arthur Krupp stepped out. Krupp glanced at his watch, took a long, quick stride toward the desk, reaching for the envelope.

"That's mine!" Will yelped.

Gretchen stood quickly and started around the desk toward Will. "He's right," she said to Krupp.

"Late," Krupp said stonily, hand still outstretched. "Give me that."

Gretchen stopped in her tracks and fixed Krupp with an icy stare. "Mister Baggett got here first," she said primly. "He wins." She leaned over and handed Will the envelope.

"Thank you, Gretchen," he said weakly.

"My pleasure." She smiled—first at Will, then at Krupp, who turned on his heel and marched back through the door to the inner office.

"Krupp you," Will said softly as the door slammed shut.

"He's not a very nice person," Gretchen said. "In fact, Will, he is one hard-assed sonofabitch." She turned from Will, opened a closet behind her desk, and took out her jacket, scarf and pocketbook. She took her time putting on the jacket while Will struggled to his feet, leaning against her desk for support. His knee screamed at him.

"Where are you going, Gretchen?" he gasped through the pain.

"Home. Or maybe to Alaska with Mister Dinkins. Are you all right?"

"I hurt my knee. I don't think I can walk."

"Shall I call an ambulance?"

"Yes," Will said with a grimace, tucking the envelope into the inside pocket of his coat, "I think that's just what I need right now. An ambulance."

————

THERE WAS A good-sized crowd at the front entrance of Channel Seven by the time the paramedics carried Will down the stairs on a stretcher. At least half the station staff were there, crowding into the lobby and onto the sidewalk outside. Applause broke out. Some of the young people from the newsroom were crying. Will smiled, waved, gripped outstretched hands. "It's okay," he said. "It's okay. God bless you all."

Then he saw the gaggle of police officers waiting just outside. There were several squad cars now, pulled up at odd angles behind the first, lights flashing, radios crackling. "Good God," Will said softly as the paramedics wheeled him through the glass double doors and into the afternoon light.

One of the officers wore captain's bars on his shirt collar. He stepped from the group, blocking the path—a big, sturdy man with arms crossed over his chest and a grim expression. The paramedics stopped. "Mr. Baggett, I'm Captain Simmons. Raleigh Police Department. We've got a problem."

"What's that, Captain?"

"Officer Pettibone here says you ran a red light . . ."

Will shook his head. "No I didn't."

". . . ran a red light and then refused to stop when he tried to question you about it here in the parking lot."

"Well, I can explain that, Captain. I was about to miss a crucial appointment, so I asked the officer to wait. And"—he indicated his recumbent form on the stretcher—"here I am. As good as my word. I would have been here sooner except for this problem with my knee. But I say again, I don't believe I ran a red light."

"My officer says you did." He pointed. "Up here at the corner of Wade and St. Mary's. Went right through the light and near about T-boned his squad car."

One of the paramedics spoke up. "Captain, you gonna arrest the dude right here, or can we take him on to the emergency room?"

"Arrest?" Will yelped. "Look, I don't have any recollection of a red light or a squad car at Wade and St. Mary's. This is just a misunderstanding, Captain."

The crowd pressed in around them now, buzzing and chattering. There was a commotion to Will's left, and Grace Hibbert, the sales department secretary, pushed her way through the crush. "Hey, that's Will Baggett!" she cried. "You can't arrest Will Baggett!"

Captain Simmons ignored her. He ticked off the charges on his fingers. "Running a red light, driving too fast for conditions, failure to yield, failure to obey an officer . . ."

Will felt a rush of panic. "That's nuts!" he cried. "Why don't you just add drunk and disorderly."

"Would you like to take a Breathalyzer test?" the Captain asked mildly.

"Of course not."

"How about it, Captain?" the paramedic insisted.

"You can't arrest Will Baggett!" Grace Hibbert bellowed again.

Captain Simmons spun on her. "You wanna join him, lady?"

Grace shrank. "No sir," she said in a small voice. But then others in the crowd took up the cry. Will looked about wildly. The noise level rose several decibels and some of it was sounding nasty.

Will raised his arms. "It's okay!" he cried. "It's just a misunderstanding! I'll take care of it! Let the police do their job!"

Captain Simmons jerked a thumb toward the ambulance. "Take him to the emergency room. I'll be right behind you." He stepped aside and the paramedics grabbed the stretcher again, front and rear, and started hustling toward the yawning rear doors of the ambulance. The crowd surged behind them.

Will heard a rapid *click-whirr* and looked up to see a photographer he knew from the *News and Observer* bearing down on him, firing off shots. "Somebody call my lawyer!" he yelled. "Morris deLesseps!" And then there were more photographers pressing in on them, toting television news cameras with station logos on the sides. Channel Seven. Channel Four. Channel Thirty-two. A couple of people with home video cameras. Will instinctively put his hands up, shielding himself.

Then he was up, into the ambulance, one of the paramedics scrambling in behind him, the doors slamming shut. The paramedic leaned over him, buckling the stretcher to the floor, strapping him in. Pandemonium outside—shouts, police radios, a siren off somewhere in the distance. Somebody pounded on the side of the ambulance. The other paramedic leaped into the driver's seat and threw it into gear. Will felt his breath coming in ragged gasps, blood pounding in his temples. His knee throbbed.

He motioned to the paramedic, who was buckling himself into a seat next to the stretcher. The man leaned closer. "Why me?" Will croaked between clenched teeth.

———

WILL AWOKE FROM a sedative-induced fog to find himself in his own bed, pajama-clad, his right leg encased in a plastic-and-canvas cast held tight with Velcro. The door was closed, dim daylight seeping in around the drawn curtains. The clock on the bedside table told him it was nearly eleven.

The rest of the world filtered in slowly: traffic on the street outside, the whine of a leaf blower in the Durkins' yard next door, the faint ringing of the telephone and murmur of the answering machine downstairs, the sound of saws and hammers and crowbars—the Christians, still happily demolishing the rear of his home. He pushed himself gingerly to a sitting position and winced as his knee protested with a stab of pain.

On the bedside table were a folded newspaper, a plastic urinal, a small brown plastic bottle of pain pills, a glass of water, a note from Clarice: SHOWING HOUSE IN CARY. BACK EARLY AFTERNOON. TAKE PILL AT TEN. P.S. CALL MORRIS.

He eased his legs over the side of the bed, peed in the urinal, took a pill, settled himself again. He felt wretched—mouth rancid, knee aching, rough stubble of beard on his face.

He sat for a moment, mind blank. Then he remembered the emergency room. Blinding light, babble of voices, intercom and police walkie-talkie. Clarice there, bending over him, her hand cool on his cheek. Morris deLesseps rushing in. "Damn, son, I told you to get the money, not start a ruckus." The pain in his knee was excruciating. A sprain, the doctor said after the X rays. No surgery needed. Couple of weeks of rest, then some light rehab. But quite painful in the meantime. "God sure did a sloppy job when he designed knees," the doctor said jocularly. A hale fellow who asked Will about the weather forecast.

They gave him a shot. The rest was a blur. Night. Home in the car. Bed. He dreamed of violent weather.

He turned on the table lamp, reached for the newspaper and spread it open across his lap. "Oh God."

The photograph was a good deal larger than the one that had appeared in the paper the day before—Will on the stretcher, half-rising, arms outthrust, hands splayed, a wild look in his eyes, Captain Simmons and several other police officers flanking the stretcher and clearing a way through the crowd. Will thought he looked like an earthquake refugee, blinded by sunlight as rescuers bore him from days beneath rubble, his clothing and skin somehow miraculously unsullied by the ordeal. But there was also a hint of white collar criminality here—perhaps, say, a crazed stockbroker captured after a gun battle with officers of the Securities and Exchange Commission who had come to arrest him for manipulating the accounts of little old ladies. The caption on the photograph read: CHARGES PENDING.

The story that accompanied the photo spoke of an "altercation" at the Channel Seven studios and reminded readers that weathercaster Will Baggett had been relieved of his duties twenty-four hours previously. It left the impression that there had been some kind of confrontation between Will and the new owners of the station and that police officers had been summoned. There was also a traffic violation involved, though details of that were not clear. None of the principals—police, Channel Seven, Baggett, lawyers—were commenting. Will read the story twice with a growing sense of horror. He had made of himself a public spectacle, a complete and utter fool. In the space of forty-eight hours, he had gone from revered celebrity to criminal laughingstock, at least in the eyes of the Raleigh public. He had lost his dignity, had taken a giant gimp-legged leap into rank foolishness.

The humiliation of it was bad enough, but there was worse. He had handed Spectrum Broadcasting his head on a platter. They had fired him and he had acted like an ass about it, at least that's what the newspaper made it look like. No amount of explaining would change the stark black-and-white image of a slightly crazed man on a stretcher, surrounded by police. And as for any interest Raleigh's other television stations might have in him—well, this sure as hell put a crimp in that, didn't it.

His bowels lurched. Nausea coursed up his throat. He fought the urge to throw up. He dropped the newspaper weakly over the side of the bed and reclined. After a few minutes the pain pill did its job and he drifted mercifully off to sleep again.

———

HE WAS AWARE OF pressure on the other side of the bed. After a while, Clarice said, "It's almost five. Don't you want to wake up?"

"No," he said. "I really don't." He reached a hand to her. She was prone on top of the covers, fully clothed. He felt silk, bone of hip, firm flesh of thigh. "You'll wrinkle your dress," he said. She didn't answer.

He opened his eyes. The house was quiet now, the Christians apparently gone for the day. Then he heard the downstairs phone. It rang for a long time and then fell silent. He imagined that the answering machine had filled up with calls and then stopped taking any more.

"How do you feel?" Clarice asked.

"Screwed."

She didn't say anything for a moment. Then: "Morris told me all about it. The paper got that part of the story wrong, didn't they. Morris called it a comedy of errors."

"I appreciate his sense of humor." Another silence. "Did you sell the house in Cary?"

"Yes."

"I'm glad."

"Will, it's not as bad as you imagine. Morris has talked to the District Attorney about dropping the charges. Mister Simpson gave out a statement saying it's all an unfortunate misunderstanding, there was no trouble with the Spectrum people."

Old Man Simpson. At home waiting to die, glad not to be around to see what hideous thing Spectrum Broadcasting would make of his television station, his life's work. Arthur Krupp should have released a statement to the press about Will's dilemma, but he didn't. So Old Man Simpson did. Still taking care of Will Baggett. Will felt the hot sting of tears. He vowed to call. To go by the Simpson home. No hard feelings, at least none serious enough to make it impossible to do the right, the decent thing.

They lay there together quietly, not touching. And then Will sat up suddenly, kicked in the gut by something that had been lurking down there since his visit to Old Man Simpson's office two days ago, something he had almost forgotten. "You know what Simpson told me?"

"What, Will?"

"He said your father called him about me."

"When?"

"Twenty years ago."

There was a long moment before Clarice said, "They were fraternity brothers at Duke."

"I know that."

"And?"

"Here, all these years, I've been under the impression I got the job on my own."

There was an edge to her voice now, impatient. And something else. "You did, Will. You got it because you were qualified. All Daddy did was ask Mister Simpson to give you a fair chance."

"You knew about it."

"Yes."

He swung his legs over the side of the bed and sat, his back to her. "But you didn't say anything."

"Will," she said finally, wearily, "I'm not going to go there. If you resent the fact that my father put in a good word for you, that's your problem. I thought, and he thought, that it was a kind and gracious thing to do. Do you think you've got to do everything in this world right by yourself?"

He shrugged. "Well, I sure got fired right by myself. I'm sure nobody put in a word for me on that."

She sat up and put a hand on his back. "Will," she said softly, "I think you need to go somewhere quiet for a while and sort all of this out. Not just the job, but how you feel about things in general."

He turned to her, catching on to the thing in her voice. "And you?"

"Maybe I could use some quiet, too."

He sat very still. *What's going on here?* He knew, of course, but then again he didn't.

She said, "Your cousin Wingfoot's downstairs. He wants to take you to Brunswick County."

"Good God."

Brunswick County. Once, a good long time ago, it had been a place of refuge. Not of his choosing back then, and certainly a time that existed bittersweet in his memory. But it might indeed be the place of quiet and recuperation he needed just now, away from prying eyes and inquiring callers. In Brunswick County, on the peaceful banks of the Cape Fear River, he might be able to put body and soul back together and figure out how the hell he was going to get his life back.

But what about this thing with Clarice? Shouldn't he stay here and thrash it out with her? Shouldn't they ever so carefully poke about in the minefield, locate the mines and disarm them? Or would that be the very wrong thing to do just now? Was it better, for the moment, while he was distraught and poisoned with dread, to put yellow warning tape around the field and step back and think about things, each of them in their own time and space? Either way might be right. Or wrong.

Clarice stood beside the bed with a rustle of silk as she smoothed her dress. "I think you should go," she said.

"But you think all those people down there in Brunswick County are crazy."

"At the moment," she said, "you might fit in just fine."

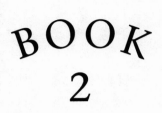

BOOK
2

5 | THE SUMMER OF 1965 was one of the hottest anybody could remember in Dysart, North Carolina. There was a string of days in early August in which the temperature regularly flirted with one hundred and the humidity was as thick as pudding. It was hot, but it was not dry. Almost every afternoon, just like clockwork, thunderheads gathered over Dysart and deluged the town and surrounding countryside with rain, gusty wind and occasional hail. Rain came in buckets, as one local put it, "like a cow pissing on a flat rock." The rain and fetid heat made Dysart's grass grow like crazy. And the rain and the heat and the grass made twelve-year-old Wilbur Baggett think he might go crazy. If he didn't die first.

On a particular Thursday afternoon in early August, Wilbur struggled across the lush fescue lawn in front of Buster Dysart's home, muttering curses at the heat, the lawn mower, the fescue, the insects that swarmed up from the grass and peppered his exposed flesh, the threatening clouds beginning to pile up overhead, and Buster. Especially Buster.

It seemed that Buster Dysart was everywhere in his twelve-year-old life. Buster owned (among other local businesses) the Western Auto store where Wilbur had purchased the lawn mower in early June, just after school let out for the summer. Rather, he had begun *paying* for the lawn mower in early June. It was a time payment plan: $20 down and the remainder of the $79.95 (plus interest) over the course of the summer in twelve weekly payments of $10 apiece. Wilbur was no whiz at math, but even he could figure out that

Buster would make a handsome profit from the lawn mower. Buster was no fool as a businessman. Dysart might be a pissant town, hardly a speck on the map, but Buster, latest in the line of Dysarts who had founded it, owned most of the place and profited thereby.

Buster also owned the most handsome home in Dysart, this red-brick-and-white-columns monstrosity with its lush expanse of fescue lawn where Wilbur labored now. Buster had other people who seeded and fertilized the lawn and kept it free of crabgrass and insects and fungus. But only to Wilbur Baggett did he entrust the mowing of the lawn because Wilbur Baggett worked cheap and Buster Dysart was one cheap sonofabitch. Most of Wilbur's customers paid him to mow their lawns once a week, an average of two dollars per lawn. Buster insisted on his being mowed every other week. And he paid three dollars for a lawn that was twice as big as any other in town. "Take it or leave it," Buster had said. Wilbur took it because at the time, when June was just beginning and Wilbur was just starting out with a brand-new lawn mowing business, a customer was a customer. Every two weeks, as the summer progressed, he regretted it.

"Sonofabitch," Wilbur yelped as the lawn mower choked down for the umpteenth time. It was not much of a mower—he had realized that almost as soon as he forked over the down payment and began to trudge from lawn to lawn. He had bought one of the cheapest models at Western Auto, with a lightweight aluminum frame and a dinky engine: just dandy if you intended to occasionally trim up around your back-yard swimming pool, but no match for a town full of rain-fed fescue, especially the yawning front lawn at Buster Dysart's house where the grass was five inches high and thickly matted. There were big chunks of aluminum missing from the mower's frame, victim of rocks lurking in the grass; and the engine, victim of two months of rugged work, wheezed and rattled and died at the slightest provocation.

Wilbur backed the mower away from the clot of grass that had bogged it down and reached for the starter cord. He reached, but he couldn't quite reach it. His body just wouldn't move anymore. He felt light-headed. Spots danced before his eyes. He sank to his knees, shoulders slumped, and stayed there in just that position for what seemed a great long while — eyes closed, mind entirely blank. The sweet-tart odor of fresh-cut grass, engorged with precipitation and fertilizer and herbicide, made him nauseated. Every inch of him was sweat-soaked — cutoff-jean shorts, grubby T-shirt, sockless sneakers, the goofy narrow-brimmed hat his mother made him wear. He felt entirely drained, entirely empty, entirely lost in a sea of grass that stretched so far ahead of him that he could barely see September off there in the distance. September, when school would start and the final payment would be made on the mower just as it died completely and went to the scrap heap behind the Western Auto store. Next summer, he would have to start all over again. That is, unless his father, Tyler Baggett, came home and rescued him from all this — from lawn mowing, from Dysart, from yawning uncertainty.

It was, he reckoned, just after five o'clock in the afternoon. He had been at it since early morning, trying to get a head start on the worst of the heat and humidity. He had twelve soggy dollars in his pocket, the result of an unceasing day in which he had stopped only long enough to drink an RC Cola and eat a package of cheese crackers he had bought at the tiny corner grocery store next to Old Lady Bentley's house. Old Lady Bentley had plied him with ice water when he mowed her lawn at 11:30 and had given him a quarter tip, which he had spent on the RC and crackers.

Five o'clock in the afternoon, his body and soul drained and shriveled, still more than half of Buster Dysart's lawn left to cut.

And then the rain started. It came without warning — none of the rumble of thunder or gusts of wind that usually preceded the late-afternoon summer downpours. It just started raining — a steady shower that pattered on his hat and shoulders and drummed quietly on the aluminum frame of the lawn mower. He roused himself long enough to take off the hat and the T-shirt and toss them aside in the grass. He turned his face skyward and let the rain beat against his face and bare shoulders. He opened his mouth and stuck out his tongue and tasted the warm wetness and let it soak into his skin and mingle with his honest sweat. There would be no mowing the rest of Buster Dysart's grass this August afternoon, not with it five inches high and rain-soaked. So Wilbur Baggett rose unsteadily to his feet and pushed his mower homeward.

It was a square cinder-block building with a low-sloping roof on a potholed, unpaved street on Dysart's outskirts. There was a garage on one side and a weed-choked vacant lot on the other. The garage, tended by two middle-aged brothers, was noisy with the clang of metal and the rumble of engines from early morning until early evening, after which the brothers began drinking and arguing, activities that would take them well past dark. The vacant lot on the other side was quiet, but snake infested. Wilbur's mother, Rosanna, had killed some kind of reptile with a hoe in their back yard just days ago. After Rosanna got through with the snake, Wilbur couldn't tell whether it was poisonous or not.

Buster Dysart owned everything on the street—garage, house, and vacant lot. And now, as Wilbur approached, pushing the lawn mower through the rain, Buster Dysart's big-finned Chrysler was parked in the twin ruts next to the house that served as a driveway. Buster's car was the only one there, of course, because Wilbur's father was using the family automobile on a business trip. Tyler had been gone for three months.

Wilbur stowed the lawn mower next to the house and covered it with a ragged piece of tarpaulin and went in through the back door, letting the screen slam loudly behind him. When he got to the living room, Buster was headed for the front door, filling it with his big round butt as he said over his shoulder, "Monday, Miz Baggett. That's it. Monday, or I'll put you out." And he was gone into the late-afternoon drizzle.

"Asshole," Rosanna said softly. She was planted firmly in the middle of the room, back to Wilbur, arms encircling her torso in a tight grip. Her shoulders were shaking.

"Mom . . ."

She didn't move. He crossed to her, touched her arm. He thought maybe she was crying, but she was dry-eyed when she turned to him. There was a deep flush in her high, fine cheekbones. She took a long, deep breath and her arms dropped to her side. She looked him over. "You're drenched."

Wilbur looked out the front door, out to where Buster's Chrysler was backing into the street. "Asshole," he said.

She put her arms around him, drenched and all, and hugged him tightly for a good long moment. She was still shaking just a little. He could feel it all through himself.

A month behind on the rent, and another payment due Monday. Buster Dysart wanted all of it, all one hundred ten dollars of it. All they could scrape together, as they sat at the kitchen table that evening, was forty-two, and that included the twelve Wilbur had brought home in the pocket of his cutoff jeans.

"How many lawns tomorrow?" she asked.

"Just two. And finish Mister Dysart's. That's"—he did the math—"seven dollars. I could do the Mondays on Sunday."

"Not in Dysart," Rosanna said with a wry smile. Wilbur and Rosanna didn't belong to a church, but it seemed as if everybody else in town did. Dysart was as dead as roadkill on Sundays.

"When do you get paid?" he asked.

"Next Friday."

Rosanna worked checkout at the Winn-Dixie, a couple of blocks' walk from their house to the main street that served as the downtown business district. Whenever Wilbur started feeling sorry for himself, trudging along behind his lawn mower in the heat, he thought of Rosanna standing there at the checkout counter for eight hours a day, ringing up everybody else's groceries, then walking home with a small sack of their own just after five o'clock—likely as not just as the daily rain shower hit. He had bought her an umbrella for her birthday the end of June, but a vicious gust of wind during an afternoon storm had ripped it from her hand as she tried to juggle it and a sack of groceries and it had sailed under the wheels of a dump truck.

"Forty-two and seven. That's forty-nine."

"Uh-huh."

"We could go next door and stick up the garage," Wilbur said.

"We don't have a gun."

"Maybe they'd lend us a tire tool."

Rosanna laughed. She had a soft, easy laugh, even when she was sixty-one dollars in the hole with no prospects. "Headline in the *Dysart Tribune*: GARAGE ROBBED WITH BORROWED TIRE TOOL."

"Dysart doesn't have a *Tribune*."

"But," she said, "Dysart does have an asshole who wants a hundred and ten dollars by Monday."

They sat for a while thinking about it and then Wilbur went to the refrigerator and opened an RC Cola and put ice in two glasses and halved the soda between them and they sat and sipped on it, making it last, while they thought about it some more. There was one thing that hung in the air between them, and that was Tyler Baggett. But neither one spoke of that. After they finished their RC Cola, Rosanna stood up and said, "Come help me wash my hair."

It was long and straight and fine and hung mane-like down her back. She knelt next to the bathtub and he straddled her back, piling the wet hair on the back of her head and kneading in the shampoo, using strong, hard pressure the way she liked it. She always looked small and frail to him this way, with thin shoulders and the knobs of her spine poking the flesh above the strap of her bra, and the hair, wet and plastered, exposing a skull that was almost tiny. But she was not frail at all, not in the least. She was strong and sturdy in her wiry smallness, and she had strong opinions about things and people, and when she spoke, it was in a firm, strong voice that made her twelve-year-old son feel anchored and rooted, at least in her presence. She was always very much a mother and put up with no foolishness, but she spoke to him as if he were older. In some ways, he supposed, he was.

"It's been three months," he said.

She cocked her head to the side. "What? I can't hear you for the water."

Louder. "I said it's been three months."

"Yes."

"Maybe he'll get here this weekend."

"Uh-huh." The way she said it, it didn't sound like she was counting on Tyler Baggett to show up in the nick of time. Tyler Baggett wasn't a nick-of-time kind of guy. When he showed up, it was usually at odd moments.

When she spoke of Tyler to Wilbur, she pulled no punches and made no excuses. She called Tyler what he was, and he was a golf hustler. At least, that was what he worked at.

He had come back from Korea with a chestful of medals and a steel plate in his head—both medals and steel plate the result of an act of singular bravery. He had been the pilot of a tiny, slow-moving plane, an aerial artillery spotter. On a frigid, snow-swirling after-noon, as a Red Chinese human wave attack threatened to overrun a Marine Corps position near the Chosin Reservoir, Tyler kept his plane in the air above the battlefield while the Chinese riddled it with shot and shell, calling in artillery fire that broke apart the enemy formations. The plane finally gave up the ghost and spiraled down to a grinding crash just behind the American lines. The Marines pulled him out of the wreckage—one side of his skull split open, one leg shredded, life oozing out of every bodily opening. Somehow, he survived the grievous wounds and the jostling of the litter-bearers who toted him back to a first aid station and the trip by ambulance over rugged ground to a field hospital where doctors managed to save the leg and patch the hole in his head. He spent six months in a hospital in Japan and then he came home and took up golf on a course near the Veterans Administration hospital in Salisbury where he completed his recuperation.

From what Rosanna had learned from Tyler Baggett's family, the man who returned from Korea was a good deal different from the one who left. He had been quiet, bookish, introspective—

headed for, they expected, a career in law or medicine or perhaps a college professorship in one of the social sciences. Now he was voluble, quirky, charmingly outgoing, a man with a quick laugh and an odd glint in his eye and an astonishing talent for striking a golf ball. His older brother, French Baggett, had once opined that the Chinese bullets and the crash had altered Tyler's entire neuro-motor makeup, scrambling signals and re-wiring his brain and body in an odd way that established some almost mystical connection that ran from eye to hand to tee to green. Tyler Baggett loved golf and loved life and loved easy money, especially the kind you could win from other golfers.

In the early years he had worked the Carolinas, the country clubs and public courses, anywhere he could find a golfer willing to wager on his prowess. He walked the fairways gimp-legged from his Korean leg wound, and that helped sucker the unsuspecting. He won a great deal of money and made sure he spent whatever was in his pocket at any given time. He and Rosanna had met in a bar in Greensboro on an evening after he had made a sizable raid on the bank accounts of several of Greensboro Country Club's members. They had married shortly thereafter, when she turned up pregnant, and after several years of bouncing from one town to another, he had settled his wife and son in Dysart, which was sort of neutral ground. It had no golf course, thus nobody to hold a grudge over losing a thousand-dollar nassau. And it was centrally located in the Carolinas. Tyler could toss his clubs into the trunk of the car and be anywhere from Boone to Charleston within hours.

Nobody in Dysart knew what Tyler did for a living. Rosanna and Wilbur simply told folks that he "traveled." And Tyler was never there long enough for anybody to ask many questions. He would swoop back in periodically with cash in his pocket and they would have a high old time—going to movies and eating at nice restaurants in Charlotte and Winston-Salem and Raleigh, jaunting around the Carolinas to places like Myrtle Beach and Grandfather Mountain and sometimes even farther than that, to Hot Springs or

New Orleans, one time all the way to San Francisco. Then one day the cash would be mostly gone and they would be deliciously exhausted from the spending of it and Tyler would be gone again, leaving them with what little cash was left. It was never quite enough to sustain them until Tyler got back again, and so Rosanna worked at the Winn-Dixie for sixty-five dollars a week and Wilbur mowed lawns, and together they usually had enough to scrape by. Usually.

Tyler was quite up-front with his son about what he did out on the road. "I fleece suckers," he told Wilbur, "and I'm damn good at it." The way he said it made it sound like the most natural thing in the world.

Tyler found a lot of suckers, he said, many of them at country clubs. "Now, there's nothing wrong with country clubs. Plenty of nice people belong to country clubs. But some of 'em are fellows who've got new money in their pockets. Doing pretty good at some kind of business, driving a fancy car, living in a big spread, wangled their way into a country club membership. They take up golf and take a few lessons and get to whacking the ball around pretty well. And pretty soon they think they're hot stuff. A guy with new money in his pocket is apt to think he's bullet-proof."

"And then you come along," Wilbur said.

"Yessir. Just wander into the pro shop and strike up a conversation. Or get into the dollar-ante poker game in the locker room. And one thing leads to another and first thing you know you're out on the course. After nine holes, I'm down three and spraying the ball all over the place and cussing to myself. New Money thinks he's found a patsy. Okay, let's double the bet over the back nine. I lose another hole and New Money's already counting his winnings. Down four holes with eight to go. I change putters and pull a new two-wood out of the bag and suddenly I'm making some shots. On the seventeenth, I've pulled even. Everything riding on the last hole. New Money's got his ego sitting on one shoulder and a monkey on the other. Double the bet again. I hit my drive about two-fifty straight down the fairway with a little fade on the end and I look at New Money and I can see it in his eyes. He's a dead duck. He hits his drive into the trees and then catches a fairway bunker and before we even reach the green he's paid up and headed for his car. I don't give a damn what he tells the guys in the clubhouse. I'm out of there."

"Ain't that gambling?" Wilbur asked. Gambling, he knew from character study at school, was sinful and illegal and addictive and led to other kinds of licentious living. A fellow who started out playing poker for nickels could end up a hippie or a free-love Communist.

"I think of it as social work," Tyler said. "When I leave New Money standing in the parking lot, he's a wiser man. At least he knows he ain't bulletproof. I may have saved him from making the same kind of mistake in his business. His wife can keep going to New York to shop and his kids can get a Chapel Hill education and he'll keep his fine house and his big car. Well, *usually* the car. I've won a couple of those, too."

Over the years, of course, the Carolinas golfing community had caught on to Tyler Baggett. He roamed far afield now. He had set out for Kentucky three months ago and had called only once, from Pine Bluff, Louisiana. Things were not going well. His putting stroke had deserted him. But he was pressing on. And meanwhile, back in Dysart . . .

"Okay," Wilbur said. "Rinse."

Rosanna leaned under the faucet, letting the gush of lukewarm water carry away the shampoo. He guided the water with his hands, filtering it through his fingers into the fine strands of hair and then squeezing it out. He turned off the taps and handed her a towel as she rose, rubbing vigorously at her hair, turning to face him. He felt his face flush, seeing her here in her brassiere, trying not to look.

She smiled, reading him. "Are you getting a little old for this?"

The blush deepened. She touched his cheek, then punched him oh-so-lightly in the tummy. "Funny feelings?"

He nodded mutely.

"You're almost a teenager. Not my little boy any more. When Dad gets home, you two need to talk."

She left the bathroom to him, and by the time he had showered and changed clothes she had supper ready. They took their plates to the living room and sat together on the sofa and watched an *I Love Lucy* re-run on the black-and-white while they ate and laughed at Lucy working on an assembly line in a cake factory and trying to put cakes into boxes while the line kept going faster and faster. It was a disaster, a wonderful mess, cakes going everywhere and Lucy ending up covered with cake and the studio audience and the folks in Dysart all in hysterics. Pure slapstick, just the way they liked it.

Later, in bed, he started thinking about Lucille Ball and how it might be to have a television show like that and make a mess with cakes and have everybody laughing, and then when the show was over you could just go home and let somebody else clean up the mess. If you had your own television show, and made people at home feel good, they would send you cards and flowers and maybe name their kids after you. There were probably all sorts of little Lucilles all over the country. And the people who owned the television station would pay you enough money so that you wouldn't have to kiss the ass of somebody like Buster Dysart. The thought of Buster Dysart soured the good feeling he had about Lucille Ball. Big Butt Buster Dysart loomed like a hungry beast out there on Monday.

The thought of Buster Dysart brought on the thought of Nell Dysart, Buster's daughter, who was in the same grade with Wilbur and, at one point toward the end of the school year, had thought he was cute, which was exactly what he thought of Nell. Wilbur had discovered in the past couple of years that he had a knack for mimicry. He could do Elvis Presley and Ed Sullivan and Cary Grant, and he had this whole routine he had thought up where Ed Sullivan doesn't want Elvis Presley on his television show, but Elvis shows up and starts singing and gyrating, and before it's over, Ed

Sullivan is singing and gyrating right alongside him. He had performed it for Rosanna, who laughed until she cried, and then at a
Wednesday assembly and the kids thought it was a riot, but the
principal summoned him to his office right after assembly and told
him he didn't want to see anything like that in his school again. The
principal was a deacon at Dysart Baptist.

Nell Dysart was one of the kids who thought Wilbur was funny,
principal or no principal. She sat right across the aisle from him in
Old Lady Bentley's English class and they passed notes back and
forth while Old Lady Bentley wasn't looking until she caught them
one day and made Wilbur, who was the author of the particular
note she confiscated, stand with his nose pressed against a circle she
had drawn on the chalkboard. After class, Nell had said she was
sorry he was the one who got caught, because if it had been *her* note,
Old Lady Bentley probably wouldn't have done anything because
Buster Dysart was the chairman of the School Board and the top
deacon at Dysart Baptist.

Nell had freckles and reddish hair and a nose that turned
up right at the tip, and when she brushed her hand lightly against
his in the hallway outside Old Lady Bentley's room, it made him
feel incredibly nice. At home that night, Wilbur thought about
washing Nell Dysart's hair and his penis made a tent out of his
pyjamas, and after that it made him self-conscious about washing
his mother's hair when she was wearing nothing on top but her
brassiere.

On the last day of school, when they were sitting in Old Lady
Bentley's class waiting for final report cards to be passed out, Nell
passed him a note. I'M HAVING A PARTY AT THE SWIM-
MING POOL TOMORROW AFTERNOON. 5:00.

He had spent all the next day mowing lawns, juggling his schedule so that the last customer of the day was Fatboy Gaines, the
police chief, who lived just a block from the swimming pool. He
stowed the mower behind Fatboy's garage and headed for the party.

There was a squat two-story building at poolside—concession
stand and dressing rooms on the ground floor, a big open room on

the top with a pinball machine, jukebox, and Ping-Pong table and a sign above the door that said DYSART MUNICIPAL RECREATION CENTER. Fatboy Gaines's brother, Solly, was the pool manager and he presided over a booth at the pool gate where he stopped Wilbur in his tracks. "Hey, where you going, sonny?"

Wilbur pointed up at the recreation center, where Elvis Presley's "Teddy Bear" was drifting from the open windows. "Nell Dysart's party."

"Twenty-five cents," Solly said.

"But . . ."

"Twenty-five cents."

Wilbur fished in the pocket of his cutoffs and handed Solly a crumpled dollar bill and got three quarters in return.

He climbed the steps and stood for a moment at the screen door, listening to Elvis and chattering laughter and Nell Dysart's tinkling lilt. Then he opened the screen and stepped inside. There were fifteen or so kids there, drinking Cokes and playing games and jostling each other. Nell was standing by the pinball machine, watching Joe Curtis as he pulled the lever and sent a ball spinning into the maze and did a little body English jive to get the ball to give him a hundred million points. Nell had her hand on Joe Curtis's shoulder.

Wilbur headed straight for the pinball machine and reached it just as Joe hit the jackpot and lights started flashing and bells started dinging. "Oh, Joe!" Nell cried. "You're the champ!"

"Nell . . . ," Wilbur said.

She turned with a jerk and stared at him.

"I made it," he said, grinning. She kept staring and he felt his grin freeze on his face and turn to something more like a grimace as her upper lip curled slowly up and up, toward her nose.

"You stink," she said, loud enough for everybody in the room to hear it, and all of the other noise stopped except for Elvis and the pinball machine. They all stared at him. Then he fled as the laughter began, flaying his back. He didn't even stop to get his twenty-five cents back from Solly Gaines.

He sobbed in Rosanna's arms when she got home from the Winn-Dixie, sobbed with impotent humiliation.

"Honey, I'm sorry," she said as she cradled him on the sofa and brushed the hair back from his forehead. And then, ever so gently, "Didn't you think about coming home and taking a bath first?"

"No. I just went."

"You were excited."

"Uh-huh."

"You like her."

"Did. Not anymore. She made me feel like I'd been wallering in shit."

Rosanna was usually pretty firm about four-letter words, but this time she didn't say anything. She held him and rubbed his forehead and patted his arm and let him be miserable and then later fixed banana pudding, his favorite, for dessert. It helped, helped a lot, but it didn't anywhere near make up for the sting of public shame. It was his fault, of course. He had made a terrible mistake and opened himself to being the butt of laughter and ridicule. But that didn't excuse Nell Dysart, who should have taken him by the arm and walked him to the door and gently said, "Why don't you go freshen up and come back later." That's what his mother would have done. His mother was a lady who knew what to say and when to say it and how to make somebody feel okay even when things weren't going so swell. He thought of all sorts of things he could do to Nell Dysart, like sneaking into her house in the middle of the night and setting her hair on fire. Instead, he just kept to himself as the summer wore on and the fescue grew and Tyler Baggett was gone, gone, gone.

One thing he would not do again, he vowed, was entertain any snot-nosed Dysart kids with his imitations. It was an odd thing about performing, he had thought when he started doing it—a way to get people to like you, and yet at the same time a way to hold them at arm's length, just beyond the outer boundary of whatever it was you were doing that they weren't clever or talented enough to do. Close, but not too close. Well, screw 'em. Let 'em get their Ed Sullivan and Elvis Presley somewhere else.

―――――

SATURDAY. Wilbur mowed lawns and Rosanna checked groceries and at the end of the day when he headed home, he stopped just out of sight of the house, around the corner from the garage, and took a deep breath. *Be there*. But there was no car in the yard. When Rosanna got home a half-hour later, he could tell that she had been a little hopeful, too.

―――――

SHE HAD A SURPRISE for him on Sunday. She had arranged with Dooley Potts, an old guy who bagged groceries at the Winn-Dixie, to take them to Asheboro, twenty miles away, to a movie. Dysart had a movie theater, but it closed on Sunday in deference to the church crowd. Folks in Asheboro were a little more liberal-minded.

"We can't afford to go to a movie," Wilbur said. "We've got rent to pay."

"We don't have the rent money whether we go to the movie or not. So why not enjoy a movie?" She was, he thought, a little like Tyler. Spend it while you had it. Let tomorrow be tomorrow.

"What are we gonna do on Monday?"

"Maybe something will turn up," she said with a wave of her hand. "A bag of cash will fall out of an airplane into the yard. If you don't want to go to the movie, you can stay here and wait for the airplane."

They drove over in Dooley's old Ford and saw the re-release of *Gone with the Wind*. Dooley had a good sense of humor, despite the fact that he had lost his wife to cancer a couple of months before, and he cackled every time the black maid, Prissy, came on screen. On the way home, Wilbur did imitations. *"Lawd, Miz*

Scarlett, I don't know how to birth no baby." And Elvis, appearing on Ed Sullivan's show. Dooley howled. "You oughta be in showbiz, kid."

Dooley let them off in front of the house. The yard was still empty. They went in and fixed RC Cola over ice and sat at the kitchen table with an oscillating fan running on the counter to stir the early evening heat. The cinder-block house trapped it and held it and even with the fan running and all the doors and windows open, it was like an oven. It would have been a little cooler outside, but you couldn't sit outside in Dysart in August because of the mosquitoes. They were plentiful and they were big. Dooley Potts said he had waked up the night before to hear two huge mosquitoes talking at the foot of his bed. "Do you want to eat him here, or carry him off in the woods?" Wilbur thought he might work it into a routine sometime. But not for the snot-noses in Dysart.

They sipped on their RC Colas and sat very still, making small, economical movements. But even so, Wilbur could feel trickles of sweat down his back. "Maybe he'll be here tomorrow," he said finally.

"I don't think so," Rosanna said. Then after thinking about it for a moment she added, "He must be doing all right. Winning some money. When he's got his game going . . ." There was a quiet, distant look in her eyes, as if she were out there on the road or on a fairway with him, following along while he fleeced the suckers with a long, straight drive and a little fade at the end. She had gone with him a few times at the beginning, she said, before the baby came. One time she watched from the woods near the eighteenth green at a country club in Fayetteville while he won twelve hundred dollars and a Rolex wristwatch.

"I don't think he's coming tomorrow," Wilbur said, "just like he didn't come yesterday or the day before or anytime for three months. What if he doesn't come back at all?"

She turned with a jerk and stared at him as if he had just struck her a really underhanded, cheap blow, as if he had just asked the most ridiculous question in the world, as if he were a little twelve-year-old snot-nose who didn't understand a thing in the blessed world. But she didn't say a word. She got up and went to the back door and stared out across the yard, sipping her RC Cola, her back very straight. He could see the ridges of her spine through the thin dress and the way her hair fell mane-like across her shoulders.

"I'm going to town," she said after a while.

"What for?"

"To use the pay phone."

"Do you know where to reach him?"

"No." Then, "I'm gonna call your Uncle French."

"Aw gawd, Mama. Not again."

"Just for a little while, until Dad gets back."

"They act like we've got some kind of social disease or something."

"French doesn't. He's always said, 'If you need me . . .'"

"But Aunt Margaret. She thinks her shit smells better than anybody else's."

She turned abruptly. "Watch your mouth, bub. That's no way to talk around a lady."

She didn't say, he thought, talk *about* a lady.

"Anyway," she said firmly, "there's nothing else to do. I won't give Buster Dysart the satisfaction of kicking us out." There was nothing resembling defeat in her voice. Just doing what had to be done. That was the way she was.

————

FRENCH BAGGETT, Tyler's older brother, was there with a truck late on Monday afternoon, and he had Wilbur's and Rosanna's things — the few items of furniture and boxes of clothes — loaded by dark.

"What about this lawn mower," he said, peering out the back door.

"Leave it," Wilbur said. "It's about shot anyway."

"No," said Rosanna, "you take it to Mister Dysart. It's not paid for. It belongs to him."

"Aw, Mama."

She pointed. He went. He was back in twenty minutes.

"Did you take it to his house?"

"No, to the Western Auto."

"It's closed. Did you just leave it?"

"Yes ma'am. I set the sucker on fire, and then I just left it."

6 | IT WAS A FINE HOUSE—two stories of white-stuccoed brick with thick round columns across the front, set back about a hundred yards or so from the Cape Fear River in a shelter of towering trees with a magnificent, spreading live oak in the front yard between house and river's edge. There was a plaque by the front door that said Baggett House was on the National Register of Historic Places, which meant that you couldn't ever tear it down or pee in the front yard. Not that Uncle French and Aunt Margaret would ever think of doing either, nor would their daughter, Minerva. Their son, Wingfoot, now that was another matter. Wingfoot had built a ramshackle tree house in the live oak, and he didn't care whether the place was historic or not. Uncle French had tried to get him to tear it down and rebuild it in a tree someplace else on the property, but Wingfoot was, at fifteen, rock-solid stubborn and (as Aunt Margaret put it) "as slippery as mud and as hard to handle." Wingfoot would go up in the tree early in the morning with a jug of iced tea and a couple of ham sandwiches and stay there all day. Sometimes, when the weather was warm, he stayed all night. When he had to pee, he just let 'er rip into the yard.

"Can I come up?" Wilbur asked as he stood at the base of the live oak the morning after they arrived.

"You're too young," Wingfoot said, peering out the tree house window. It was reached by a rickety ladder that Wingfoot could pull up after him. Wilbur thought he could probably shinny up the tree if he wanted, but Wingfoot was making a statement with the ladder business.

"I'll be thirteen in two weeks," Wilbur said.

"Okay. When you're thirteen you can come up. You can spend the night when you're thirteen. That'll be your birthday present." He disappeared inside.

"What do you do up there?" Wilbur called out.

Wingfoot just laughed. It sounded wicked.

Uncle French was a tall, thin, quiet man. There was a quality about him that reminded Wilbur of gauze, sort of transparent and wispy. But that could fool you, because French seemed to know his own mind and keep his own counsel. Wilbur never heard him argue with Aunt Margaret or Min or Wingfoot. He just went about his business.

French called Wilbur to his study on the day after he fetched them from Dysart.

It was the largest and most elegant room in the house, even more so than the dining room with its huge crystal chandelier that Aunt Margaret said had been imported from Paris when the house was being built in 1761. (Aunt Margaret seemed to know as much about the history of the house as Uncle French, and carried on about it at the slightest provocation. Wilbur thought she seemed more of a Baggett than her husband.) The study—actually, a library and office and sitting room all in one—had dark wood-paneled walls and a lot of leather furniture and a huge oak roll-top desk and bookcases that soared to the ceiling, filled with old books that gave the room a slightly musty smell. There was a big bronze coat of arms mounted on one wall, paintings on the others: a scene of a harbor with tall-masted sailing ships, gloomy portraits of men and women in old costumes. Despite the dark walls, it was well lit by the tall windows. And it was a neat and orderly room except for the mass of wooden crates and cardboard boxes stacked along one wall and on a leather settee. One box was open on the long table where Uncle French was working, sorting through a tall pile of papers, another next to the oak rolltop where Min was going through another stack. Min rose when Wilbur entered the room. "I'll let you two menfolks be," she said, and she gave him a wink as she closed the door behind her.

Uncle French had a nice, gentle smile. "Sit down," he said, indicating a tall leather chair with curved wooden arms. Wilbur's feet barely touched the floor. He sat quietly for a time, studying the room while French kept at the pile, perusing each sheet and consigning it to one of the several smaller stacks spread across the table. "September fourteenth, eighteen sixty-two," he said, his voice breaking the quiet and startling Wilbur a bit.

"Sir?"

French was reading from a piece of yellowed paper.

"Dear Mama and Papa,
We have just been through a hot time at a place called Chancellorsville. The Yanks were just about on us, and fighting as well as we've seen them since the beginning, but then General Jackson came up with some more of our Carolina boys and rallied us and we carried the day. I'm sorry to say that Pierce Bledsoe was mortally wounded and I hope you will visit with his folks and express my condolences. He was a brave fellow and often entertained the boys around the campfire with his fiddle."

French looked up. "That was from your great-great-grandfather. Lieutenant Sprague Baggett. Do you know what was going on in 1862?"

"The Civil War?"

"Some folks around here refer to it as the War of Northern

Aggression. I think of it as the War of Misplaced Southern Honor."

"He was in a battle?"

"Several of them, until he lost his leg at Cold Harbor."

"Did he die?"

French chuckled. "In his bed, upstairs in this house, at the age of eighty-five."

Wilbur looked over at the stack of boxes and crates. "Is all of this stuff about the Civil War?"

French rose and walked over to the stack and placed his hand on one of the crates, as if testing its warmth. "Actually, very little of it. Most of it is pretty ordinary stuff. Bills of lading, receipts and invoices, picture postcards and recipes, sheet music and dance programs, love letters and newspaper clippings."

"Are you cleaning it out?"

"Oh, no. I'm writing a family history. Or at least, organizing the pile to try to make some sense of it. Min's helping me catalog things. Baggetts have never cleaned out much of anything, just tossed it all in boxes and crates until the weight of it threatened to collapse the attic." He looked straight at Wilbur. "Are you much interested in history?"

Wilbur wanted to be helpful, but this mass of stuff was more than he could comprehend. This seemed to go back to the dinosaurs. No, he wasn't much interested in history.

"Well," French said without waiting for him to answer, "it matters, and then it doesn't." He sat back down at the table and leaned across it toward Wilbur. "I think a fellow ought to know where he came from, because that gives him an idea of where he stands. But a fellow's history ought not to be a burden to him. He can either use it as a guide or set off on his own direction."

"Yes sir."

"Like your father has done."

Wilbur looked over at the stack again. There didn't seem to be anything there, or in fact anything in this particular place on earth, remotely connected to Tyler Baggett.

But instead of going on about Tyler, French gave him a brief family history lesson. The Baggetts, he said, had been among the first settlers on the Cape Fear River, not long after the explorer Verrazzano had found the place in the early 1600s. They had started with a grant of land from the English king and established their fortune with rice crops, and by the time the rice business petered out, they had land holdings and businesses in and around Wilmington, just upriver. Baggetts spread out all over southeastern North Carolina. But there was a straight line running from the original Baggett settler to Uncle French and an iron-clad family tradition that the oldest son of each generation always occupied the big house. "As a caretaker," he said. "Of the house and . . ." He waved at the boxes and boxes of family history. The pile.

"Two things stick in my mind when I think about the Baggett family going back in history," French said. "Baggetts have always been enterprising folks. And we've had a streak of orneriness, too. Sometimes those things come together. There was apparently a falling-out over some aspect of family business not long after the Civil War and some of the Baggetts left in a huff and settled over in Pender County, well up the river to the northwest of here. They haven't fared as well as the branch that stayed here, but it seems to have been important that they struck out on their own. My own father referred to them as the Trashy Baggetts. That was probably unfair. I'm sure there are some fine people among the Pender County Baggetts."

It occurred to Wilbur that Uncle French was talking to him as if he were an adult, just two Baggett men sitting here in this manly room surrounded by ages and ages of family history that you could take or leave. He sat up a little straighter.

"So the Baggetts are enterprising people," French said. "Your father is, in that sense, very much a Baggett. He lives by his wits and his skills."

"And," Wilbur put in, remembering the other half of the equation, "he's a little ornery."

French nodded. "Some years ago, he set off on his own direction.

He has never let this"—he indicated room, house, land, history—
"tie him down in the least."

"Dad says a fellow has to tend his own fire," Wilbur said.

"And I respect him mightily for that," French agreed.
"Although, that manner of getting along can, on occasion, cause
difficulty for those about him."

"Yes sir."

French leaned back in his chair and made a steeple of his fingers.
"I believe your mother is more than adequate for the challenge," he
said with a smile. "I have thought that from the first. More than
adequate."

"Yes sir."

"I just want you to know, Wilbur, that you are always welcome
here. This is Baggett House and you are a Baggett. Don't let that be
a burden, but rather an opportunity."

"I will."

"You know where your name comes from, don't you?"

Wilbur gave him a blank look.

"From the very beginning. The first Baggett to set foot on this
land was Squire Wilbur. He built a small fort out of logs on this
very soil. And then a hurricane came along and washed it away, and
along with it, his wife and small daughter. But he just hitched up
his britches and went on. He had a streak of . . ." French raised his
eyebrows, waiting for him to finish it.

"Orneriness."

"Exactly."

———

"I'LL GET WORK," Rosanna said at the dinner table. "We don't want
to be a bother."

"That won't be necessary," Aunt Margaret piped up. "I'm sure
you'll be back home before you know it." What she said and the
way she said it, Wilbur thought, were two entirely different things.
There was a saccharine surface to it, but lurking just underneath
was all sorts of rough-edged junk. Translation: *You're a nuisance and*

*a bother and an embarrassment to the fine, upstanding, cultured side of
the Baggett family and the sooner that no-account husband of yours
comes to fetch you, the better.*

"You're welcome here as long as you need to stay," Uncle French
said directly to Rosanna, leaping gracefully over Aunt Margaret
like a deer bounding across a pasture. "And with your retail experience, I could sure use you at the store. If you think that would be
suitable."

"Of course," Rosanna said with a sweet smile. "I'd be delighted.
And grateful." Wilbur could hear in his mother's voice a tit-for-tat
response to dear Aunt Margaret, who was sitting there at the foot of
the table with her lips pressed primly together and some tiny muscles fluttering like little animals under the skin of her temples.

Rosanna spoke directly to French, but then she turned her smile
on Margaret. "And if there's anything I can do around the house,
you just let me know. You're so gracious to make us feel at home
here." Translation: *Your name's Baggett because you married one, just
like I did. And nothing—name or otherwise—makes your doo-doo
smell any better than mine.*

"I can mow the lawn," Wilbur put in. "Anything to help out,
Aunt Margaret."

Aunt Margaret didn't respond, but then at that very moment she
had found something terribly interesting among her green beans
and was giving it her full attention.

"I think that would be just fine, Wilbur," French said. "That's
one of Wingfoot's chores, but he's been a little negligent about it
lately. Maybe you and he can divide the duties."

"Yes sir. We'll sure do that."

Wilbur didn't dare give Rosanna a look, but she reached under
the table and gave his knee a squeeze.

Later, when he and Rosanna were alone, he said to his mother,
"Aunt Margaret is a pickle. Sometimes, I could just smack her."

"Listen," she said, taking his face in her hands, "we're here by the
grace of God and the goodness of your Uncle French and Aunt
Margaret."

But there was, he thought, just a touch of sarcasm in the way she said it. Maybe even more than a touch.

"I'll remember that, Mom," he said in mock-earnestness. "Yassum, I shore will."

She gave him a wink. Yep, it was sarcasm, all right.

———

IT SEEMED THAT WILBUR AND ROSANNA were the only folks at Baggett House these days who had no particular agenda. Uncle French was running his business and working on the family history. Aunt Margaret bustled about being a Baggett and supervising the hired help—a cook, a maid, and a part-time gardener who tended the extensive landscaping on the sprawling grounds that surrounded the house. Min and Wingfoot were busy making plans. It was a far cry, he thought, from mowing lawns and checking groceries at the Winn-Dixie and waiting for Tyler Baggett to show up.

"I'm going to Chapel Hill," Min announced as he poked his head warily into her bedroom on the evening after his arrival. "I've already been admitted. And I'm going to be an ADPi."

"What's an Eighty Pie?" he asked, holding the door slightly ajar.

She looked at him as if he had just been dropped out of a spaceship. "A sorority," she said. "Every Baggett woman who has gone to Chapel Hill has been an ADPi. I'm a quadruple legacy. If they didn't pledge me, they'd have to shut the chapter down."

Wilbur had only the vaguest idea of what a sorority was. It sounded like life-and-death stuff, the way Min put it. "Can I come in?" he asked.

"I suppose. And the word is *may*. 'May I come in?' But don't touch anything."

The room was awash in blue—Carolina blue. The bedspread and pillows, the curtains, even a lamp shade with UNC TARHEELS printed on it. There were UNC banners on the walls and a framed watercolor of the Old Well on the Chapel Hill campus and another frame that held an old, yellowing diploma awarded to one Edwina French Baggett in 1874.

"Don't you have a closet?" Wilbur asked as he made a brief tour of the room, as much of it as you could get to with all the items of clothing lying about—dresses, coats, shoe boxes, stacks of blouses and slacks and some stuff he thought might be undergarments—covering bed and chairs and dresser top, boxes stacked in the corners. It was a bit overpowering, all this blue and all these garments and all the exotic smells—cologne and powder and frilliness and God knew what else that was girl-mystery. He had never been in a girl's room before. His mother's, of course, had its own good smells, but her wardrobe fit easily into a small closet and a couple of dresser drawers.

"Of course I've got a closet." Min was seated at a vanity, her back to him but watching him in the mirror while she brushed her hair. She was a sturdy girl, just a tad on the thick side, but she had a nice, pleasant face that bordered on pretty, with soft brown eyes and a sprinkling of freckles about her nose and cheeks. She carried herself well, with just a touch of Aunt Margaret's air of refinement, but she seemed somehow more approachable. If she hadn't, Wilbur would never have dared to invade the sanctuary of her room.

Min swung around to him on the vanity stool. "This is my college wardrobe," she said with a sweep of her hand. "Mother and I just got back from shopping in New York."

"When are you leaving for college?"

"Not for another year. I'm a senior in high school."

"Oh."

She turned back to the mirror.

"Who's this?" he asked, examining the framed diploma on the wall.

"It's my great-grandmother. And yours too, I suppose. She was one of the first women to graduate from Chapel Hill."

"Was she an Eighty Pie?"

"She was there before the ADPi's had a chapter. But if they'd had one, she would have been one."

He stood awkwardly in the middle of the room. There was no place to sit, and even if there were, he had the feeling that Min didn't intend for him to stay long enough to take a seat. Still, he wasn't ready to go yet. He breathed deeply, taking in the smells, watching as Min drew the brush easily through her hair, over and over. It made him a little light-headed. And he had a funny feeling somewhere down below his stomach, the same kind he got when he thought of Nell Dysart, even though she had turned out to be a shit.

"I'll be thirteen next week," he said for no particular reason.

"Congratulations." She was smiling at him in the mirror, but he couldn't tell exactly what kind of smile it was. Min was hard to read, he thought. She seemed to keep a lot to herself. It might be a warm smile or a mocking smile. Maybe she thought being thirteen wasn't such a big deal.

"I don't know where I'll go to college," he offered.

She stopped brushing and turned again to him and studied him for a moment. He fidgeted under her gaze. "Baggetts go to Chapel Hill," she said.

"Actually, I may not go at all."

"Why not?"

"Well, I doubt Mom and Dad could afford it." He could imagine himself standing with his old cardboard suitcase on the sidewalk outside some college's dormitory, evicted because Tyler Baggett hadn't showed up in the nick of time. "Mom says," he added, "that we're here by the grace of God and the goodness of your family." He put on what he hoped was the same sweet smile his mother had used on Aunt Margaret at the dinner table.

Min studied him for a moment and then something about her face softened, just a slight easing of lines and angles. "Wilbur," she said, "don't pay any attention to Mother."

"I'm going to West Point," Wingfoot announced.

If Min's room was a shrine to the Tarheels and Eighty Pies, Wingfoot's was an armed camp. The air above the furniture was a war zone of model airplanes and helicopters, suspended by fishing line from the ceiling. Tanks and armored personnel carriers, artillery pieces and plastic soldiers campaigned across the desk and chest of drawers. The walls were covered with maps and Army recruiting posters. The bookshelves were filled with old military manuals and novels such as *The Hardy Boys at West Point* and *Dress Gray* and Shelby Foote's three-volume history of the Civil War. A sword dangled from the ceiling in one corner and an ancient musket was suspended above the fireplace.

"Don't touch anything," Wingfoot commanded.

"That's what Min said about her room."

"Her room's just full of girl shit. This one's booby-trapped. Mess with anything and you'll blow your fuckin' hand off."

"Well, how am I gonna share your room and not touch anything?"

Wingfoot grinned. "Very goddamned carefully."

Wilbur noted two things about Wingfoot: he had an exceptionally foul mouth and he was taking this military thing very seriously, even more seriously than Min was taking Chapel Hill. This was a house full of obsessed people, he thought, the children even more than the parents. There was something both alien and exotic about the place and its inhabitants, a constant electric current that seemed to hum and throb through the house. Especially Wingfoot, who seemed wired directly into a socket. He was short and muscular with close-cropped hair, almost a buzz cut, and intense gray eyes. He could, if you took him as seriously as he seemed to take himself, make you nervous.

Wingfoot was sitting at his desk, tinkering with something in a cardboard box. There were wires hanging out of it, but Wilbur couldn't see what was inside. A book was open on the desk next to the box. "Whatcha doing?"

"Building a bomb."

"For real?"

"I'm gonna blow up that fuckin' alligator."

"What alligator?"

"Barney. He sleeps in the reeds down next to the river. You better stay away from there. He'll eat you, just like he ate Petunia."

"Who's Petunia?"

"Mama's dog. She got loose and went down by the river and the goddamned gator came up out of the reeds like he'd been shot and gobbled her little ass down in one gulp. I saw it all from the tree house."

"What did you do?"

"Not a goddamned thing. I couldn't stand the little shit. She'd jump up on the couch between Mama and me when we were watching TV and curl up in a ball, and then after a while she'd cut a fart. I never smelled such a big fart from such a pissant little dog. And Mama would make like she didn't smell it. Mama's like that."

"I'll bet," Wilbur agreed. "Do you always talk like that? I mean, all the cussing?"

"I'm practicing."

"For West Point?"

"Vietnam."

The room wasn't really booby-trapped, as Wilbur figured out after several days of residence, during which time he had it almost entirely to himself. The weather was nice and Wingfoot spent most of the time in the tree house, coming inside for an occasional meal and bath and change of clothes. Wilbur made himself at home, though he was careful not to mess with Wingfoot's stuff. Just in case. There was a double bed, and the first night he spent in it, he felt a lump under his pillow. His hand found the unmistakable hard steel of a pistol, a huge one with an enormously long barrel. He lay there frozen with fear for a long time, then eased his head off the pillow and eased the pillow off the pistol and, holding it by the tip of the butt, placed it gently in a drawer of Wingfoot's desk.

The gun, as Wingfoot told him the next day, was not loaded. Bullets were in the closet where Wingfoot could get to them quickly (he didn't explain why that might be necessary) but the gun was not loaded. The bomb was another matter.

The blast shook him upright in bed and he grabbed his head with both hands, probing frantically for the bullet he was sure was embedded in his brain. There was no hole, no blood. But there was, within an instant, a great commotion throughout the house. Lights came on, feet thundered up and down the hall, muffled shouts rang out. He sprang from his bed to join them.

The acrid smell of cordite drifted up on the light haze of smoke from the river's edge, where they found Wingfoot standing with a flashlight, probing the reed-clogged water's edge.

Uncle French, for the first time, seemed to have lost his air of genteel calm. "What in the name of God is going on down here?" he said as he scrambled down the slight incline toward the river, waving to the rest of them to stay back, up on higher ground.

"He got away," Wingfoot said, disgusted.

"Who?"

"Barney."

"Goddamn," Uncle French barked.

"French, I don't think we need any blue language," Aunt Margaret called down.

"Margaret, shut up."

"All right."

French came back with Wingfoot's collar clutched tightly in his right hand, the flashlight in his left. He shined the light into Wingfoot's face. "Do you want to tell the rest of the residents of this household what in the hell you've been up to?"

"I built a bomb," Wingfoot said simply. "I set it off."

French shook him. Wingfoot's head wobbled crazily. "You could have gotten yourself killed."

"Well, I didn't. But the mission wasn't a total failure. The bomb worked just like the book said."

"I swear," Aunt Margaret put in, "sometimes you act just like your uncle Tyler."

Wilbur, standing with Rosanna's arm around his shoulders, could feel her stiffen. But she didn't say anything.

"Where did you get the . . . whatever blew up?" French demanded.

"Dynamite," Wingfoot said. "There's a couple of cases of it in an old shack over by the lighthouse."

"Good Lord." French released him. Wingfoot shook himself and stood military-erect. "What am I going to do with you?" French asked.

"Be patient," Wingfoot said calmly. "Give me a couple of years and West Point will take over."

Aunt Margaret grabbed Wilbur's arm. "Did you know anything about this?"

"Of course not," Wingfoot said quickly. "You think I'd tell a twelve-year-old I was making a bomb?"

But Wilbur could tell that Aunt Margaret didn't believe it, or didn't want to believe it. Everything about her since his arrival had said that he was on probation here and always would be. Why? Well, that remark about "Uncle Tyler" said everything. He bristled with indignation, but his mother's firm hand on his shoulder and her own silence kept him from saying anything.

"You'll sleep in the house from now on," French said to Wingfoot. "Where we can keep an eye on you."

"Yes sir."

Wingfoot slept nude. Wilbur was stunned when he pulled off all his clothes and tossed them in a corner and climbed into the bed, the twin globes of his bare ass disappearing under the sheet. "Turn out the light," he said, his back to Wilbur, who was still standing in the middle of the room.

"Don't you . . ."

"No."

"Why?"

"So I can get to my willie when it needs workin' on."

"You mean . . ."

"Yeah. Don't you?"

"Well . . ."

"I'll show you sometime."

Wilbur got reluctantly into bed, but he perched precariously on the far edge away from Wingfoot, who seemed to him a great deal older and wiser in the ways of the world. He probably knew some stuff Wilbur wasn't quite ready to get into yet. But one thing for sure, if he went to Vietnam and slept like this, some jungle thing was likely to get hold of his willie.

———

AT DINNER ONE EVENING, Aunt Margaret said something about Min "coming out."

"What's she coming out of?" Wilbur asked.

Margaret's nose curled up a couple of centimeters. "She's coming *into* society." The way she said *society* made it sound like something just short of being a movie star.

"Then why don't you call it coming in instead of coming out?"

"Wilbur, that's enough," Rosanna said. She explained later that Min was a debutante and that it was a big deal for girls of Min's age from prominent families in the Wilmington area. They went to lots of fancy parties, and then the whole thing—the "season," they called it—wrapped up with a fancy dress ball where everybody was really gussied up. The debutantes were thus formally introduced into Wilmington's social life and then were expected to meet some eligible young Wilmington man and marry (after they had finished being Eighty Pies at Chapel Hill) and have daughters who would come out in their own time. Or come in, as it were.

Each family with a debutante daughter hosted one of the summer parties, and the Baggetts were to have the last one before the big fancy ball at the end of August. Aunt Margaret said it was an acknowledgment of the Baggetts' long-standing social prominence that they were chosen for the honor of giving the last party. Wilbur wondered why, if it was such an honor and all, Aunt Margaret had her asshole so puckered up about it. She was like a tornado, tearing through the house from dawn until late into the night during the week before the party, ordering everybody about, seeing to caterers and decorators and a professional cleaning service that scrubbed the house from top to bottom, inside and out, even though the party was to be on the lawn where two huge open-sided tents were set up, one for dining and the other for dancing.

"Mama, it's just a party," Min said to Margaret at dinner.

"No it's not," Margaret said emphatically. "When you're a Baggett, you have obligations and duties that other people don't have. Everything has to be just right. There's a standard that's higher than everybody else's. You must always remember who you are. Isn't that right, French?"

"I suppose so," French said, sort of noncommittally.

"Of course it is," Margaret emphasized.

Uncle French found a great deal to do with his business interests in Wilmington, and when at Baggett House stayed mostly in his study, working on the family history and writing checks to the legion of workers Margaret had hired. Rosanna worked lengthy hours at French's store out on Highway 133. Wilbur (whose offer to mow the lawn had been rejected by Margaret) and Wingfoot retreated to the woods and marshland between the house and Orton Pond, where Wingfoot instructed Wilbur in guerrilla warfare, which involved a good deal of crawling on bellies while pretending that live ammunition was being fired overhead. Wingfoot ate grasshoppers. Live ones, for God's sake. Just protein, he said. It made Wilbur sick, just thinking about it.

Wilbur's thirteenth birthday would fall on the same day as the party, but when he mentioned that to Rosanna, she advised him to keep quiet about it. They would have their own celebration later, she promised.

Margaret had decided on a Mexican theme. The decoration ran heavily to gaily colored blankets, which were draped from the front windows of the house, and tons of flowers, delivered fresh-cut on the morning of the party. The guests arrived in costumes which rivaled the blankets in gay color, the debutantes themselves attired in dresses with wide flouncy skirts and tops that showed a great deal of flesh across shoulders and upper torso. A little mishap with elastic, Wilbur thought, and you could really get a look at something. It was sexy-looking enough as it was.

Tables set up under the tent and the live oak tree were laden with mounds of food—tortillas, tacos, frijoles and tons of guacamole dip. A black fellow dressed in starched white jacket dispensed mar-

garitas from a bar to the adults and fruit punch to the young
ladies and their dates. A mariachi band—some local guys wearing
serapes and fake moustaches—wandered through the crowd
playing guitars and fiddles and making a brave attempt at "La
Cucaracha" and "Allá en el Rancho Grande." Wilbur and Wingfoot, attired in white shirts and sombreros, were pressed into service
to pass amongst the guests with trays of finger food. They had been
warned by grim-lipped Aunt Margaret to behave themselves or die.

"What a great place for tear gas," Wingfoot said as they surveyed
the scene from the front door. He was still mad because, over his
heated protests, Margaret had insisted on having the tree house in
the live oak dismantled for the occasion. He could build it back
after the party, she said. But he wasn't mollified.

"Or a dog with firecrackers attached to his tail," Wilbur offered.
Several days of crawling around the grounds with Wingfoot had
gotten him into the spirit of mischief, if not the practice of it.

Wingfoot's eyes lit. "I know where there's a dog."

"Well, I don't have any firecrackers," Will said quickly and set
off with his tray.

The party began at six o'clock in the evening, and by the time the
sun had set back beyond the house, it was going full blast. The
debutantes and their dates were sneaking margaritas from the bar
and transferring them to fruit punch cups. The mariachi band had
changed into more casual attire and shed their fake moustaches and
were belting out rock and roll under the second tent, where young
and old were packing the dance floor. It was a soft, beautiful
evening, the lawn bathed in the gentle glow of fading daylight and
a couple of hundred Chinese lanterns strung about (Margaret
couldn't find Mexican lanterns anywhere in the two Carolinas, and
said that by the time everybody had plenty to eat and drink, they
wouldn't know the difference anyhow). Min wore a lustrous smile
and a gardenia in her hair. Margaret warbled and glowed. Uncle
French, pretty well into the margaritas himself, floated through the
crowd with a vague smile on his face, chatting up the adult guests.

Wingfoot and Wilbur, finished with their finger food duties, retired to a corner of the porch to watch from a safe distance.

And that was when Tyler showed up. There was first the insistent honking of a car horn that caused heads to turn, and then the longest automobile Wilbur had ever seen rounded the corner of the house and kept coming across the parking area and up onto the grass and stopped right in front of the front steps. It was a huge car, an ocean liner of a car. And it was a convertible. With the top down.

"Godawmighty," Wingfoot said softly. "That's one sonofabitch of a car."

Tyler stepped nimbly out, looked around, spotted Wilbur. "Yo, Birthday Boy!" he called out.

Wilbur met him at the steps.

"You thought I forgot," Tyler said, wrapping him in a huge hug, then stepping back and holding him at arm's length. "I brought you a present."

Wilbur could feel the mass of the party moving their way, and when he glanced in the direction of the tent he saw Aunt Margaret at a full gallop.

"A present?"

Tyler indicated the car with a grand sweep of his arm. "A Cadillac."

"Holy shit," Wingfoot said from somewhere behind him.

"Where did you get it?" Wilbur asked.

"Well, it used to belong to a fellow in Hopkinsville, Kentucky, whose inflated opinion of his game was exceeded only by his hook. That there automobile comes courtesy of a twenty-two-foot putt on the eighteenth hole."

It was magnificent—a beautiful light blue with sweeping lines and big fins on the rear. It was polished to a fare-thee-well and it glowed like a humongous gem in the lantern light.

"Mine?"

"Yessir. 'Course you aren't old enough to drive it just yet, but I'll keep it up for you until you turn sixteen. Can you imagine, tooling around in something like that? You'll have to drive fast to stay ahead of the mobs of women."

"Tyler!" the shrill voice of Aunt Margaret bearing down on them. "Everybody's supposed to park up the road. There's a shuttle bus. French, do something . . ."

"I missed you," Tyler said, looking straight down into Wilbur's eyes, his hand resting firmly on the top of Wilbur's head, like a preacher performing a baptism. Wilbur could feel something warm and powerful flowing through the hand and into his head and all down his body. Everything was okay now. Tyler was back and they could go somewhere and be just the three of them and leave Aunt Margaret with her society shit and Uncle French with his piles of history and Min with her Eighty Pie business and Wingfoot with his bombs. They would take a trip somewhere and be almost normal.

"I missed you, too," Wilbur said. He put his arms around his father and held tightly to him as the crowd surged up around them.

"Hi, Margaret," Tyler said, across the top of Wilbur's head. "Damn good of y'all to throw such a nice party for my boy. It ain't every day you turn thirteen."

By the time the party broke up near midnight, Tyler Baggett had utterly charmed the crowd, had taken carloads of debutantes for rides in the Cadillac, and had arranged a golf game the next day with several of their fathers. He and French and Wilbur stood at the porch saying goodbye to the guests. Aunt Margaret was upstairs with a headache.

Tyler and Rosanna appeared arm-in-arm in the dining room for breakfast the next morning. She glowed, clinging to him, her eyes smiling and her mouth soft. Watching them, Wilbur felt something inside himself ease off a little. Things would be okay, he thought. At least until next time.

7 | It was a good nine months. Tyler took them to Waxhaw, a little town just below Charlotte near the South Carolina line, where they rented an old house across the road from the railroad tracks that split the town. They enrolled Wilbur in the seventh grade (a couple of weeks late, of course, after they made a trip in the Cadillac to Lake of the Ozarks and then on to Chicago, where Tyler bought him a whole new wardrobe for school). Tyler played some golf and was gone for occasional stretches of a week, two weeks, but he was around the house a lot, too. His game, he said, had never been better. He and Rosanna talked about maybe buying the house, staying put while Wilbur finished junior high and high school. There seemed to be plenty of money. Rosanna stayed home. When spring came, nobody said anything about Wilbur mowing lawns all summer.

Tyler took up flying again. Refresher lessons at the airport in Charlotte, then a physical to make sure Korea hadn't impaired his ability to pilot a plane, and finally renewal of his license. On a lovely early spring day he took Rosanna and Wilbur for a ride. They flew all the way to Roanoke, Virginia, had lunch, and flew back. Wilbur sat up front, wearing an extra set of headphones and listening to all the radio traffic and feeling more important than he had ever felt in his life. Important and rich, in a way that went far beyond money.

———

ON ONE OF TYLER'S ABSENCES over the winter, he had gone to the coast and talked to French about trying to qualify for the pro golf tour. French encouraged him. He had friends in Wilmington who might put up some sponsorship money.

And then Tyler had cooked up a trip to Augusta for the Masters — just the brothers and their wives. French was reluctant.

He was up to his eyeballs in business affairs these days. But Tyler talked him into it. So in May they were back at Baggett House to drop off Wilbur for the weekend and then head south in a rented plane.

Tyler insisted they drive to the little airport near Southport in the Cadillac, all seven of them jammed in, with the suitcases in the trunk. In deference to Aunt Margaret, he left the top up. She was out of sorts, glum and snappish, walking like she had a carrot up her butt. She didn't care much for golf and fretted about getting runs in her stockings hiking all over the golf course. But Tyler was working on her non-stop, buttering her up and complimenting her summer dress and her new hairdo and carrying her suitcase for her, assuring her that the Masters course was safe for her stockings as long as she stayed out of the azaleas. Wilbur bet himself that by the time they landed in Georgia he'd have her all sweet and nice. Tyler could do that. He had even held out the possibility that she might meet Arnold Palmer. Tyler knew a fellow who had played golf on the college team at Wake Forest with Arnie, who was favored to win this year.

Wilbur and Wingfoot helped the men carry the luggage to the plane and stow it in the compartment in the back. Margaret had brought enough for a couple of months, but they managed to get everything packed in except for one small bag, which Rosanna offered to carry in her lap.

Rosanna looked awfully pretty this morning. She had gained a little weight over the winter, just enough to fill in the worry lines and give a soft glow to her face. She gave Wilbur a hug and said, "We'll see you Sunday night."

Uncle French put his arm around Min's shoulder. "Min's in charge," he said, fixing Wingfoot with a stern look. "No trouble." He waited for a moment and finally Wingfoot said, "Yes sir."

"That goes for everybody," Aunt Margaret piped up, putting the evil eye on Wilbur.

"Yes ma'am," he said.

"Y'all use the Cadillac all you want," Tyler said. "Min, if a pack of girls start chasing you, put these two fellows in the trunk. I don't want lipstick on my seat covers. And if a pack of boys start chasing you—well, use your own judgment."

"Yes sir," Min said solemnly, even though Tyler gave her a big wink. She was a serious girl with a bit of a squint about her eyes as if she were trying to look off there in the future and see if the Eighty Pies really would ask her to join and if she'd meet that eligible Wilmington boy and settle down and have lots of little debutantes. She would be going off to Chapel Hill in August, and she was mostly packed already.

The four adults climbed in and closed the door of the plane and Tyler sat at the controls and checked everything out, then cranked her up and the engine turned over with a cough and a backfire and caught with a roar. They all waved to one another, and the plane taxied down to the far end of the runway where Tyler gunned the engine and tested the flaps and then it came barreling back down toward them, gaining speed and lifting off just past where they stood. Min and Wilbur waved and waved and Wingfoot snapped off a salute. They stood watching as the plane climbed and banked and headed south, a diminishing speck and sound that finally disappeared over the horizon.

They walked back to the Cadillac and Min asked Wilbur, "Do you know how to let the top down on this thing?"

"I sure do," he said with a grin.

After lunch they got the Wilmington paper and looked at the movie schedule. Wingfoot wanted to see *Seven Days in May* with Burt Lancaster and Kirk Douglas (a general takes over the country), but Wilbur sided with Min on *Mail Order Bride* with Buddy Ebsen and Lois Nettleton.

"Sissy shit," Wingfoot muttered.

Min gave him a hard look. "Wingfoot, Papa left me in charge. If I have any trouble out of you this weekend, or if you utter another word of profanity, I'll tell Mama what I found in that box under your bed." Wingfoot turned a little pale. Later in the afternoon,

Wingfoot showed Wilbur the magazines. Some pretty hot stuff, Wilbur thought. Not the kind of thing Wingfoot would want Aunt Margaret to see.

They were just about to leave the house, shortly after six o'clock, when Aunt Grace and her husband, Harbert, from Wilmington arrived with the news that the plane was missing.

———

A NIGHTMARE OF FLAME, stench of smoke searing his throat and burning his eyes. He flailed at a crush of debris—twisted metal, daggers of glass. Blood. A severed arm. He screamed.

A hand on his shoulder, clutching him firmly, pulling him away from the wreckage. He woke and looked up to see Wingfoot in the dim light of the spare bedroom, leaning over him.

He began to sob again, though he had thought when he finally collapsed into sleep somewhere in the emptiness of early morning that he surely had no tears left in him and never would again.

Wingfoot slipped into bed beside him and wrapped his arms around him. They clung desperately to each other and Wingfoot's hot, salty tears ran down his face and mingled with his own.

"Please," Wingfoot whimpered, "don't tell anybody I cried."

He never did.

———

THE SEARCH FOR THE PLANE went on for more than a week. No one had seen it since it took off into the flawless May morning, headed west-southwest toward Augusta. The flight path should have taken it between Columbia and Orangeburg, but an air traffic controller in Columbia had noticed the blip on the radar making a broad, sweeping turn just after it passed Sumter, curving back toward the coast in the general direction of Charleston. Since Tyler hadn't filed a flight plan, there was nothing about the plane's course to raise curiosity.

The search concentrated in the wooded expanse of the Francis Marion National Forest where a hunter had reported a smudge of smoke on the horizon the day of the flight. But the Civil Air Patrol and volunteers on the ground could find nothing. The smudge had come from a campfire. The Coast Guard combed the Atlantic waters offshore, but they too came up empty-handed. Newspapers and broadcasts were full of the story, and some of the rampant speculation—public and private—bordered on the bizarre. Was it a suicide pact? A hijacking? Had the occupants bailed out somewhere over land to begin new lives under assumed names? Was organized crime involved? The CIA?

When the search was finally called off, an expert from the National Transportation Safety Board concluded that, in all probability, the plane's engine exhaust system had malfunctioned, the cabin occupants were overcome by carbon monoxide fumes, and the plane flew pilotless until it finally ran out of fuel and went down in the Atlantic. With no plane and no occupants, no one would ever be able to say with absolutely certainty. But, bizarre possibility aside, it seemed the only logical explanation.

For Wilbur, numb with loss, the details didn't seem important. He sat for hours at the edge of the marshland down by the Cape Fear River, staring off in the direction of the Atlantic. He never once imagined that the plane would suddenly come into view, restoring safety and sanity. No, his parents were gone. What filled his imagination was an ongoing replay of the terror that had awakened him the first night—smoke and flame, and then as the week wore on and a crash in the Atlantic seemed likely, visions of a violent plunge into rock-hard water, the plane coming apart and settling beneath the waves where fish began to rip at dead flesh. He could not make it go away.

At night, with the river quiet and dark, there were twin red pinpoints of light hovering in the air across the Cape Fear. Wingfoot told him they were warning beacons on radio station towers. But they seemed to him, in his grief, somehow connected with Tyler and Rosanna, out there far beyond his reach. He tried to think of them in heaven. He could only think of them as dead and himself as utterly lost and alone.

———

"PAPA LEFT ME in charge," Min said firmly.

They sat in the front parlor of Baggett House—Min and Wingfoot and Wilbur, Aunt Grace and Uncle Harbert from Wilmington. Grace was Margaret's sister, and certainly not a Baggett, but she had taken charge of things. She had stayed at the house, presiding with calm efficiency over the rituals of mourning. Aunt Grace was the closest relative Min and Wingfoot had. But since she was Margaret's sister, not French's, she was no kin at all to Wilbur. He felt eyes on him, studying him—orphaned child of the family's black sheep. He knew nothing of these people, even the ones with the same name as his. Grace was sweet. She hugged him a lot. But it didn't help. It just made things worse.

Now, with the search ended and the conclusions drawn and the memorial service over and done with, they talked about what next.

"But Min honey, you can't take care of a house and two boys."

"Can and will," she said. There was a fierce glint in her eyes and her hands gripped the handkerchief in her lap, squeezing and squeezing all the tears out of it as she had squeezed the tears out of her eyes and replaced them with this stubborn thing.

"But you're going off to Chapel Hill in a couple of months."

"No, I'm not."

Uncle Harbert spoke up. "Min, let the boys come stay with us. There's plenty of room. You've got to go on with your life."

"This is my life," she said. And then again, "Papa left me in charge."

"You're still a minor," Grace said. "Eighteen years old."

But she didn't seem that way, Wilbur thought. She seemed to have grown up all of a sudden—the girl with the room full of Carolina blue and frilly dresses for Eighty Pie replaced by someone much older and more serious. She had spent unflagging hours in the parlor in the days after the plane's disappearance, greeting the flocks of people who came bringing enormous mounds of food, many of them Baggetts from the Pender County bunch. She had sheltered Wingfoot and Wilbur from the curious. She grieved, but she did it behind the locked door of her own room. Wilbur could hear her quiet sobs in the dead of night. But when she emerged each morning she was dry-eyed and calm and seemed quite sure of who she was and what she was supposed to do. As she seemed just now.

"Uncle Harbert can write the checks," Min said. "But we intend to stay here in this house. I intend to finish raising these two boys. Wingfoot is as wild as a buck and this is about the closest thing Wilbur has ever had to a home."

That wasn't really true, he thought. The house in Waxhaw had been becoming a home, with Rosanna there all the time and Tyler spending long days with them and an easy peace settling about the place, maybe even a sense of some permanence. But that, of course, was all gone.

His mother's family? That wasn't even a remote possibility because Wilbur had no earthly idea who they were. He had asked her once about them. All she told him was that they were in Louisiana. "I don't want to think about them, and you don't either." There was, he understood, some bad business there. The Louisiana people weren't an option. And neither was anybody else. So if he were to have any home at all, this would have to be it.

"Min honey, I just can't in good conscience let you do this," Grace said. "Margaret would . . ."

"Margaret is dead," Min said flatly. "And Papa left me in charge," she said for the third time. Wilbur thought it sounded like something from the Bible or the legislature, and that maybe she should have it lettered on a sign she could wear around her neck. She did, indeed, seem very much in charge. "Aunt Grace, if you fight me on this, I'll make a stink." The look on Aunt Grace's face said the last thing she wanted was a stink.

Min stood up now, and Wilbur and Wingfoot, who were seated on either side of her on the sofa, stood up, too, and she put her arms around both of them and pulled them close to her. And for the first time, Wilbur thought there might be some hope, that he might get over feeling utterly lost and scared to death.

———

THE NEXT MORNING he emerged from the back door and stood there for a long time trying to figure out what was wrong. Then it came to him: the Cadillac was gone. There was only Uncle French's Ford station wagon in the garage behind the house.

"Uncle Harbert took it to town to sell," Min said as she stood at the stove frying bacon. "The money will go toward your college education."

"But I'm only thirteen," Wilbur protested.

"It will be here before you know it."

"But that's my dad's car."

Min dropped her fork with a clatter and turned with a sudden fury that stunned him. "I don't ever want to hear Tyler Baggett mentioned in this house again."

For a moment, he couldn't speak. The bacon sizzled and popped in the frying pan. "But . . ."

"He was an irresponsible no-account who never did an honest day's work and left his mess lying around for other people to pick up." Her eyes blazed—the muscles around her neck and jaw taut, her face wild and twisted. "He killed my parents." The words were jagged stones, dropped from a great height, gathering speed until they smashed against him.

"Min, please . . ." He felt tears, very close.

"No!" Her voice a lash that made him cringe. "I'll give you a place to live and I'll raise you right, Wilbur. But I won't have that sonofabitch Tyler Baggett hanging around here. Do you understand that?"

"What about Mama?" he asked, his voice shaking, barely a voice at all.

There was a long, unyielding silence and then she repeated, "Do you understand?"

He nodded. And then he fled.

He cowered in his room—wretchedly, physically ill.

He thought of leaving—packing some stuff and standing out on

Highway 133 with his thumb out. Just disappear, the way Tyler and Rosanna had done. But to where? And what?

No, he was trapped—weak, helpless, dependent on Min, who needed somebody to blame for the unthinkable thing that had happened to her. And, in a way, wasn't she right? It was Tyler who wanted to go, Tyler who piloted the plane, Tyler who was instigator and instrument of tragedy. Sure, it was a senseless, fickle twist of fate. And there was enough grief to go around for all the survivors. But Min's bitter, wrathful blaming towered over everything, shutting out all the rest. He huddled in its shadow.

He would have to stay. And in staying, he would have to abide by her terrible rule, keep his mouth shut, not utter the unutterable, suffer his own private grief in his own private way until he was old enough to make his own rules, make his own way. At thirteen, that seemed a long way off.

He was still on probation here, just as he had been when Aunt Margaret was casting her evil eye on him. Would he ever in his life get off probation?

Aunt Grace came and stayed with Wilbur and Wingfoot while Min and Uncle Harbert went to Waxhaw. They took the station wagon. It was all they needed. They were back by nightfall with Wilbur's things. Min never said what she did with all the rest of it. And he didn't ask.

———

IN THE FALL, Wilbur and Wingfoot rode the bus to school in Southport—Wingfoot to the high school, where he was in tenth grade, Wilbur to the seventh at the junior high, where the bus stopped first. When Wilbur started to get off the bus, Wingfoot said, "You have any trouble with anybody, tell 'em to come see me."

But he didn't have any trouble, and if he had, he sure wouldn't have involved Wingfoot. He got along on his own, as he had learned to do with all the moving around they had done during his elementary years, rarely in the same school for more than a year at a time. He had no trouble talking to people, and he had a fairly quick wit about him. He supposed he had gotten that from Tyler. And he could do imitations. By the end of the first month he had the principal and a couple of the teachers down pat, and of course he had his old repertoire of Elvis Presley and Cary Grant.

The thing to do was keep your eyes open and your mouth shut at first, get the lay of the land, figure out who was who, not try to shoehorn yourself into any established cliques, smile (but not too much so you didn't appear too eager), avoid confrontation, and join the band. Sports would have helped, but he was too much of a runt for that, a late bloomer. So he played saxophone, which he had learned in elementary school. It wasn't an especially difficult instrument, and most school bands had an extra saxophone lying around somewhere, since he couldn't afford one of his own. At least, he couldn't until he started Southport Junior High. He came home at the end of the first day and told Min he had joined the band. When he arrived the next afternoon, there was an instrument case on his bed, and he opened it to find a gleaming gold sax nestled in a bed of velvet. It was the most beautiful thing he had ever seen. Min was matter-of-fact about it. "Baggetts don't use junk." He thanked her and gave her a hug.

Another thing he had learned about getting along in a new school was to pick out a girl — not the most or least beautiful or the most or least popular, but somebody in between — and befriend her. And keep it on a friendship level, at least at first. A girl like that, right at the middle of the scale, didn't threaten anybody else and provided connections. It was a delicate thing, not letting it develop into anything serious, at least not at first, and not being such a bosom pal with the girl that the guys thought you liked girls (and guys) for the wrong reason.

He picked out Glenda Turnipseed, who played clarinet. She had a nice smile and a flat chest and she rode a different bus. She made good grades, especially in math and science, which were Wilbur's weakest subjects. And she didn't mind making good grades, though she didn't flaunt it, either. Wilbur was a middling student.

All that moving about, and missing big chunks of school time when Tyler would be taking them on jaunts, had given him a sketchy background in the basics. Glenda helped him with math problems in study hall, patiently explaining things like integers that gave him a headache.

Junior high, he thought, was goddamned complicated. Everybody trying to figure out who the hell they were and trying not to be pigeonholed as one kind of oddball or another. You really had to be careful, especially if you were a new kid. Here, too, he was on probation.

One thing he had going for him was that he was something of a curiosity: the kid whose parents disappeared in an airplane. He played on that a little, feeling a bit guilty about it. But by the end of the first month the novelty had worn off and people had stopped either giving him strange looks or coming right out and asking him about it.

Wingfoot was a help—not because he was physically present in the junior high building, but because he was making a mark for himself over at the high school. During the first week of school he had left a garter snake in an English teacher's desk drawer, been caught with a wad of chewing tobacco tucked in his jaw at lunch break, and booby-trapped the janitor's closet with a smoke bomb that went off when the door was opened. The junior high kids thought all that was pretty awesome, and Wilbur benefitted from the kinship. Then in November, Wingfoot went out for basketball. He was, the coach told anyone and everyone, the most talented sophomore who had ever played at Southport High. "We'll win the regionals," the coach said, "if I can keep the little sonofabitch out of detention, and if I can get him to stop fighting on the court. He acts like basketball is hand-to-hand combat."

Wingfoot's best friend was Billy Hargreave. He was a year older than Wingfoot, already established as both a big man on campus and a college prospect in basketball. North Carolina State was already showing some interest. Billy had both a level head and the sharpest elbows in the region. The coach assigned him to keep

Wingfoot out of trouble, at least enough so he could remain on the team. When it appeared that Wingfoot was about to strike a blow on the court, it was Billy's job to wrap his long arms around him until he cooled down.

Billy was also nice to Wilbur. The first time Wilbur met him, he poked his head into Wilbur's room one afternoon after school as Wilbur was practicing scales on his saxophone. "You're pretty good," he said. Wilbur's mouth dropped open. Billy Hargreave was the tallest boy he had ever seen. "Want to shoot some hoops?"

"I'm not very good at it."

"Aw, come on. I'll teach you a hook shot."

The three of them played for a half-hour at the goal attached to the rear of the garage, Billy keeping Wingfoot partly under control and letting Wilbur get off some shots. He never did sink a hook, but he vowed to practice before Billy came home with Wingfoot again.

Wingfoot left for the bathroom and Billy and Wilbur sat down on the hard clay with their backs to the garage wall and Billy spun the basketball on the end of his index finger.

"I hear Wingfoot's pretty good," Wilbur said.

"Coach says he has court sense. You know what that is?"

"No."

"He knows where everybody is on the court every second—our five guys and theirs—and where they're gonna be the next second. Sometimes he makes passes to places where there ain't nobody, and suddenly there's somebody there to catch it. And on defense, he steals a lot of the other guys' passes because he knows what they're gonna do before they do. It's like he can read your mind or maybe even control your thoughts. Like he's playing some sort of basketball that ain't been invented yet. If he keeps improving and quits fighting, the college coaches are gonna be slobbering over him next year."

"He's going to West Point."

"Yeah," Billy said. "What a waste."

But for now, Wingfoot was anything but a waste. Just his mere presence over at the high school was a boon indeed to Wilbur. He eased into life at the junior high, kept a low profile, and enjoyed the light and warmth of Wingfoot's reflected glory.

———

HE ARRIVED HOME from school (and he had finally begun to think of it as home) on an October afternoon to find Min in the study, hunched over some papers at Uncle French's rolltop desk. "Min . . . ," he said from the doorway.

"I'm busy," she said, but she didn't tell him to go away, so he slipped inside and closed the door behind him. The first thing he noticed was that all those boxes and crates French had been working on were gone.

"Where's the stuff?" he asked.

She didn't look up. "In the attic."

"Aren't you . . ."

"Not now."

"I thought you were all into that history business."

She looked up at him then and he saw that her face was white and drained and there was a strange hollowness around her eyes. It startled him. "Min, what's wrong?"

She stared at him, or rather stared through him, for a long moment. Then she shook her head, a quick side-to-side jerk, and told him, "Sit down."

He took a seat in the leather chair next to the desk and waited. She looked again at the papers. Then, "There's not as much as I thought there was."

"As much what?"

"Money." She held up the papers. "Uncle Harbert brought these over today. They probated the will and Papa's lawyer went through his holdings and wrote everything down. There's . . ." she laid the papers gently on the desk ". . . a good bit of debt."

She explained it all to him in great detail, much of which he couldn't follow, but he understood that she needed to say it all to somebody and he was the only one around. Some of it was just thinking out loud, he thought, getting all of it straight in her mind.

There had once been a good bit of land here along the Cape Fear River and some commercial real estate in Wilmington and a business that involved selling things to the shipping industry. And there was the small general store out on Highway 133 between here and Wilmington. The store had no connection whatsoever to the rest of the family's business interests, but Baggetts had always operated a store on Highway 133 from back in the long-ago years when rice had been grown on the place and the Baggetts were the wealthiest and most prominent landowners in Brunswick County. So there was never any thought of *not* operating a store because that's something that Baggetts just did. But now, the store was the only solvent enterprise. The Wilmington business had taken a downturn in concert with a slump in the shipping business. There were loans, and banks wanted their money, and the commercial real estate would have to be sold to satisfy them. The business would be shut down.

Out here on the Cape Fear, there was less land than Min had thought. French had been selling off pieces of it for years. Aunt Margaret had expensive tastes and French had tried mightily to keep her happy. The long and short of it was, there was the store and there was the house and about a hundred acres of land around it. And what was left of the Baggett House Baggetts would have to make do with that.

"What are we gonna do?" Wilbur asked.

"Run the store."

"Do you know anything about running a store?"

"I'll learn. You can help after school. It'll be good experience."

"For what?"

"Later, when you go into business."

"What about Wingfoot?"

"He's got other things to do."

Min got up from the desk and walked over to one of the tall windows and stood there for a long while looking out at the live oak and the river beyond. "We've faced adversity before," she said. "Squire Baggett had this whole place blown away by a hurricane. And Doster Baggett had to stare utter ruin in the eye when the rice failed." She turned back to him with a defiant jerk, something almost wild in her eyes. "This will get Uncle Harbert and Aunt Grace out of our business. It's just us out here, and the rest of the world can go to hell. We're Baggetts, and we don't need a thing from anybody. Not a damned thing. I'm not going to fail my mama and daddy, Wilbur. I'm not. And neither are you."

———————

"I HAD A TALK with Min last night," Wingfoot said. "She says I've got to get my shit together." It was late summer. Wilbur would start the eighth grade in another week and Wingfoot would be a junior. They stood on the banks of Orton Pond, fishing. Min had given Wilbur the afternoon off from the store. Wingfoot had rigged up some makeshift gear from instructions in a jungle survival book — a piece of vine for string and hooks made out of sapling branch with sharpened points on which he had impaled crickets. The fish in Orton Pond didn't seem to think much of the rigs.

"What did she mean, get your shit together?"

"Well, she didn't say it exactly that way."

"I didn't think so."

"She said if I've got any hope of getting into West Point, I've gotta get my grades up and stop carrying on a lot of foolishness."

"What do you have to do to get into West Point?" Wilbur asked, pulling his line out of the water and studying the drowned cricket.

"Take an exam, get a lot of recommendations . . ."

"Like teachers and stuff?"

"Yeah."

That, Wilbur thought, might take some doing. Wingfoot, from all reports, was not a favorite with the faculty over at the high school. Some of them docked his grades as punishment for his unruly and unpredictable behavior. It had almost gotten him kicked off the basketball team at midseason. The coach had had to personally plead for him.

"And then I get a nomination from somebody in Congress. Fill out all these forms, take some tests. It's pretty competitive. Min says if I don't get my shit together, I won't make it."

"When did you start wanting to go to West Point?" Wilbur asked.

"Daddy took me up there one time when I was a little kid. He said I had a rebellious streak about a mile wide and just enough sense to be dangerous. He thought the military might be good for me. Lots of Baggetts have been military men."

Wilbur remembered the portraits hanging on the walls of Uncle French's study. A couple of them were of men in uniform. Uncle French had been in World War Two. And of course there was Tyler, with the medals and the plate in his head.

"What's it like? West Point?"

"It's awesome, Wilbur. All these guys marching around in their gray uniforms and all these old stone buildings and the parade ground and Michie Stadium and the Hudson River. And the museum. Godawmighty. Military stuff that goes back to the Egyptians. Did you know that George Washington thought West Point was the key to defeating the British in the Revolution?"

"No, I didn't know that."

"He had a big garrison of troops there, and they put this huge chain across the river so the British ships couldn't use it."

"Well, I'll be damned," Wilbur said. He replaced the cricket with a live one from the box they had brought and tossed the line back in the water. "If Uncle French had taken you to a landfill when you were a kid, would you have wanted to be a garbage collector?"

Wingfoot gave him a disgusted look. "Do you know who I'm named for?"

"No."

"Colonel Wingfoot Baggett. He went to West Point. When we went up there, we saw the room where he stayed when he was a cadet. But when the war broke out, he quit the Army and came home and fought for the South. A guerrilla fighter. Some guy at Chapel Hill wrote a book about him. *Wingfoot Baggett, Southern Marauder.* It was all about how he and his men hid out in the Great Dismal Swamp and ambushed Yankees. There was a price on his head. A thousand dollars for Wingfoot Baggett, dead or alive. But they never caught him. Daddy gave me the book when I was ten years old. I've read it a hundred times. He said Colonel Wingfoot was the best of the Baggetts. He was one tough sonofabitch. If he'd stayed in the Union Army, he'da been a general. That's what I'm gonna be. One tough sonofabitch of a general. It's what I'm supposed to do, Wilbur."

Wilbur thought it sounded a lot like Min saying, "Papa left me in charge." Biblical. Carved in stone. He remembered the little lecture Uncle French had given him in the study, about how you can appreciate your history without it being a burden to you, and about how a fellow could strike off in his own direction if he wanted, like Tyler had done. French left all sorts of room for taking your history or leaving it. But neither of his children seemed to have gotten the message. Wingfoot sounded like he was toting some old dead Confederate around on his shoulders. And Min was toting the whole damn Baggett family, bag and baggage. Surely, Uncle French hadn't intended for that to happen. But Uncle French wasn't here to set 'em straight.

"If I was you," Wilbur said, "I'd lots rather go to State and play basketball than go someplace and get my ass shot off."

"Well, Wilbur," Wingfoot said, "I can't imagine you doing either one. Maybe you'll be a hustler like your old man."

Wilbur flung down his fishing line and barreled into Wingfoot's midsection so fast that he caught him completely off guard and was sitting astride his chest, pummeling him with his fists, before Wingfoot knew what hit him. "You take that back, you goddamned sonofabitch!" he screamed.

Wingfoot tossed him off easily with a twist of his body. Wilbur landed in the soft mud at the edge of the water, scrambled to his hands and knees and headed for Wingfoot again. This time Wingfoot was ready. He held out a long arm and grabbed Wilbur vise-like on the shoulder and held him at bay while Wilbur swung his fists wildly, flailing air, cussing and screaming. "Take it back, you motherfucker! Take it back!"

"Okay. Okay. I'm sorry." He pushed Wilbur away with a shove.

"You better be! Goddamn you!"

"Really. I mean it." He rubbed his stomach and his mouth twisted into a grin. "Damn. That was a pretty good pop."

"Don't laugh at me."

Wingfoot's grin disappeared. "Wilbur, I really am sorry."

"Don't you ever say anything about my dad again."

"Okay. Calm down."

They glared at each other for a while and then both sat down on the long grass. Wilbur could feel tears stinging his eyes, but he fought them back. He was fourteen years old and he was goddamn well not going to let this sonofabitch make him cry. They sat there for a long time, not speaking. Finally Wingfoot said, "Min shouldn'ta done that."

And then the tears came anyway, and there was nothing he could do about it. He had been holding a lot inside for a good while. Wingfoot let him cry. And after couple of minutes, when the sobs had subsided, Wingfoot said, "Well, it's okay if you talk about 'em around me. I ain't Min."

"It wasn't their fault."

"It just happened, Wilbur. It wasn't nobody's fault."

"Then why does Min . . ."

"I guess she's gotta have somebody to blame. Don't take it personal."

"How else am I gonna take it? She makes me feel like my mom and dad are terrible bad people."

"Well, they weren't. No more, no less than anybody else."

They sat for a while longer and then Wingfoot rose and picked up the two makeshift fishing rigs and gave them a fling out into the lake. He looked down at Wilbur. "She's holding this whole fuckin' business together, Wilbur. The place, you and me, everything. She's had to give up just about everything she ever wanted. So cut her some slack. You need to talk about your folks, you come to me. You're in my platoon."

Wilbur didn't say anything.

"Do you know what the motto is at West Point?" Wingfoot asked.

"No."

"It's Duty, Honor, Country. It's a good motto. I like it. I intend to abide by it, and I'm gonna get my shit together like Min said so I can be the best, meanest goddamn general in the whole fuckin' U.S. of A. Army."

"I sure hope you do, Wingfoot."

"And Min feels sort of the same way about things. Without the 'Country' part, of course."

"You and Min both, you make all this sound like, well, like Moses gave it to you on a tablet or something."

"Something like that, yeah. And maybe one of these days, you little fart, you'll find something you just gotta do, something you care so much about you'll move heaven and hell to do it. Maybe Moses will hand you a tablet. People that don't have a tablet . . . they're just blowin' in the wind, Wilbur. Blowin' in the wind."

8 | WINGFOOT'S TRANSFORMATION INTO a prospective West Point cadet was awesome to behold. He went at it with an iron will and a religious fervor. He became a model of comportment at school. He bore down on the books and his grades improved. He stopped fighting on the basketball court. He went out for football, because the West Point application form said it was good to be athletically versatile. He joined the Glee Club and the Debate Team, where his stubborn tenacity served him especially well. Teachers were aston-

ished, and because the contrast with his previous behavior was so remarkable, they gave him more credit than they might have otherwise. At the end of his junior year he was inducted into the National Honor Society and was elected senior class treasurer. He could have run for president of the class, but he told Wilbur that it showed more responsibility to be entrusted with money.

At home, he gave Min no lip and no trouble and made sure Wilbur didn't, either. He rose early, did thirty minutes of calisthenics in his room, and then bolted from the house for a five-mile run along Highway 133. Some mornings he dragged Wilbur, bleary-eyed and protesting, from his bed to time him with a stopwatch. He improved his time so much that he became the star distance runner on the track team and placed second in the three-mile run at the regional meet, just behind a kid who had gotten a partial scholarship to Virginia Tech. To the rippling muscles of his frame, he added lean sinew. There was not an ounce of fat on him. Warm weather or cold, he ran without a shirt. "You are built," Wilbur said, "like a brick shit-house. And you stink like one, too."

Wingfoot didn't smile. It seemed to Wilbur that he had put aside, along with his foolishness, his sense of humor. He was unremittingly grim about this West Point stuff. He wasn't much fun anymore. But what he was doing, the way he was making himself over, was astonishing. Wilbur could only look on in amazement.

The basketball team went to the state tournament, where they lost to a team from Winston-Salem that went on to win the championship. Billy Hargreave, by now six feet five and quick of foot for such a big guy, signed with North Carolina State. The coach named Wingfoot captain of the team for the upcoming senior season.

In the fall of Wingfoot's senior year, he was visited at home by Norm Sloan, the basketball coach at State. Billy Hargreave came, too. Wilbur helped Min serve coffee and homemade cinnamon rolls and then they sat down and listened to Coach Sloan offer Wingfoot a full scholarship.

"I'm going to West Point," Wingfoot said. "They have a basket-ball team."

Norm Sloan shook his head. "What a waste." He looked over at Billy Hargreave, who shrugged. "Like I told you, Coach, I think he's got his mind made up."

"Baggetts are stubborn people, Coach Sloan," Min said. "Always have been."

"A streak of orneriness," Wilbur chimed in, but Min gave him a frosty look and he didn't open his mouth again.

Coach Sloan said, "If you change your mind, son, or if your plans don't turn out like you hope, the scholarship's waiting. I'll hold it for you as long as I can. We'd sure love to have you. With you and Billy, we can win the ACC. Maybe more than that."

"No need to hold the scholarship," Wingfoot said. "I'm going to West Point."

By the time Coach Sloan came to call, Wingfoot had done most of what he needed to do to get admitted to West Point. His grades were respectable. He had gotten nominations from the local congressman and both of North Carolina's U.S. senators. His basketball coach at Southport High had given him the standard West Point physical fitness test and he had turned in an astonishing performance—twenty pull-ups, a nine-foot standing long jump, a three-hundred-yard shuttle run in fifty-two seconds, and eighty-six pushups in the two-minute time allotment. Plus, he had thrown a basketball ninety-two feet from a kneeling position. The basketball coach at Southport High had written to the basketball coach at West Point, who was said to be salivating over the thought of Wingfoot Baggett.

Wingfoot was prompt about everything in the application process except the Scholastic Aptitude Test. He was nervous about that and kept putting it off until January of his senior year, the last opportunity, stared him in the face. On a Saturday morning, he rose early, rousted Wilbur from his bed to time his five-mile run in a cold drizzle, showered and clothed himself, threw up, and drove to Wilmington in the station wagon alone. In the late afternoon, he appeared at the store, ashen-faced but calm. When the test results arrived two weeks later—his scores well within the acceptable range—he went out to the tree house in the live oak and stayed for twenty-four hours.

The only thing left to do was take a medical examination, and the Army scheduled that for him at Fort Bragg on a Saturday in April. He boarded a bus for Fayetteville. He planned to go by the Post Exchange while he was there and buy a pair of second lieutenant's gold bars. When he graduated and got his commission, he said, Min and Wilbur could pin them on his uniform. One on each shoulder.

Wilbur was at the house alone late that afternoon with a long list of chores that would take him all weekend. He was out front, trimming shrubbery, when he heard the phone ring.

"Wilbur . . ."

Something in the voice sent a chill through Wilbur. "Wingfoot, what's wrong?"

"I can't go. They won't let me go."

"What . . . ?"

"They won't let me go to West Point."

"Why not? God, Wingfoot . . ."

"I failed."

"What, the exam?"

"I failed."

He was going off someplace, he said, someplace where he could think. Don't try to look for him, he said. Just tell Min he was okay, he said. And he hung up.

I failed. And Wilbur Baggett, who didn't know shit from Shinola, was smart enough to know that he meant a lot more than just a medical exam.

Min was wild with grief and worry. She called Uncle Harbert in Wilmington, but she was incoherent. Wilbur took the phone and told Harbert what Wingfoot had said. Harbert had political connections. He was the one who had gotten Wingfoot's nominations from the congressman and senators. He'd call the governor right away, he said. The Highway Patrol would find Wingfoot. Everybody should just sit tight and stay calm.

Wilbur hung up. Min had collapsed in a chair, sobbing into her hands. "Min," he said gently, "it's gonna be okay. He's just upset. He'll be back."

She didn't seem to hear him. "Papa left me in charge," she kept saying over and over.

————

IT TOOK TWO MONTHS to locate Wingfoot. He was in Morehead City, living in a boardinghouse and working as a laborer in a boatyard. An assumed name. Harbert also found out what had happened at Fort Bragg. Wingfoot had something called premature atrial contractions in his heart. Palpitations. Benign, the Army doctor said — nothing life threatening or even alarming, though unusual for an eighteen-year-old. But West Point wouldn't take him with premature atrial contractions.

Wilbur was unpacking a case of canned green beans when Harbert came into the store to tell Min. "What do you want me to do?" Harbert asked.

"Nothing," Min said. "Wilbur, go get in the car."

She closed up the store, right then and there in the middle of the afternoon, and they drove to Morehead City. Wingfoot was just getting off work, walking out of the boatyard shed, when the station wagon pulled up. It was late June, the air hot and sticky with the smell of rank salt water, diesel fumes, resin, freshly sawed wood. Wingfoot stopped in his tracks when he saw the car. Nobody moved. They all just stared at each other. Wilbur thought Wingfoot looked older. He had let his hair grow. It was over his ears, crawling down the back of his neck. He reached in his shirt pocket for a pair of sunshades and put them on. Min started crying. Wingfoot walked over to the car, leaned inside and hugged her.

She didn't fuss at him, as Wilbur thought she ought to. He had scared the hell out of them, running off like that. If anybody could take care of himself, he'd kept telling Min, it was Wingfoot. But just disappearing — well, anything could happen to you. Hitch-hiking, probably. And he had a heart condition, she kept saying. Wilbur hadn't tried to argue with her. He had stood somewhere at the fringes of her grief for a month, afraid to say much of anything, feeling alone and, at times, a little pissed off. Would she have carried on like this if he'd been the one missing?

But now, for all she had been through, she didn't fuss. She looked up into Wingfoot's face and caressed his cheek and patted his hair and cried. Wingfoot was stone-faced, and whatever was going on behind the sunshades, you couldn't see. He might have glanced over at Wilbur, or he might not have. Wilbur wanted to say something, anything, but he couldn't for the life of him think of a thing. He was still out here on the fringe of things.

"Come on," she said finally, "let's go home."

Wingfoot withdrew his head from the car. "I'm okay," he said. "Just let me be. I'm not ready to go home."

"Wingfoot . . ."

"It's a big old empty hole, Min. I can't go to West Point. I can't be a soldier. They won't even let me be a private. I was" — he held up his hand, a tiny space between thumb and forefinger — "this close. And now it's gone."

"I called Coach Sloan," she said. "He's still holding the scholarship."

Wingfoot shook his head. "You don't get it, Min." Then he turned and walked away.

They were almost home before she broke the silence. "Well, it's just the two of us now."

I'm not much at math, he thought, *but I know that one and one ain't always two.*

———

GLENDA TURNIPSEED RODE the bus home with him after school one afternoon during the spring of his junior year to study for an English test. Actually, a performance. Their teacher had decreed that every student would memorize Marc Antony's funeral oration from *Julius Caesar* and recite it in front of the class. Glenda was petrified. She was quiet and shy, a tall girl who was self-conscious about her height.

She and Wilbur had kept an easy, casual friendship. He had grown a foot since junior high. His voice had deepened. He was mildly popular. At the junior class Follies he had brought the house down with a dead-on imitation of Jeffers, the principal. He played saxophone. His grades were okay. Not spectacular, but okay.

"Stand up straight, Glenda," he told her. She stood in the middle of the parlor, slumped at the shoulders, hands clasped in front of her and writhing like small animals. She straightened just a bit. "More," he said. "You're a nice-looking girl when you're not all bent over like some old person. That's it. Throw your shoulders back. You're gonna be magnificent. Now. Let 'er rip."

"Friends, womans, countrymen,
Lend me your ears."

"It's Romans, Glenda. Not womans."

"Did I say womans?"

"Afraid so."

"If I do that in front of the class, I'll die."

"Remember the Bible. The book of Romans, not Womans."

"Friends, Romans, countrymen,
Lend me your ears.
I come to praise Caesar, not to bury him."

"Actually, it's the other way around. I come to bury Caesar . . ."

"Oh."

"I come to bury Caesar, not to praise him."

"Bingo. And why don't you try a little dramatic thing with your hands.

She stared at her hands.

"When you say 'bury Caesar,' do a little downward sweep with your right hand. Like this. Like you're indicating the hole in the ground where they're gonna put old Julius. And then when you say 'praise him,' lift your other hand up, like you're indicating the sky. Get your whole body into it."

"My whole body?"

"Yeah."

Glenda stared at the floor. "I can't do it, Wilbur."

"Yes you can," he said firmly.

"You try," she said. And she sat down on the sofa. "Show me."

Wilbur stood in the middle of the room and looked Glenda squarely in the eye. "I am Mark Antony. A bunch of other guys have just stabbed my best friend to death in the Roman Senate. I didn't really take part in the foul deed, but I didn't do anything to stop it, either. And now they've asked me to do the oration at the funeral. There's no way I can make up for betraying this guy, but I know how to give a good speech. And I'm clever. I'm gonna tell 'em I didn't come here to praise Caesar, and then launch into doing that very thing." He placed one hand on his hip and lifted the other slightly toward his audience, assuming what he imagined to be a tragic pose.

"Friends . . . Romans . . . countrymen . . ."

He went through the whole thing, using his hands and a little body English and inflection. Glenda sat there, spellbound, her mouth slightly open. And when he finished on a high, tremulous note, his voice full of the pathos and passion of the moment and then lowered his arms slowly to his side, she didn't speak for a long time.

"You have a really nice voice, Wilbur," she said after a while.

"Thank you." He sat down beside her on the sofa and picked up his English textbook from the coffee table to see if he had gotten all the words right. She took the book away from him and closed it and put it back on the coffee table. Then she kissed him. She tasted of Juicy Fruit and smelled of White Shoulders. "I love you, Wilbur," she said. "I've been in love with you since the first time you spoke to me in the hall in junior high."

"Well . . . oh."

"You don't have to be in love with me. I don't want you to be in love with me unless you really mean it."

What was he supposed to say—that he was in love with her, too? He wasn't, not in the way she was talking about. He didn't know anything about being in love with somebody. Anybody. But he owed her something, he supposed.

He thought about it for a long time. Finally, he reached across the sofa for her hand. To his surprise she drew it back. There was an odd look in her eyes and he could see that she had been watching him, studying him, while he agonized over this business of loving.

"There's something missing with you," she said quietly. "I thought maybe it was like, you know, how an artist will paint over a canvas, put a new picture on top of an old one. You wonder what's down there where nobody can see it. But maybe there's not anything at all."

She got up and left him, walked out of the house and down toward the river. He watched her for a long time through the window, standing there with her shoulders hunched over, as if she might bump her head on something if she stood up straight and tall. Then she straightened up and he could see her arms moving about and he realized that she was doing Julius Caesar. Doing just fine without him.

A little later, Min came in from the store and offered to drive Glenda back to Southport. Did Wilbur want to go? No, he sure didn't.

Min was back in a half-hour. "I don't think you ought to be spending time with that girl, Wilbur. She's . . ." Min waved her hand, and the gesture said everything. Glenda's father operated a boat, taking tourists deep-sea fishing. Wilbur had never been to her house, but he could imagine it—probably something like the little cinder-block oven he and Rosanna had lived in in Dysart while they waited for Tyler to come home.

"You have to remember who you are," Min said.

"A Baggett."

"Yes."

"How could I forget?"

———

OVER THE NEXT YEAR, Wilbur puzzled frequently over what Glenda had said. Was there something missing? Was he missing something?

But hell, he kept telling himself, he was seventeen years old. You weren't supposed to know everything about yourself when you were seventeen. Maybe later, you might find some missing stuff. It might suddenly appear, like something that had been lost in the Bermuda Triangle. But if it wasn't all there right now, at seventeen . . . well, hell.

He wondered about Wingfoot, what he knew of himself, what he had learned by aiming at something like a powerful guided missile and then exploding in midair, almost to the target. Wingfoot called occasionally, just to let them know he was alive and okay. He worked at the boatyard in Morehead City, on a state highway crew at the other end of the state near Asheville, on a Christmas tree farm in the mountains outside Boone. He was doing okay, he said. Making it. But the calls were brief. If you said anything even obliquely about coming home, he hung up. If he was finding out anything about himself, he sure wasn't sharing it with anybody at Baggett House.

And what about Min? At twenty-three, did she know all about herself? If she did, she didn't reveal any more than Wingfoot did. She was mostly pleasant. She would occasionally unwind and joke around a little. But there was always a distance, a line she had drawn somewhere that he was careful not to approach. She worked hard at the store and he helped in the afternoons and evenings and on long days during the summers. She provided the things he needed, at least in a physical sense. But what they said to each other, that was all pretty much on the surface, and carefully said at that.

So here he was, Wilbur Baggett, seventeen years old, an uncharted island in the midst of a blank sea. Who was he? What was he? Was he simply whatever he could touch and see? Or was some part of himself, as Glenda had accused, really closed off and painted over? And if so, what?

The answer came to him on a spring afternoon in his senior year.

He heard the splash of water from the half-opened door of the bathroom as he mounted the stairs and started down the hallway toward his room.

"Wilbur . . ."

He peeked in. She was bent over the tub, rinsing shampoo from her hair, a towel draped over her shoulders. "The conditioner . . ." She was pointing to the shelf on the far wall. "Pour some on and work it in," she said when he tried to hand it to her.

He froze, assaulted without warning by a powerful, sudden memory. He felt weak in the knees, the floor about to drop out from under him. "I can't," he said, barely above a whisper.

She turned to look up at him. "What?"

He stared at the bottle of conditioner. "I used to wash my mother's hair."

He set the bottle down on the rim of the tub and bolted, slamming the door behind him. He made it as far as the stairs and collapsed on the top step, head in hands. He heard the bathroom door open and close, Min's footsteps in the hall, heading back toward her room. Then he got up and left the house and hid away in Wingfoot's house up in the live oak tree, collapsing in a corner, feeling the structure shift precariously under him. He didn't care if the whole goddamn thing fell out of the tree. He was near panic, brain roiling, breath coming in gasps.

He had tried so hard to keep the past at bay, to play by the rules and not make any mess and be a good kid and be grateful for a place, any place, so that he could carry on his own pitiful, inconsequential little life. He had done what Min had told him he must do. He had come to accept, in a way, her version of things. Tyler at the controls. But he could see now that acceptance had come at a terrible price. He had betrayed his parents, had denied them, Judas-like, had given them up to save his own stinking ass. He hated Min for what she had done to him, but he hated himself a lot more for letting her do it. Maybe it was Tyler at the controls, but Wilbur was the one who had killed his parents, over and over, in every instance that he had pushed them to the back of his mind or given over to Min's version of things. They weren't lost at sea, not at all. They were here, in graves far too shallow to keep the wolves away. They rose up now to accuse him.

Glenda Turnipseed was right, and she was wrong. There wasn't anything missing. It was all there. And the sudden, searing knowledge of what was down there, what had been painted over, drove him into the corner of the tree house, terrified and wretched. He curled up into the tightest ball imaginable, head buried between his knees, and sobbed.

Darkness came. His body gradually unwound, the tight spring of a clock coming slowly apart until time disappeared. Every muscle, every nerve ached. He rose to his knees and looked out through the window that faced the river. He could see the winking red lights of the radio towers off yonder across the river, could hear the Cape Fear itself, a murmur, more like a vibration, so low that you had to be very still and quiet to catch it.

The fever subsided, the ghosts receded into the darkness, leaving him lost and utterly drained. Exhausted, he slept.

———

"MIN," HE SAID at breakfast several days later, "I've been accepted at Chapel Hill."

The tiniest flicker of something — pain, fear, disappointment, regret? — crossed her face and then was gone. He felt a quick thrill of satisfaction at the wounding, and then he regretted it. She hadn't intended to damage him, he was pretty sure of that. Maybe she had, as Wingfoot said, just done the best she could. He was the one who had done the damage.

"I've got a loan for the tuition and I'll get a job."

He hadn't told Min a thing about applying for admission. He just sent off for the forms, signing "Tyler D. Baggett" where it said "Parent or Guardian," and then watched the mailbox up by the road to intercept the package when it came.

Min rose and busied herself clearing the table. She didn't say anything for a good long while. Finally, "Why don't you take the afternoon off," she said. "I can manage the store." Then she was gone and it was time for the school bus.

———

MIN CAME TO HIM in late August with a check for six hundred dollars. "It's from the car," she said. "I told you I'd save it for your college education."

That was all that was said. The next morning he hitchhiked to Southport and went to a used car lot and bought a 1954 Plymouth. It wasn't a Cadillac convertible, but it would do. There was enough money left over for a tank of gas and a few bills in his pocket. He drove it home, packed it up, and set out for Chapel Hill.

As he drove through the afternoon he made a pact with himself. He would leave Baggett House and all it represented there on the Cape Fear with its shallow graves and its great legion of ghosts. He might forever be a Baggett, but he would not be a prisoner of the name, would not be shackled by anybody's past — his own or anyone else's. See what it had done to Min and Wingfoot? No, he would make his own way, as French had said long ago he might, as Tyler had done. It was, perhaps, a way of atoning in part for his betrayal.

He would save himself. He would be somebody, by God. One thing for damned sure, he wasn't going to spend his life being disappointed. Or on probation.

BOOK
3

9 | THEY TOOK INTERSTATE 40 toward Wilmington — Wingfoot driving the Ford van, Will propped in the bucket seat beside him with plenty of room for his leg to stretch out — but then they veered off after a while onto the old back way, Highway 421.

"Why are you going this way?" Will asked.

"Are you in a hurry?"

"Not really."

"That's good, Wilbur. A fellow ought not to be in a hurry."

Will smiled to himself. *Wilbur. Nobody's called me that in a good long while.* Not since he had gone off to Chapel Hill and introduced himself as Will Baggett, not Wilbur, because he wanted to get a fresh start. The other thing — well, yes, he supposed he'd been in a powerful hurry for as long as he could remember. But here on Highway 421 in the dark, cruising mostly on two-lane toward Clinton and Delway and Harrells, it seemed to make sense not to be in a hurry. He decided to give himself over to the novelty of it. They rolled the windows down and let in the night air, cool and spring-laden, and they turned on the radio and got an AM station out of Richmond that was playing country music for truckers.

He looked over at Wingfoot, who drove in a half-slouch, elbow resting on the open window, right hand draped over the steering wheel. Will hadn't seen him in more than four years, not since he had turned up unexpectedly at Palmer's graduation from high school. The other surprising thing, besides Wingfoot showing up, was that he had been entirely at ease around Palmer and Clarice and Clarice's folks, the Greensboro Palmers. He wore a nice navy blue suit and a yellow tie and his shoes were shined and he looked and acted right at home with the rest of them. He still had that fit, erect military bearing about him and he moved with the ease and grace of an athlete, but there was none of the old white-hot intensity. He seemed like a man who had made some accommodation with himself. Will had meant to visit with him, to ask him how his life was going, but when the ceremony was over and the photos taken, Clarice's family had hustled them off toward Greensboro where luncheon waited at the country club, and Wingfoot had headed on back to the Cape Fear, where he said he was living then, off and on. There hadn't been occasion for them to be together since then.

"You look good," Will said now.

"How so?"

"Fit. Solid. Like you've come to grips with yourself."

"How about you, Wilbur?"

"Well, since the last time I saw you, I've gained weight, lost my job, and made a goddamn fool of myself."

Wingfoot looked over at him. "All sorts of shit has hit the fan, huh?"

"All sorts." He stared out the window at the passing lights of farmhouses and crossroads stores and the blur of plowed fields in moonlight, waiting for the planting of a new tobacco crop. On the radio, Hank Williams junior was singing a song about getting buck naked. Finally Will asked, "Why?"

Wingfoot knew what he meant. "Min thought a fellow in your sorry shape should come home."

"For what?"

"Sympathy, rejuvenation, blueberry pancakes . . ." He shrugged.

"I haven't had any communication with Min, except for Christmas and birthday cards, for a couple of years. Is she okay?"

"I suppose," Wingfoot said, "you'll have to judge for yourself."

They fell silent then and Will leaned back and let April blow fresh on his face. He had taken another pain pill just before they left the house and his mind mellowed and eased into untroubled sleep.

He woke as they reached Wilmington and passed over the Cape Fear River where the gray hulk of the battleship USS *North Carolina,* outlined in twinkling lights, hunkered at its memorial park below the bridge.

Wingfoot recalled how, as a child, he and his elementary school comrades had collected nickels and pennies to help save the old battlewagon from the scrap heap. From his perch in the big live oak next to the river, he had watched as the ship glided past, nursed by tugboats, on the final leg of its journey from Bremerton, Washington, to its resting place. "It was the most magnificent sight I'd ever seen," Wingfoot said. "It made me downright giddy and I had to hold on tight to the live oak to keep from falling out."

"Did it make you want to be an admiral instead of a general?" Will asked. He was not sure he ought to broach what might be an old, painful subject with Wingfoot, but in his half-fog, just easing out of sleep, his voice took its own path.

"I thought about it for a little while," Wingfoot said, "but then not long after that was when Papa took me to West Point. I decided that if I was gonna buy the farm, I'd rather get it on a battlefield, where I could fight back, instead of being torpedoed or eaten by sharks."

"But you did neither."

"We can talk about that sometime," Wingfoot said. "I'm okay with it."

They turned south on Highway 133, paralleling the Cape Fear for several miles, passing Min's store on the left and, a mile later, turning on the old plantation road. Then it was hard-packed sand under the canopy of moss-dripping trees, until they reached the place where the road emerged from the trees and there was the house and the long sloping lawn and the live oak and the expanse of river and marshland and the twin lights of the radio towers winking across the way.

The house was ablaze with light and Min was standing at the

back door peering out. She came to the car and opened the door and helped him out and got him situated on his crutches and then hugged him for a long time.

He breathed deeply of the night air, warm and soft as only mid-April along the Cape Fear River can be. Smell of the river, tinged with the slightly brassy aroma of marsh—a river both tart and sweet, where salt water from the Atlantic mingled with fresh from upstream. It was, he thought suddenly, something he had missed without knowing it. It might be a place to heal. And then get back to his life.

When Min finally pulled away a bit he could see the glint of tears. "Come on in the house." She tugged on his arm. "It's good to have you home."

———

HE WOKE THE NEXT MORNING to the smell of bacon and eggs and pancakes. When he opened his eyes he had the strange, momentary thought that he was in a museum. Then he remembered that they had set up a cot for him in the study so that he wouldn't have to negotiate the stairs with his bum knee. The room was exactly as he recalled it from that first visit years ago, when he had listened to Uncle French tell about the Baggetts and their baggage: paneled walls, mahogany and leather furniture, the oil-on-canvas visage of Squire Wilbur Baggett peering benignly down at him. It had been unchanged when he went off to college and it was unchanged now. Everything clean, neat. Just as it was.

When he hobbled into the kitchen on his crutches, Min was at the stove. Billy Hargreave was at the kitchen table, hunched over a mounded plate, attacking it with gusto. Billy waved a fork. "The walking wounded." He was in dusky green uniform with dark green epaulets, a Sheriff's Department Brunswick County patch on one shoulder and a silver nameplate that said simply, SHERIFF HARGREAVE.

"Morning."

"Wilbur!" Min called happily, jabbing the air with the spatula she was using to turn the pancakes. She had matured into a sturdy woman with strong gray hair that she kept close-cropped. "Sit down. I'll have you a plate in a second."

Will eased into a chair across from Billy, propped his crutches against the table, and stretched out his bum leg, encased in the plastic-and-Velcro cast. It was still pretty sore, but he wasn't feeling any of the sharp knife-thrusts of pain. "What time is it?"

Billy checked his watch. "Almost eight."

"You show-business people—up all hours and sleeping away half the morning," Min said. "How do you feel?"

"A little groggy. I think I'll lay off those pain pills."

Billy peered over at the cast. "Looks like you come in second in an ass-kicking contest," he said around a fresh mouthful of pancake.

"Billy, if you're going to be crude, you can eat out in the yard," Min said from the stove.

"Yes ma'am."

Min brought Will a huge plate of food—a stack of pancakes, already slathered with butter and maple syrup, a mound of scrambled eggs, several pieces of bacon and sausage.

"Good Lord," Will said. "Are you trying to finish me off?"

"Shut up and eat," she commanded. Will shrugged and started working on the breakfast. Min brought her own coffee to the table and sat down with them, watching the two men. "Is it any good at all?" she asked Billy.

"Tolerable," he said with a grin.

"Is Wingfoot sleeping in?" Will asked.

There was a moment of silence, just enough to make Will notice. "Wingfoot has his own agenda," Min said pleasantly. And then she rose quickly and took the coffee cup to the sink and poured out what was left. "Well, I've got to get moving. See what that Pakistani is up to."

"Who?" Will asked.

"Hired help at the store. No telling what kind of mess he's made. I usually open up so people can have their fresh coffee and cheese biscuits on the way to work. But with company this morning . . ." and she was gone, down the hall and up the stairs.

"Who's this Pakistani?" Will asked.

"Actually, he's from Lebanon," Billy said. He was mopping up egg yolk with a biscuit.

"Is he legal?"

"He's got papers."

"How long has he been working for Min?"

"Couple of years. She still refers to him as the Pakistani."

"To his face?"

"Yeah. He gave up trying to tell her. You know, when Min gets something in her head . . ."

A few minutes later, Min breezed back through the kitchen, purse in hand. "See you tonight. You know where everything is." She bustled out the back door and in a moment he heard her car crank and pull away.

Billy pushed back from the table, wiped his mouth with his napkin, and dropped it onto the plate. "Damn!" he said with a satisfied smile. "That woman can flat cook a breakfast." He rose and poured himself another cup of coffee and stood looking out at the morning through the window above the sink.

Will picked at his food, but he really wasn't very hungry. The aftereffect of the pain pills, probably. And all the rest of it. Maybe he would get in the habit, in his few days here on the Cape Fear, of eating less. Lose a little weight, get rid of the fleshiness around his chin and midsection before he went back to Raleigh. By the time his non-compete clause was up and he was back on the air, people would say, "Doesn't Will Baggett look fit."

"Haven't seen you in a good while," he said to Billy's back as he pushed the plate away.

Billy turned to him and leaned against the counter. "Four or five years, prob'ly."

In the vertical, Billy Hargreave filled up a room. Six feet eight or nine, Will estimated, broad in the shoulder and now, at middle age, a good-size paunch bulging the uniform shirt and easing over the wide leather belt at his middle. Imposing, the kind of law officer you probably didn't want to mess with. At North Carolina State, he had been a bruiser on the basketball court (his teammates had named him Takeout because of his knack for doing grave damage to opposing teams' best players). He had returned to Brunswick County after college, dabbled in business for a while, and then run for sheriff. Wingfoot had related to Will that Billy was very good at it. He carried no gun and wasn't in the habit of chasing folks down with warrants. If Billy wanted to see you, he just sent word. But as big and imposing as he was, he had a gentle air about him, an easy smile.

There was a time, while Will was off at Chapel Hill, that he heard reports that Billy—newly returned to the county—was spending a good deal of time at Baggett House. If he was sweet on Min, nothing ever came of it. Billy had instead married a girl from Maryland he had met in college. But now, here he was in Min's kitchen this April morning, having devoured an enormous breakfast that she had prepared for him and leaning against the counter sipping on his coffee as if he were right at home and always had been. Will wondered if the girl from Maryland minded. *Was* there something? Whatever, it wasn't any of his business.

"How's the sheriff business?" Will asked.

"Tolerable. The usual stuff—some drugs, not too bad, kids with too much money, tourists that don't know how to behave, occasional shooting or cutting, domestic stuff. Keeps us hopping."

But Billy didn't seem to be in a hopping mood this morning. He sipped on his coffee, looking over the top of the cup at Will. After a moment, he set the cup down on the counter and unlimbered himself. "Ready?"

"For what?"

"I'm your nursemaid this morning. I'm gonna get you a bath and change your diaper."

Will rode piggyback up the stairs and Billy helped him into the tub and left him to soap and soak for a while, then hauled him out and helped him get dressed from the suitcase Min had left open on the bed in his old room. Will felt a little self-conscious about it, but if it bothered Billy, he didn't show it.

He looked about the room as he struggled into his clothes. It, too, like the study downstairs, seemed unchanged from the day he had left to go to Chapel Hill. Old high school textbooks on the desk, his saxophone in its case in a corner. Odd. Almost a time warp. Things preserved in amber. The difference here was himself—middle-aged, a few pounds overweight, unemployed, battered about the head and shoulders. A refugee, in a way, the same as he'd been more than thirty-five years ago when he and Rosanna had come here to Baggett House because there was no place else to go. *At least,* he thought, *this time I'm not on probation.*

"You know how to handle yourself on those crutches?"

They were standing at the top of the stairs now. "Not really. They showed me at the hospital, but I was pretty doped up and I don't remember much about it."

Billy took the crutches and Will steadied himself with a hand on the banister. "Broke my foot one time when I was at State," Billy said. He had to bend way over to get his armpits on the crutch pads. "When you're going down the stairs, the crutches go first, then the foot. Like this." He clumped down a couple of steps, then turned back. "Going up, it's foot first, then the crutches. And be sure to keep your weight forward so you don't topple over backwards." He handed the crutches to Will. "You try it."

Will peered down the stairwell. It seemed a great long way to the bottom. "Crutches first, then the foot."

"Yeah," Billy said. "Get it backwards and you're likely to bust your ass."

"Maybe I should give it a couple of days . . ."

"Nope. Just go ahead and do it, Wilbur. You only get a nurse-maid for one day. After that, you're on your own."

While Billy fetched folding lawn chairs, Will leaned against the live oak tree and gave the house a good looking-over. It had sagged and deteriorated even more in the four or five years (he couldn't remember exactly) since he had last been here. Large chunks of plaster were missing, and what remained was dingy and moss-splotched. Paint was flaking from eaves and windowsills. Some of the fascia boards beneath the roofline showed signs of rot. He remembered it from his youth as a grand, even forbidding place. But he had begun to notice signs of decay the first time he had brought Clarice here, a couple of months after they were married. They had driven down from New Bern, and as they approached, she peered through the windshield of the car at the aging, sagging house and said, "It looks like a . . . tumor." It was much worse now. And the lawn, once lush and green and immaculately kept, was a straggly stretch of sand and patches of grass. When Billy brought the chairs they turned them so that they faced the river.

Will studied the clouds — wisps of high, thin cirrus against pale blue, drifting in from the Atlantic. No rain there. A dry, mild day in the making, though that could change pretty quickly along the coast. If you got a front moving in from the west, things could deteriorate pretty quickly. Gusty wind, heavy rain, a surf advisory out at Wrightsville Beach. He didn't know about all that, though. He hadn't seen or heard a forecast in a couple of days. He hadn't wanted to. But he couldn't help studying the clouds. Always the weatherman. Maybe for the few days he was here along the Cape Fear he would just let the weather happen, simply go on instinct — the taste and feel and smell of what it was like outside, not satellite photos or prognosis charts with their snaking lines of isobars and millibars.

A freshet of breeze drifted in off the Cape Fear, rustling the tall marsh grass at water's edge.

"Is that old alligator still there?" Will asked.

"Barney." Billy grunted. "Hunh. Haven't been down there in years to look. Could be. I don't know how long alligators live."

"Wingfoot tried to blow him up one time."

Billy chuckled. "I know. I was with Wingfoot when he found the dynamite in that old shack up by the lighthouse. He wanted to see if he could take out a bridge, but I talked him into going after the gator."

"Where *is* Wingfoot, Billy?"

Billy scratched his chin, as if trying to decide what to say, how much. "Like Min says, he's got his own agenda."

"Which is?"

"I guess you'd better ask him about that."

"Does he live here?"

"Off and on."

Will felt a little nibble of irritation. Whatever Wingfoot was up to, Billy wasn't revealing. And no telling where Wingfoot was or what he was doing. Whatever it was, it couldn't be any more of a surprise than his showing up unannounced and unexpected in Raleigh to haul Will off to Brunswick County. "Well, I don't want to get stuck down here. I've got things to take care of."

"So I hear."

"Do you know all the gory details?"

"Pretty much. It was in the paper down here, too."

"My God. Well, don't believe everything you read in the paper. When you've got a couple of hours, I'll tell you my version." Will cupped his bum knee with his hand and rubbed it gingerly. "The doctor said I can start putting weight on the knee in a couple of days. A week or so, I ought to be a lot better."

"And you don't want to be stuck down here."

"No."

"Well, Wilbur, no sense in being in a rush. You might find you like it. Might want to stay on for a good while." He turned and looked at Will, a straight-on look sort of like the kind Will imagined he might give a suspect he was questioning. Was this a question? Was Billy fishing for something? It was unsettling. But then, he was aware of a vague but gathering notion of unsettlement that had begun when he had waked a couple of hours ago in the time capsule that was Uncle French's study. Billy just added to the feeling.

"I don't think so, Billy." Then, "What's going on here?"

Billy pursed his lips fish-like and held the expression for several seconds. But he didn't say anything. After a moment he rose and hitched his britches, snugging them up under his paunch. "Guess I'd better get on over to Southport and see what kinds of atrocities the criminal element of Brunswick County are committing this morning. You'll be okay?"

"Sure. I can get around."

"Remember what I said about those crutches. We don't want to find you at the bottom of the stairs with your neck broke."

"Okay," Will said. "*Don't* tell me what's going on. I guess I'll have to figure it out for myself. But do you have any advice?"

Billy smiled down at him benignly. "I'll tell you like I tell my deputies when they go out on a domestic disturbance call. Keep your head up and your ass down."

———

HE SPENT THAT NIGHT in his old bedroom, easing slowly and carefully up the stairs on the crutches with Min just behind, her hand at his beltline, steadying him. He slept well and woke the next morning to the soft sound of rain.

It rained for the rest of the week — a thick soup of fog and drizzle, interspersed with galloping downpours. The radio said a front had stalled along the coast.

Will had the house mostly to himself. Min left early for the store and returned after dark to fix supper (she insisted on calling it supper in the old-fashioned way), which they ate at opposite ends of the big table in the dining room, the vast expanse of mahogany keeping conversation rudimentary, like two people calling to each other from opposite banks of a river. He wasn't much help in the kitchen while the meal was being prepared, but he insisted on cleaning up, propping on the crutches at the sink. It took a good while but he was happy for the simple activity of it, and by the time he had finished, Min was gone, up to bed.

During the day he clumped about the house, rubber-tipped

crutches squeaking across the polished heart pine floors, and began to negotiate the stairs fairly nimbly. He worked diligently at his rehabilitation, pushing himself, occasionally overdoing it a bit and having to rest for several hours and take aspirin. By the end of the week he was putting a good deal of weight on the knee and had discarded one crutch. Early next week, he vowed, he would walk on his own.

While he rested, he read. Among the books that lined the shelves in the study were the complete works of James Fenimore Cooper. He spent hours with Cooper's Chingachgook, outwitting the wily Indians. A man could survive and thrive in all kinds of wilderness, he thought. Even with a bum knee.

It was the first time he had been physically restricted in years, since the day he had wrenched his back lifting a lawn mower from the trunk of his car. He had lain abed most of the rest of that Saturday and all day Sunday, but he had insisted on going to work on Monday afternoon (Clarice, shaking her head in disbelief, had had to drive him and then pick him up at 11:30), shuffling along half-bent, smelling of Icy Hot, moving stiffly at the weather map and joking with the viewers about the dangers of yard work.

Now, he decided not to let the bum knee cloud his thinking.

Or the weather, as morose as it was. The rain continued, unabated. The Cape Fear swelled and ran sluggishly brown and debris-logged, but much of the time he could barely see it for the shroud of mist that hung about it. When the downpours came, they were wind-lashed, whipping the limbs of the live oak in the front yard between house and river, scattering bits of branch and leaf across the yard.

On television, he had made light of long, water-soaked stretches like this, inventing an imaginary celebration he called the Raleigh Mold and Mildew Festival. Anytime the weather was damp for more than three days at a time, he hailed the beginning of festival days at six. During one especially lengthy rain event he had gotten the mayor to issue a proclamation. Channel Seven printed T-shirts which went to lucky viewers who submitted their names on postcards for a nightly drawing. The weatherman couldn't let the weather get him down. Or his viewers. A little humor went a long way.

So he wasn't going to let a bum knee or bad weather get him down. Or this business back in Raleigh. As the week went on he tried to work his way mentally through it, to look it straight in the eye and figure out exactly what it was and how he ought to act. There were aspects of utter disaster, of course—lost job and dignity, appalling publicity, humiliation and dread and yawning uncertainty. He wallowed in that for a while, but as the week wore on he decided that there was nothing to be gained by wallowing. He was by nature an upbeat and optimistic man. Old Man Simpson had been right: stay calm. Watch and wait. Clean up the debris and rebuild. All right, so he was out of commission as a Raleigh weathercaster for a year. There were other things he could do, or he could do nothing. There was no problem with money. They had some savings. He had a check for fifty thousand dollars, which he had won by what he was coming to think of as physical combat. He had scars to prove it. And of course there was Clarice the real estate whiz. But they wouldn't need to get into that. He had always provided. He still would.

Two telephone calls helped considerably to boost his spirits.

On Thursday, Morris: "I think you need to fight this thing, son."

"I thought you were working something out with the district attorney to drop the charges."

"Well," Morris drawled, "the D.A. is between a rock and a hard place on this, Will. If he drops, the police department and the paper are gonna be all over his ass. Favoritism for a celebrity, you know. And he's got an election coming up."

"I don't know, Morris. I just want to get it over with. Plead guilty, if that's what it takes."

"But you say you didn't run the red light."

"I don't remember running a red light."

"Then it's just one cop's word against yours. Cops make mistakes all the time. Maybe the light was yellow and he thought it was red."

A long pause. "They don't have any witnesses. The D.A. did tell me that."

"What if the judge believes the police officer and not me?"

He heard Morris's chair squeak and he could picture him easing back in it, propping feet on desk, maybe reaching for the pipe. "Look, old son, I've had this conversation with the D.A. Let me be circumspect about what I say here. He can't drop the charges, but he's . . . ah . . . I get the distinct impression he won't be too upset if he loses the case. You get me, tiger?" Then there was the click of Morris's lighter. Yep, he had the pipe, all right.

"Puff on your pipe for a moment, Morris, and let me think about this."

"While you're thinking, add this to the pile. I wasn't going to say anything about it, but I had lunch today with Charlie Timkin from Channel Thirty-two."

"Why weren't you going to say anything?"

"Didn't want to get your hopes up."

"I could stand some up hopes, Morris."

"Well howsomever, they're interested. More than interested. They'd like to sign you up right now, get the public relations goody out of it, maybe even put you on retainer, and wait a year while your non-compete runs out."

"Can they do that? The non-compete says I can't help another station during the year."

"I doubt Spectrum would challenge you on it." Will could hear him take a puff, let the smoke out easily. "I get the impression they consider you damaged goods. If you went on the air at Thirty-two right away, they'd sue. But just an announcement that you plan to in a year . . . probably not."

"I see."

"But here's the hitch. Charlie Timkin is concerned about these court charges. More publicity, you see. He'd like to see you cleared."

"And the only way to do that is fight it."

"Seems to be."

Channel Thirty-two. It wasn't much of a station, mired in third place in the local news ratings, plagued by aging equipment and a listless staff. Compared to Channel Seven, it was a dump. But it was a job and it was in Raleigh. And Will Baggett could be a hero at Channel Thirty-two. Raleigh's most popular TV weatherman, boosting an also-ran to respectability.

"Did you talk money?" Will asked.

"Low six figures."

"Uh-huh."

"And there's this one other thing, Will . . ."

"What's that?"

"Politics. I had lunch yesterday with the chairman of the county Democratic Party. Republicans have been eating their lunch in Wake County. So he's practically salivating at the thought of Will Baggett at the head of the ticket. He wants to meet. After we get this thing behind us."

"Meaning . . . no record."

"Yessirreeebobtail," Morris said brightly. "You're coming on strong, son."

"How soon do I have to decide this?"

"Sometime next week I need to tell the D.A. what our intentions are. He's willing to put it high on the court calendar, get it taken care of."

"Okay, Morris. I'll call you next week."

"Think about it, son. As your attorney, I'm advising you to put your dukes up. You're gonna win this one. Tie things up in a neat little package and get on about your business."

"Let me just ask you this, Morris."

"Shoot."

"Did you get a couple of free lunches from Charlie Timkin and the chairman of the Democratic Party?"

Morris just laughed and hung up.

The second call, on Friday morning, was from Clarice. It was raining in Raleigh, too, she said, had been most of the week. But the foul weather didn't seem to have gotten her down. Her voice was light, buoyant. Nothing much in the mail. Some cards and letters for him. She was keeping them in a box. The phone calls had pretty much stopped. No more stories in the paper. She had hired a neighborhood boy to mow the lawn as soon as the rain quit. Everything taken care of. He was not to worry. She didn't mention the construction project. Could you demolish the backside of a man's house in the rain? He didn't ask.

"We're going to Cincinnati," she said.

"What for?"

"A seminar on selling on the Internet."

"Who's we?"

"Several of us from the firm."

"When did this come up?"

"Oh, we've had it on the calendar for a couple of months."

"You didn't tell me." Silence. "How long are you going to be there?"

"We'll be back next Wednesday. So, no need for you to hurry back to Raleigh. Stay there and recuperate. How's your knee?"

"Much better. How do you sell real estate on the Internet?"

"That's what we're going to find out. We've got a Web site, but Fincher says we're not getting all the benefit from it we should. He said there's a way you can put virtual tours of homes on your site. You know, you click on a picture of the house and a video comes up and it's like you're just wandering through the house. Fincher says it can save a lot of time for us and our clients. If you like what you see on the video, you go look. But you can eliminate a lot of what doesn't suit." She was almost breathless when she finished.

"I see."

"So . . ."

"Have a good trip. I imagine we'll arrive back in Raleigh about the same time."

"That's good. You just relax and rest up. Don't push too hard."

"I love you," he said.

"Of course you do." And she, like Morris, rang off with a laugh.

He mulled it. She had sounded chipper, almost playful. That laugh at the end. It wasn't what you would call a gales-of-mirth laugh, but it was the first time he had heard any kind of laugh at all from her in a long time. It was, at least, a laugh that gave him a good, solid notion that things would be okay. It would take some work, but they would be okay. Another week and he would be mostly healed and much rested and he could return to Raleigh and get his life back. That is, if he could locate Wingfoot. Min hadn't mentioned his name all week, and neither had Will.

That business—Min, Wingfoot, this house, the larger thing all that might represent—was the one part of his present circumstance that he couldn't get a handle on. There was, he was dead certain of it, something unsaid, unapproached, hanging in the damp gloom of this cavernous old house. The first time he got a real peek at it was on Friday evening. He was sitting at the kitchen table while she worked at the stove, her back to him.

"It's been a good while since you've been to visit," she said.

"Well, here I am."

"Didn't they give you any vacation at that TV station?"

"Sure."

"Where did you go?"

"Usually, I just took a few days to putter around the house. With Clarice's business, it got to be pretty hard to arrange a trip."

"Do you still go to Nags Head with those Greensboro people?" she asked.

"The Palmers," Will said.

"I never can remember their names."

"Palmer," Will repeated. "My son is named after them, remember?"

"How's Palmer doing?"

"Fine. First year of med school is pretty rugged. We don't see much of him."

"A Duke man," Min said.

It didn't seem to matter that Palmer was now in med school at Chapel Hill. To Min, he would apparently always be a Duke man. A Tarheel fan to the bone, she harbored a deep and abiding enmity for everything associated with Duke. They had argued quite heatedly about it five years before when Palmer had chosen Duke for college. She hadn't shown up for Palmer's high school graduation and he hadn't been back to Baggett House since. It wasn't worth arguing about now, but it reminded Will how prickly she had become in middle age. Duke-Carolina wasn't the issue. But what was, and why? Maybe it was menopause, or being by herself so much in this big, sagging house. Did it have something to do with Wingfoot? Did it have something to do with Will—resentment, perhaps, over his success, his celebrity? All of the above? Or something even deeper? Whatever, he didn't have any appetite for getting into it. He had too much else going on in his life that needed his time and mental energy. He had his own agenda. Didn't everybody?

The morning after their set-to five years ago they had patched things up, at least on the surface, and had parted cordially. But he hadn't been back and she hadn't been to graduation. Wingfoot came, but not Min. The relationship had been distant since then. Until she had sent Wingfoot to fetch him.

"Yes, the Palmers still have the place at Nags Head," Will said now, heading the conversation away from Duke. "We go sometimes."

"Well, you could have come by here on the way to Nags Head."

"It's not on the way to Nags Head," Will said. "It would be like going through Chicago to get to New York."

"Sometimes," Min countered, "you have to go out of your way." She paused for a moment, and then, for the very first time in the entire conversation she turned from the stove and faced him. She smiled pleasantly, at least with her mouth. "But let's not get into that."

———

THE CONVENIENCE STORE was closed on Sunday. Baggetts had never operated a store on Sunday and never would, Min said. So she was at home all day. She bustled about the house—cleaning, mopping, dusting. He helped a little, polishing the silver tea service in the dining room. They were massive, heavy, ornate pieces—coffee and tea pots, cream pitcher, sugar bowl, all of it on a huge tray with the Baggett name and family crest etched in the metal. Squire Baggett, the original Wilbur, had it shipped from England when he built the house, Min told him.

"This stuff must be worth a fortune," Will said to Billy Hargreave when he stopped by at midday. Billy was sitting at the other end of the dining room table. Min had set him to work cleaning crystals she had removed from the chandelier.

"The house is full of it," Billy said. "Silver, porcelain, furniture, paintings. No telling how much."

Will looked around to make sure Min was nowhere near. He could hear the vacuum cleaner running back in the study. "Doesn't Min worry about somebody breaking in?"

"If she does, she doesn't tell me about it."

"Don't you? Worry? You're the sheriff."

"Will, you've been here long enough this visit to get a good look around. Do you notice any changes from the time you were a teenager?"

"No."

"Well, there aren't any, not as I can see."

Will thought about it. "When I woke up the first morning, I thought for a moment I was in a museum."

"You were. Are."

"Why?"

"Min likes things just so."

"What about the outside of the house? It looks pretty desperate."

"I guess Min's just doing the best she can, Will. It's not something she talks about. But you're family. Maybe you oughta bring all this sort of thing up with her."

"How does that fit into your advice to keep my head up and my fanny down?"

"Hmmmm." Billy hummed. But before he could answer, the vacuum cleaner shut off and they could hear Min's footsteps in the hall. Billy gave him a wink. What did that mean?

*   *   *

Late on Sunday afternoon, in response to Will's inquiry about whether there was anything to drink about the place, Min brought out an ancient bottle of scuppernong wine from a storage room off the back porch. The bottle was caked with dust. He decided not to ask its age. But the wine had a surprisingly nice, gentle taste to it. She transferred it to a crystal decanter and served it in elaborate wine glasses on a silver tray. There was another tray of assorted cheeses and fruits. They sat in the front parlor and nibbled and sipped as darkness began to settle over yard and live oak and river. Outside, it was still raining. The wind had picked up during the afternoon and occasionally it lashed against the windows. Five straight days of rain with little letup. Billy Hargreave had said there was flooding in low-lying areas in the counties around Wilmington.

They chatted amiably, mostly about the past. Min was an encyclopedia of Cape Fear history—the families that had settled the riverbank, their commerce and social life, the imprint they had left on the land, their tales of elegance and tackiness.

"When you put down roots and cling to a place over time and protect it and nurture it, it means there's something solid about you," she said. "Most folks aren't solid. They buy and sell places like they were some kind of cheap commodity. They pick up and move on a whim. They don't have a sense of one place where they belong. And without that, you're apt to act like there's nothing solid in the rest of your life. You just gallop off in all directions at once."

"Like me?"

"I suppose you've made the best of being stuck up there in Raleigh," she answered mildly.

"I've never thought of it as being stuck. I chose Raleigh. Both Clarice and I wanted it."

"Clarice wanted to go to Greensboro," Min said. She said "Greensboro" the same way she did "Duke people."

"Well, she's close enough. And now that she's doing so well in real estate, she's perfectly happy in Raleigh. Selling big houses to all those rootless people. We're both happy there. We have a nice home in a nice neighborhood. We wish you'd visit sometime."

She sipped on her scuppernong wine and munched on a slice of apple, and then she said, "All that work you do in the yard. It proves my point."

"Which point is that?"

"About attaching yourself to a plot of ground. You're trying to put your mark on it."

"Is that what I'm doing? I thought I was just trying to keep out the crabgrass."

"So you're going to stay in Raleigh?" It was the first time—almost a week gone by, and the very first time—she had brought up the subject of his job and general disaster. That, too, was part of the unspoken thing in this house, the thing that hovered. Not just Min's agenda, but also his own. He would have appreciated at least an acknowledgment of his dilemma. But he had bided his time.

"Of course I'm going to stay in Raleigh," he said, perhaps a little more adamantly than necessary. Who was he trying to convince?

"And what are you going to do in Raleigh?"

He gave her a brief recitation of the bare facts—the non-compete clause, all that business. Then, "Until something in television opens up—and I've already had some feelers from other stations—I'm open to possibilities. I've even considered politics. Morris—you remember Morris—mentioned my running for mayor."

"Baggetts aren't politicians. Well, there was a distant cousin somewhere back in the twenties. He ran for Congress, I think."

"And?"

"Lost. He got on the wrong side of the evolution debate."

"He was . . ."

"For it."

"Well, I'm glad that's no longer an issue. Most folks seem to have come to grips with the idea of monkeys in their past. At any rate, I've never heard of it being discussed at a Raleigh City Council meeting. I think they're more into things like traffic and garbage pickup."

Will speared a small cube of cheese with a toothpick, placed it squarely in the middle of a Triscuit, and ate the whole thing in one bite. It was good cheese, a variety of local cheddar that Min brought home from the convenience store. She bought it by the large hoop and measured out whatever a customer wanted. A way, she said, of maintaining some touches of the old crossroads country store of the Baggett family's past, even though it now had plate glass across the front and bright overhead fluorescent lighting and plastic bags for your purchases.

"It's the best thing that ever happened to you, Wilbur," she said.

"Political consideration?"

"Losing that TV job."

"I loved that job," he said quietly. "The way you love this house."

"No," she said, "it's not anywhere near the same."

"Well, maybe not." He took a deep breath and stepped gingerly into uncharted waters. "I think you can hold on to something too long, Min."

She stared at him for a long time, stone-faced. It was so quiet that a rattle of wind-driven rain against the parlor windows sounded like musket fire. Finally she said, "Do you want to elaborate on that, Wilbur?"

"This place," he said with a sweep of his hand. "I know, it's been . . . well, all you've said it is. But it's so big. And all this stuff. God, I can't imagine what it would appraise for. And you, here right by yourself—I mean, I know Wingfoot comes and goes, but still, a lot of the time . . . Anyhow, you work so hard down at the store. Long hours and all. And I know from the local news in Raleigh that working in a convenience store can be dangerous sometimes, especially if you're there by yourself. I mean, somebody can walk in and hold up the place and if he's high as a kite on some kind of junk, you don't know what the heck he'll do." He could hear himself talking faster and faster, his voice rising, and he thought that he should probably back way off from this, but he was in pretty deep now and he didn't know how to extricate himself without just going ahead and blurting the whole thing out, the thing that he had been mullling over all afternoon.

"I asked Billy this morning if you don't worry about somebody breaking in here."

"Why don't you just ask me, Wilbur?" she said. Her voice was flat and hard.

"Well, don't you?"

"No." There was another long silence. He waited. "You don't know anything about this place or my life here, or Wingfoot's life, or any of the rest of it. You've spent the last umpteen years over there in Raleigh being Mister Television Personality. We're just common folks here, Wilbur. Just living our common ordinary everyday lives in rural Brunswick County without benefit of celebrity status."

"You're anything but common folks, Min. You're the Baggetts. I've had that drummed into me . . ."

"And you're not? No, I guess you're not. You've forgotten what it means."

He put up his hands. "I'm sorry. I didn't mean to cause a ruckus."

"No," she said, "that's quite all right, Wilbur. Let's just go ahead and get this said. If you're so worried about me, and about the store, and about the house, what do you think I should do? Give me the benefit of your carefully considered opinion."

"Forget it."

"No," she said sharply. "I insist."

He chewed on it for a minute or so while she waited. "All right. You could deed the house to the county historical society. Take a huge tax write-off. Sell some of the contents. Sell the store. You'd have enough to be absolutely comfortable. Take a trip. Go around the world, for gosh sakes. If you stay here, it's just gonna become more and more of a burden. I mean, look at all the work it needs right now."

Min leaped to her feet, eyes blazing. "This is our home! If you don't like it, get out!"

"Min . . ."

"It's your fault! If you'd done what I asked you to do, we wouldn't be in this situation."

He gaped at her, open-mouthed. "What on earth can you possibly mean by that?"

An angry toss of her head. "I tried to get you to study business at Chapel Hill so you could come back and take over and get things back on track. But no, you had to study show biz."

"Broadcast and film, Min. It's a business, too."

"Show biz, Wilbur," she spat. "And then you ran off to be Mister Celebrity and left me here holding the bag. Well, I've done the best I could. I've done just fine. I don't need you. In fact, you've been nothing but trouble from the beginning. You and your god-damned . . ." She was fairly screaming now, fists clenched, face red and blotched.

"What, Min? Me and my goddamned what?" He was on his feet, ignoring his knee, halving the distance between her chair and his.

"You and your goddamned father!" she cried.

"It was an accident! It just happened. It was nobody's fault."

"He was flying the plane."

"Min, dammit, you're not gonna do that to me again, not like you did when I was a scared, miserable little thirteen-year-old boy. I've put all that behind me because I couldn't be halfway sane otherwise. But you . . . you've had it stuck in your craw for thirty-five years. Truth of it is, you're just plain stuck. Your daddy left you in charge, and so you're stuck here in some sort of nutty time warp. Nothing can change. It all has to stay just the way it was when he left you in charge. You can't *do* anything, so you just have to look for some-body to blame. Well, blame God if that'll help you. But don't blame the dead!"

She started to say something, but whatever it was strangled in her throat. Instead, she burst into tears and bolted from the room, leav-ing him standing there tottering on unsure legs, shaking with anger, shaken with the rage of her outburst. That, and the sheer disaster of having finally, after all these years, openly confronted that terrible thing between them. That unsaid, unapproached thing. It had hap-pened so fast. Such an enormous thing, and so fast. The beast, dor-mant this great time, had come uncaged in the blink of an eye.

He staggered backward, slumped in his chair, lowered his face to his hands, made a blackness there and sat staring into it. With all that had happened to him, all of the disasters piling one upon another, now this. Why now, when it—added to the crushing weight of everything else—was simply more than he could handle? A few hours ago, he had been full of hope and optimism. All of the rest of it would work out, he just knew it. But this—well, it had cast a pall over everything. Why? Maybe it was because this was so basic, so ancient, so at the core of who he was and all he had tried to be. If it made him feel so desolate and drained now, what effect had it had on him all these years? What kind of baggage had he toted around, not realizing that it was baggage, and that what was inside was so lethal?

He raised up finally. It was dark outside. The rain had stopped. He rose wearily, climbed the stairs, and went to bed. It was not until he was under the covers that he realized that he had left the crutches in the study, that he had mounted the stairs entirely on his own. His knee ached a bit now, but he couldn't remember whether it had hurt as he climbed or not. The rest of him was just numb.

It took a long time for sleep to come. He kept thinking, over and over, *I've got to go home. I've got to go home.* But then, he couldn't quite figure out where home was. Maybe he had never truly had one.

10 | WILL WOKE THE NEXT MORNING to the sound of bumping and scraping overhead. He thought at first of a storm-blown limb, but then he saw the brightness at the edge of the curtains. He realized that the bumping and scraping was coming from the attic. He

threw back the covers, swung his legs over the side of the bed, and hobbled to the window. He pulled back the curtains and was momentarily dazzled by sunlight. Overhead, something hit the floor with a thud.

"Min . . . ," he called tentatively.

"Down in a minute," she sang back.

He stood at the window for a while. New sun danced on droplets of water still hanging from the leaves of the maple tree just outside and on the puddled yard below. He tugged at the window, trying to open it. Stuck. He banged on the frame with his hand to loosen decades of dried paint, then tried again. It came free with a loud crack as he heaved upward, opening the room to the wet, juicy smell of late spring. The window screen had long ago rotted away, so there was nothing between him and the morning. He leaned far out and took a deep breath, inhaling the rich blooming scent of azalea and jasmine, hearing the buzz of insects around the honeysuckle that grew wild at the edge of the yard.

He heard the door open behind him and turned to see Min reaching into the room with a cup of coffee. She placed it on a table next to the door. "Breakfast is almost ready," she said.

"Min . . ." But she was gone.

When he got to the kitchen several minutes later, she was at the stove, laboring over grits and scrambled eggs. The back door was open, letting the morning in. He stood in the doorway and watched her for a moment. "Min . . ."

She turned to him then, reaching for the coffeepot. "Sit down and have another cup. I'll be finished with this in just a minute."

He sat, staring at her, while she filled his cup and then went back to the stove. Not a twitch of muscle, not a thing out of place betrayed the slightest hint of what had gone on in the study hours before. She looked fresh, well-rested, glad unto the morning. Good God. Had it not happened? Had he just imagined or dreamed it because it was something that was stuck in his own craw that needed to get out? Did it really have nothing to do with Min?

"What was all that noise?" he asked finally.

"Go to the study after breakfast. You'll see."

"Don't we need to talk, Min?"

"Not now. Later. After." But she didn't say after what.

She brought their plates to the table and they bowed their heads and she said grace and then they ate. She chatted amiably about the welcome break in the weather, the barge traffic on the river, the employment situation at the Sunny Point Military Terminal just downriver, the wholesale price of groceries, the Pakistani who helped her in the store. Will watched her in astonishment.

"I see you're without your crutches," she said.

"Yes. Last night . . ."

"That's good. You're on the mend. Maybe it wasn't as bad as you thought."

What?

"I guess I'll be able to get on back to Raleigh pretty soon."

"Why hurry? You said Clarice is away on a business trip. And there's nothing for you to do there. Take your time. Maybe you'll find some other things here to occupy your time and mind." She bit off a chunk of toast, washed it down with coffee, and then jumped up. "Well, I better get on to work and find out what kind of mess that Pakistani has made of things this morning. I swear, it's hard to get good help . . ." and then she was gone, her sturdy shoes clumping down the back hall and up the stairs.

She was back in a few minutes with her purse. "The study," she said as she headed for the back door. "Call me if you have any questions."

He sat there, flabbergasted, for a while longer. And then he got up and went to the study.

Time warp? He wondered if he were somehow twelve years old again, entering the study at Uncle French's bidding to hear a capsule history of the Baggetts and an analysis of the family psyche. All that was missing was Uncle French. There were the museum-like furnishings, of course, but there was also the great collection of crates and boxes he remembered from that long-ago visit. So that's what Min had been dragging down from the attic this morning.

He stood in the doorway, immobilized for a time by the sight of it. The family pile, packed away all these years. Blasted loose by that explosion in the parlor yesterday evening?

The top of Uncle French's grand mahogany desk was bare except for a legal pad and a row of freshly sharpened pencils and a single sheet of white paper with some writing on it. He gathered himself and walked to the desk and picked it up.

Wilbur,

It would do you a world of good to have a true appreciation for the Baggett family history. It is all here, and it just needs to be cataloged and put in some chronological order so that it can be turned into a historical document. You are a communicator, and I know that you have the smarts and the talents to do that. And now you have the time to devote to it. I wouldn't trust just anybody to do this.

Min

He laid the sheet of paper gently on the desk and looked about at the boxes and crates stacked one upon the other, the ancient, musty mass of it crowding the parlor like a convention of moldering ghosts. He opened the box nearest the desk and gazed in at the jumble. He opened another, and another, digging down into the contents with a sort of horrified fascination—letters and documents, leather-bound ledgers and receipts, deeds and invoices, wills and testaments, books and diaries, manifests and calendars. "My God," he said softly. "French was right. These people never threw anything away." *These people.* His people. But he felt no connection to them. A gene pool, but what else?

The sheer mass of it drove him from the room. He opened the French doors that led to the front porch and then wandered out across the limb-strewn yard, past the live oak, down to the river. It was still swollen and turgid. Out in mid-current, a tugboat struggled against the red-stained mass of water, pushing two barges laden with huge boxy metal containers. The doors of the wheelhouse were open and he could hear the faint, unintelligible snap and crackle of the tug's radio.

SOS. SOS. I am adrift in a sea of paper history. Maybe I should bring it all down here and toss it. Too bad there's not anything in there for old Barney to eat. But then, he'd choke on all that stuff.

He stood there for a while and then his knee began to ache and he hadn't figured out anything by staring at the river, so he went back into the house. He made a wide detour of the study, and went instead to the kitchen where he made another pot of coffee. He drank two cups at the kitchen table, washed the breakfast dishes, took out the garbage, picked up a few wind-blown twigs by the back door.

Back inside, he turned on the radio on the kitchen counter and listened to a talk show on a Wilmington station. Doctor Laura was dispensing no-nonsense advice to a woman who was involved in the latest in a string of messy, destructive relationships with men who couldn't quite get free of their mothers. Dump him, Doctor Laura said. Get the heck out of there. Doctor Laura took a break and a local announcer read the forecast — sunny to partly cloudy for the next two days with a steadily warming trend.

He turned off the radio with a sigh and emptied the remains of the coffee in the sink and went back to the study.

It looked like the aftermath of an eviction — a business gone bust, deputies arriving with legal papers and emptying the offices of the company's records, piling it all unceremoniously on a sidewalk while passersby gawked and clucked in sympathy. The sheer volume of it was daunting. How had the attic stood the accumulating weight over the years? It was a wonder the entire house hadn't collapsed in on itself, reducing the family to litter and rubble.

Finally, he cleared a place on the leather sofa and sat down, rubbing his knee and flexing his leg. He opened the box next to him on the sofa and took out the top sheet. It was a bill of sale for two mules, made out in now-fading ink to Lemuel Baggett on April 27, 1873, and signed by one Fonzell McQueen of Burgaw. April 27. He realized with a start that it was today's date. More than one hundred twenty years ago on this very day, Lemuel Baggett had paid thirty-five dollars for two mules. Lemuel and his mules were long departed, but here was evidence of their existence, of money and goods fairly traded.

He remembered with sudden vividness something he had said to Clarice years ago when they were in the first mad throes of love. She had asked him about his family, his history. "I have no history," he had said to her, "not in the sense you think of." What history he had, he had shaped himself, and it began the day he climbed in the 1954 Plymouth with a full tank of gas and headed off for Chapel Hill. But now here he was, surrounded with this vast archaeological dig of paper, this chaotic mass of family detail. It made him weak, just looking at it. What did Min expect him to do with it? And why? Was it penance? *Here I am on probation again. I'm going to spend my whole life on probation.*

He got up from the sofa and poked around the room until he found the volume of James Fenimore Cooper. He took it to the front porch and sat in a rocking chair and started reading. Chingachgook. Outwit the Indians and save the settlers. A simple life.

————

HE HEARD A CAR around back. A few minutes later, men's voices in the front hall, detouring through the study. Then Wingfoot appeared in the doorway, Sheriff Billy Hargreave looming tall behind him. Wingfoot glanced back into the study. "You look like a man who could use an outdoor burning permit," he said.

"Where in the heck have you been?" Will asked.

Wingfoot ignored the question. "Billy was at the store this morning. Min told him you're writing a family history."

"You're kidding."

"Ummm-hmmm," he grunted, then turned to Billy. "Billy, what did Min say?"

"That Wilbur's writing a family history."

"Ummm-hmmm."

"Did Min say . . . anything else?" Will asked.

"Nothing in particular," Billy said. "Well, she said the Pakistani messed up the cash register again."

"About me?"

"Only that you were writing the family history."

"Shit," he said softly. This was all just too much. Should he tell Wingfoot what had transpired last evening? Would Wingfoot give a damn? No, Wingfoot had his own agenda. "Wingfoot, I've got to go home."

Wingfoot said. "Come with us."

They rode for more than an hour, Billy Hargreave driving his Sheriff's Department cruiser, Will sitting beside him in the front seat, Wingfoot lounging in the back and reading a pamphlet from the State Agricultural Extension Service: "Everything You Need to Know About Nematodes."

Wingfoot and Billy had hustled him out of the house, fairly kidnapping him. Shouldn't he call Min, tell her where he was going? Where *was* he going? "Never mind all that," Wingfoot said. "Billy will take care of it." So he and his suitcase were in Billy's cruiser, heading away from Baggett House, away from ruckus and history. Will felt a great sense of relief.

They meandered upcountry, heading generally northwest through the Cape Fear lowlands, sharing the back roads with pickups and logging trucks and an occasional school bus full of wilted children. It was mostly pine trees and marsh and low scrub growth, an occasional small frame house along the roadside. Will tried to make conversation for a while, but Wingfoot said, "Wilbur, this ain't tee-vee. Silence is perfectly okay." So he shut up and watched the scenery. They rode with all the windows rolled down, the wind rushing easily past the car. It mussed Will's hair, and he didn't even care.

It was a fine spring day, the landscape straining for as much lushness as the sandy soil would allow. He watched a pair of hawks circling lazily over a field freshly plowed for soybeans, spotted a thick-bodied water moccasin crossing the road just ahead of the cruiser, Billy slowing the car to let him clear the road and slither into tall grass. Will thought he probably would have tried to run over the snake, but for Billy, the act of mercy seemed offhandedly natural, done without comment. Live and let live.

They skirted the Little Green Swamp and then followed busy U.S. Highway 74 west for a few miles, past a sign that said WELCOME TO COLUMBUS COUNTY. "Aren't you out of your jurisdiction?" Will asked Billy.

"Anybody asks, I'll tell 'em I'm transporting a prisoner," Billy said.

"Who's the prisoner, me or Wingfoot?"

Billy just laughed.

They rode on, turning north again into Bladen County, crossing the Cape Fear River. Will pondered the strangeness of it, this easing off into remoteness and uncertainty with not the foggiest idea where he was headed or why. And with no deadline, no schedule, no real purpose. No schoolchildren for the Weather Wizard to entertain, no red light blinking on the front of a studio camera to display him to the world, no family history to chronicle. He was unfettered. It was a novel idea. *Go with the flow, Will. Go with the flow.*

He jerked awake with a start, realizing that he must have nodded off not long after they crossed the river. They were bumping along a narrow sandy road now, a winding cut between stands of tall pine that loomed on either side of the car. "Where are we?" he asked.

"Almost there," Wingfoot answered.

They emerged after another minute or so into a broad clearing and the cruiser pulled to a stop in front of a green-and-silver mobile home. A green canvas awning stretched across the entire length of the trailer, providing a sort of open patio. Beyond the trailer were two large glass-enclosed greenhouses, and past that, several acres of open ground where shrubs and plants grew in well-tended rows. Wingfoot's van and a large stake-body truck were parked in the bare sandy yard of the trailer.

As Billy killed the engine of the cruiser, Wingfoot stepped from the rear and called out, *"Muchachos, vengan y miran a la curiosidad que he traido de la ciudad."*

"He's speaking Spanish," Will said to Billy.

"Yep."

"What did he say?"

"I caught the *muchachos,* but that's about all."

"I told 'em to come see the freak I brought from the city," Wingfoot said.

"I didn't know you spoke Spanish," Will said out the window.

"Well, ain't much call for it back at the big house," Wingfoot answered.

A short, stocky man emerged from the nearest greenhouse, and after a moment, a teenaged boy. They waved happily to Wingfoot. *"Buenos días, Wingfoot,"* the man called. *"Han traido alguien para tocar el violin?"*

"Lamentablemente no. No mas es un cojo destituido y sin trabajo. Se me ocurrío darle un balazo, pero decidí enseñartelo primero. Para mi es igual si lo quieres blazear."

"What?"

"Pedro asked me if you play the violin. I told him no, you're an unemployed homeless man with a bad leg and that we probably ought to just shoot you."

"Violin?"

"Well, fiddle. In these parts, we refer to it as a fiddle."

The man and boy walked over to the car as Will and Billy got out. "Will Baggett, meet Pedro Esquivel and his son, Cisco,"

Wingfoot said. *"Muchachos, mi primo Will Baggett, antes era un famoso actor de televisión en Raleigh."*

"I got the television actor thing," Will said.

Fernando stuck out a hand. *"Eres un luchador?"*

"What did he say?" Will asked.

"He wants to know if you're a wrestler."

Will shook hands with Pedro and Cisco. *"Buenos días,"* Will said, remembering a bit of his college Spanish. *"Me llama Will.* No wrestler." What was that word? he asked Wingfoot.

"Luchador."

"No luchador."

Pedro and Cisco looked a little disappointed. They chattered with Wingfoot in Spanish for a moment, then turned with a wave and headed back toward the greenhouse while Billy opened the trunk of the cruiser and handed Will his suitcase. "You coming tonight?" Wingfoot asked.

"Might," Billy said. "Depends."

"We're trying out a new song," Wingfoot said.

"Well, in that case . . ."

Billy got back in the cruiser and cranked the engine. Pedro and Cisco had almost reached the greenhouse when Pedro turned back and called, *"Sheriff Billy es como los Dukes de Hazzard."* Billy looked to Wingfoot, who made a siren sound. Billy grinned and turned on the flashing blue lights on top of the cruiser, and then, as he pulled away, heading along the sandy road, the siren split the air with a *whoop!whoop!* Pedro and Cisco laughed and cheered, and then disappeared into the greenhouse as Billy's car vanished into the pine forest.

Will stood there for a long moment with his mouth open and his suitcase in his hand, feeling Wingfoot's eyes on him. "All right," he said after a while, "what the hell is this?"

"My adobe hacienda," Wingfoot said, indicating mobile home, greenhouses, field and woodland.

"Yours?"

"Like Thoreau, I went to the woods."

"Where . . . who . . . what . . ."

Wingfoot started for the trailer. "Come on in and take a load off. I'll explain while I cook supper. Peachy'll be here in a little while, and if supper ain't ready, she'll whip my butt. She gets real ornery when she's hungry."

"Who's Peachy?"

"You'll see."

11 | WILL SET THREE PLACES at the table, then sat and watched Wingfoot tend a sizzling pan of stir-fry—chunks of beef and assorted vegetables—and a steaming pot of rice. Wingfoot lifted the lid briefly and peered in, then put the lid back.

"Where are we?" Will asked.

"The backside of East Jesus," Wingfoot answered. He reached into a cupboard for a jar of garlic salt and sprinkled it liberally over the stir-fry.

Will looked out the window next to the table. Dusk was settling over the neat rows of plants that stretched from the rear of the trailer to a stand of pines a couple of hundred yards away. Mexican music drifted from the nearby greenhouse. An overhead light was on out there and he could see Pedro and Cisco moving about inside, tending tables crowded with potted plants. Come Sunday, Daylight Saving Time would go into effect and this hour of the day would be bathed in late sun. But now, at just past five o'clock, the fading light was softening everything with shades of gray.

"Yours?" he asked, turning back to Wingfoot.

"Partly."

"You have a partner."

"Peachy. And the bank, of course."

"How much land?"

"About seventy-five acres here, bigger place down the road a ways."

"I hope you don't mind all these questions. I'm just . . . well, a little astonished."

Wingfoot opened the refrigerator and pulled out two bottles of beer, twisted open the caps, and handed one to Will. He took a deep pull. Ice cold. The best thing he had tasted in a good while, though the scuppernong wine hadn't been half bad. Scuppernong wine. The thought of it, of Min, of the sudden violent eruption in the parlor twenty-four hours ago, made his stomach knot. He took another swig of the beer.

Wingfoot leaned back against the counter and slugged at his own beer and let the stir-fry sizzle in the skillet behind him. "Shoot," he said.

"How long?"

"You mean the place here? Or Peachy?"

"Both."

"The place . . . ten years. Peachy . . . a year, two months, thirteen days, and"—he glanced at his watch—"about three hours."

"Sounds grim, Wingfoot."

Wingfoot just smiled.

"Tell me about her."

"Just wait," Wingfoot said. "I don't want to color your first impression."

"Okay, what about the place?"

Wingfoot turned back to the stove and stirred the stir-fry. "Well, it's pretty much as you see, Wilbur. Several hundred acres in pines, and we sell off some of 'em every once in awhile to International Paper. But most of it is the nursery. Grow stuff, sell it all over the south and east. We've got Pedro and Cisco out yonder and a couple of dozen more down at the other place."

"Mexicans."

"Yeah. They're terrific people. Work hard, make no trouble, send most of their money back south to their families. All of 'em are legals. We make sure of that. No sense in getting yourself crossways with the law when there's plenty of legals around."

"And you speak Spanish."

"*Si si.*"

"How did you learn about all this?"

"Just picked it up, I guess. You can read how to do just about anything. You just got to figure out what it is you want to do."

"Uh-huh."

"Take you, for instance. You figure out what you want to do with the rest of your life, then go look it up."

"I don't have to look it up," Will said. He took another big swig of beer. "I know exactly what I want to do. The same thing I've been doing. It's the only thing I know how to do. And tomorrow, I'm going back to Raleigh and do it."

Wingfoot took three plates from the cabinet next to the sink. He spooned heaps of rice onto the plates, then sprinkled on a generous helping of Chinese noodles, and topped the whole business with stir-fry meat and vegetables. He glanced again at his watch. And that was when they heard the throaty roar of a car's engine coming fast down the road toward the trailer.

"You'll want to watch this," Wingfoot said.

Will opened the trailer door just in time to see a vintage Triumph Spitfire two-seater sports car skid to a stop, throwing up a rooster tail of sand and fine dust. The driver-side door swung open. It took her a while to unravel herself from the car because there was a great deal of Peachy to unravel. Incredibly long legs, encased in faded jeans so tight they could have been painted on. An orange tank top that was filled to capacity. And finally, a tousled head full of wind-blown jet black hair. Peachy stood. And kept standing. She had a clean, angular face—a bit too large to be called pretty, but definitely handsome. Will looked her up and down. Six feet two, he guessed. The word "statuesque" came to mind. "My goodness," he said softly.

"Hi," she called. "You're Wilbur."

"I sure am," Will said.

Peachy grabbed a backpack from the car and shoved the door shut with an incredibly sexy movement of her right leg.

"Has that rascal Wingfoot got supper ready?"

"You bet. He said you'd whip his butt if he didn't."

"Peachy Delchamps," she said, striding toward him with her hand outstretched.

Will took it. It swallowed his own. "Charmed," he said.

Peachy moved with an athlete's swift grace, pulling him with her into the trailer, where Wingfoot was putting the plates of stir-fry on the table along with fresh bottles of beer. "Hi," she said. And the way they looked into each other's eyes made Will tingle. She was a bit taller than Wingfoot, so she had to bend a little to give him a peck on the cheek. The movement tightened the fabric of the jeans across her rear end even more, and Will felt a rush of pure desire. Peachy turned just in time to catch him looking. She smiled a great big knowing smile.

She was, she told him over dinner, the former Miss Greater Greenwood. She had been born and raised in Greenwood, South Carolina, and was the tallest girl to ever enter the Miss Greater Greenwood Beauty Pageant. "There was this one other girl who had a shot at it," Peachy said. "I told her if she'd drop out, I'd teach her how to yodel, and if she didn't, I'd whip her butt."

"She dropped out," Will guessed.

"Yeah. But she went to Nashville and she's doing backup vocals with Aaron Tippin."

Will didn't know who Aaron Tippin was, but it sounded impressive. "And let me guess again," he said. "She yodels."

"Like a songbird."

"And after Miss Greater Greenwood?" Will asked. "I hope that wasn't the end of your beauty career."

"I came in third runner-up in the Miss South Carolina Pageant. And then I got a scholarship to play basketball at Clemson."

"She invented a move," Wingfoot said. He had been deep in his stir-fry, but he looked up now and winked at Peachy. "Show him."

It was a lightning-fast head fake and double-clutch glide to the basket, she explained, and she stood and gave a demonstration.

"The Peachy Pump," Wingfoot said. "Imitated by female basketball players, and some male, all over the Atlantic Coast Conference."

"We won the ACC championship my junior year," she said, looking down at him after she had jammed an imaginary basketball through an imaginary hoop with such vigor that it made the floor of the trailer shake.

Wilbur stared, realizing his mouth was open, hoping he wasn't drooling. He had his chair tipped precariously far backward, looking up at her.

"You ought to see her do it in bed," Wingfoot said.

She rapped him on the top of the head with her fork as she resumed her seat. "Mind your mouth, Wingfoot."

"Yes ma'am," he said with a grin.

They finished dinner, and while Peachy was back in the rear of the trailer freshening up, Will helped Wingfoot clear the table and do the dishes.

"Goddamn, Wingfoot," he said. "Can you handle that?"

"I reckon," he said. Then he gave Will a long look. "Don't get the wrong idea about her, Wilbur. There's a lot going on there."

"I can see there is."

"No, I don't mean that. She graduated magna cum laude in finance at Clemson. When I met her last year she was one of the top brokers at the Merrill Lynch office in Wilmington."

"Then why the hell is she out here on the backside of East Jesus messing with the likes of you?"

Wingfoot lowered his voice conspiratorially. "Because I think she's in love."

"Where are we going?" he asked when they left the trailer an hour later—Will and Peachy in the Spitfire, Wingfoot, Pedro and Cisco following in the van. Peachy drove fast but well, both hands firmly gripping the steering wheel. Even with the seat pushed back as far as it would go, she was folded under the wheel like an accordion and she had to shift her weight to move her right foot from gas pedal to brake. That didn't matter a great deal, however, because she rarely used the brake. They sped along a rural two-lane black-top at near seventy, the wind howling in the open windows and rattling the canvas top of the Spitfire. They had to shout to hear each other.

"We're going to see your cousin," she said.

"Min?"

"No."

"Who?"

"Another cousin. Don't ask so many questions, Wilbur."

"That's how you find out things," he said. "I confess, this whole business has me pretty flabbergasted. Wingfoot said you gave up being a stockbroker to raise nandinas and stuff."

"Well, that's not the only reason."

"What's the other?"

"Wingfoot plays drums," she said, beating a little tattoo on the steering wheel.

"I'm not even gonna ask about that."

"Don't. Just keep your eyes open."

"My head up and my ass down?"

"That, too."

Will gave himself over to the wind and the highway and the rich smell of Peachy sitting thigh-to-thigh beside him there in the Spitfire, making him jump every time she reached to shift, brushing against his leg. She had changed before they left into a pair of jet-black jeans, also skin-tight, and a loose-fitting blouse affair with a lot of fringe on it and a good bit of shoulder showing. He couldn't remember when he had had so many of his senses engorged at once.

Where in the hell were they? He was so far off the beaten path that he had absolutely no sense of geography or direction, physical or mental. Physically, he guessed they were somewhere in the general vicinity of Pender County, and confirmed it when he got a quick glimpse of a road sign at an intersection: BURGAW 10 MILES, with an arrow off to the right. Burgaw, he knew. He had judged a cornbread cook-off there a couple of years before as a representative of Channel Seven. But they weren't headed for Burgaw.

"May I just ask you one more question? What's your real name?"

"Peachy."

"That's on your birth certificate?"

"Yep."

"Let me guess. Your father grows peaches."

"Nope."

"Well then . . ."

"Mama went through sixteen hours of labor when she had me. Daddy fell asleep. When the doctor woke him up and told him he had a daughter, he said, 'That's peachy.' And that's what they put on the birth certificate. Don't you think I'm peachy?"

"Yes ma'am," Will said, "I sure do."

———

THE BIG RED-AND-WHITE NEON mounted over the front door read BAGGETT'S PLACE. EAT, DRINK AND BOOGIE DOWN. There was a brightly lit sign on a small two-wheeled trailer sitting out front of the place: APPEARING TONIGHT: PEACHY DELCHAMPS AND MINOR AILMENT.

"Appearing . . . ," Will said.

Peachy wheeled the Spitfire into the gravel parking lot. It was jammed with an assortment of automobiles, pickup trucks, vans, all-terrain vehicles, and a dump truck. "The boys and I are the 'boogie down' part," she said.

They parked around back, the van pulling alongside the Spitfire. "You wanna help us?" Wingfoot asked as he and the Mexicans climbed out. "Just take some of this light stuff. Don't strain your knee." He handed Will a cardboard box full of microphone cords and assorted electronic gear. Wingfoot grabbed a guitar case and headed for the back door. Will followed.

He was assaulted by an explosion of noise and beer-and-grease-and-sweat smell and a thick pall of cigarette smoke that made his eyes water and his throat constrict. It was a single cavernous room with a wide bar at one end and a dance floor and stage at the other. In between was a sea of tables and a seething mass of people—men in jeans and overalls, bright flowered shirts and cowboy hats; women packed into tight pants and blouses and industrial-strength makeup; waitresses struggling through the crowd, precariously balancing platters of food and beer bottles. Recorded music—Clint Black, he thought—thundered from a huge set of speakers on the stage, competing with the shouts and laughter of the crowd.

They cut around the edge of the dance floor and deposited the guitar case and the cardboard box on the stage. Will looked out at the crowd. Rowdy, raucous, loud, joyous. The music pulsed, making the smoke-riven air dance and setting off ripples in the stir-fry in his belly. He felt a little woozy. Wingfoot clamped a firm hand on Will's shoulder. "Wilbur, this could be a life-altering experience here tonight. You might find salvation. A state of sublime grace."

"Or I might throw up," Will said. "I've never heard so much noise in my life."

"Well, get ahold of yourself. If you throw up, just don't do it on anybody's woman."

Wingfoot turned loose of his shoulder and plunged into the crowd and Will had no choice but to plunge after him. They emerged after a moment in front of the bar. "Cousin Norville!" Wingfoot shouted over the heads of the people pressed up close.

There was another crowd behind the bar, a whirlwind of arms dispensing beer and food as fast as they could manhandle it from the taps and the open window of the kitchen beyond. A stocky, balding man wearing a white apron popped up. "Hey Wingfoot! Did you bring him?" Wingfoot pointed to Will.

"Say hello to Cousin Norville while I help Peachy and them set up," Wingfoot yelled in Will's ear, and then he was gone back into the mass.

"Norville Baggett," he bellowed over the noise when Will had made his way behind the bar. He offered a beefy hand. Will judged him to be about sixty.

"Will Baggett."

Norville's handshake was firm and manly. "The family celebrity."

"Well . . ."

"Damn, you look like your daddy."

"I do?"

"Spitting image. What's your handicap?"

"Well, I have this bum knee . . ."

"No, I mean golf."

"I don't play."

A middle-aged bleached-blond woman with large braless breasts straining to escape from her barely-buttoned denim shirt leaned across the bar, waving a beer mug. "Norville, are you gonna get me a beer or ain'tcha?"

Norville beamed at her bosom. "Maylene, you look like you're smuggling grapefruit."

Maylene looked down at herself. "Why thank you, Norville. Ain't you the sweetest one."

Norville took Maylene's mug and filled it from the Pabst Blue Ribbon tap, slid it across the bar to her, and rang up her dollar bill in the cash register. Then he filled another mug and shoved it into Will's hand. "Hope you like it on tap." Before Will could answer, Norville grabbed him by the elbow and steered him to a corner of the bar, out of the traffic pattern. "It's a little quieter over here," Norville said. Will couldn't tell any difference. Noise crashed against them like rough surf and he and Norville had to stand close and talk loudly.

"You're just about the only famous Baggett I know," Norville said.

"Well, it's just local TV . . ."

"Last year when we opened this place, I started to send you an invitation. But Wingfoot talked me out of it."

"Why?"

"Well, this is the trashy side of the family."

"How big is the trashy side of the family?"

"Well, there's Min and then there's the trashy side."

Will took a sip of beer. Norville grabbed a handful of redskin peanuts from a bowl on the shelf behind the bar and started popping them into his mouth one by one. "Want some peanuts?"

"No thanks."

Norville seemed to be studying him, sizing him up. Will looked out across the dance floor where a woman in pedal pushers and high-heeled shoes was dancing on the top of a table. Music exploded from the speakers at the far end of the room. Mary-Chapin Carpenter now. *I feel lucky* . . . Norville polished off the fistful of peanuts and wiped his hands on his apron. "Wingfoot said Min was trying to get you to write a family history."

"News travels fast," Will said.

"So we figured if you were gonna write the family history, you might as well know about the whole family."

"I reckon so."

Norville winked. "Are you into municipals?"

"What?"

"Bonds."

"No."

Norville swept the air with his arm. "I owe a lot to municipals."

"Is that so?"

Norville held up a stubby finger. "Correction. I owe a lot to Peachy."

"She's quite a girl," Will agreed.

"You ever heard of Microsoft?"

"I think I have."

"She got me into Microsoft six years ago. Put every dime I could scrape together into it. I said to Peachy, 'Peachy, if this don't work, my tit's in a wringer.' And Peachy said to me, 'Norville, I'm the one with the tit.'"

"You did okay, I take it."

Another sweep of his arm, taking in the entire premises. "What you see is the house that Microsoft built. I was barely scraping by in a little hole in the wall over at Moore's Creek until Peachy introduced me to Microsoft. We cashed in, built this place, and put the rest into municipals. So you see, even the trashy side of the family can do all right for itself. All we need is a little sound investment advice."

"So you've known Peachy for six years."

"I was the one who introduced her to Wingfoot. She taught him to play drums."

"I'll bet. And the rest, as they say, is history."

Norville gave him a broad grin. "Yep."

"It's quite a place," Will said.

"Lyle Lovett was in here a couple of months ago," Norville said, just as the speakers erupted in a crash of Garth Brooks sound. *"Shameless!"* Garth bellowed.

Will couldn't quite make out what Norville said. "Who?"

"Lyle Lovett. The country singer."

"Oh, yeah."

"He was making a movie over at the studio in Wilmington and somebody told him about this place and he and a whole mob of the movie people came over here one night."

"Did he sing?"

"No, but he did say he might record one of Peachy's songs."

"Oh?"

"It's the one called 'Shit Fire.' Maybe she'll sing it tonight."

"I sure hope so," Will nodded. "She writes songs?"

"Writes 'em and sings 'em. She's damn good, boy."

"And she sure does fill up a pair of britches," Will said, taking a big swallow of beer.

"You bet your booties, Wilbur. Are you gonna write all this down, what you see here tonight? For the family history?"

"Well," Will said, "I don't think I'll have any trouble remembering it." He drained his beer and handed the mug to Norville. "I think I'll have another one. Can you run me a tab?"

Norville smiled and clapped him on the shoulder. "Hell boy, you're family."

Billy Hargreave showed up a half-hour later, wearing a Hawaiian print shirt, jeans and cowboy boots. He threaded his way to the bar and waved to Will, who was on his third beer and feeling quite nice.

"Hey! Sheriff Billy!" Will called out, "do the Dukes of Hazzard. *Wooooaaaahhhhh.*"

"Norville," Billy said, "give me some of whatever that boy is drinking."

Will and Billy Hargreave had a ringside seat at a table right in front of the stage. A waitress brought a fresh pitcher of Pabst Blue Ribbon and two ice-cold mugs.

Norville took the stage with a flourish, bouncing nimbly on the balls of his feet and holding his thick arms wide to take in the whole rowdy crowd. "Everybody happy?"

"Yeah!" they roared.

"Well, put your hands together and welcome the best damn country music band that ain't made it to Nashville yet—Peachy Delchamps and Minor Ailment."

And then Peachy and Wingfoot, Pedro and Cisco came in from a door just behind the stage through the wall of cheering. Cisco slid onto a stool at a portable keyboard while Wingfoot took his place

behind the drum set and Peachy and Pedro plugged into ampli-
fiers—Pedro cradling a bass, Peachy running her fingers up and
down the fretboards of a double-necked guitar. Peachy stepped to
the microphone. "Awright," she thundered, "y'all shut up and sit
down. We're gonna play you some music."

The crowd answered with a roar. Nobody sat down and the
noise just got louder. Will was on his feet, pounding his hands
together.

Peachy slashed a chord from her guitar. Will sat down and
topped off his mug from the pitcher. "This is a brand-new one,"
Peachy said, "and it's for all you sorry-assed men who came here
tonight looking for sympathy. You ain't getting any, y'hear?" She
turned to the band. "One, two three . . ." and they launched into a
hard-driving country rock beat that seemed to suck the air from the
area in front of the stage. Will's eyes went wide and he looked over
at Billy Hargreave. Billy winked. And then Peachy leaned into the
microphone . . .

I see you lookin' at me across the dance floor;
I see that mournful teardrop in your eye.
You look like you been had
By a woman that's mean and bad;
But let me tell you this before you cry:
I'm the kind of gal that likes to have a good time;
When the party starts I'll always do my part;
I'll laugh and dance and sing,
I'll do most anything,
But I ain't baby-sittin' no broken heart.

Peachy had a strong, clear, resilient voice that wrapped around a
song and squeezed it and made it part of her. She closed her eyes
and made love to the microphone, and then stepped back wide-
eyed, grinning at the crowd, and ripped off lightning runs on the
guitar, her fingers a blur on the strings and frets. She and the band
played nonstop for two hours and her voice never seemed to lag or

waver. She sang a few old Patsy Cline songs, some Loretta Lynn and Dolly Parton, and a new thing by the Dixie Chicks. But mostly, she sang her own — songs about losing your love and breaking your heart, about cheating women and hard-drinking men, and they fit right in with all the old stuff. It was pure, old-fashioned country music straight from its roots, none of the clever ditties you heard on the radio these days backed up by lush symphony strings and a chorus that sounded like the Mormon Tabernacle Choir. Not that Will had ever listened to much country music on the radio. But here tonight, he decided that he had missed a lot by not paying much attention to it. He found himself singing along with the choruses of songs he barely knew. The beer pitcher was always full and Billy Hargreave kept transferring it to his glass. He thought at some point in the evening that he should probably stop drinking, but the surging beat of Peachy's upbeat numbers and the lonesome ache of her ballads and a glass full of beer just seemed to go together, to fit.

Peachy sang a song she had written about country music stars who want to be in the movies and make videos for the Nashville Network:

> *Nashville's going to Hollywood*
> *And country's going to hell.*

Another, to the tune of George Hamilton IV's "Abilene" that was a spoof on country songs used in TV commercials:

> *Havoline, Havoline,*
> *Best motor oil I've ever seen;*
> *It'll keep your engine clean,*
> *Havoline, my Havoline.*

And an aching, wistful ballad about a woman who looks back on what her life might have been like if she hadn't run off and gotten married to a no-account man:

And sometimes in the evening
I listen to the wind
And wonder 'bout the girl I might have been.

The crowd loved her. And so, quite obviously, did Wingfoot Baggett, who hammered away at the drums but rarely took his eyes off Peachy Delchamps, a sly smile playing at the edges of his mouth. *I believe,* Will thought to himself, *that Wingfoot Baggett has at long last found peace and grace. Amen and Amen.*

Toward the end of the evening, Peachy surprised Will by calling him up onstage. "We've got a special guest here tonight. If you've spent any time in Raleigh, you know Will Baggett, Raleigh's most popular TV weatherman. Well, he's taking a break from the weather these days, and he's here tonight visiting the trashy side of the Baggett family. Tonight, he's Cousin Wilbur. Wilbur honey, come on up here."

Will hesitated. "Go on," Billy insisted, grabbing him by the elbow and propelling him out of his chair. He stood, a bit unsteadily, and grasped Peachy's outstretched hand and let her pull him up onstage. A big cheer went up from the crowd. He turned to them and waved. And then Peachy thrust something into his hand. A tambourine.

"Wilbur's gonna join us on a few numbers before we call it a night," she said. "Wilbur honey, whop that thing against the palm of your hand."

Will gave the tambourine a tentative smack. "Aw come on." Peachy laughed. "You can do better than that."

Will tried again, a little more forcefully. The tambourine rang out across the room.

"That's the way. Now get us a little rhythm going." She took the tambourine from him, popped it against her hand once and then gave it three shakes—*whang, jingle, jingle, jingle.* Will took it back and imitated her motion. "A little faster. Yeah!"

The band ripped all of a sudden into a hard-charging beat, grabbing the rhythm he was beating out and turning it into a powerful surge of sound that pulsed someplace way inside of him that he hadn't known was even there. Then Peachy started singing.

I was born to boogie,
I was born to jive;
So if you want some boogie love
Just get yore ass in line.

The crowd went crazy.

"Yeeeeehah!" somebody yelled in Will's ear. Then he realized it was coming from his own throat. But it wasn't a voice he had ever heard before.

———

A PHRASE CAME TO MIND, bubbling up from his distant past. *I lay near death . . .* Flashes of memory. An apartment in Chapel Hill, smell of stale beer and cigarettes, weak Sunday morning sunlight at the edges of the window shade. He tried to turn his head away from the light, but then his head came loose from his body and fell from his bed and bounced along the floor to the bathroom where it disintegrated in spasms of nausea, ridding itself of all it had consumed the night before. *God,* he thought now, *I haven't been this near death in thirty years.*

It took him a bit to figure out where he was—the fold-out couch in the living room of Wingfoot's trailer—and to reconstruct enough of the night before at Baggett's Place to remember approximately how he had brought himself to such wretchedness. It took a bit because he had to be very careful with this process called thinking. Thoughts, even small and benign ones, were painful in the extreme, ricocheting around inside his head like pinballs.

A voice at his ear: "Wilbur . . ." It was Peachy. He remembered Peachy, that was for sure. How could he forget Peachy? He would have asked her to sing to him, but he wasn't sure he could stand that much racket. Even Peachy's singing would amount to racket to someone as near death as he.

"I lay near death," Will whispered.

"Yes hon, I can see that."

"I hate to be rude, Peachy, but could you please go away and leave me alone?"

He heard a door close. It sounded like the last door on earth.

Time passed, but he had no idea how much. He was aware at times of the muffled sound of machinery, the murmur of voices, outside. A gaggle of crows roosted at some point in a nearby tree and yammered for a while, the sound of it almost making him cry. He rose periodically from his bed of nails, staggered to the bathroom at the rear of the trailer, hugged the toilet bowl as if it were made of precious metal, and then crawled back. At some point, his body finally rid itself of poison and he fell into a profound, dreamless, exhausted sleep.

When he awoke again, it was late afternoon. He felt hollow, drained of all that he had ever been. The air inside the trailer was hot and still — the only sounds, a drip from the kitchen and some Mexican music from the general direction of the nearest greenhouse.

He found his clothes in a pile on the floor, pulled them on gingerly over inflamed skin. Thirst raged in his belly and he rummaged in the refrigerator until he found a carton of orange juice. He drank straight from the carton, just a little at first, testing his stomach. The orange juice stayed put. A good sign. Carton in hand, he walked to the trailer door and stood there for a long while, summoning the courage to open it. When he did, the light was soft and gentle and he gave thanks for that.

The van and Peachy's Spitfire were parked in the yard, but the only sign of life was Wingfoot, hunkered on a bench under the awning, tinkering with a piece of machinery. He looked up at Will. "Behold, the tomb is empty and the stone has been rolled away. My Lord has risen. Glory, hallelujah."

Will eased down the steps and took a seat on the bench next to him. "We can talk," Will said, "but it will have to be very softly."

Just then, Pedro poked his head around the corner of the trailer.

"Señor Wingfoot . . ." Then he saw Will. *"Ayyy, caramba!"* He shook his head mournfully and disappeared.

"What's that you're working on?" Will managed after a moment.

"Water pump. Needs a new gasket."

Will watched, sipping on the orange juice, while Wingfoot worked at the pump with wrenches, pliers, a screwdriver. He had a bad moment when Wingfoot opened a can of gasket sealer and the pungent fumes escaped. He rose, walked a few steps away, fought down the nausea, then waited until Wingfoot had re-sealed the can before he sat down again. There was a bit of a breeze now, stirring the still-warm air and sighing softly in the tops of the tall pines at the edge of the clearing. Will communed with his emptiness and began to entertain hope that he might yet live to see another sunrise.

Wingfoot reached into his back pocket and pulled out a pouch of chewing tobacco. Will put a firm hand on his arm. "Please."

Wingfoot smiled and stuffed the pouch back in his pocket. They sat there for a while longer before Wingfoot said, "I don't suppose you want to hear how it all ended."

"Probably not."

"One minute you were doing a tambourine solo, and the next minute you were passed out on top of an amplifier. It happened real fast."

"A tambourine solo."

"First one I've ever heard. You insisted."

"What was the song?"

"Shit Fire."

Wingfoot sang softly, off-key:

Strike a spark, light a fart
And shit fire.

Wingfoot nodded. "It's a crowd favorite. You'll have to admit, Peachy does have a way with lyrics."

"I didn't," Will said.

"You did."

Will took another sip of orange juice, then set the carton down on the bench beside him and leaned forward, staring at the ground, thinking of this place (and he included the big house on the Cape Fear) as an island in his life, a time away from time, wholly unconnected to all that stuff back in Raleigh.

"I feel like I've been on a long trip to a foreign country," he said.

"And you're not just talking about last night."

"No."

Will raised up and looked around. "All this, Wingfoot . . . I had no idea. Does Min?"

"I don't know, and that's the honest truth, Cousin Wilbur. She doesn't ask much about how things are going with me and I've learned over the years not to volunteer much."

"Why?"

"Because I think Min gets along, deals with things, by compartmentalizing. She's got me in a little cubbyhole that works for her."

"Do you spend much time over there?"

"I come and go on a regular basis. I try to look after Min as best I can, as best she'll let me."

"You're all she's got, I guess."

"Well, there's Billy," Wingfoot said. "He goes by several times a week."

Wingfoot finished with the water pump, wiped it off with a cloth, and set it aside.

"You know we had a fight," Will said.

"I could tell on the phone that something wasn't quite right. But she didn't give me any details. And frankly, Cousin Wilbur, I'm not just dying to know."

"She still blames me, Wingfoot."

"Not you."

"Well, not directly. But I'm the one who got left holding the bag."

Wingfoot stood. "Well, you and Min will have to work that out." He disappeared into the trailer and came back with two bottles of beer. Will held up his hands in protest. "Just sip on it," Wingfoot said. "It will do you a world of good."

Will tried a tiny taste. It was ice cold, water droplets beading on the outside of the brown glass. It went down okay. It stayed down. Wingfoot pulled on his bottle and looked out across the yard toward the road.

"Where's Peachy?" Will asked.

"Gone down to the other place to pick up some plants. She's taking 'em to Rocky Mount tonight. She'll drop you off in Raleigh."

"That's good. I need to get back."

"For what?"

For what, indeed. "Well, for one thing, I've got a court appearance. And once I get that behind me, I'm going to get my life back."

Wingfoot gave him a long look as he took a swig of beer. "Do you like being famous, Wilbur?"

"I like my job—or, what was my job. I guess the famous part just goes with it. But yes, I enjoy it. Maybe more than enjoy it."

Wingfoot got up, strolled around to the corner of the trailer, peered out toward the greenhouse, and shouted something in Spanish to Pedro and Cisco. Then he came back and sat down and polished off the beer. "Want another one?" he asked Will.

"No sir, I sure don't. But this one is just fine."

"Hair of the dog that bit you."

"I suppose so."

Wingfoot stared at his empty beer bottle for a moment and then set it down beside the bench. He leaned forward, propping his elbows on his knees. "Wilbur, you're a grown man and much too old to be in the market for advice. But I'm gonna tell you something I've learned. I've learned that if you want a thing so bad that it takes over your life, you better be damn sure you get it."

"West Point."

"In my case, yep." He looked over at Will. "How about yours?"

"I got what I wanted," Will said flatly.

"And got it taken away from you."

"And I'm gonna get it back."

"And if you don't?"

"Well, I won't get the exact same thing I had, but something like it."

Wingfoot smiled. "I sure hope you do, Wilbur. I sure hope you do. But if you don't, be giving some thought to what you'll make of yourself. I don't just mean a job. I mean your other life."

"What other life?" Will asked.

"Everybody has two lives, whether they know it or not. The one you have and the one you might have. It's what you would be if you weren't who you are."

Will felt an irritated buzzing at the back of his brain, like a bumblebee trying to drill through his skull. He was in no mood for this. "Most people," he said, "don't have a secret existence, Wingfoot, some place they disappear to, or flee to, whatever the motivation is in your case."

"Maybe not as obvious as this, maybe not a physical place, but everybody's got one. Another life."

"My God," Will groaned, "you've turned into an existentialist philosopher. I haven't heard this kind of woolly-brained nonsense since Chapel Hill. And it doesn't make any more sense now than it did then." He stood, a bit too abruptly. A stab of pain raced through his head and a meteor shower of black dots stormed in front of his eyes. "Shit," he said, and sat back down. He was very still for a long time, waiting for the attack to subside.

"Did you have a good time last night?" Wingfoot asked after a moment.

"I made a goddamn fool of myself."

"But did you have a good time doing it?"

"I don't remember. Shut up, Wingfoot."

Wingfoot laughed. "You sure looked like you were having a good time. Especially when you started taking off your clothes."

"I didn't!"

"No, but you looked like you might have at any moment."

"If this gets back to Raleigh . . ."

"So what."

"So, I'm trying to get my act back together in Raleigh," he said. "I've got a wife and a kid in medical school and a house and a yard and I did have a job. And intend to have another one."

"How is Palmer these days?" Wingfoot asked, throwing him entirely off track.

Will realized with a pang that he had not given his son a moment's thought for some little while, not since they had talked briefly by telephone the day after Will's firing from Channel Seven. *Don't shit me, Dad,* Palmer had said then. It was a strange thing to say, and recalling it now, he still didn't know what to make of it. Or Palmer, for that matter.

"Fine," Will said. "Palmer's just fine. Studying hard. First year of med school, you know . . ."

"That's good," Wingfoot nodded. "You and Palmer ever get shit-faced together?"

Get shit-faced with Palmer? It was so thoroughly alien an idea that he couldn't get his imagination to make even an oblique approach to it. He could imagine Palmer in the bar at the Greensboro Country Club, having a circumspect scotch and soda — just one — with the Greensboro Palmers. He would be wearing a neatly pressed pair of chinos and a Ralph Lauren knit shirt, possibly even a navy blazer. He would sip his drink and make polite conversation with soft edges and pleasant digression. *Another?* His grandfather might ask when his glass was empty? *Oh no,* he would say, *one's my limit.* That might not be the precise truth. He might have more than one in the company of friends, but not sitting in the walnut-paneled bar of the Greensboro Country Club with Daddy Sidney. And even with friends, not getting shit-faced, falling-down, toilet-hugging, knee-walking drunk. Palmer was a polite boy, deferential to his elders, correct in his manners, neat in his dress. He was not the shit-faced kind. And what would he say if somebody told him that his father had gotten shit-faced last night? He simply wouldn't believe it, wouldn't be able to conceive it, any more than Will could conceive of Palmer doing the same thing. The difference was that Will had. He had been royally shit-faced and was still paying the price for it. But what the heck. Once in thirty years?

"No," he said to Wingfoot, "Palmer and I have never gotten shit-faced together. I don't suspect it's the kind of thing he'd enjoy doing with me."

"Or you with him." Wingfoot nodded.

Will shrugged. After a moment he stood, slowly this time, testing his equilibrium. "Wingfoot, I've got to go home. "

Wingfoot slapped his knees with both hands. "You're right, Wilbur. You've got to get home. I sure hope you get your life back, as you say. Whatever that means."

———

"HOW'S YOUR KNEE?" Peachy asked. She drove, one hand draped over the steering wheel, elbow propped at the open window. She handled the big truck like she did her guitar. They had the windows rolled down and some Waylon Jennings on the CD player.

Will rubbed his knee. He hadn't given it a thought in the past day or so. "It's feeling pretty good. I don't think I'm up to dancing yet."

Peachy laughed. She had a wonderful, throaty laugh, like something warm cascading over you. "It sure didn't affect your tambourine playing."

Will laughed back. "I don't remember. Wingfoot said I looked like I was about to take off my clothes. Just before I went down. I hope I didn't mess up the song."

"We just went right on," she said.

A large, juicy bug splattered itself on the windshield right in front of Will. His stomach lurched. He was still a little queasy.

"Sometimes you're the windshield," Peachy sang, *"sometimes you're the bug."*

"Is that one of yours?"

"I wish. Mary-Chapin Carpenter. She and the guy who wrote it have both made a mint off it."

"I like your stuff," Will said. "What I remember of it. That one about not baby-sitting no broken heart."

Peachy sang it all the way through, keeping time on the steering wheel. She was really good, Will thought. Even though he didn't much care for country music. "Where did you get the idea for that one?" he asked.

"Wingfoot," she said.

"Really?"

"When I met him he was a mess, Wilbur. Well, in some ways he had his act together. He had the nursery, or at least the part the trailer's on now. Making a living. But the heart and soul part? A mess. Just drifting. Like he had some part of himself stashed away where he wouldn't have to look at it."

"You know about the West Point business."

"Oh yeah. Anyhow, I told him right off that if he wanted me around, he'd have to be honest—with me, with himself. I told him I wasn't baby-sitting no broken heart."

"And . . ."

"I think he's making progress. At least I got a song out of it."

They rode on through the night. Peachy stuck to Highway 421, the route Will and Wingfoot had taken on the way to Brunswick County more than a week before, keeping the speed down below fifty-five so the wind wouldn't damage the plants crammed into the back. Peachy kept switching CDs—Faith Hill, Reba McEntire, some old Porter Wagoner and Johnny Cash. Will found himself paying attention to the lyrics. They made sense, he thought, not like a lot of the stuff you heard on the radio. People telling stories. He thought he might listen to the country station in Raleigh when he got home.

"And what about you, Peachy?" he asked. "You've got a great voice. You write good songs. Where's it going?"

"I may be singing at Baggett's Place the rest of my life. Or I might get a break. I've sent tapes, talked to some folks. There's lots of people out there with great voices and good songs that never make it beyond places like Baggett's. But who knows. I'd love to get a break."

"Nashville?"

"Sure. You know," she said, "I'da probably have been better off without being Miss Greater Greenwood. I shoulda let Marva win the damn thing and I shoulda gone off to Nashville and yodeled."

"But then," Will said, "you wouldn't have invented the Peachy Pump. You'll always have that on your resume."

"That's true." She did a small version of the Pump, as much as you could do in the confines of a truck cab.

"What does Wingfoot think about all that? The Nashville business?"

"He won't say."

"Wingfoot says you ought not to want something so bad that it messes you up if you don't get it . . . or words to that effect."

"He told you that?"

"Yeah."

"Well, the only thing I want that bad is Wingfoot."

Will drummed his hands on the dashboard. "I hope you get it because"—he sang badly, off-key—"*I ain't baby-sittin' no broken heart.*"

"Stick to weather, Wilbur."

"Yes ma'am," he said. "I intend to."

———

IT WAS ALMOST ELEVEN when they pulled up in front of the house on LeGrand. "Doesn't look like anybody's home," Peachy said.

"My wife's in Cincinnati. At a real estate thing. She'll be home tomorrow."

Will climbed out, retrieved his suitcase from the back among the plants, and went around to the driver-side window. "Thanks for the lift."

"Sure. Enjoyed the company."

"You staying over tonight?"

"No, I'll drive on back. Fellow's gonna meet me to help unload."

"You're quite a girl, Peachy. I'm glad Wingfoot found you. And I hope you get that break you're looking for."

"You, too, Wilbur. If you don't—well, you may have a future as a tambourine player."

She put the truck in gear and pulled away, leaving him there in the street. Will stood there for a moment, watching the taillights as she turned the corner a block away. Then he stepped up on the sidewalk and looked for a moment at his house. Coming home late again, he thought, just like always.

Then he thought about where he had been, the things he had said and done the past week or so. A far country, yes. An island, yes. He had almost been a different person. Or maybe he had, just a little, been something of a person he used to be. But that was all behind him. He was back now.

12 | "YOU CAN STILL COP A PLEA," Morris deLesseps said. They were standing on the steps of the Wake County Courthouse. It was almost nine o'clock, the morning warm and dry, a perfect sky overhead. A day to get your blood up.

"But you said I shouldn't. Have you changed your mind?"

Morris held up his hands. "I'm just presenting you with the option." He was in rumpled tweed this morning, a shapeless grayish sport coat, a windowpane-checked shirt, a nubby brown tie that looked like the product of an inept attempt at crochet. A touring cap and pipe completed the outfit. Instead of toting a briefcase, he had a stack of legal pads and manila file folders tucked underneath an arm. Morris had recently begun teaching a night class at the Chapel Hill law school and he was affecting professorial attire and demeanor. "My friend, I am here to defend your honor and good name to the best of my ability. I will stand with you before the bar of justice. We will smite the legal system hip and thigh. If possible."

Will was casually dressed, as Morris had advised. He wore charcoal gray slacks, an open-necked blue oxford cloth shirt, loafers, and a lightweight jacket from the front hall closet he had added as an afterthought just before he left the house. It was a nice medium shade of green with a polo player stitched on the front. It was Palmer's jacket, the kind of thing you might wear into the casual bar at Greensboro Country Club at cocktail hour.

"You don't want to look like Will Baggett the weatherman," Morris had said.

"Why not?"

"Because this judge is a no-nonsense sonofabitch. He dislikes everybody, especially the noteworthy. I once saw him rip the mayor to shreds in an annexation case."

The judge was one Broderick Nettles, and as Morris told it, the Wake County legal community referred to him behind his back as "Nettlesome Nettles." On his best days, he was barely civil to all who appeared before his district court bench—lawyers, defendants, even the bailiff and clerk. According to Morris, he didn't have many best days.

Will was in district court because that was where all but the most serious traffic-related charges were heard. The officer who had filed the charges would be present in court to testify to Will's arrogant and high-handed (as Morris put it, in his most professorial tone) behavior. The *News and Observer* notwithstanding, it would be Officer Pettibone's word against Will's. Judge Nettles would have read the paper, of course, but he would have to rule on the evidence, and that alone. He was a mean sonofagun, Morris said, but he was fair. That's all they could ask for.

Will said, "I don't think I ran a red light."

"Then that's how you shall stand. And of course there's such a thing as honor, in whose name the late lamented Confederacy suffered grievous defeat."

Will thought about it for a moment, then squared his shoulders. "Screw 'em."

Morris shrugged. "All right, then. We shall go henceforth in harm's way and hope for the best. One last piece of advice. Keep your mouth shut. Let me do the talking unless the judge asks you a direct question."

"Hip and thigh, you say," Will said.

"With the jawbone of an ass."

A portly middle-aged man wearing Bermuda shorts and calf-high black socks above jogging shoes labored past them up the courthouse steps, glanced at Will as he passed, then stopped and stared. "Hey, you're that fellow on TV." He plucked at the air with thumb and forefinger, searching for a name. "Uh . . ."

"Will Baggett."

"No," said the man, "that ain't the one," and kept moving.

Will stared after him.

"How soon they forget," Morris said.

————

THE COURTROOM WAS CROWDED with as motley a collection of humanity as Will had ever seen in one place—unshaven men in faded jeans and shirts that bulged over potbellies, hard-faced women with stringy hair. In one corner was a gaggle of men in orange jumpsuits with INMATE WAKE COUNTY stenciled across the back, watched over by two beefy deputies who stood cross-armed against a nearby wall.

"Rode hard and put away wet," Morris observed drily.

"Yeah," said Will. "My fellow dee-FEN-dants."

The lawyers were likewise a somewhat scruffy lot, most of them in ill-fitting suits and ties that clashed with their shirts. They lounged about in the jury box, chatting idly with each other, making an occasional foray into the spectator section to confer with one defendant or another. There was another group, somewhat younger and better attired, whom Morris identified as representatives of the District Attorney's and Public Defender's offices. They all, in Will's estimation, seemed disturbingly nonchalant about the dispensing of justice, as if this were some sort of assembly line in which widgets were pieced together, then inspected and either passed on to the outside world or consigned to a scrap heap. It occurred to Will that it was his very first time in a courtroom. It was not what he had imagined from civics class.

He cut a quick glance at Morris, who—having exchanged cursory pleasantries with a few of the fellow attorneys he knew— had a faintly distasteful look on his face, as if he had smelled something rank. The aroma of the courtroom was, in fact, part unwashed flesh and part sullen attitude. Morris, he of the upper crust of Raleigh's legal community, did not practice in a court like this, did not deal with the likes of this sad collection. He was doing it only as a favor to his longtime friend and sometime client Will Baggett.

They took seats on a bench at the front of the courtroom, two of the few empty ones left. Will's fellow accused seemed to shrink from justice, preferring to slouch on the back rows or against the rear wall. Some of them reminded him of the crew from Christian Renovators, who were well into their task of demolishing the rear of his house. Furniture from that area had been removed to the garage, flooring ripped up, walls covered with dust, the whole business sealed off from the rest of the house by huge sheets of opaque plastic. They had been at it again early this morning, but this time they didn't wake him. He was up already, on his third cup of coffee, moving briskly about the house and girding himself for court, when they started their sawing and hammering.

Morris must have caught the look on Will's face. "Criminal court," he intoned somberly. "These days, about two-thirds of the docket is minor drug cases. Most of the rest are offenders of various traffic laws, ranging from driving under the influence to driving with a revoked license."

"No murderers or rapists?"

"Those go to superior court. Actually, they're a better-looking lot. Defendants and attorneys."

Behind him, Will detected a growing buzz of conversation, and long experience told him he was being recognized. Somebody tapped him on the shoulder. He turned to see a middle-aged woman with soda bottle–thick glasses and bad teeth. She was leaning toward him. "You the weather fellow, ain't you."

"Yes ma'am," he said. "How are you this morning?"

"Not worth a shit," the woman said with a crooked grin. "They got me on possession. I told the cop I was just holding it for Percy while he went to take a leak, but I was the one that got charged. Percy got off scot free. He's at the beach."

"Is that so?"

"What you in here for?"

In here? It sounded like jailhouse talk. Will looked around the room. For most of these poor wretches, he thought, it probably was. *God, the messes people get themselves into.* "Well . . ."

Then there was a sudden scuffling of bodies. Everybody was standing. Will rose alongside Morris to see a uniformed bailiff emerge through a doorway behind the bench, and right on his tail, the tall, scowling, black-robed personage of Judge Broderick Nettles.

"Hear ye, hear ye," the bailiff intoned. "Court is in session, the General Court of Justice, District Court Division, Wake County, North Carolina, the Honorable Broderick E. Nettles presiding. May God have mercy on this Honorable . . ."

"Yeah, yeah, yeah," the judge interrupted, settling himself with a rustle of cloth in his high-backed leather chair and dropping a thick stack of manila file folders on the desk in front of him with a thump. The bailiff looked up at him, shrugged, and edged off to the side of the bench. Judge Nettles glared at the stack of folders, as if contemplating the dire consequences awaiting those poor souls whose names appeared therein. Everyone in the courtroom remained standing. "Sit down," he commanded, his voice like a lash across the crowd. Everyone sat.

"It's not," Morris said very quietly, "one of his best days."

The courtroom had no windows, but by late afternoon Will could almost feel lengthening shadow stretching across the room as one woeful case after another paraded in front of Judge Broderick Nettles, many of them exiting through a side door in the custody of a deputy sheriff. Possession of controlled substance. Possession of controlled substance and paraphernalia with intent to distribute. Driving while under the influence and without valid license, fourth offense. Communicating threat with intent to do bodily harm (this, a plump, pleasant-faced woman in her sixties who wore a fake rose blossom in her hair, which Judge Nettles summarily ordered her to remove and hand to the bailiff, who held it for a moment uncertainly until the judge thundered for him to put it in a wastebasket). Several cases were set for jury trials, which would begin the next day. The more Will saw of Judge Nettles, the more he wondered if he might not be better off with a jury. It was a possibility which Morris had raised, then dismissed as being the greater of two jeopardies. "Some folks just love to stick it to a celebrity," he said.

One thing about Judge Nettles, Will thought: he's dogged. He heard cases steadily until noon, took a thirty-minute recess, and then was back at it. Will barely had time to grab a sandwich and soda at the courthouse coffee shop and escape with them to an empty cubicle in the Registrar of Deeds' office, away from the glad-handers who spotted him and wanted to know about the weather. A couple even asked for autographs. Nobody mentioned his sacking at Channel Seven. One man said, "I watch you every night." *No you don't,* Will started to say, but thought better of it.

Morris took the half-hour to dash to his office a block away and then joined Will in the hallway outside the courtroom. "When?" Will asked simply.

"No telling. Judge Nettles likes to jump around on the calendar. Keeps him from getting bored."

"What if I get bored?"

"For God's sake, don't show it," Morris said. "He'll crawl your fanny if you even look like you're not paying attention."

It wasn't, Will thought, as if there wasn't anything to pay attention to. Watching the parade of down-and-outers with their violations of North Carolina's drug and traffic laws was sort of like being an onlooker at the scene of a bad wreck, the road littered with mangled debris and humanity. But after several hours of it, the spectacle took on a wearying and depressing sameness. And Judge Broderick Nettles was letting him—making him—sit there and endure it. He had given absolutely no sign that he recognized Will, not even a glance in his direction. He could have called Will's case first thing, but he didn't. Whatever the reason, Judge Broderick Nettles let Will sit and stew and watch an endless parade of human folly while his rear end went numb and his brain atrophied and his personal attorney sat calmly at his side, running up a bill of well more than a hundred dollars an hour.

It was almost four o'clock before Will got his turn. The courtroom was almost empty now. Without its crowd of miscreants it was a stark, cold place—harsh fluorescent lights, pale paneled walls lined with the stern visages of former judges who had dispensed justice from the Wake County Courthouse, the resigned mutter of attorneys and defendants, the defeated shuffle of the convicted. The woman who had sat behind Will and Morris at the morning session had failed to reappear after lunch, thus forfeiting her bond and incurring the terrible wrath of Judge Nettles, who had a warrant issued for her arrest. The judge was so exercised by her blatant disregard of his authority that Will half expected him to issue a shoot-to-kill order. Will sank lower on the hard bench, filled with gloom. He glanced at Morris, who wore a bemused expression.

"State versus Baggett," the bailiff's voice rang out. It didn't quite register until Morris elbowed him in the side and they both rose briskly and walked together the few paces to one of the two large tables in front of the bench. Morris motioned Will into a chair while he stood in front of another, spreading legal pad and file folder on the table in front of him. A young prosecutor—barely out of law school, from the looks of him—was at the other table. He and his colleagues had worked their way through a huge stack of folders as the day had progressed, and the young fellow, who had seemed full of vim and purpose at the start, was now beginning to droop a bit. Morris looked as fresh as ever.

"Who's representing the state here?" Judge Nettles asked.

"Finley Sinclair," the young prosecutor answered.

Morris looked over and gave him a tight smile, then gave to Will the merest hint of a wink. *Young pup. I'll have his ass for dinner.*

Judge Nettles peered over his half-glasses at Morris. "Counsel for the defense?"

"Morris deLesseps, Your Honor."

"It's been a good while since you've appeared as counsel in criminal court, Mister deLesseps. Practicing rich folks' law these days?"

"Mainly civil matters, Your Honor."

"It's good to see that you have not appeared today in buckskin, Mister deLesseps."

"Upon Your Honor's strict admonition," Morris said with an absolutely straight face.

Will cut a quick glance at prosecutor Sinclair, who was making a brave effort to stifle a smile.

"Why are you cluttering up my court with this case, Mr. deLesseps?"

"My client feels he is entitled . . ."

Nettles waved him to silence and leafed quickly through Will's file. "Wilbur French Baggett." He didn't look at Will.

"Yes, Your Honor," Morris said.

Nettles ticked off the charges in a monotone. "Running a red light, failure to yield right-of-way, leaving the scene, failure to obey an officer, obstruction of justice . . ." Now he looked down at Will. "Mr. Baggett, how do you plead?"

"Not . . ."

"Stand up when you address this honorable court," Nettles ordered.

Will stood. "Not guilty, Your Honor."

Nettles picked up the file and waved it. "All this is just a . . . fabrication?"

"I can explain."

Nettles let the file fall from his hand. It landed with a soft smack on the desk. He shook his head. "Maybe a script for a TV show, Mr. Baggett. *Law and Order*? Or maybe *Truth or Consequences.*"

Will managed a weak smile. Judge Nettles didn't return it.

"You have witnesses, Mr. deLesseps?"

"Mister Baggett is our sole witness."

He turned to the prosecutor. "And the state?"

Sinclair was looking back toward the spectator section of the courtroom. He turned with a jerk. "Your Honor, our witness . . ." He made a helpless gesture. "Officer Pettibone doesn't appear to be in the courtroom."

Will looked. He had spotted Officer Pettibone at the rear of the room this morning—trim and crew-cut, a poster boy of a policeman—but he hadn't seen the man since the lunch break. There was, at the moment, not a single uniform in the courtroom except for the bailiff.

"Hot damn," Morris said softly.

"What was that, Mister deLesseps?"

"Nothing, Your Honor."

"I hope not."

"If I could have a moment, Your Honor . . ." The prosecutor looked stricken, shuffling about desperately among his papers as if hoping he might uncover a hole into which he could disappear.

"No," Judge Nettles said simply. "If you ain't ready, you ain't ready."

"Then the state would move for a continuance."

"Denied."

"Defense moves for dismissal," Morris spoke up.

"On what grounds?"

"Defense avers that Mister Baggett did not run a red light, did not do any of those other things that he's accused of. The state is obviously unprepared to present any evidence to the contrary. No tickee, no washee." Morris was on his feet now, looking positively magisterial. Will felt a rush of exhilaration. Was it really going to be this easy?

"Don't you try to foist any of your homespun levity on this honorable court, Mister deLesseps."

"No, Your Honor. Beg pardon."

"So that's what you aver, Mister deLesseps?"

"Absolutely."

"That's a good old-fashioned word, 'aver.' I haven't heard it used in my court in years."

"One tries to raise the level . . ."

"And what do you aver, Mister Sinclair?"

Sinclair could only shrug.

Nettles glared at them all for a moment, then furiously slashed the air with his hand. "Get up here. You, too, Mister Baggett. I want you to hear this."

They all scrambled toward the bench, Morris and Will and the young prosecutor bumping into each other in haste. They arrayed themselves in front of the bench, looking up at the wrathful, glowering face of Judge Broderick Nettles. He fixed them all with a furious stare. And then his gaze jerked away. "Bailiff, what's the matter?"

"Your Honor . . ." They all turned to look at the bailiff, who was rising from a crouch, holding a small plastic bag that he seemed to have retrieved from the floor.

"What's that?" Nettles demanded.

The bailiff opened the bag, sniffed, then reached inside and plucked out a pinch of withered brown substance. "Based on my previous experience," the bailiff said somberly, "I'd say it's marijuana, Your Honor."

"Where did it come from?" the judge asked, his voice rising.

"Mister Baggett's jacket pocket."

There was a long, terrible silence and then Morris said softly, "Will, I don't believe I'da done that."

Will stared. He could feel the floor opening up beneath his feet, could hear a thundering roar in his ears like waves crashing. "Oh my God," he said.

"That's right," Judge Broderick Nettles agreed. "Oh my God."

———

THEY ALLOWED HIM one phone call. He called home, of course. He got the answering machine. If Clarice was back from Cincinnati, she wasn't at home. But then, what would he say if she had answered? He wasn't ready to say anything just yet—not to anybody, including Clarice. He needed some time to think. So he hung up without leaving a message, a little relieved. Morris could break the news to Clarice.

After that, Will sat, miserable and frightened, in a holding cell for two hours. A jailer brought food. Will politely declined. Finally, Morris showed up with the news that Judge Nettles had refused to set bond, at least immediately. He would consider that tomorrow. Meanwhile, Will Baggett, who had committed the unpardonable outrage of showing up in the good judge's courtroom with marijuana in his pocket, could just cool his heels in jail overnight.

"For God's sake, Morris," Will croaked as he felt his throat constrict and his rectum tighten, "horrible things happen to people in jail."

"Yeah," Morris said, looking around at the holding cell where, for the moment, Will was the only occupant. "This place'll start filling up before long, I imagine. Drunks, bad-asses, the dregs of humanity." Morris had dropped his professorial air and now had a wry, worldly-wise demeanor about him.

"Maybe I can work something out," Morris said. He left and came back with a jailer who took Will to a regular cell with only one other occupant, an emaciated young man of perhaps twenty with a wisp of a goatee, wearing knee-ripped jeans and a leather vest over bare torso. He gave Will a disinterested glance as the jailer clanged the door shut behind him. Morris stood in the hallway outside and Will had to talk to him through a small square of barred window. "Am I gonna be okay?"

"I think so," Morris said.

"You think so."

"You'll be fine. You're bigger than he is. If he messes with you, beat the shit out of him."

"I tried to reach Clarice. She's not home. Will you call her?"

"Sure," Morris said.

"What'll you tell her?"

"That you're in jail. And why. Is there anything else you want me to tell her?"

"No."

They had taken his watch, wallet and belt. He was thankful not to have been strip-searched and made to wear one of those orange jumpsuits with INMATE on the back. They had said that overnight guests were allowed to keep their own clothes. If he came back for a longer stay, he would get a jumpsuit, just like everybody else.

"What time is it?"

"Almost seven."

"Tell Clarice I'm okay. Not to worry." He tried to picture her hearing the news. And then there were the Greensboro Palmers . . .

"Do you need anything?"

Will glared at him. "That is the stupidest question I have ever heard you ask, Morris."

Morris smiled. Then he went away again.

The cell had the barest of furnishings—long metal benches securely bolted to opposite side walls, thin cotton mattresses, a metal toilet at the rear. The place smelled of human waste and despair, and Will couldn't tell whether the odor emanated from the premises or from his fellow inmate. Probably both.

Will took a seat on the bench opposite the young man.

"Hey man."

Will tried to ignore him, but he got up from the bench and

plopped down next to Will. He smelled rank, all right, but no worse than the cell itself. *Okay,* Will thought, *here it comes. Ain't you that fellow* . . . He didn't want to be recognized, didn't want to be singled out, just wanted to melt into a gray anonymity, keep his mouth shut and his pants firmly about his waist, and get the hell out of here as quickly as possible. He edged a couple of inches away on the bench.

"Got a cigarette?"

"I don't smoke. Sorry."

The young man shrugged and returned to his own bench where he stretched out and went promptly to sleep.

Will sat perfectly still, listening to the alien sounds of the jail — inmates and jailers yammering at each other, the hum and clank of electronically controlled doors, harsh laughter and ragged curses, the snoring of his cellmate, all of it echoing along the steel-and-concrete hallways and splintering into a thousand jagged pieces that sliced through him and left him shattered and bleeding. And then it got worse. The catcalls started. "Yo, Will! What's the weather? Will Baggett. Yo! Will baby, wanna see my lightnin' rod?" *Well, the word is out.*

It went on for a long time. Will kept absolute silence.

There was another sound, a voice in his head. *You can save yourself,* it kept saying over and over. *Just tell 'em.* Well, he would have the long night to think about that.

But he didn't. He couldn't. His mind wouldn't focus on it. It was just all too insane. At some point, after the jail had settled down to a dull whimper, he drifted off to sleep.

He awoke sore and stiff on the metal bench and lay there, numb and empty, for a long time until the jail woke around him. Still, he couldn't make much sense of things. There was a lot of stuff careening about in his head like space junk, one thought clanging against another, but he was too busy dodging the junk to bring any order to it, not here in the Wake County Jail at six o'clock in the morning when he was sore and weary and desolate with worry.

So he decided that for the time being, he would say nothing. Tell no one. Leave everything open. It was just the best he could come up with right now.

———

IT TOOK ALL MORNING to secure Will's release.

Morris showed up at ten with news that Judge Nettles was having one of his best days and had, without a great deal of bitching and moaning, agreed to set bond. Two hundred fifty thousand dollars.

"Isn't that a little steep?" Will asked.

"Outrageous."

"I don't have two hundred fifty thousand dollars." He didn't think he knew anybody who did, not anybody he knew well enough to ask. Well, there were the Greensboro Palmers . . . *Will who? Never heard of him.*

"Oh," Morris said airily, "you don't need that much in cash. A bondsman will secure it for fifty thousand."

"I don't have . . ." Then he thought about the check from Spectrum Broadcasting, his hush money. It was still in the drawer of a bedside dresser at home. With all that had happened, he had forgotten to deposit it.

"I'll call Clarice," Morris said.

"Have you talked to her?"

"Yes."

"What did she say?"

"I suppose you could say she's in a state of shock."

"Is she coming to get me?"

"I think so."

The thought of finally facing Clarice filled him with dread. But at least there was no need to approach the Greensboro bunch. At least not for money.

Morris was back at eleven with the check, which Will endorsed to the Ace Bail Bond Company. An hour later he returned to fetch Will. "Clarice isn't here," Morris said.

"Why?"

"I advised against it. There's a pretty good crowd outside. Oh, and I have some good news."

"I could use some."

"Judge Nettles has dismissed the other charges. The red light, all that stuff."

"As you say," Will said, "that is good news. I now have only this felony charge to worry about."

It was raining, but that apparently hadn't put a damper on the curious, which included a fair-sized contingent from Raleigh's news media, all of them shouting questions at Will as Morris sped him out of the jail doorway and across the sidewalk toward a car parked at the curb. Will felt the splat of raindrops on his face and thought with a sense of wonder that he had been totally disconnected from the commonplace world for almost twenty-four hours, suspended from ordinariness, from the mundane human traffic that was the stuff of just getting along in a slightly skewed world. *So that's what it means to be locked up. Ah, how blessed is the mundane.* The reporters jostled and cursed each other, sticking microphones and recorders in his face, shouting questions. He kept his mouth shut, as Morris had ordered. He felt the rough edge of a microphone scrape past his ear. They moved en masse like a swarm of bees surrounding a queen, darting about and buzzing angrily. Then they were in the car—Will in the front seat beside the secretary from Morris's office who was driving, Morris in the rear. He had to shove a radio reporter out of the way to get the door closed. When the car pulled away from the curb, they heard a bellow from the sidewalk. "Sonofabitch! You got my mike cord!" They stopped abruptly and Morris opened the door and freed the cord, then slammed the door again. They roared away. They were only a block from Morris's office, but they weren't going to Morris's office. They were going home.

All the way there, nobody said a word. When they pulled into the driveway, Will turned and looked into the back seat. Morris was in repose, eyes closed, arms crossed, head tilted back against the seat rest. "Morris . . ."

Morris opened his eyes and blinked. "It's one of the more interesting cases I've had in some time," he said. "Not like your usual charitable remainder trusts and bankruptcy proceedings. Although bankruptcy can, on occasion, have its roguish moments." He was the professor again. "Go talk to your wife. I'll see you tomorrow."

Will got out of the car and stood next to the driveway as it backed out and headed down the street. The rain had stopped, leaving a fresh-scrubbed aftertaste. He looked at his lawn—lush and weed-free here in the fullness of mid-spring, freshly mowed sometime during his brief incarceration. Then he spotted a flaw, knelt and plucked a mere infant of a crabgrass plant from the narrow gap between concrete and fescue. A lawn was an exquisitely simple thing. So simple it made him want to cry.

13 | HE FOUND CLARICE IN BED, the shades drawn against the day, the only sound the faint purring of the clock radio. He sat on the edge of the bed next to her and put his hand on her cheek. "I have a headache," she said. "No, that's not entirely right, Will. I have a *sick* headache." Her voice seemed to float up to him from a distance, almost as faint as the clock.

"I'm not surprised," he replied, trying to keep his own voice light. It would be a way to approach this, he thought, at least for now, at least until he had some more time to think things through. He sat there for a moment and then said, "I think I'll go take a shower. I didn't get one last night. In a place like that, you don't want to take a shower if you don't have to." But he made no move to get up.

Clarice was having none of it. "Do you want to tell me what in God's name happened?"

Well, God is not involved in this at all. Blind, stupid bad luck, maybe. But that isn't the same as God, at least not like I think of God.

"Clarice," he said slowly, drawing out the words, "could we just put what and why on hold for a little while?"

She sat up then, slid back in the bed with her back against the headboard. It was difficult to see her in the dim light, to see what was moving about on her face. "Is it okay if I turn on the light?" he asked.

"No."

Well, he could *hear* it clearly enough. Hurt, anger, disappointment.

"I think I'm going to throw up," she said.

"I'll get you a cold washcloth," he offered.

"No."

They sat, neither moving, for a minute or so. "I suppose it's all over the paper," he said.

"The front page."

"I'm becoming a real regular."

She massaged her temples and forehead. "I'm going to ask you again, Will. What happened?"

Will took a deep breath. "I'm not ready. Not just yet."

"Not ready?" She lowered her hands to her lap and tried again. "What the paper said . . . ?"

He didn't answer that.

"When are you going to be . . . ready?"

He didn't answer that, either.

At the end of the next long silence she said, "Is that what two weeks in Brunswick County did for you?"

He almost laughed, but managed to check it. *So that's what she thinks. My crazy family, weird and dysfunctional, and now into controlled substances.* That, at least, would help explain things to someone like Clarice who had no frame of reference to understand people like the Brunswick County Baggetts, much less the other, upriver bunch, Cousin Norville and his clan.

"Could I fix you a bowl of soup?" he asked. "It might help."

"As opposed to an explanation?"

"No, just as a love offering."

"I'd rather have an explanation," she said quietly.

"As I say . . ."

"You're not ready."

"I just don't want to rush into anything."

"That's a very odd thing to say, Wilbur."

"I suppose it is."

"Do you have any earthly idea what this does to us? To all of us?"

He reached to touch her cheek again, but she turned away from him. And it was more than that. A turning-away and a sliding-away, both a twist of her head and a shift of her body, much as Will himself had done in the jail cell when his fellow inmate sat down next to him. A sliding-away from . . . what? In his case, it had been fear. What was it with Clarice? She hadn't done that before, even at times when she had been terribly exasperated with him. She always stood her ground and fought, though they rarely had what you could call a real fight. But now, she had . . . what? Was *recoiled* too strong a word? No, it wasn't. It was the smallest of movements, but she had indeed recoiled. Not just from conflict, from confrontation, from shock and embarrassment, but from *him*. From his very person.

It terrified him. For a brief instant he thought that he might tell her everything, at least the unadorned facts of the case, unburden himself completely, and make it okay. Tell her and tell her quickly and then deal with the fallout of all that.

But he stopped himself. There was more to this than a matter of a plastic bag of marijuana, a great deal more, and telling her the unadorned facts of all that would not begin to address this larger and more profound thing between them, the thing that had made her recoil. What had happened in court was, in a sense, irrelevant, and telling her about that would *not* make it okay. He knew, as much as he had ever known anything in his life, that in the ever-so-slight turning away of his wife's body, they had crossed some Continental Divide of the heart, going in opposite directions.

His breath caught in his throat with a strangled gasp. Clarice gave no sign that she noticed. He felt himself rising, stepping back from the bed, turning and moving toward the door. Even with his back to her, he sensed that she wasn't watching him, only feeling him go with her head still turned away.

Just before he stepped into the hallway Clarice said, "How could you do this to Palmer?"

There was no answer whatsoever for that. He closed the door behind him.

———

CLARICE WENT TO GREENSBORO for the night. He heard her descend the stairs and pause in the kitchen, and then she passed through the front hallway without looking into the living room where he sat and went out the front door. He found the three-word note she had left him in the kitchen. GONE TO GREENSBORO.

He went back to the living room, newspaper in hand. The *News and Observer* had given it a big headline and a detailed account that began just below the masthead on the top left of the paper and cascaded down the length of the page and spilled over to page 2A. It was complete with photos—Will at the Channel Seven weather map, Will on the stretcher in front of the Channel Seven studios surrounded by gawkers and law enforcement officers, a mug shot of Judge Broderick Nettles and another of attorney Morris deLesseps. It didn't take much of the story to recount the facts of Will's arrest, but the paper had taken the opportunity to regurgitate all of the other sordid details of his unpleasantness. Reporters had scoured his neighborhood for reaction: *I'm shocked. He seems like such a nice guy. You see him out in his yard all the time.* . . . Had they nosed about the house and yard, looking for anything growing illegally? Had they been through the garbage?

He read the article twice through in the stillness of the living room. Then he put the paper down and stretched out on the couch and went to sleep. He was vaguely aware of the doorbell several times during the afternoon, but he didn't rouse himself. Every phone in the house was unplugged. Clarice had done that before he got home. When he finally awoke it was almost dark outside. He sat up, blinking in the dimness.

He realized that he was still wearing the lightweight jacket— the one with the polo player stitched on the front, galloping jauntily across the polished green fabric, mallet at the ready, poised to slam one home for the old boys at the riding club. He shoved his hands in the pockets, marveling that he had never done that yesterday when he put it on, when he wore it in court. Never put his hands in the pockets. How do you wear a jacket and never put your hands in the pockets? There had been something in there that he should have known about, and one simple movement that would have taken all of two seconds could have saved him. Astonishing.

And that, the act of jamming his hands deep into his pockets, was what finally brought his mind to bear on things, to begin to put some order into the swirling cosmos of space junk. He had been circling for hours with sideways glances at the thing that was his dilemma. Now he looked head-on.

All right, Wilbur. You are facing serious criminal charges, of which you are entirely innocent. Well, technically, mostly innocent. You were in possession of marijuana in Judge Nettles's courtroom. There's no denying that. But it wasn't your marijuana. It belongs to your son, whose jacket you were and are wearing. Your son the doctor-in-training. That, by God, is the bare-bones truth, and we have to start with that, don't we?

Now. Next. What will happen if you just tell it exactly like it is, come completely clean? The doctor-in-training will be ejected from medical school in the time it takes them to hustle him out the back door. And that's some more of the bare-bones truth.

So . . . isn't that exactly what he deserves? It's his mess and he should have to clean it up himself. He's a big boy.

Will sat quietly for a minute or so, letting his mind digest that. Fact and logic. You could chart a reasonable course if you had fact and logic on your side. It was neat and clean.

But then there was this other thing that had nothing to do with fact and logic, but instead with those murky, intangible things that mucked up a good, neat, clean line of thought. It was like carefully writing things on a sheet of paper and then having somebody spill milk on it. Ink runs and words blur and pretty soon you can't make out a damned thing.

Your son the doctor-in-training, the architect of this incredible mess, is also the golden child, repository of all his mother and his grandparents are and aspire to be: smart, handsome, well-spoken, lithe of body and keen of mind. He has inherited all of the best in them and none of the worst in you. They worship him. And if you come clean, you destroy that. You destroy them.

He remembered a time at Nags Head when Palmer was perhaps five. They were there for the week at the Palmers' elegantly weathered cottage. At midmorning he sat in a sand chair absorbed in a spy thriller novel, only vaguely aware of the gentle wash of wave against sand, the scurrying of sandpipers at surf's edge, the fluttering of the fringe of his umbrella in the brisk sea breeze. Movement caught his eye and he looked up from his book to see them trooping down the path that snuggled between two sand dunes—knobby-kneed Sidney in the lead in plaid Bermudas and a wide-brimmed Panama hat, Consuela wrapped in a terrycloth smock, Clarice breathtakingly slim and erect in a one-piece bathing suit. Palmer trudged along between his grandparents, holding on to both, while Clarice carried his small yellow inner tube and a beach bag full of suntan lotion, books, towels, plastic pail and shovel. They marched along in soldierly fashion, taking possession of sand, sky, ocean. All of a piece, the four of them. He watched Palmer—already a stunningly handsome boy with a thick shock of hair and fine, almost dainty Palmer family features. *He's theirs, not mine,* Will thought with a sudden pang. His breath caught achingly in his throat and he had to look away. He had never, in all his life, felt so alone, not even in the worst moments following his parents' disappearance. This was different. This was loss of the living.

It was partly his fault, Will thought now, that there had been that distance, that wariness, between him and Palmer during the years of his son's growing up. Will had tried to bridge the gap, but had he tried hard enough? Or had he just accepted it after a while and then gone about immersing himself in his career, his celebrity, all the things that told him he was okay, that he wasn't alone, that lots of people thought he was pretty goddamned special?

Theirs, not mine. Do I resent that? Of course. Is that a good reason to tell? Or is it a perfectly good reason not to?

Of course, there was another practical thing: he might tell for naught. Judge Nettles might look down from the bench in his mighty wrath and say, "Are you trying to palm this off on your *son?* Despicable. That'll be an additional five years in the slammer, Mister Baggett. Good God!"

But that was really beside the point. He couldn't decide what to do based just on what was practical or logical. The real business was the murky stuff.

So, what was he going to do? Well, he still hadn't decided that. He had considered a lot, and that was a big step. But he couldn't decide until he looked Palmer in the eye in a way he hadn't done for a good many years.

For now, he sat here in his living room in the gloom of late afternoon with his hands jammed into the pockets of Palmer's green jacket. One pocket was empty. In the other was the remains of a packet of sugarless gum with one spongy stick left. He unwrapped it and popped it into his mouth, chewing thoughtfully until long after the flavor of it had passed.

THE CHRISTIAN RENOVATORS WERE there the next morning, demolishing and reconstructing the rear of his home as if nothing had happened. From the spare bedroom where he had spent the night he heard their hammering and banging, the whine of an electric saw of some kind, a constant faint undercurrent of country music from the boom box.

The bedroom door opened, throwing a shaft of light across the bed. Will blinked. It was Morris deLesseps.

"Every phone in the house is unplugged," Morris said irritably. "Nobody answers the door. How am I going to defend you if I can't reach you?"

"Morris, you are — if nothing else — persistent."

Morris waved a hand in the direction of the renovation project. "What in the dickens is going on back yonder, son?"

"We're building an addition on the house to hold my newspaper clippings."

"Get up," Morris ordered. "We're going for a ride. You can't hear yourself think around here with all that damned ruckus going on."

Will raised up on his elbows. "Are there reporters outside?"

"No," Morris said. "You're yesterday's headline."

They drove into the countryside north of Raleigh in Morris's Saab, out Highway 401 and then up a two-lane road to a little community called Walker's Crossroads where Morris was to look over some farm acreage for a client, a developer who was considering a subdivision. Clarice would be up here before long, Will thought, selling houses as the sprawl from Raleigh crept even farther north into territory that had so far pretty much escaped.

It was a splendid day, the air clear and warm after yesterday's rain. Morris drove with his window down. He was still in tweed, but he had left his touring cap behind. Will wondered how long he'd be able to hold out in tweed, what with the Raleigh weather getting warmer by the day. Soon they would have a heat wave. It always happened this time of year, a brief reminder of what lay ahead. But for now, things were just about perfect. Will breathed deeply. Morris didn't bring up the legal business, and Will was grateful. He wasn't ready to get into that with Morris, any more than he had been with Clarice.

Morris was in good spirits. He was considering part interest in a sailboat, a forty-five-footer anchored now at Oriental on Pamlico Sound. Will could almost hear the sound of salt spray crashing against the bow in Morris's voice. Would he trade tweed for nautical attire—whatever you wore around the yacht club? Would he ask people to address him as Commodore?

Morris had come prepared with hiking boots and overalls—two pairs of each. They changed and tramped together across the property, gently rolling hills and creek bottoms, part hardwood forest and part pasture, the ground spongy and sweet, ripe with spring, pasture grass in lush growth, dogwoods sprinkling the woodlands with white blossoms.

They stopped in the early afternoon at a barbecue restaurant near the crossroads, the parking lot still crowded with pickup trucks and vans. Morris fetched sandwiches, chips and iced tea and they ate in the car, watching the ebb and flow of the midday lunch crowd—lean, weathered farmers, big-bellied plumbers and electricians, a state highway crew in a yellow Suburban. The Saab drew some curious looks, but nobody came over. Will was wearing a baseball cap and sunglasses and hadn't shaved since Monday morning, just before he left for court. It was apparently enough to make him incognito, at least when viewed through the windshield of a Saab. It was just fine that nobody came over.

"These are your folks," Morris said.

"Mine?"

"Your audience. Salt-of-the-earth people who watch Channel Seven every evening."

"*Used* to be my audience."

"Will be again, old bean," Morris said, "when this all blows over."

Will thought he might be using it as an opening to talk about the court case, but instead he launched into a lengthy story about how one of the other prospective owners of the forty-five-foot sailboat at

Oriental had once met Walter Cronkite, who was an avid sailor and put into port occasionally along the North Carolina coast. From all reports, a regular fellow, Morris said. Just like Will Baggett.

It was nearly three o'clock when they got back to Morris's office. The receptionist and secretaries were adroit in pretending that nothing whatsoever out of the ordinary had happened to Will Baggett. They greeted him heartily but respectfully, as if he were there to discuss the negotiating of a new contract or to seek advice on wills and testaments. Well, Will thought, people in a law office were used to dealing with all sorts of people and their disasters. *Oh, Mister Jones. Haven't seen you since you murdered your boss. How are things at the office?*

They settled in Morris's plushly paneled and upholstered sanctuary, Will on the sofa just beneath the oil painting of Cochise the Indian chief that Morris had acquired during his most recent western phase, Morris in a leather chair with massive rolled armrests, a legal pad and freshly sharpened number two pencil in hand. "All right," Morris said, "let's have it."

Will hiked one leg over the other and crossed his arms over his chest in what he hoped was sufficiently negative body English. "I'm not ready to say. Not just yet."

Morris's pencil hovered over the legal pad. He looked at the blank page, then up at Will.

"And when will you be ready to say?"

"I don't know. I don't want to rush into anything."

Morris studied his fingernails for a moment. "That's the same thing you told Clarice."

"You've talked to Clarice?"

"Yes."

"When?" Will asked.

"Last night."

"From Greensboro."

"Yes. She called me from Greensboro."

Morris put down his legal pad on the coffee table between them, placed his pencil neatly beside it, crossed his arms over his chest, leaned back in his chair, and stared at Will. Will looked away, out the window, catching a glimpse of the state flag fluttering gracefully in the spring breeze in front of the capitol building down at the other end of Fayetteville Street. There was a good long silence, broken at last by a knock on the office door. Morris's secretary poked her head in. "Clerk of court's on the line. About the arraignment."

"Take a message," Morris said.

"Can I bring you guys some coffee?"

"Scotch," Will said.

She gave Will an odd look, then glanced at Morris for guidance. "Go away," he said pleasantly. She closed the door.

"Arraignment?" Will asked.

"There is a fairly standard legal procedure here, Will, a sequence of events in which you will be involved. You will be arraigned on the charge, the judge will again consider the size of your bond, you will plead not guilty, and the case will be set for trial. At any and all points along the way, I can as your attorney ask for continuances, thus prolonging the process before the inevitable moment when the case is actually heard and a jury of your peers, based on your testimony, sets you free." He picked up the legal pad and pencil again. "In the meantime, it's necessary for me, as your attorney, to hear a recitation of the facts which I will use in your defense."

"What are the terms of my bond?" Will asked.

"You stay in Wake County, stay out of trouble, show up in court on the appointed day."

"If I do all that, do I get my money back when it's over?"

"Less ten percent. Bondsman's fee."

"Five thousand dollars?"

"Yes. And if you violate the terms of the bond, they come after you for the whole quarter million."

"Okay." Will sat there for a moment, hands on his knees, then rose. "In good time. But I don't . . ."

Morris sighed. ". . . want to rush into anything."

"Yes. Can you take me home?"

"No. I'm representing a client before the Planning Commission at four." He glanced at his watch. "The fellow who's buying the land we saw this morning."

"It was a nice trip," Will said. "I enjoyed the barbecue."

"My pleasure."

Will started toward the door.

"There's another thing, Wilbur."

"What's that?"

"Clarice wants a divorce."

THEY WERE ON THE SIDEWALK in front of Morris's office building. Morris was reaching for him, trying to hold him back. Will was staying just out of his grasp, striding along the Fayetteville Street pedestrian mall. "I've got to go see my wife. If you won't let me use your car, I'll find a cab."

Morris put a hand on his shoulder. "Will, let's talk about that."

"I don't want to talk to you. I want to talk to Clarice. Where is she?"

"Will, Clarice doesn't want to see you," Morris said. "She doesn't want any communication. Not right now."

"To hell with what she wants," Will cried. "Do you realize what's happening here, Morris?"

"Yes I do."

Will stopped abruptly. Morris almost ran into him. "No you don't. Clarice is upset. I don't blame her. Every few days I'm on the front page of the *News and Observer* looking like I've just robbed a bank or been caught exposing myself to a busload of schoolkids. And things haven't been quite right between us for some time now, things in general. But divorce? No. It's nowhere near that bad. Clarice is a reasonable woman. We've just got to talk this out."

Morris sighed. "I'm afraid it's not quite that simple."

"What then?"

"I'm not altogether sure. Exactly."

"You sound like that goddamn rental car commercial. Not

exactly," Will said, waving his arms. Passersby were giving them odd looks. He was being recognized. To hell with passersby. "Well, I want to know *exactly* what the hell is going on here." He started off again down the sidewalk. Morris followed. They were at a brisk lope now.

"Will, as your attorney, I'm advising you to lie low for a while until things cool down a little. Then I'll talk to Clarice's attorney . . ."

"She's got a lawyer?"

"In a divorce proceeding . . ."

"There's not going to *be* a divorce. Two reasonable people can work out their differences without lawyers getting involved."

"Will . . ."

Will looked back. Morris had stopped. He was standing there, hands on hips, wearing his best professor-with-dull-student demeanor. "Will, I'm telling you . . ."

"Later, Morris. Tell me later."

He strode briskly on, watching for a taxi, and finally hailed one near the capitol building, driven by a tiny bald-headed man who leaned out the window and yelled, "Yo! Will Baggett! What's the weather?" The sign attached to his dashboard announced that he was one Arthel Sutley, and he pronounced himself pleased as punch to have a celebrity occupy his cab. He was one of those people who assumed that if you appeared on television, you knew everyone else who appeared on television. He peppered Will with questions about Dan Rather and a woman who had a cooking show on Public TV, but the traffic was fortunately light and it took only a few minutes for the taxi to reach LeGrand and pull into the driveway. The Christian Renovators were gone for the day. It was almost four o'clock.

Will reached for his wallet. It wasn't there. He must have failed to take it with him when Morris picked him up. Morris had paid for lunch.

"I don't have my wallet," Will said. "It must be in the house."

"I'll wait," said Arthel Sutley.

Will climbed out of the cab, fished in his pocket for his keys, and inserted the house key into the front door. It wouldn't turn. He tried again. Nothing.

Arthel Sutley was watching him through the windshield of the cab. The engine was still running. Will shrugged in Sutley's direction and went around to the back of the house. His key didn't work in the back door, either. And the Christian Renovators had quite efficiently boarded up their demolition site with big sheets of plywood reinforced by cross-members of two-by-four. He went to the garage for a crowbar and found that it, too, was locked. He tried the garage key. Nothing. His car was in the garage.

Morris, you sonofabitch. You had me traipsing all over north Wake County with you this morning, hiking and eating barbecue, while Clarice was having the locks changed. You, Morris, you sonofabitch, are aiding and abetting my wife in this foolishness.

He should be truly pissed, he thought, standing there beside the garage with his useless key in the lock. But instead he felt a rush of love for Clarice, an intense and urgent need to protect and comfort, to reassure, to make things once again whole and right. They would go away for a while, away from lawyers and the rest of the madding crowd. He would take her in his arms and comfort her. He would tell her whatever she wanted to know. What had happened to him, this embarrassing ruckus and this larger thing, this slow shifting of cosmic forces that left them, their marriage, suddenly teetering on the brink of disaster . . . they would mend and heal. Whatever it took. He could not, would not, lose her. He would fight for her. He would take the first step—and the last, too, if that's what it took. Right now, he must see her, touch her.

He went back to the cab. "I can't get in the house," he said. "I can meet you somewhere later with the money."

Arthel Sutley shook his head slowly. "Can't do that. Comp'ny rules."

"Look, you know me. You know where to find me. Do you think a celebrity would try to gyp you out of a fare?"

Sutley turned off the engine. "Yep," he said, "happened before."

He sat back in the seat, hands firmly gripping the steering wheel as if suspicious that Will might reach in the window and try to wrest it from him.

Will flapped his arms in frustration. "What do you want?" He reached for his wrist. "My watch?"

"Cash," said Sutley.

"Well, I don't have any cash," Will barked. "My cash is locked up in the house and I can't get in."

"Your wife changed the locks?" Sutley had a look that said he had seen all this before.

"It appears that way."

"And where's your wife?"

They arrived fifteen minutes later at the offices of Snively and Ellis Realty.

It was a couple of miles out Glenwood from the center of down-town—a fairly new structure, but built in the fashion of a rambling old farmhouse with a wide front porch (with a row of rocking chairs), a tin roof, and dormered windows peeking from the second story. It was a good location, out here on Glenwood, out toward all the falling-all-over-itself growth that made North Raleigh a boom area and made Old Raleigh cringe. The office nestled comfortably on a modest expanse of immaculate lawn and perfectly tended beds of shrubbery and annuals. The parking lot was tucked discreetly to one side behind a screen of cypress and holly. It was the kind of place that gave the impression of homespun efficiency, the kind of neighborly place where people didn't sell houses, they fitted you lovingly into the perfect home where there would always be cookies baking in the oven and a large, long-haired dog lounging in front of the fireplace.

It was the first time Will had actually been to the headquarters of Snively and Ellis. He had escorted Clarice to company Christmas parties and summer picnics, but they had always been held some-where else. There had never been any reason to come here.

Will felt a pang of guilt. Okay, he had been too wrapped up in his own career. He hadn't paid proper attention to Clarice's, hadn't given proper credit to the charm, cleverness and hard work that had led to her considerable success. But that would change. Now that he had the luxury of time, he would be a regular visitor here, arriving to take her to lunch, sending flowers that the entire staff could enjoy. That is, if he wasn't in jail. He still hadn't figured that one out, but he thought he might have to pretty quickly, now that he was here.

Will checked the parking lot. Clarice's car was there.

Tina, the receptionist, met him at the front door. He remembered her vaguely from the previous Christmas party, where she had consumed a trifle too much champagne punch and had giggled as she told him of her ancient grandmother in Goldsboro who had somehow gotten it into her dotty mind that Will Baggett was not only her weatherman but also a long-lost cousin who had left for Argentina in the thirties. Here, four months later, Tina seemed to have put on a bit of weight and was now a rather formidably sturdy, no-nonsense presence filling the doorway.

"How are you, Tina?" he asked pleasantly.

"Mrs. Baggett isn't available," Tina said.

Will tried to peer around Tina into the office interior. Tina shifted slightly, blocking his view. "I know she's here. Her car is out back."

"She isn't available," Tina repeated.

Will felt the hairs on the back of his neck prickle, but he kept his voice calm and even. "Just tell her I'm here, and I'd like to speak to her. As soon as possible. If she's busy and can't speak to me right away, I'll wait."

Tina took a deep breath, and Will thought she was about to say something definitive. Instead, she stepped back inside, closed the door behind her, and deadbolted it. "Shit," Will said softly. When he tried to peer through the glass, Tina lowered a blind. There was a big plate-glass window just to his left, but as he turned to it, blinds came down there, too.

Will tapped on the door glass—lightly at first, then harder.

Then he rapped his knuckles forcefully against the wood frame of the door. And then he banged on it with his fist. He could hear voices inside.

A voice behind him: "Did you get the money?" Will turned to see Arthel Sutley standing at the bottom of the steps. Will had forgotten about him. "Meter's still running," Sutley said. "She's up to thirty bucks now."

"Then let it run," Will said. "This may take a while." Sutley shrugged and headed back to the parking area.

Will banged again, even harder this time. The glass in the door rattled precariously. Next, he thought, he would put his fist through it. Blood everywhere. He would sue for damages.

Then he heard the deadbolt unlock and the door opened a few inches and Fincher Snively, managing partner of Snively and Ellis, peered out. "Will!" he said brightly, as if suddenly discovering who was banging the hell out of his front door. Will could see movement behind Fincher, could hear the urgent murmur of voices.

"Yes Fincher, it's me, good old Will," Will said. "I've come to see my wife."

"Will, she's just not available at the moment."

"That's what Tina said."

Fincher shrugged. "I can ask her to call you."

"I want to see her in person."

Fincher glanced back into the room. Then he lowered his voice conspiratorially. "She's with some clients right now. A big sale."

"I don't care if she's with the Shah of Iran . . ."

"The Shah's dead." Fincher smiled, all charm and affability.

Will put a hand on the door and gave a light but firm push. Fincher jammed a foot behind it and pushed back lightly but firmly. Will pushed harder. So did Fincher. "Will," he said, "let's don't have a scene here."

Will took his hand away from the door.

"I'm sure we can be reasonable . . ."

"Fincher," Will said evenly, "I don't feel very reasonable right now. You have a size and strength advantage on me. I've seen you in those tank tops at the company picnics with your pectorals bulging, so I don't have any illusions about being able to whip your ass in a fair fight. But I am prepared to arm myself with a tire tool from the taxicab which brought me here and beat on this goddamn door, and you, if need be, until I am allowed to talk to my wife."

Fincher's eyes narrowed. "Will, you have just communicated a threat. That's a punishable offense. And given your current, ah, situation, I don't think you need any more punishable offenses."

They stared at each other. Will smiled. "I withdraw my threat, Fincher."

"I salute your good judgment," Fincher said. "I'll tell Clarice you were here." He closed the door.

Will stood there on the porch for a moment, at a loss. He had not expected this, not this throwing up of barricades by a goddamn bunch of realtors. He had intended to rush here and take her into his arms and beg her to come home with him, and once there they would make love and begin to rediscover what it was they had lost. And he would set the record straight if need be. Whatever it took. But this . . .

He turned away from the door and walked down the steps and stood on the lawn looking out at Glenwood Avenue. Across the divided six-lane was a strip shopping center, and one of the occupants was a Kinko's copy center. Will considered things for a moment, then made for the road.

He had some change in his pocket, enough to purchase a large sheet of poster paper and two magic markers—a red and a black. Then he re-crossed Glenwood, dodging the traffic that was beginning to pick up here in the late afternoon. He returned to the front steps of Snively and Ellis and sat for several minutes fashioning a sign. Big black letters, accented with red. He worked diligently, somewhat surprised at what he was doing but either unwilling or unable to stop. He couldn't tell which, exactly.

Arthel Sutley appeared before him again. "Meter's up to forty-five now," Arthel said.

Will peered up from his work. Sutley was looking at the sign, trying to read it upside down. Will tilted it up at just enough of an angle that Sutley couldn't see. "Look at it this way, Mister Sutley. As long as I'm running up a bill, you don't have to pick up any more fares, one of which could be an armed robber who would take everything you've got, including your cab, and might even put a bullet in your brain. This is the easiest, safest money you'll make all day."

Sutley shook his head and went back to his taxicab. Will finished the sign, going over the letters several times to make them as big and bold as possible. Then he tossed the markers into the shrubbery next to the porch and walked with the sign to the curb alongside Glenwood. He faced left toward the oncoming traffic and held the sign aloft. He thought for a brief moment that he should probably feel ridiculous. But he didn't. And if he looked ridiculous, he didn't care.

It took twenty minutes for Morris deLesseps to get there. In the meantime, Will created a fair-sized commotion along Glenwood as the rush-hour traffic piled up. Passengers gawked and pointed, and behind the closed windows of their air-conditioning he could see them mouthing the words of the sign: SNIVELY & ELLIS SUCKS. The sign got them first, and then, more often than not, they would recognize the holder as none other than Raleigh's (former) most popular TV weatherman, the fellow who kept turning up on the front page of the paper. There was a good deal of horn-honking and window-rolling-down-and-waving-and-shouting—*Yo, Will!*—along with several near-collisions. Across the street at the strip shopping center, clerks and customers came out of the stores and stood watching and pointing. Somebody, Will figured, would go back inside and call Snively and Ellis Realty. Or the cops. Or both. He felt like an ancient barbarian, laying siege to the place.

Will spotted Morris's Saab a good way off. Morris was honking the horn now, flapping an arm out of the driver-side window, motioning for Will to get away from the curb. Will stood his ground. Finally the Saab reached him and Morris flung the passenger-side door open. "Get in!" he barked.

"I'm busy," Will said. Traffic backed up. A school bus full of rowdy kids was just behind the Saab. The driver bore down on the horn, drowning out whatever it was that Morris said next. Morris pulled away and made a sharp turn into the Snively and Ellis driveway, stopped, leaped out, and started loping across the lawn toward Will. "Are you crazy?" he cried.

Morris lunged for the sign, but Will made a quick, neat move, blocking Morris with his body. "I just want to see my wife."

"Put the sign down. She'll talk to you on the phone." He pulled a flip phone from the pocket of his tweed jacket.

"I want to look her in the eye, Morris."

Morris's eyes were bulging now, his face blotched with red. "Look, you stubborn sonofabitch, if you don't cut this out . . ."

"Are the cops on the way?"

"No," he said between clenched teeth, "but they will be. And if they come and arrest you, Judge Nettles will revoke your bail, you'll lose your bond money, and you'll rot in jail. Good God, Will, you're making an absolute ass of yourself!"

Will lowered the sign.

Morris started punching numbers on the flip phone. "Fincher? All right. The sign's down. Put Clarice on."

He handed the phone to Will.

"Go away," Will said firmly. "I want to speak to my wife without some goddamn lawyer listening in on the conversation."

Morris made a face and walked away toward his car.

Will put the phone to his ear. "Clarice . . ."

"Wilbur," she said, "go away."

He turned, saw her standing at one of the front windows of the realty office. He took a step toward her.

"Clarice, please . . . let's talk. Just give me . . ."

"We don't have anything to talk *about*. "

"I know I've embarrassed you, honey."

"You're embarrassing me right now."

"I'm sorry. About everything. Look, is it about what happened in court? If it is, I'll tell you whatever you want to know."

"No," she said, "it's not about what happened in court . . ."

"Look, honey, I know we've got a lot to work on."

"What did you just say?"

He hesitated. "I said we've got a lot to work on. But we can fix this."

Her voice rose an octave. "Are you listening to yourself, Wilbur? Fix it? Work on it? My God. Mow the grass, clip the shrubbery, deliver the forecast, fix Clarice!"

"Honey," he said softly, "it's not like that. I love you, Clarice. I just want us to get straightened out. Whatever it takes. It's my fault. I'll take all the blame. I know things haven't been right. And all this business the past couple of weeks—Jesus, I'm sorry. I know you're embarrassed. And your family . . ."

"Don't bring my family into this," she said sharply.

"Okay. But don't give up on us, Clarice. Just tell me what to do." He could feel himself close to tears now, a naked pleading in his voice.

There was a lengthy silence and then she gave a long, slow sigh. Even through the cell phone he could feel the weariness, the resignation. "Will, I'm just tired."

"Of me?"

"Of all of it. I can't handle it anymore. I want out. And I want you to go away and leave me alone." He could see her clearly through the front window of Snively and Ellis, using one long, elegant index finger to punch the button on her own telephone. *Click.* She turned away from the window. *Wait a minute! I've got one more question before you shut me out of your life! Is there somebody else?* But someone closed the blinds and she was lost to him and whether there was someone else or not was almost beside the point.

Morris was back. Arthel Sutley was with him. Sutley said to Morris, "Are you with him?"

"Unfortunately."

"Well, it's up to sixty-five dollars."

"Pay him," Will told Morris. "You owe me."

Morris made a wry face. He knew exactly what Will meant. While Morris pulled out his billfold, Will sat down on the curb. Traffic eased by, inches from his feet. He thought briefly of flinging himself in front of one of the vehicles, but they were moving too slowly to do more than nudge him. And besides, he had already been run over several times.

14 | "YOU SET ME UP," Will said. "That trip today, traipsing around the countryside . . ."

Morris made a helpless, supplicating gesture. "You should have heard Clarice on the phone last night. I've never known her to be so wrought up. I thought the best thing to do was to get you out of the house. Let things cool down. It's a common technique in transactional negotiation, Will. Separate the warring parties."

"We're not at war. We're at . . . well, I don't know what we're at. Impasse, maybe, but not war."

"I'm just trying to be helpful here. You're both my friends, have been for a long time. I dated Clarice before she met you. Remember? I'm in an awkward position, Will. Kinda caught in the middle. I want to do what's right for both of you."

"Did you know she was having the locks changed?"

"Well . . ."

"You sonofabitch."

"If it helps you to take it out on me, go ahead," Morris said. "But I'm hurt."

"Good."

Morris was helpful. Guilt, whatever. He arranged for a motel room for Will and retrieved his car and several changes of clothes from the house on LeGrand. He took Will to dinner at a nice restaurant. And then he took him back to the motel and advised him not to do anything stupid overnight.

He got Palmer's answering machine, which kicked in on the first ring. Palmer's mechanical voice said simply, "Leave a message."

When the machine beeped he said, "Palmer, this is your father. If you're there, pick up." He waited for perhaps ten seconds, and just as he was about to hang up, Palmer answered. He didn't say anything, just picked up the phone.

"Is that you?" Will asked.

"Yes."

"Don't you think we need to talk?"

There was a long silence, and then Palmer started crying.

————

PALMER LIVED IN A two-bedroom brick bungalow a mile or so from the edge of the Chapel Hill campus. He had shared an apartment with several fraternity brothers during his undergraduate years at Duke, but when he started medical school he wanted his own place with quiet and privacy. Clarice found the house through a realtor friend in Chapel Hill and Sidney Palmer bought it with the understanding that Palmer would live there rent-free until he finished medical school. Sidney had also given him a new BMW 325i as a graduation present. The car was dark blue. Duke blue, not Carolina blue. The house, which Will had seen only once — shortly after Palmer moved in the previous August — was spiffed up and newly furnished throughout. There was leather furniture in the living room and the spare bedroom was equipped as a study/office with a new computer and an antique oak rolltop desk.

Sidney, the consummate Duke man, complained good-naturedly about being a Chapel Hill property owner, but it was Chapel Hill's medical school, not Duke's, which had accepted his grandson. Palmer was properly appreciative, as he had always been whenever his grandfather opened his wallet. Throughout his Duke years, he had phoned Sidney at least once a week and driven to Greensboro at least once a month for lunch at the country club. Palmer spent as much time in Greensboro as he did in Raleigh.

Palmer's education (or at least the paying for it) had been a sore subject between Will and Clarice. "We could handle Duke," Will had said when Clarice told him that her parents wanted to foot the bill. But they both knew that it would have meant sizable debt. Not for Sidney.

"Well, we're not going to handle Duke," Clarice said. "I don't know why you have to be so defensive about my family."

"I'm not being defensive."

"Can't you just accept the fact that they love Palmer and want to help him?"

"And I don't?"

"I don't see your family offering to help."

There was no answer for that. *Your crazy family.*

And then there was the car.

Will had been on the verge of buying a car for Palmer a year before—a sleek, low-mileage Pontiac that a young woman in the Channel Seven newsroom had for sale. The timing was perfect. She had put a note on the newsroom bulletin board on a Friday in early April. Will took the car for a test drive and offered the young woman a hundred dollars less than her asking price. She accepted. He would bring a check for the full amount on Monday, he said. But when he arrived home from work that midnight, the BMW was sitting in the driveway. It glowed like a dark pearl in the soft light from the nearby street lamp. Will stood for a long time looking at it, feeling resentful and then feeling guilty about his resentment. It was a joyous time in the Baggett household—Palmer on the verge of getting his undergraduate degree with honors from a fine university, accepted already into medical school. It would be unfair, petty, tacky for Will to cast a cloud over the harmonious atmosphere. Clarice watched him carefully for reaction, but he made the proper exclamations of admiration when Palmer showed off the car the next morning.

———

IT WAS AFTER TEN when Will pulled into the gravel driveway behind Palmer's BMW. The house was dark.

Will didn't knock. He pushed open the door and peered inside and was assaulted by the unmistakable odor of marijuana. And mixed with it, the smell of staleness and stagnation—drifting like toxic vapor from the abode of his son the medical student: he of the Ralph Lauren jackets and Calvin Klein slacks and Bass Weejun loafers, he of the carefully cultivated air and manner of the Greensboro Palmers. Will recoiled from it, taking a step back, almost losing his balance at the edge of the stoop, a hand going up reflexively to ward off whatever was inside.

"Palmer," he called after a moment. Maybe Palmer would come forth and they could parley out here on the stoop or in the yard where there was light from the nearby street lamp and the air was cleaner. But there was no answer. Will took a deep breath and stepped into the living room, leaving the door open behind him. As his eyes adjusted to the dimness, he turned to a table next to the sofa and clicked the switch on a lamp. Nothing.

"The electricity's off," Palmer said, startling Will. He looked up to see Palmer's dim form in the bedroom doorway.

"Why is the electricity off?" Will asked.

"I forgot to pay the bill."

They stood there for a good while, not speaking. Will's eyes gradually adjusted to the gloom and he could see that Palmer was wearing only boxer shorts.

"False alarm," Palmer said finally, his voice flat and lifeless. "You can go back home now."

"No," Will said, "I think I'll stay a while."

He turned to the window behind the sofa and raised the blinds, letting a little more of the light from the street lamp into the room. When he turned back, the bedroom door was empty. Palmer came back in a moment, wearing jeans and a T-shirt, but still barefoot.

"Is there . . ." Will hesitated ". . . someone else here with you?"

Palmer had a steady girlfriend—Anna, a tiny brunette from Hickory, both doll-like and vibrant, a gymnast on the Duke women's intercollegiate team. They had met during Palmer's senior year. They would, Will assumed, someday marry. In the meantime . . .

"No," Palmer said. "It's just us guys."

"You want to tell me what's going on here?"

"There's nothing to tell."

"The place smells like a homeless shelter, you haven't paid the electric bill, you're stoned, and you're crying on the phone. And there's nothing to tell." Will sat down on the sofa. "I think I'll just sit here and give you time to reconsider that."

Palmer stood there for perhaps another minute, then crossed to the sofa and sat down on the other end. Will leaned back with one elbow parked on an armrest, waiting. Palmer slumped forward with his chin in his hands. They sat there for a long time.

There was a sudden burst of noise from Palmer's bedroom—the phone, then the answering machine. Palmer's recorded message: *Leave a message. BEEP.* Then Clarice's voice. Will was off the sofa and into the bedroom, his hand reaching for the receiver, freezing in midair as Clarice said, "Palmer, pick up the phone." A long pause while she waited. Will could imagine her drumming her fingers on the kitchen counter, a habit she had picked up since she had gotten into real estate. Clarice was not the patient person she had once been.

"Palmer, if you don't call me back by eight in the morning, I'm going to get in the car and come over there. I need to talk to you. I know you're busy with school, but you can take a few minutes to call me. I mean it. I'm not kidding." Another long pause. Then she gave up. *Click.*

Will turned to see Palmer in the bedroom doorway, framed by dim light. He looked thin, almost frail.

"Palmer, how long has it been since you've talked to your mother?"

"About a week, I guess. She's been out of town."

"How long has she been trying to call you?"

"Couple of days."

"Where have you been the last few days?"

"Right here. Haven't been outside in a week."

"And no electricity."

"No."

He doesn't know. He doesn't know any of it. And she doesn't know. It is, indeed, just us guys here.

————

"I'VE SCREWED UP," Palmer said.

They sat at a table tucked into a corner of a coffee shop on Franklin Street across from the campus. Students drifted in and out. Some read or tapped on laptop computers at the other tables. Will sat with his back to the room, hoping to avoid being recognized. It wasn't the best place in the world to talk, but Will couldn't abide staying at Palmer's house, dark and odorous. Palmer smelled faintly rank himself. The jeans and T-shirt didn't appear to have had a recent washing. They sipped coffee and stared into their cups.

"How did you . . . screw up?"

"I haven't been to a single class in two months."

"Well, you told us that some med students never go to class. They just get the notes . . ."

"I don't have any notes. I haven't opened a book." Palmer looked up at Will now, his face bleak, defeated. Will was having a hard time getting past the sheer strangeness of it. He realized that he had not looked directly into his son's face for a long time, and that seeing it now, bleak defeat was the last thing he would have imagined.

"I've lied and covered up until I've gotten myself trapped in a corner and I don't know how to get out," Palmer went on.

"Does your mother have even the faintest notion of what is going on?"

Of course Clarice didn't know, and Will didn't need Palmer's silence to tell him that.

"Your grandparents?"

"God, no."

"What happened?" Will asked.

"I guess I just sort of gave up. First semester of med school was the worst thing I've ever been through."

"You've always been a good student," Will said. "The best. You wouldn't have gotten into med school in the first place if you weren't smart and disciplined."

Palmer shook his head. "But it's always been easy before." He waved his hands weakly. "I really never had to break a sweat."

"And med school is so much different?"

"Yeah. Hard. And so goddamn much of it. You go to class, come in and start studying, and before you know it, it's five o'clock in the morning and you've got another class at eight. So you get a little sleep and drag yourself back to class and do it all over again, and at the end of the week you're farther behind than ever. It's just . . ." His voice trailed off and he looked at Will with a look of utter bafflement.

"But you passed," Will said hopefully. "Your first-semester grades were okay."

"Okay," Palmer agreed, "but just barely. When the semester was over, I should have been glad that I survived. That's how everybody else seemed to feel. But I just felt so . . . I don't know, empty. Like I had been fucked over or something and couldn't do anything about it. Scared."

It was, Will thought, another measure of how odd, even bizarre, this conversation, this situation, was. He could never, ever remember Palmer using the phrase "fucked over" around him, or anything remotely resembling it. They had been excessively polite to each other these last few years. Wary. They took each other's pulse from a safe distance. But here was Palmer feeling "fucked over" and admitting it to Will, saying it right out like that. *He's desperate. He has absolutely no other place to turn. If he did, I wouldn't be here.*

"What about Anna?" Will asked.

"She's disgusted with me," Palmer said flatly. "She told me to get the hell out of her life if I couldn't straighten myself out. I heard she had a date with a Delta Chi last weekend."

He remembered now how pointedly cheerful Palmer had been at home over Christmas break. He had slept a lot the first few days, but Will and Clarice had put that off to sheer exhaustion. After that, there had been a sort of frantic brittleness about him—a nervous laugh, a distracted air. He had driven several times to Greensboro and then on to Hickory to spend time with Anna. Right after New Year's, he had hastened back to Chapel Hill. He needed to get ahead of things, he said. Since then, he had remained almost incommunicado. He called, but he made excuses not to come home. It was two months since Will and Clarice had seen him. Two months since he had been to class.

"Well," Will said, "I guess you're right. You screwed up. Question is, what are you going to do about it?"

"I don't know. I feel . . . paralyzed."

"In deep shit."

"Yeah. Real deep."

"What can I do for you?"

Palmer shrugged. "Look, just forget it. Get in your car and go back to Raleigh. I'm sorry I blubbered on the phone. I made the mess and I guess I'll have to clean it up."

"How?"

A look of exquisite pain crossed Palmer's face. "Tell 'em. Isn't that what I've got to do?"

Well, this is it. Draw a line under all the practicalities and the logic and the murky stuff and say, "Okay. Here's what I'm going to do with his life and mine." I've looked him in the eye and the bottom line is, he needs me. He's hanging by the bloody tips of his fingers from a sheer cliff and

I'm the only one who can do anything about it. We've never been here before, he and I. And I've only been here once before myself, a long time ago when I had a chance to defend the honor and memory of a man and a woman who flew off in an airplane. Had a chance, but didn't.

"No," he said to his son. "Lie like a dog."

Palmer squinted at him, brow furrowed. And then a look of sheer relief flooded his face.

"Someday you will have to own up to your sins," Will said. "It's the honorable thing to do. But for the time being, no. See what you can salvage before you go spilling the beans and letting people who love you think you're a liar and a slacker and a pothead and that you lack grace and courage."

Palmer flared. "If you're gonna preach . . ." He started to rise, but Will clamped a firm grip on his arm and Palmer eased back into his seat.

Will released Palmer's arm and took the last of his coffee in a large gulp. "I'm not through. Here's what I want you to do. In the morning, call your mother and tell her you love her and you're sorry you've neglected her for the past week. Take a bath, put on a coat and tie, and go see the dean of the medical school. That is, unless you no longer want to be a doctor."

Palmer thought about it. "Yeah. I do. It's just . . ."

"Uh-huh. So, go to the dean and throw yourself on his mercy. Tell him you have had a momentary lapse of . . ."

"Judgment?"

"Don't use the word 'judgment.' Doctors aren't supposed to have lapses of judgment. Just tell him you've had a temporary crisis of spirit. Personal problems. Your father lost his job, et cetera, et cetera. Anyhow, you wish to be forgiven this semester's disaster and allowed to resume your studies in the fall."

Palmer nodded. "What if he says no?"

"Take it one step at a time. I doubt you're the first person in the history of American medical education who's had a crisis of spirit. Surely there's some mechanism, some process. If it's a medical school worth its salt, it's run by people with a sense of perspective and compassion. What you have to do is give the appearance of someone who, with a little grace and mercy, will make a dear and glorious physician."

"I guess I could do that," Palmer said. He ducked his head and gazed into his nearly empty coffee cup.

"Want some more coffee?" Will asked. Palmer didn't answer.

Will looked around. The place was almost empty now. Behind the counter, a young woman was cleaning the cappuccino machine. Will glanced at his watch. They would be closing in ten minutes. He and Palmer would have to get up and leave. Go on to the next thing and the next.

Will rose. Palmer looked up at him, then got to his feet. They stood facing each other across the table. Palmer said, "I guess I owe you."

"And you're not talking about for the coffee."

"No."

"Well," Will said, "you don't know the half of it."

———

MORRIS DELESSEPS's PENCIL hovered over the legal pad on his desk. He hesitated, then jotted down a single word. "Do you know what I just wrote here?"

"What?"

"'Bullshit.'"

"I repeat, I'm guilty," Will said firmly. "I appeared in court in possession of a controlled substance—to wit, as you lawyers like to say, marijuana, a plastic bag of which fell from the pocket of my jacket and was promptly and correctly identified by the bailiff, whereupon the judge threw my ass in jail." He paused for effect. "That's my story and I'm sticking to it."

Morris tossed the pencil onto the pad, leaned back in his chair, and grunted with exasperation. "All right, Will. You're paying for every second of hogwash you're dishing out here, so I'll humor you and we'll spend some more of your money. How did you come to be in possession of said . . . controlled substance?"

"I bought it?"

"From whom?"

"It was dark. I couldn't tell."

"Did you have any idea what it was when you bought it?"

"Of course. I specifically asked for marijuana. 'Gimme some real good stuff,' I said. I would so testify if the case came to trial. But it won't come to that. I intend to plead guilty."

Morris leaned forward and picked up the pencil again. "No you're not. I'm going to put up a spirited defense for you, and you're going to help me."

Will sighed. "There's nothing to defend, Morris. I intend to throw myself on the mercy of the court."

"Judge Broderick Nettles has no mercy. He will have your fanny for lunch."

"Active jail time?" Will asked.

Morris thought about it for a moment. "Oh, yes. Along with probation, a fine, maybe community service."

"Would he let me do the community service as the Weather Wizard?"

"Goddammit!" Morris exploded. "What in the hell is going on here?" His eyes blazed. Will halfway expected him to hurl the pencil and legal pad against the wall. Or maybe even at Will. But Morris got hold of himself after a moment. "I woke up in the middle of the night wondering why in the deuce that bag of pot was in your jacket pocket, how it got there, if you knew it was there, if somebody planted it. 'Morris,' I told myself, 'there is no way Will Baggett would intentionally take a bag of pot to court. Maybe he smokes a little bit of it at home, back behind the garage away from prying eyes. Maybe it puts old Will in the right frame of mind to do the fucking weather on TV. Morris,' I told myself, 'sometimes people you think you know will surprise you.'" He stopped for a moment and glared at Will. "Hell, I've smoked a little myself from time to time. But take it to court?"

When Will didn't say anything, Morris placed the pencil back on the legal pad and stood slowly. He leaned across the desk, palms flat on the top of it. "You realize that this really rips it."

Will met his stare. "Yes."

"TV or any other kind of responsible job, politics, teaching a Sunday School class, you name it."

"Yes."

"Possession of marijuana is a felony offense under North Carolina statute."

"Yes." He tried to sound final, unequivocal. Amen and Amen.

Morris reached for the phone. "I'll call the District Attorney and tell him you want to plead guilty and get it over with."

"That's okay. If I'm going to jail, I want to start serving the sentence as soon as possible. Tomorrow would be just fine."

"You're either incredibly stupid or you're some sort of misguided hero," Morris said.

"Hero?"

"I think I know what happened," Morris said quietly. "I'm pretty sure of it."

Will shrugged. Morris stared at him for a moment longer and then started dialing.

Will studied Morris's desktop while Morris waited for the District Attorney. It was neatly arranged—pencil holder, desk lamp, a wooden carving of a donkey he had brought home from the Democratic National Convention the year they nominated Walter Mondale, an inch-high stack of legal-size file folders, a brass desk lamp. Morris was a neat man who—despite whatever persona he might have chosen for himself at any given moment—was a fine attorney. He deserved better than this. Some day he might share a thing or two with Morris deLesseps. But that would be a long way off.

BOOK
4

15 | HE WOULD ALWAYS ASSOCIATE HER with John Coltrane. That's what was playing on the stereo when he first laid eyes on her. Coltrane, making loose and funky on the sax. And there was Clarice, standing in the open front doorway just behind Morris deLesseps, looking a bit bewildered.

It was an aging, dilapidated farmhouse several miles out of Chapel Hill toward Pittsboro where Will lived during his senior year simply because it was cheap and he was having to pay most of his way. Since he had changed his major from business to broadcast and film, the monthly checks from Min had dwindled. She was mad at him, but he had stood his ground about that.

The occupants were an eclectic bunch—a goateed sociology graduate student, an artist, a musician (owner of the Coltrane album and a devotee of classic jazz, rock and big band music), a Ferlinghetti-inspired poet from the creative writing program, Will and another guy from broadcast and film, a non-student who drove a bread truck.

The bread truck driver owned the place. It was habitually grubby and litter-strewn. They had cleaned up a little for the party, at least moved stuff into piles. It was mid-March and there was an early warm spell that held promise of spring. Will was thankful. The drafty house had been gripped through the winter by an abiding chill that overwhelmed the small kerosene heater in the living room. In Will's tiny bedroom off the kitchen, formerly a pantry, he slept under a mound of blankets. But this Friday night all the doors and windows were open. The farmhouse had been airing out all day and some of the stagnant smells of winter — stale food, stale beer, mildewed furniture and bedclothes — had dissipated a bit.

She was tall enough that she could look over Morris's shoulder as he stood in the front doorway. Tall and angular, strikingly fine bones in her face, a swath of soft golden hair that swooped down across her forehead, almost covering one eye. She kept flipping it back with her right hand, a movement so utterly graceful that it took Will's breath. She blinked into the crowded room and there was a sort of *What on earth?* look on her face. Will was on the far side of the room, a bottle of Budweiser raised almost to his lips. She was framed by Morris's shoulder and the doorway, stunning in the pale light from the single bare bulb that hung over the crowd in the living room. Will was talking with the sociology graduate student, who was carrying on drunkenly at some length about a certain professor's bizarre grading habits. Will was on his third Budweiser, a pleasant buzz tickling the back of his brain. "My God," he said softly. John Coltrane hit a high note, making the sax squeal with ecstasy. "My, my God."

"Yeah," the sociology major said. "That Coltrane. He's a bitch."

It took him several minutes to corner Morris, who was by now in the kitchen making daiquiris. He had left the girl in the living room, where she stood near the door, looking as if she might take flight at any moment. Morris had brought everything for the daiquiris in an Igloo cooler — rum, frozen pineapple concentrate, ice, even a blender for God's sake. Everybody in the place drinking Budweiser or cheaper, or smoking joints, and here was Morris making daquiris. Morris was a Phi Gam. If you saw him on campus during the week, he would be dressed in fraternity uniform — khakis, madras shirt, Weejuns, often a navy blue blazer with the Phi Gam crest on the breast pocket. But on Friday nights, he was more likely to show up at the farmhouse than the Phi Gam house. He was fascinated by the kinds of people who gathered there — the campus off-beats, the artists and sociologists and writers, the retro musicians, the broadcast and film people. He and Will were friends, though Morris was a year older and Will wasn't a fraternity man. Morris was just barely a senior because he kept changing majors. He had been, at one time or another, in psychology, premed, chemical engineering, finance and art history. He was now back to psychology and thought he might go on to law school. Morris's Friday night farmhouse dates ran by habit to plain-faced girls with long, straight hair and long, straight tie-dyed dresses who played guitar and read poetry. Not tonight.

"Who *is* she?" Will demanded.

Morris poured rum into the blender, a good deal of rum, fitted on the rubber top and flipped the switch. It whined and rattled. "Who?" he asked over the racket.

"That incredible creature." Will pointed to the living room where he could just see the top of whoever-she-was's head through the pall of smoke that hung over the crush of bodies. Coltrane was making the air shimmer.

Morris gave him a close look. "Down, boy. You're drooling."

"Who?" he demanded.

"Clarice Palmer. Duke. Of the Greensboro Palmers. She's out of your league, son."

"The hell you say."

"Want a daiquiri?"

"No, Morris. That is definitely not what I want."

"You're with Morris," he said.

"Yes."

"Slumming?"

She gave him a puzzled look, then caught his meaning. She looked over his shoulder, her gaze sweeping the room. "Morris said there's nothing like this at Duke. He's right." She had a rather small voice, almost timid, but it had an incredible timbre to it—rich, colored with soft browns and umbers, a half-octave lower than you might expect. He could hear the colorings in it even if he couldn't understand exactly what she was saying.

"I'm Will Baggett."

"Oh. Yes. Morris told me about you."

"Morris says . . ." Coltrane's sax screeched and Clarice's eyes went wide. A deer caught in headlights. He took her elbow and guided her out onto the front porch. He thought she might resist, but she didn't. "Morris says you're out of my league," he said when they were outside.

"What league is that?"

He looked back through the open door at the living room—packed to capacity, everybody shouting to be heard over the music, the conversations intense, the Coltrane pulsing. The walls of the old house seemed almost to bulge. At a party two weeks before, a piece of ceiling plaster had collapsed onto the crowd and a girl had been knocked cold. It was a jazz crowd, even the bread truck driver's friends. There was some Charlie Mingus and some Modern Jazz Quartet and some Brubeck all stacked on the stereo, waiting for Coltrane to finish. The musician had a nice collection. He played trombone.

He turned back to her. "I live here," he said. "These are my people."

"I can see why Morris likes it. There seems to be one of each."

"And Morris is all of the above."

She laughed. "Or none. On any given day."

They just looked at each other for a moment, but you wouldn't call it an awkward silence. A sizing-up, maybe. Then she said, "I've heard you on the radio."

He worked the night shift at a Chapel Hill station, Sunday through Thursday. He played jazz, folk, some light rock—an odd mix, maybe, but students liked it. Local businesses liked it because the students listened, and they bought a lot of advertising on his program. The station manager told him he could play recordings of pigs grunting if that's what the students and the advertisers wanted.

"You've got a good voice," she said.

"Not as good as yours. You could talk on the radio and melt butter in Raleigh."

They looked at each other some more. "Do you date many Chapel Hill men?" he asked.

"Do you date many Duke women?"

"Never have felt the need until just now."

She was amused. She had a nice smile that went nicely with her rich voice. She was wearing a yellow dress with some green and blue figures on it, cut low across the front, but not so low as to be bold. She was, he thought, probably the only woman here who owned a bra. He had never seen anything quite like her, not this incredible package of stunning looks and graceful movement and yet a certain air of vulnerability, uncertainty, that made him want to touch her cheek, to reassure her that he would make everything all right.

He was working on his fourth beer. He might never lay eyes on her again. "Come home with me," he said.

"You are home," she answered.

And then Morris showed up with the daiquiris.

Hours later, when the party had mellowed out and everybody was drunk or stoned or both, the musician got out his trombone and played along with an old Tommy Dorsey Orchestra recording of "Mood Indigo." And then the crowd began to yell for Will and the musician turned off the stereo and Will did some imitations—John Wayne doing Shakespeare, *tubbee or not tubbee, that's the question, Pilgrim,* and a new routine he had worked up, Senator Sam Ervin questioning Nixon at the Watergate hearings while Tiny Tim sang "Tiptoe Through the Tulips" in the background. He could see her at the back of the crowd, daiquiri in hand. She was laughing.

Two o'clock in the morning. Morris was in the kitchen. He had run out of daiquiri ingredients and was drinking one of Will's Budweisers and carrying on a heated argument with the musician that had something to do with Fats Domino's piano technique. It didn't make much sense to Will. He went looking.

He found her on the front steps, the yellow dress drawn up around her legs. The air was cool. It was, after all, March. She looked up at him, bored and tired. The swath of hair cascaded across her forehead. She pushed it back. He thought, *Please don't*. He brought a jacket and draped it over her shoulders and she gave him a grateful smile.

He sat down beside her. "How long have you known Morris?"

"Since his art history phase. Was that last year or the year before?"

"With Morris, it's hard to remember. What're you studying?"

It was such a lame line, he thought, such a shopworn opening gambit. Surely, she was used to better. But it wasn't an opening gambit. He had already opened, and now he was exploring. She didn't seem to mind. "Elementary education," she answered. "You?"

"I started out in business, but then I got a job pushing camera at the Public TV studio and decided that's what I wanted to do. So I switched to broadcast and film."

"I suppose you want to own NBC or something like that."

"Not really."

"Then what?"

"Maybe program a network. The stuff that's on prime time now— I could do better."

"I'm afraid I don't watch much television."

"You're not missing anything."

"What would you put on?"

"Something to make you think. You know, in there tonight . . . ," he waved a hand toward the living room ". . . did you listen to the conversation?"

"It was sort of hard," she said.

"Well, it was mostly people talking about other people. A little about places and things. Not much about ideas. And these are fairly intelligent people."

"What does that have to do with television?"

"I want it to be about ideas."

He was looking out across the yard, elbows propped on the top step, legs stretched out in front of him, but he could feel her eyes on him. He turned to her. "Do I sound incredibly Boy Scout?"

She smiled. "No." Then, "You were funny in there tonight. But that was mostly about people."

"Not really. You can entertain people and still be about ideas. Watergate? That wasn't about Nixon, it was about faith."

"Faith?"

"You get in your car in the morning and you put the key in the ignition and turn it and you have faith that the car will start. You elect a president and you have some faith that he won't try to steal the country from you. Make fun of Nixon and you show people how ridiculous he is, and it's not far from that to showing how he broke faith. Ideas don't have to be boring. It depends on what you do with them."

"If you make fun of Nixon on television, even now that he's gone, a lot of people get . . ."

"Pissed off."

"I really don't like that word."

"Sorry. They get upset."

"Yes."

"Disturbed."

"Yes."

"Well, television ought to disturb people sometimes. Television's too damned timid."

She smiled. "And you're going to change all that."

He returned the smile. "Maybe you're right. Maybe I ought to own NBC."

Then there was a noise at their backs and he turned to see Morris lurching through the door with the Igloo cooler in his arms. "Goddamn Fats Domino," he said. Then he looked down at Will and Clarice there on the steps. "Son, are you trying to snake my date?"

"Yes," Will said matter-of-factly, "I sure am."

———

HE CALLED MORRIS FROM the radio station Sunday night. "I'm in love," he said.

"I told you, she's out of your league," Morris said.

"I don't think so. I can offer her things you can't."

"Such as?"

"NBC."

Morris grumbled, but he finally gave Will the number.

She was alone in her room. Her roommate was engaged and out with her fiancé for the evening. They talked while the records were on and then she listened to the radio while he ad-libbed ads for bookstores and coffee shops and introduced the next number. Four hours later, toward the end of his shift, he said, "Well, we can just keep talking on the phone or I can ask you for a date."

"Yes, you could."

"Friday?"

"The farmhouse?"

"No. I don't think so."

He picked her up at Duke and they went to dinner and a movie. He kissed her good night and they held the kiss for a good long while, not anywhere near the usual first-date good-night kiss. On Saturday night he borrowed the apartment of a friend who had gone home for the weekend. He put some Coltrane on the stereo and made whiskey sours. And sometime not long after midnight they made love.

———

WILL MOVED OUT of the farmhouse and into another apartment, this one sublet from another friend who had come down with mononucleosis and had gone home to Tarboro to recuperate. The farmhouse was no place for a nice girl. And Clarice Palmer was, despite the complete abandon with which she gave herself to him, the nicest girl he had ever met.

They were both giddy with their discovery of what they could do to and with each other. Sex seemed almost a thing apart from both, in which they each came as a pilgrim, worshiping at the shrine of it and receiving its blessing and benediction. There is this *thing,* and there are our things, and we engage our *things* in this *thing* and our *things* disappear into this *thing* and . . . He tried to articulate it. She told him to shut up and just do it. She had, he discovered, despite her abiding air of vulnerability, a good sense of herself and a way of saying something quite forcefully when she made up her mind. He was intrigued.

Yes, she was the nicest of girls, in the old-fashioned sense of the word, from the finest of Greensboro families, in the old-fashioned sense of the word. Morris told him a good deal about her. President of the Kappa Kappa Gammas at Duke. A former Greensboro debutante. Recipient of the DAR Good Citizenship Award. Presbyterian. And she had come to him as a virgin, Will was pretty sure of that. The stunning thing was not so much that she devoured sex, but that after twenty years of chastity in a strictly codified Presbyterian-Kappa-DAR-debutante world, she had so utterly and happily abandoned chastity *with him.* He felt quite rare.

Was it love? They were surely in love with each other's bodies, with curve and hollow and orifice and protuberance and with eruption and pyrotechnics. They might even be in love with each other. Everything was happening so fast, and so spectacularly, he gave little thought to love as anything more than what they were doing and saying to each other here and now. For one of the first times in a great long while, Will Baggett didn't feel as if he was on probation. He felt totally, unquestioningly, accepted by a magnificent young woman who was both beautiful and passionate. Morris was dead wrong. She wasn't out of his league at all, nor he out of hers. He asked no questions about why. He just gave himself to it completely. And if that, the complete giving, was love, or at least part of it, fine. Let it be love.

———

AT THE SAME TIME he was pursuing Clarice Palmer, he was, with graduation looming, pursuing a job.

There was an opening at the television station in New Bern, near the coast, for a "production assistant"—a camera-pushing, broom-wielding flunky. He sent resumes and letters of recommendation from faculty members, telephoned at least once a week. Virtually every other prospective graduate in the broadcast and film curriculum was after the same position. The job market was tight in local television and the competition for entry-level openings, even at bare-bones stations like New Bern where the facilities were primitive and the pay was minimal, was fierce. The station manager got weary of hearing from the horde of applicants and sent word back to Chapel Hill that anybody who contacted him directly would be automatically eliminated from consideration.

Will drove to New Bern on a Friday night in early April, went to the station, found the production supervisor, and offered to work on weekends without pay. "Just looking for experience," he said. Throughout April and May he made the trek, sleeping in his car in the station parking lot, operating a camera on the weekend news shows and doing odd jobs about the studio, returning to Raleigh in time for his Sunday evening shift at the radio station. Clarice complained about his absences, and he missed her terribly, but this was about the rest of his life. Maybe she was, too, but she wasn't a job, a way to make a living. Anyway, without a job, there could be no Clarice.

On a Sunday afternoon in mid-May, with graduation only two weeks away, he rounded a hallway corner into the front lobby and almost ran into the station manager, who glared at him and demanded, "Who are you?"

"Will Baggett."

"When did I hire you?"

"You haven't. Yet."

"You're one of those Chapel Hill pests."

"Yes sir."

The station manager looked him over with a sneer. "One lousy job opening that any idiot off the street could fill, and I've got half the Chapel Hill student body asking for it. What makes you so special?"

"I'm eager, ambitious, and terribly earnest. Sir."

"And why the hell do you need a college education to push a camera in a rinky-dink television station?"

"I don't," Will said. "But I'm gonna do something important in television someday. I've got to start somewhere. I'll give you two of the best years of my life, and then I'm out of here."

The station manager stared at him. *I am either a brash genius or a complete fool,* Will thought.

"Are you the doofus that's been working for free?"

"Yes sir."

The station manager stared for a moment longer. "Okay." He brushed past Will and headed for the front door.

"Does that mean I'm hired?"

"What the hell," the station manager said with a wave, and was gone. On Tuesday, Will got a formal job application in the mail. He would start full-time in New Bern as soon as he could finish his final exams. He wasn't planning to hang around for graduation. Why bother? Min had shown no interest in attending, and at the moment, he hadn't the foggiest idea where Wingfoot was living. The last Will had heard, he was at Hilton Head Island doing construction work. But that had been a year ago. Wingfoot remained elusive.

So, Will Baggett had a job. And now he would see about Clarice Palmer.

16 | ON A WEEKEND IN MID-MAY Clarice invited him to Greensboro to meet the Palmers. She hadn't said much about them, just that the family had been in Greensboro for several generations and that her father and brother were involved in some kind of business in which they handled money. It took about fifteen minutes from the time of his arrival for Will to understand that they were Old Greensboro, and wore the title and aura with an air of carefully cultivated grace. Clarice's mother, Consuela, nonchalantly dropped nuggets of Palmer bona fides into the introductory conversation. Palmer ancestors had been among the founders of Greensboro Country Club, where they would be lunching on Sunday after church at First Presbyterian. Their home, a sprawling two-story cedar-and-stone, was at the heart of Irving Park, Greensboro's most prestigious neighborhood. Politically, they were conservative Democrats who had no truck with activists, social engineers or professional do-gooders.

As the weekend wore on, Will observed that Sidney and Consuela moved and spoke with exaggerated ease and seemed to go to great lengths to cultivate an air of not having to try hard at anything they did or were. The mantle of gentility appeared tailor-made for their shoulders. Greensboro Palmers, Will surmised, might work like the dickens to maintain their status—financial, social, political. But you'd never see one of them sweat.

Consuela (her mother had had a weakness for Spanish novelists, she said) reminded Will a bit of Aunt Margaret, who had seemed more Baggett than the Baggetts, though Consuela was less obvious about the status she had attained by marriage. Consuela was Old Greensboro in her own right, she made clear. Will caught the underlying message: Old Greensboro girls married Old Greensboro boys. *Morris was right,* Will thought. *I am indeed out of my*

*league. But to hell with it. I am damned determined not to be on proba-
tion here, not even for the weekend.*

Clarice's older siblings lived in Greensboro—brother Donald and
his wife, Pookie; sister Fern (two years out of Sophie Newcomb,
dabbling in art, waiting for a suitable match with one of Old
Greensboro's eligible young men)—but they didn't make an
appearance during the weekend, nor were they included in Sunday
lunch at the country club. That would have made it, Will suspected,
too much of an occasion.

The table Sidney had reserved was off to one side of the dining
room, next to double French doors that looked out on the practice
putting green. It was a spectacular day. Dogwood and azaleas were
in full bloom across the club grounds, their aromas drifting in to
mingle with the scents and muted voices of their fellow diners,
dressed and coiffed and powdered in Sunday best. The Palmers
seemed as essential a part of Greensboro Country Club as the paneled walls and damask drapes and Oriental rugs. Will, though
wearing a new suit and tie, though he felt fairly confident that he
was using the silverware correctly, was on edge. Probation, no. But
he still wanted to make a decent, or at least not indecent, impression
on these people. He had labored for twenty-four hours to maintain
an air of casual cheer and good manners without seeming to toady
to the Palmers. Sidney had been watchful and distant, peering at
Will occasionally over the top of whatever issue of the *Wall Street
Journal* he happened to be reading at the moment. The weekends,
he said, were when he caught up on his *Journals*.

Will knew, of course, that he was being measured, as any man
would measure a young buck who panted after his daughter. But
Consuela had obviously decided to make no great fuss over this particular young buck. Her air was lighthearted, as if Will were some
distant cousin's boy who had popped in for the weekend and would
vanish into family obscurity when it was over. She had asked only
the most cursory questions about his background and none about

his breeding. "I'm from the Wilmington area," he said. It seemed to be quite enough for Consuela. Everything about her said, *This is nothing of consequence.* Ah, but it was. And if Will needed anything to remind him that it was something of consequence, it was the wrenching effort he and Clarice had made in trying to keep their hands off each other, at least in the presence of the elder Palmers.

So here was Will, at lunch with the Greensboro Palmers on a spectacular spring Sunday in the elegant dining room of the Greensboro Country Club, his beloved sitting across the table from him, her stockinged foot rubbing lightly against his trousered thigh, his erection threatening to make him faint into his soup. At any moment, he half expected Sidney Palmer to lean over to him and say, quite evenly, "Young man, that faint line of perspiration on your upper lip gives you the look of someone who might be diddling my daughter."

Instead, Sidney Palmer said something else. "Are you a golfer, Will?"

"Hah! Huh?" He dropped his spoon with a clatter and turned to stare, not at Sidney, but at Consuela, sitting at the end of the table to his left. Gay, lighthearted Consuela, clad in floral print—sufficient for a Presbyterian Sunday, but nothing so dressy as to suggest there was anything remotely serious about this young man with whom the Palmers were sharing lunch. "Sorry," Will said. He made to pick up his spoon, but thought better of it. A man in social peril with a hard-on shouldn't try to eat soup. Clarice's foot slid another inch toward his crotch. "A golfer!" Will cried, his voice a couple of octaves north of normal. "No! I'm not a golfer."

Silence settled over the table. Will stole a glance at Clarice, who gave him a quick wink. A waiter approached with the main course, the centerpiece of which was a thick slab of prime rib.

At the other end of the table, Sidney Palmer suddenly roused himself. "Speaking of golf . . ."

"Yes dear." Consuela smiled at him.

"There was a Baggett fellow here at the club some years ago," he said.

"Clint Baggett," Consuela said. "The oil distributor."

"No, that wasn't his name. And he certainly wasn't into oil. This fellow was a hustler. Showed up one weekend and damn near cleaned out a couple of the members playing five-hundred-dollar nassaus. He left just ahead of the sheriff. I was the one who called the sheriff."

Will wasn't paying much attention. He stared at the prime rib on the plate in front of him, pink in the middle, oozing fragrant juices. His erection ratcheted up another notch. It was becoming painful.

"Oh, that one," Consuela nodded. "I remember Maude Fletcher talking about him. Right handsome, Maude said. But," she added quickly, "not the kind you'd want . . . Talbert . . . Tolbert . . ."

"Taylor. No, Tyler. Tyler Baggett."

Will's head jerked up.

"Killed in a plane crash, as I remember," Sidney said. "Flying drunk, probably."

Will stared at Sidney. "No, he wasn't drunk. It was the exhaust system. They all passed out and the plane kept flying."

Sidney stared back and his face drained of color. "Tyler Baggett . . ."

"My father," Will said. Clarice withdrew her foot. The steel thing in his lap melted into limp noodle.

From the other end of the table: "Oh my God." Gay, lighthearted Consuela looked stricken, as if a pigeon had dive-bombed her gazpacho.

Will looked across at Clarice. Her lips were pursed, her brow furrowed. *What's going on here? Where did all this come from?* He had told her little of his background, only that his parents had been killed in a plane crash when he was thirteen and he had been raised by a cousin. In truth, they hadn't really talked about much at all, what with all their groping and entering and ecstasy. And it shouldn't matter, he thought now. None of it. But obviously, it did.

Something akin to grief settled over the table. They were all witnesses at the scene of a bad wreck. And not just any wreck.

Something both horrid and distasteful, like an overturned chicken truck, all feathers and runny doo-doo. Sidney and Consuela uttered barely a word for the rest of the meal, and precious few as they rode back to the house in Sidney's Mercedes.

When he descended the stairs with his suitcase, Clarice was emerging from the study, closing the door behind her. They stopped in the front hallway, just looking at each other. Her hand went to her hair. She tugged, swept it back over her ear, tugged again. "I'm . . . I'm going back to school later."

"Your car's there," Will said. He had planned to drop her off at Duke, then pack his car in Chapel Hill and drive on to New Bern. He started work in the morning.

"Daddy will take me. I've got some things to do here."

"Clarice . . ."

She kissed him, but it was just a light kiss, on the cheek. "It's okay, Will. Let me handle this."

———

HE CALLED HER ROOM at Duke, where final exams were still under way, on Wednesday. She was out, studying in the library, her room-mate said. He left his new number in New Bern.

She finally called on Saturday night. She was crying. It took him a minute or so to get her calmed down enough to understand her. And then she said, "I can't marry you, Will."

Time seemed to stop. He had no idea how long he held the phone, listening to her sobs, feeling physically ill and humiliated and angry and trying to figure out who to blame: Tyler Baggett? The snotty Greensboro Palmers? Clarice? Himself?

Finally he said, "Who said anything about marrying?" His voice was hard and cold, floating up from the wretched icy pit of his heart.

"Will, please, try to understand . . ."

He hung up. Then he collapsed against the wall next to the phone and let his feet slide out from under him until he hunkered there, back to the wall, in utter desolation. "Goddamn 'em!" he cried out. "Goddamn 'em all." But there were no tears. He wasn't about to give them that satisfaction.

———

THERE WAS THE JOB, and he immersed himself in it. He learned all he could about studio production and pestered the rest of the staff with questions about newsgathering, advertising sales, promotion, station management. He had a timetable, a plan. Two years in New Bern, as he had promised the station manager, learning as much as he could about the basics of TV station operation. Then a larger market—maybe something like Charlotte or Des Moines or even a place as big as Miami or Chicago. And then a network job, working his way up the ladder to the seat of power. He wanted to run things, to have his hand on the throttle where he could make a difference.

At midsummer, though, something happened that altered his course. An opportunity fell at his feet in the form of Grady Lee Potts.

Grady Lee was the weathercaster—a portly, balding man with bad breath and a terrible temper who had been a fixture in New Bern television from the day the station went on the air. In a station that small, he performed a variety of duties ranging from weathercasting to hosting an afternoon kids' cartoon show dressed as Truffles the Clown, all done with ill humor that he concealed from the audience but spewed generously over the young men and women of the production crew. He suffered terribly from heartburn and popped Rolaids like candy. The crew members referred to him fondly as "Acid Ass."

One sultry night shortly after eleven, as Grady Lee was delivering the weather, delineating the sweeping line of an occluded front on the map with a magic marker, he stopped suddenly, lowered his arm, and turned very slowly to Will, who was serving that evening as floor manager—giving time cues and indicating which camera was taking a shot at any particular moment. Grady Lee's mouth curled into what appeared to be the beginning of a snarl. Will's stomach lurched. *Oh God, what have I done now?* Then Grady Lee's eyes rolled back in his head and his legs buckled and he pitched face-forward, out of the camera shot. The lapel microphone he was wearing picked up the WHUMP as he smacked into the floor, his head bouncing a couple of times on the linoleum, blood spurting from his nose and mouth.

There was stunned silence for a long moment. "Holy shit," one of the cameramen said through his intercom headset.

"What the hell's going on out there?" the director barked into their ears from the control room.

"Want me to get a shot of him?" the cameraman asked.

"No," Will said calmly. "I think the sonofabitch just died. Go to commercial."

While commercials played, Gordon, the news anchor, bustled over as Will and the other crew members knelt over Grady Lee. Will pressed a finger against Grady Lee's neck, probing for a pulse. "Yep," Will said, "dead as a doornail."

"What're we gonna do?"

They looked at Gordon. "I don't know a damn thing about weather," he protested.

"What the hell," Will said with a shrug. With a grunt, he rolled Grady Lee over, unclipped the microphone from his lapel, and clipped it onto the front of his own shirt. He pried the magic marker from Grady Lee's hand, then stood and faced the camera. He took off his headset and handed it to the cameraman. "I'm doing the weather," he announced. And he did, standing over Grady Lee Potts's body, finishing the drawing of the occluded front and pointing out to an astonished audience at home that this particular weather feature would mean intermittent showers for Massachusetts and Rhode Island, but not a darn thing for the good people of New Bern, North Carolina, who could expect continued hot and muggy weather because of a large and stubborn Bermuda high pressure area hanging around in the Atlantic.

As Will rambled on, essentially repeating what Grady Lee Potts had told the audience at six o'clock (the weather rarely changed from early to late evening this time of year anyway), he felt a rush of something almost sexual—a kind of raw power that began some-where down very deep in him and flowed freely from his mouth and through the magic marker onto the weather map. He smiled into the camera. *Listen up out there. I've got something you need.* And, it struck him as he finished and the red light on top of the camera winked off, *You've got something I need.* The studio burst into applause. Gordon rushed over and pounded him on the back. Outside the studio building, he could hear the faint sound of the ambulance approaching, coming to tote old Grady Lee away. It was as fine a sound as Will Baggett had heard in a long time.

"Who the hell do you think you are?" the station manager bellowed into the telephone after the newscast was over.

"Your new weatherman," Will said. "I work cheap, and as you saw on the air, I can handle it."

"Do you own a suit?"

"One."

"Well, get another one. Dark blue, single-breasted. Five blue shirts, five ties. Charge 'em to the station. Three hundred bucks max. And get a haircut that doesn't look like your wife did it."

"I don't have a wife," Will said.

"Try not to," the station manager said gruffly, and hung up.

————

HE DIDN'T SEE HER at first. She was standing in the shadows next to the stairway as he started up toward his second-floor apartment.

"Will," she said softly.

He stopped, hand on the railing, heart in his throat. She moved from the shadows and touched his hand. For a moment, that was all. He understood in a flash of revelation that this, as much as the still form of Grady Lee Potts on the studio floor just an hour ago, was the rest of his life. She waited. She waited for *him*. She had come for him, despite everything, and she was waiting. He hadn't had anyone wait on him like this since he was thirteen years old. He turned his hand over so that their palms were together and gripped hers. And then he took her in his arms and things began to break loose inside him and the humiliation and the pain and the anger went away. Well, most of it.

———

THEY DROVE TO NAGS HEAD on Sunday afternoon. Her parents were there, midway in a two-week stay at their cottage. They found Sidney and Consuela on the beach, perched in sand chairs under an umbrella. Consuela was absorbed in a novel. Sidney was reading a *Wall Street Journal,* the corners of which fluttered in the sea breeze. A stack of *Journals* was beside him in the sand. He was the first to look up, and then he said something quietly to Consuela and she very, very slowly closed the book with her finger keeping her place and turned to Will and Clarice as they reached the umbrellas. They stopped a couple of yards away and stood there, holding hands. Consuela looked as if she couldn't decide whether to be stricken or to do her gay, lighthearted, this-is-of-no-consequence routine.

Clarice didn't give her time to decide. "Well, what's it going to be?"

Sidney cut a quick glance at Consuela, who didn't return it. Will felt the hair on the back of his neck prickle. This thing, this quite obvious struggle of wills, was between the two women, and he and Sidney were just bystanders. My God, she was magnificent. For all her air of vulnerability, the smooth curve and soft sheen and seeming pliability of her, she had incredible backbone, or at least she did here and now. He understood completely what was at stake. She was fighting for him, she was defying not just her parents, but all of Old Greensboro. And Consuela Palmer knew it.

"A good old-fashioned Greensboro wedding?" Clarice asked. "At least six bridesmaids and a five-tiered cake? Or . . ." a long pause ". . . shall we elope?"

Consuela touched her chin delicately with the finger that had been marking her place in the book, which fell to the sand. "Clarice, can't we discuss this later?"

"No, Mother," Clarice said, "we can't. If a wedding is just too much for you, Will and I can drive to South Carolina tonight and get married. And then"—she smiled—"you can have a small reception for us later at the club. A chance for a few of your friends to meet my new husband." She tightened her grip on Will's hand. He felt a great rush of love for her.

And then she said, "Will and I are sleeping together. My idea, not his."

Sidney made a small move, hands tightening on the armrests of his chair, and Will thought that he might suddenly heave himself up and chase Will down the beach, scattering gulls and kicking up divots of hard sand at water's edge. But he didn't. The tightening of hands and an almost imperceptible tightening of jaw, that was all. Then his hands relaxed. Consuela gave a tiny shudder. They had both taken the blow full-on and weathered it. It occurred to Will that it was the supreme test of all that it meant to be a Greensboro Palmer. They passed magnificently.

"Are you . . ." Consuela made a little fluttering motion with her hand.

"No," Clarice and Will answered at once.

"Well, that's nice."

There was a long silence, undergirded by the splash of surf and the cry of birds. They were, the four of them, alone on the beach.

Consuela took a breath. "A wedding would be just fine," she said easily. She turned to Sidney. "Don't you think?"

Sidney cleared his throat, picked up one of the unread *Journal*s, put it back down in the sand.

Clarice looked to Will. His turn. "October?" he said without really knowing why.

"How about November," Consuela suggested. "So many people spend October in the mountains. Leaf season, you know."

"Or New England," Sidney added. "Some go to New England."

"November." Will nodded. "That sounds like a good month. When everybody's back from the mountains and New England."

Sidney and Consuela rose now, together, as if cued by some offstage manager. Sidney stuck out his hand and Will took it. Sidney's grip was quick but firm. So was Consuela's hug. Will tried to summon a sense of triumph. Instead, he just felt a flood of relief.

————

THE WEDDING WAS an Old Greensboro production — stylish, graceful and Presbyterian, without a hint of the kind of ostentation you would have expected had the Palmers been "new money." Consuela engineered every aspect and Clarice gave her mother free rein — penance, perhaps. The crowd was mostly from Greensboro. Will was joined by a few of his Chapel Hill classmates. And Min and Wingfoot.

Will was a little nervous about Min, but she arrived in Greensboro in good spirits, and after she had adroitly dropped a few tidbits of Cape Fear Baggett family history, she and Consuela got on well. Consuela helped with arrangements for the after-rehearsal party at the country club, which Min was to host as Will's next-of-kin. Min pronounced Clarice pretty but a bit thin. Clarice just smiled.

Min played the gracious hostess at the after-rehearsal affair. She rose to represent the Baggett family and welcome the guests, which she did quite pleasantly. But then she launched into a lengthy account of her one previous visit to Greensboro when she was eight years old. Her parents had brought her and Wingfoot to the city on a business trip. It was summer, and frightfully hot. They stayed in a rather fancy downtown hotel where children were sternly admonished by hotel staff not to run in the halls. "In fact," she said, "they made it quite clear they didn't like children at all. I felt like some sort of foreigner just off the boat." At dinner in the hotel dining room, she had ordered seafood Newburg and had been stricken during the night with food poisoning. A doctor was summoned. The hotel management apologized profusely, paid for the doctor, and offered an extra night of lodging at no cost. The Baggetts refused and decamped back to Brunswick County the next day with Min, still weak and disoriented, swathed in blankets in the back seat of the car.

Min recounted the entire business with what seemed light-hearted good cheer. But Will knew better. He knew Min, who obviously had taken stock of the Greensboro crowd—Palmers and all—and found them not quite as bona fide as they might think they were. Not, in short, as bona fide as Baggetts. When Min finished and sat down, Clarice leaned over to Will and whispered, "I wonder what Daddy's going to say to top that?"

Daddy Palmer had, to his credit, been exceedingly gracious. "Miz Baggett," he said with a smile, "I hope your future visits to Greensboro are more like this one than the first." The pleasantly blank look on Min's face said she didn't expect to be making any future visits to Greensboro.

Morris deLesseps was his best man. He would have asked Wingfoot, but he didn't know quite how to locate him, and he didn't care to broach that subject with Min. So he enlisted Morris and invited several other Chapel Hill classmates to be groomsmen. Morris and the rest of the Chapel Hill bunch, to a man, got stinking drunk at the after-rehearsal party and afterward when they took Will out for a bachelor evening. He slipped away early. Morris and the rest turned up for the wedding the next afternoon pale but vertical and, observing the old-line Greensboro gentry who filled the church, were on their best behavior except for the giant pink foam rubber penis Morris stashed in the back seat of the honeymoon car.

To his surprise, Wingfoot showed up. When Will and Morris entered the First Presbyterian sanctuary from a side door, there sat Wingfoot in a next-to-front pew with Min. He was neatly dressed in a blue suit and burgundy tie, shaven and shorn. Will thought he looked quite handsome, and apparently so did a couple of unattached young ladies, who gravitated toward him at the reception afterward.

Will finally cornered him in a hallway of the country club. "Thanks," he said. "For coming."

"Why wouldn't I?"

"Well, Wingfoot, I don't rightly know how you feel about things these days. We haven't had a conversation worthy of the name in several years. How are you?"

"I'm making it," Wingfoot said. "In fact, I've moved back home."

"With Min? She didn't mention it."

"No, I suppose not."

"Are you two getting along?"

"Mostly."

"Is Min all right? Last time I was over there she seemed . . . well, a little odd."

"As in . . ."

"I don't know. Distant. Moody."

"Well, that's Min. I wouldn't worry about it. Carry on with your life, Wilbur. That's a helluva good looking woman you've got there. Can you handle her?"

Will smiled. "I'm working on it." He hesitated. "Wingfoot, I should have . . ."

"No you shouldn't," Wingfoot interrupted. "Look, you went off to school and made your own way, Wilbur. Hell, I understand you aren't even Wilbur any more. Will, is that right?"

"Yeah."

"Everybody has to hitch up his own britches and tote his own load in this world . . . Will. You've done that so far. Keep doing it."

The Palmers *mater* and *pater* floated through the entire business on a cloud of elegant, reserved ease. Was it breeding or Valium? Will caught a final glimpse of them, standing at the top of the front steps of the country club, waving demurely as he and Clarice drove away in her car, a new Buick that had been a graduation gift from Sidney and Consuela. It would hardly have done to use Will's ancient Plymouth, long in the tooth when he bought it four years earlier, now rust-riven and mechanically uncertain. It would have scandalized the Greensboro Country Club crowd. So he agreed to use Clarice's car for the honeymoon, but declined Sidney's offer of a trip to Bermuda. Instead, they would spend a week at the Palmers' cottage at Nags Head. That much, he could afford himself. A new husband, he told Sidney, had to learn to pay his own way. He even offered to rent the cottage, but Sidney wouldn't hear of it.

The Palmers were the subject of their first serious argument, and it came on the second day of the honeymoon. Clarice was attempting hamburgers in the cottage kitchen. Will was in the den, leafing through an old issue of *Southern Living*. "Shit!" he heard from the kitchen. He flew to her rescue.

She was at the stove, wearing nothing but an apron. He was wearing nothing at all and the sight of her incredible behind peeking out from the open rear of the apron brought him instantly to attention, even though they had made vigorous love only an hour earlier. He crossed the kitchen and cupped her globes with his hands.

"Don't do that!" she barked.

He removed his hands. "What's wrong, love?" Then he peeked over her shoulder and saw what was wrong. She had the grease far too hot and it was splattering as the hamburger patties sizzled in the frying pan, already quite overcooked and curling at the edges. "Grease on your tit?" he inquired, and instantly regretted it as she turned, full of fury, brandishing a spatula. He backed away a couple of steps.

"We could have been in Bermuda!" she cried.

His erection melted. "No," he said evenly, "we couldn't have been in Bermuda. We don't have enough money to go to Bermuda."

"Just because you've got my parents stuck in your craw!"

"Do we have to talk about this right now?"

"Yes."

"Could you turn off the stove first? I don't want you getting grease splatters on that incredible derriere of yours. It would break my heart."

She turned back to the stove with a jerk, grabbed a pot holder, picked up the frying pan, marched to the back door, opened it, flung frying pan and contents into the yard, and turned back to him. He had never seen her truly angry before. It was a Clarice he didn't know. "Now," she said firmly.

He drew a deep breath. "All right. Clarice, I have been an independent sonofabitch for a long time. I intend to remain that way. I will take care of you, provide for you, cherish you, love you until I draw my last breath. I will do it on my own. So help me God."

"You don't like my parents," she accused.

"Not yet. But I'm trying. I will continue to try. I will come to like your parents in good time."

"But you don't like them now."

"What do you expect, Clarice? They take me to lunch at the Greensboro Country Club, where it's revealed that my father was a notorious golf hustler who relieved some of their friends of a considerable amount of money, and the look of horror on their faces would make you think I'd pissed on the tablecloth."

"You don't have to be crass about it."

"And then they told you you couldn't marry me because I was . . . well, what, tainted?"

"You could have told me about your . . . history," she said.

"I don't have a history, Clarice. Not in the way you and your family think of a history. I've invented myself."

"Your family has all sorts of history. Even if they are oddball."

"That has nothing to do with me."

"You think they're snobs, don't you."

"I think they have an incredible daughter with whom I'm deeply and passionately in love," he said softly.

He made a move toward her, but she turned away and bolted from the room. He heard her steps thundering up the stairs, and a minute or so later, back down again. The screen door at the front of the house slammed. Then there was silence.

He gave her a few minutes, then followed her to the beach. She was huddled on the sand, arms tightly around her drawn-up legs, chin resting on her knees, staring out at the Atlantic. She was wearing shorts and a halter top now. He had pulled on a pair of

Bermudas. He eased himself down onto the sand beside her and they sat there for a long time. Finally he said, "Clarice, I love you."

"I chose you," she said quietly. "I fought for you."

"I know you did. And that means you love me, too."

"They've accepted you because I chose you. They want what makes me happy. Maybe they didn't like the idea at first, but they've gotten over it. And now you've got to get over resenting them."

"I will. Give it some time. That's all it needs, Clarice. Some time."

He reached for her hand. She gave it to him. He kissed her. They lay back on the sand entwined. Finally he said, "Come back to the house and put on that apron again."

17 | CLARICE GOT A JOB TEACHING first grade at the New Bern elementary school, but by the middle of their second year of marriage she was pregnant, so she quit teaching and stayed home to have Palmer. Home was a cramped efficiency apartment, and there wasn't much money for anything extra, but they looked back on it later as a good time, a time of adjusting and settling into the habits of marriage and parenthood. Clarice learned to cook. Will became something of a local celebrity. People recognized him on the street.

Clarice insisted on having Palmer delivered by the family's doctor back in Greensboro, but Will sped back to New Bern with photos which he shared with his audience. Clarice and the baby stayed in Greensboro for three weeks, and by the time they were ready to return to New Bern, Will had moved everything to a two-bedroom apartment.

They stayed in New Bern for two more years — first, because Will had promised the station manager not to run off at the first opportunity for a job in a larger market. Then, too, he was learning a lot. In a small station you had a chance to do just about everything. He took over the kids' cartoon show (wearing a cowboy outfit instead of a clown suit), emceed bicycle rodeos and beauty contests, and volunteered to answer the station's viewer mail. He critiqued his weathercast every day, studying videotape to see what worked and what didn't, honing his on-air skills. New Bern was an apprenticeship. When the right opening came up somewhere else, he would be ready. All in good time.

Will also did what he had promised Clarice on the beach at Nags Head: he tried to like the Palmers. It was an uphill struggle, a work in progress. The problem wasn't that they treated him badly. Quite the opposite. They were pleasant, even cheerful, when he was around. They were ecstatic about the arrival of the baby, their first grandchild — well, as ecstatic as the Palmers ever allowed themselves to be. But there was always an air of studied reserve about them. They measured Will because they measured everybody. He could never escape the feeling of being on probation.

Will came to realize that they were not snobs. To be a snob, you had to consider the existence of people who were unlike yourself. Usually, they didn't. If forced to, as in Will's case, they simply pretended that you were enough like them to pass muster. But Will could never quite feel part of them. He was more like a small boy with his face pressed against the plate glass of a toy store, examining merchandise that was beyond not only his means, but also his understanding. The Palmers seemed to know exactly who they were. They were perfectly comfortable in their circumspect, steady, old-line lives. They were at peace with their history and their place. More than at peace, in fact. They thought it was damned splendid.

It didn't help that the Palmers made it clear they considered New

Bern an outpost of civilization, no matter that it had a rich and hallowed history, including the graceful and sturdy Tryon Palace, where a long-ago colonial governor had resided. No, the Palmers saw Greensboro as the center of the universe and their daughter as an exile. Clarice began to spend more and more time in Greensboro and, in the summers, with the Palmers at Nags Head. Will tried not to resent it, or at least not to show his resentment. Still, he felt an outsider, looking on from afar as the Greensboro Palmers meddled freely in each other's business and spoke in an intimately familiar shorthand that encompassed everything in their mutual past and their shared notion of the way things were.

The younger generation of Palmers were a mixed lot. Donald was pleasant enough, and his wife, Pookie, who had come from good Greensboro stock, occasionally drank a bit much and told bawdy jokes outside the presence of the elders. Fern had—a year or so after Will and Clarice's wedding—married a doctor named Beau, an effeminate-acting prick who ran with the runny-Brie-and-dry-chablis crowd and wore bow ties as if they were the Legion of Merit. To Clarice (who didn't like him much either), Will referred to Beau as "Doc Savage."

Will decided early on not to try to woo the Palmer family. They were, he sensed, un-wooable. He could be *with* them but never quite *of* them, but then he really didn't care to be. As long as they didn't meddle in his life, he would be okay. He might not ever really like them, but they could accommodate each other. So when he was around Sidney and Consuela and the rest of them, he tried to make himself at ease. And he avoided the subject of golf. He kissed no fanny, but he also made no waves.

———

WILL'S CONTACT WITH HIS former life on the Cape Fear River became almost cursory. He had taken Clarice to Baggett House several weeks after they settled in New Bern. It had not gone well. For one thing, the house was beginning to show signs of decay. Will hadn't paid much attention before, during the years when he had visited from college. But now he saw that it was in need of paint and repair. Not a good first impression for a girl from Irving Park.

Min worked until late Saturday evening at the store, had little to say at dinner that evening, and left early the next morning. Business in Wilmington, she said. Will showed Clarice the grounds and Barney the alligator, and after that, there didn't seem to be much to do. They left just after lunch on Sunday. Min hadn't returned.

He tried again when Palmer was two. They arrived late on Saturday afternoon and Will was relieved to learn that Min had no pressing business on tap for Sunday. They were up early and Min hauled some ancient toys down from the attic for Palmer, setting him up under the live oak tree while she sat nearby in a lawn chair reading *Retail Monthly* magazine. Will and Clarice were enjoying an especially vigorous intimate moment in his old upstairs bedroom when they heard Palmer's screams. They grabbed dressing gowns and bolted for the yard to find that Palmer had wandered away from the toys and stumbled into a patch of sandspurs.

Clarice snatched him up, glaring at Min furiously. "I thought you were watching him!"

"Well my goodness, it's just a few sandspurs," she retorted.

And then they engaged in a heated argument about the best way to treat sandspur wounds. Clarice marched off to the house with Palmer in her arms, and when Will found them upstairs, she had him calmed down and was packing their suitcases. "We're going home."

"Clarice, for gosh sakes . . ."

"And don't you"—she whirled on him with pointed finger—"say it's just a few sandspurs!"

"Okay. Let's go."

He said a hasty goodbye to Min, who didn't seem much perturbed by their departure. When they pulled away, she was still sitting under the live oak reading *Retail Monthly.*

And Wingfoot? He turned up once at the New Bern TV station just as Will was getting ready to go on the air with his late-evening weathercast. He parked Wingfoot on a stool in a corner of the studio, and when he was finished, they went for a beer at a local tavern that stayed open late. He offered the couch for the night, but Wingfoot was on his way to Richmond. A new job, he said, doing construction.

It was the week after the disastrous trip to Baggett House and Will recounted it to Wingfoot. "Min's getting peculiar," he said. "I got the impression she didn't care whether we came or went."

"Living alone will do that to you," Wingfoot said.

"And the house looks like . . . well, Clarice said, a tumor."

"If I were you, I wouldn't mention it to Min. She's pretty touchy about the house."

"How do you think I oughta handle Min, Wingfoot?"

"Carefully. That's my advice."

Wingfoot looked good, he thought. He was getting some new wrinkles around his eyes, probably from being out in the sun a lot. He had spent the past several months crewing on a fishing boat out of Oriental. But he was rock solid and he looked as if he were easier with himself. The old intensity in his eyes had softened a bit.

"Are you okay?" Will asked.

"I'm vertical," Wingfoot said with a crooked smile. And then he was gone into the night.

———

IN THE FALL OF 1980 one of his former professors at Chapel Hill called to tell him that the longtime weatherman at Channel Seven in Raleigh was getting ready to announce his retirement. The competition for the job would be fierce, so if Will was interested, he should get cracking.

Will hung up and called Clarice. "What would you think about Raleigh?"

"Well, it's not New Bern. That says a lot for it."

"I don't know if I can get the job."

"Of course you can," she said. "You're good, Will. You're ready. They'd be lucky to have you in Raleigh."

"And you'd like being closer to home."

"Of course."

He went straight to the New Bern station manager. "I'm going after the weather job at Channel Seven in Raleigh."

The station manager said, "Well, I knew I couldn't keep you. Let me know what I can do to help."

"Give me tomorrow off."

"Done."

By early afternoon the next day he was standing in front of Old Man Simpson's desk at Channel Seven, wearing his best suit and holding a videotape of his weathercast. Old Man Simpson took the videotape and added it to a pile on the credenza behind the desk, then showed Will to the sofa in the big corner office, just under the painting of long-ago governor Zebulon Baird Vance. "All right, Will," he said, "tell me why you think I should hire you."

"I'm ready. I'll do you a good job. I'll work like the dickens."

Simpson hiked one long leg over the other and gave Will a long look. "Charlie Tuttle's been doing our weather for twenty-five years. He's better known in Raleigh than the governor. You young folks in the business these days . . . you've always got your eye on the next rung up the ladder. I'm not interested in Channel Seven being a way station."

"Mister Simpson, I'll be honest with you. I won't promise to be here as long as Charlie Tuttle. But I don't have my eye on the next rung up the ladder. I've got a wife and an eighteen-month-old son and I'm not interested in bouncing all over the country with 'em. Hire me, and we'll see if we like each other."

Simpson looked over at the pile of videotapes on the credenza. "Lots of talented people, experienced people, want to be my weathercaster. This is a good station and Raleigh's a good place to live. We'll see. You'll get a fair shot, Will. Meantime, go back to New Bern and keep your mind on your work." He smiled. "And don't pester me like you did the station manager over there when you went after that job."

"Yes sir."

He heard not a word from Old Man Simpson for six weeks. Instead, he heard from Sidney Palmer. "I'd like to take you to lunch, Will."

"Well . . . sure."

"Carolina Country Club in Raleigh. Noon Saturday."

"What's this all about?" he asked Clarice when he had hung up the phone. "What's the agenda here?"

"Just go have lunch with Daddy," she said.

He drove to Raleigh Saturday morning, found the club, found Sidney waiting in the lobby. Sidney offered his hand. Will shook. Sidney had a nice, firm grip, for all his cool air of detachment. Will didn't ask how Sidney had arranged lunch at Carolina Country Club. He supposed people like Sidney had connections with people like himself just about everywhere. Hong Kong Country Club? Sidney could probably arrange lunch there, too.

"A drink?" Sidney asked when they were seated and a waiter hovered at the table. Will hesitated. "I'll have a scotch and soda," Sidney said.

All right, Sidney. Whatever the hell this is all about, let's just be us guys here. No baggage, huh? No Tyler Baggett, no deflowered daughter, no mismatched marriage. Just us guys. "Scotch sounds fine. On the rocks for me."

They made small talk over their drinks — Clarice, Palmer, beach living, prospects for the upcoming basketball seasons at Duke and Chapel Hill. Sidney was affable, almost expansive. Will tried to match his mood. They chewed over London along with their lunch. Sidney and Consuela had just returned from a two-week trip on which Consuela had, Sidney confided, acquired a rather hideous elephant-foot umbrella stand at the Saturday flea market along Portobello Road. "Sometimes we have to indulge our ladies," Sidney said with a conspiratorial smile.

Over coffee, he got right down to business. "I understand you're considering a move, Will."

"Yes, Sidney, I am."

"Raleigh's a good town. State government, the university, now the Research Triangle Park. A lot going for the place. We have friends who like living here a lot, people whose families go back generations. Old Raleigh people. They worry about the growth, all that sprawl out on the north side and the traffic and all. But all in all, a good town."

"You should be a spokesman for the Chamber of Commerce," Will said.

Sidney smiled. "But have you considered alternatives?"

"To what?"

"A job in Raleigh."

"I might not get the job in Raleigh. The owner at Channel Seven . . ."

"Barfield Simpson."

"Yes sir. He says I'll get a fair shot, but there's a lot of competition."

"So, if you don't get the job here?"

"Well, I won't stay in New Bern much longer. I'll start looking."

"But you want to stay close to . . . well, home."

"Not necessarily."

Sidney finished his coffee, wiped his mouth delicately, and tucked his napkin under the edge of his saucer. "Would you consider Greensboro?"

"I didn't know there was an opening in Greensboro."

"I mean . . . with the family business."

It took Will a good while to say anything at all. Finally he said, "I really don't know what the family business is, Sidney."

"We're investment bankers."

"Oh. I see."

"Are you familiar with investment banking?"

"Not really."

"It's really very interesting, I think. My father started the business some years ago. I came in when I finished Duke, and now there's Donald. We've been talking about bringing someone else along."

Will was thoroughly taken aback. But he had presence of mind enough to see what this was: a peace offering. More than that, a measure of acceptance. He would never be a Palmer, not in any sense of what that might mean, but here was Sidney saying that he could, if he wished, gain entrance to the inner sanctum, at least on a permanent visitor's pass. Sort of a second-tier Palmer. But did he want to be a second-tier Palmer? No, he didn't.

If there were only himself to consider, he would have told Sidney Palmer to stick investment banking up his rear end. But there was Clarice to think about. And his son. His relationship with his in-laws, or lack of one, was already a sore point, something around which he and Clarice treaded warily, something they kept shoved back in the recesses of their marital closet. He loved Clarice and she, despite her occasional streaks of rebelliousness, loved her parents. It was a dicey game they played. And handling this present business the wrong way would cause a ruckus he didn't even want to think about. So—how to decline the job without declining the peace offering?

"Sidney," he said, "I can't tell you how flattered I am. That's very generous, and more than that, it's kindhearted. But it wouldn't be fair to you and Donald—or to Clarice or anybody else in your family—for me to accept. I would be a disaster at investment banking. I have a hard time balancing a checkbook." He gave Sidney what he hoped was a self-deprecating smile. "My job is to be a good husband and father to Clarice and Palmer, and the best way I can do that is to stick with the business I'm in. It's not investment banking, but it's something I know how to do."

Sidney looked at him impassively for a long moment. Then he said, "I respect that, Will."

"I love your daughter, Sidney. I'll always take care of her and cherish her and protect her. I promise that."

"Consuela and I couldn't ask for more." He paused. "If you ever change your mind . . ."

Will couldn't, in his wildest imagination, believe he ever would.

He was braced for fireworks from Clarice when he got back to

New Bern, but she said only, "If that's what you think you need to do, Will." Odd, but he let it rest.

On Monday, he got another phone call. "Will, this is Barfield Simpson at Channel Seven. Could you get free from work and come talk to me again?"

By sundown Tuesday he was Channel Seven's new weatherman.

———

CLARICE WENT STRAIGHTAWAY TO Raleigh to look for a house while Will wrapped things up in New Bern. Consuela joined her and brought along a nanny to take care of Palmer while they toured.

By the weekend, Clarice had settled on what she wanted, and Consuela decamped back to Greensboro with Palmer and the nanny and left Clarice to deal with Will.

It was a two-story Cape Cod on LeGrand Avenue in the Cameron Park neighborhood, not far from downtown and the North Carolina State campus. A quiet and gracious street, lined on both sides with towering oaks and sidewalks. Will pulled into the driveway and they got out and stood there looking at it. "It has a nice yard," he said hopefully. But the only thing really nice about it was the size. It was shaded by two large maples between the house and the sidewalk and the undernourished grass was patchy, laced liberally with chickweed and dandelion. Whoever had planted the shrubbery years ago had started it out too close to the house and now it crowded against the brickwork of the foundation and sprawled, tired and leggy, toward the lawn, straining for light and space. The house and detached garage needed paint and Will could see signs of rot on some of the fascia board beneath the roofline. The roof itself was an ancient moss-encrusted slate thing.

The interior, if anything, was worse. The house was fifty years old and the floor plan was outdated. It had a nice-sized living room and a huge dining room, but the only thing that remotely resembled a den was a tiny room off the kitchen, barely large enough for a TV set and a couple of chairs. Closet space was miserly, the carpet was worn, and the furnace, Clarice admitted, was on its last legs. The kitchen had chipped metal countertops and cabinets and aging appliances. The fixtures in the bathrooms also looked original — huge ball-and-claw–footed tubs and pedestal lavatories.

They toured, Clarice expounding brightly on the great possibilities for the house — tear out a wall here, add a wall there, an updated kitchen, pull up the carpet and refinish the hardwood underneath, on and on. Will kept his mouth shut until they were back outside on the front walkway.

"Why?" he asked.

"Because it's what I want," she said without hesitation.

"Why?" he asked again.

She took in the street and neighborhood with a sweep of her hand. "It's a good neighborhood, Will. It's established. Not like those new places sprawling out up there in North Raleigh. It's a good place for Palmer to grow up. A nice yard, sidewalks for him to ride his tricycle. Parks, an elementary school nearby. Good neighbors."

"How do you know the neighbors are good?"

"Will," she said, "I wouldn't have even known about this place if a friend of Mama and Daddy's hadn't told us. It's not even on the market yet."

It was the first time he had noticed there wasn't a For Sale sign in the yard. "Mama and Daddy have friends here," he said. "I see."

"This is Old Raleigh, Will."

"Like Old Greensboro."

He stood there a moment longer, looking over house and grounds while she watched him. "How much?"

"A hundred twenty-five. It's a good price. Homes in this area are going for a lot more. Sure, it needs work, but there's nothing basic . . ."

"Good God, Clarice. We can't afford that. And all that work you're talking about inside . . . for crying out loud."

She shook her head and then marched back inside the house, leaving him there on the walk. He found her in the front hall, hand resting possessively on the stairway banister. "Okay, I see," he said. "Mama and Daddy."

"Just a loan, Will."

All right. Another moment of truth here, just like the one last Saturday at the country club with Sidney. I can get my bowels in an uproar over my in-laws interfering in my life, or I can keep peace and make my wife happy. And besides, I have other fish to fry.

"Just a loan," he said.

"That's all."

He crossed the hallway and took her in his arms and kissed her. She kissed him back and the kiss grew deeper and deeper until, almost before he realized what was happening, their clothing was in disarray and she was sprawled backward on the staircase and he was on her, in her, and she was crying out and he was crying out and . . . the house was theirs.

———

SO THEY OCCUPIED THE HOUSE and made it a home and seasons passed and they became as much a part of Old Raleigh as newcomers can become, more so than most. It was, as Clarice said, a good neighborhood. There were, as she said, nice neighbors. Palmer rode his tricycle and then his bicycle on the sidewalks. Clarice formed a book club. And Will Baggett threw his energies into becoming Raleigh's most popular TV weatherman.

Will got along with the Greensboro Palmers just fine. They visited Raleigh occasionally and Will and his family reciprocated, especially at Christmas and Easter. They spent summer vacation weeks at Nags Head. As Will's Raleigh career blossomed, he seemed to gain legitimacy. *Our son-in-law the celebrity.*

Clarice threw herself into updating the Raleigh house, aided by generous annual Christmas gifts from Sidney and Consuela (though Will refused to use any of that money to pay down the loan they had used to help buy the house). And she gravitated increasingly toward Greensboro, which was now only an hour and a half away. She called daily, visited often, maintained old friendships, even joined the Greensboro Junior League by special dispensation.

Will had put up no fuss when Clarice wanted to name their son Palmer, but it was unsettling to watch the way the Greensboro Palmers drew the boy into their realm. He visited for long stretches in the summer, in Greensboro and Nags Head. They immersed him in the rituals of their life: birthday parties, country club activities, ways of dressing and talking and conducting oneself. From his sixth birthday on, Palmer was at his grandfather's side at every Atlantic Coast Conference basketball tournament, to which Sidney had superb tickets through his Duke connections.

The effect of all of this on Palmer, Will thought, was to make him a snob. Unlike his grandparents, he *did* consider the existence of people unlike himself. Will made sure of that, mostly by insisting that Palmer attend public school. But when Palmer saw the real world and compared it with the one his grandparents created for him in Greensboro, he didn't like the real one very much.

All this was unsettling to Will, but he kept it mostly to himself. And the main reason he did was that he had a thorny issue of his own to deal with—the effect his job was having on his marriage.

"You're like a politician," Clarice said. "Always campaigning."

"Clarice, there's a part of me that belongs to all those people out there who watch me every night. They could watch somebody else. And new people move to Raleigh all the time. I have to woo 'em and win 'em. It goes with the territory."

"You overdo it, Will. Hanging around the malls all evening? Speaking to every five-member garden club in the viewing area? Why is there so much of you that belongs to them and not enough that belongs to us?"

"That's unfair."

"You're never here to help Palmer with his homework."

"But you are."

"And what if I'd like to go out somewhere myself at night?"

"You could always get a sitter."

"My God, Wilbur, Palmer is thirteen years old. I'm not going to embarrass him with a baby-sitter."

"Look, why don't you and Palmer meet me at the mall and we'll have dinner."

"And sit there while your public interrupts our meal and paws over you? It makes me feel like an . . ."

"Appendage."

"Yes."

Palmer took cues from his mother. "Are you coming to the band concert tomorrow night?" *Translation: I know you're not coming to the band concert because you have something better to do.*

"Son, I'm sorry, but I've got to make a speech to the Elks Club banquet. I didn't know the concert was tomorrow night. You have to tell me about these things in time for me to plan."

"Get on your schedule."

"Well, I didn't mean . . ."

Palmer would by habit shrug and walk away, leaving Will with the sour taste of guilt in his mouth.

One hard-and-fast rule Will had about his job: he didn't make weekend public appearances. Weekends were reserved for home — family and yard.

He spent a lot of time in the yard. For the first time in his life he had a piece of soil all his own and he made his mark on it.

He began with the front yard, plowing up the grass and ripping out most of the shrubbery. He seeded the lawn with a new variety of creeping fescue that grew well in shade and babied the tender shoots with water and fertilizer until they spread into a lush green carpet. He widened the shrubbery beds and installed new, low-growing plants — azalea and mahonia — and lined the beds with variegated liriope.

When he had the front pretty much the way he wanted, he started on the back, walling it in with holly and Leyland cypress and carpeting it with a tough stand of centipede grass that held up well under Palmer's childhood pounding. At the rear of the house he built a spacious deck of treated wood, doing all of the work himself from plans he got from *Southern Living* magazine. And when Palmer reached the age where water was no longer a safety hazard, Will constructed a small goldfish pond at the corner of the back yard, complete with a statue of a Greek goddess holding a pitcher from which re-circulated water gushed.

Clarice transformed the house itself. She started small: paint, wallpaper, curtains. As their finances improved, and with a boost from the Palmers' Christmas checks, her projects grew: ripping up carpet and refinishing the oak floors; re-doing the kitchen with new cabinets, countertops and built-in appliances; replacing bathroom fixtures, installing new window treatments across the front of the house, top and bottom.

They all had their lives, and sometimes they intersected and much of the time they didn't. They learned to accommodate them-selves to the things that unsettled them, to make peace (uneasy though it might be) with the thorny issues. There were things they just didn't talk about.

And as for Palmer—he reached the point, as teenagers do, where the last person he wanted to be seen with in public was a par-ent. Especially Raleigh's most popular weatherman.

It surprised Will when Palmer announced during his senior year in high school that he wanted to be a doctor. He couldn't picture Palmer caring for real, live human patients. Palmer was fastidious, given to interminable baths and excessive attention to hair and nails. Not that a doctor couldn't be fastidious, but occasionally he would have to get his hands dirty—flesh and fluid and bodily ori-fices and all that. And the thought of Palmer dealing with flesh and fluid didn't compute. A researcher perhaps, Will thought. Test tubes and laboratory rats. But the Greensboro Palmers thought medical school was just marvelous, just exactly the right thing. Among his high school graduation gifts from Sidney and Consuela was a stethoscope.

———

SO PALMER WENT OFF to Duke with the intention of becoming a doctor. And Clarice discovered real estate.

At first, it was part of her grand plan to re-make the house. But it became a great deal more than that.

She did it exactly the way she said she would. She completed the community college real estate course, got her license on the first try at the state exam, and started to work at a small firm that specialized in moderately priced residential property. She was a quick learner, patient and hardworking, adept at sizing up clients and guiding them deftly into homes that cost slightly more than they really wanted to pay. She struggled at first, slowly building contacts, listings and referrals, but over the next three years she became one of the firm's top salespersons. Then she was wooed away by Snively and Ellis. Clarice did stunningly well.

Will had mixed feelings.

On the one hand, he was genuinely proud of her. He got into the habit of rising earlier than usual each morning so he could have breakfast with her and hear reports of her dealings — some disappointments, but increasingly, successes. Clarice's commissions grew steadily. Will insisted that she keep a separate bank account. It was her money, he said. She could do whatever she wanted with it. He asked occasionally about the addition to the house. "Not just yet," she kept saying.

Work changed Clarice in other ways. Will had never thought of her as well organized. She had been prone to lose things, arrive late, forget phone messages. She had once had her car stolen when she left the keys in the ignition while she shopped for groceries. But now she was quite the buttoned-down businesswoman, leaving the house each morning with briefcase, cellular phone, Palm Pilot, and Multiple Listing Service book in hand. She couldn't afford to lose keys or forget phone messages or be late to appointments, so she didn't.

And then there was that more subtle thing. Clarice was more

confident, more self-assured, than Will could remember in years, more like the feisty young woman who had shared his Chapel Hill bed and defied her Greensboro upbringing.

"I'm myself," she said when he mentioned it casually one Sunday evening as they sat on the deck with cocktails in hand. She had spent the afternoon at an open house in North Raleigh. "I'm not just the weatherman's wife anymore," she said. "I've found some-thing that's just mine and I'm good at it and I enjoy it."

"And you didn't have to run off with a siding salesman to do it," he said good-naturedly.

"No. I considered that, but thought better of it. None of the sid-ing salesmen I've met are all that attractive."

"Well, it looks good on you."

"Yes. It does."

Another thing. Clarice stopped complaining about his job, or at least the way he approached his job. If he was working the malls or emceeing Rotary Club ladies' night, she might well be showing a house or returning calls or updating her listing book or attending a Board of Realtors meeting. Or if she happened to be at home in the evening, she seemed perfectly happy with the peace and quiet after a busy day of coddling clients and coaxing lenders.

The downside to all of this was the way Will spent his mornings. Clarice was usually away before nine, and the hours between then and his departure for work could be interminable. He puttered in the yard when the weather was good and in the garage when it was bad, even helped out with clothes-washing and house-cleaning. But as Clarice's car pulled out of the driveway each morning, the empty spaces seemed to expand around him, amplifying the house noises. He found himself welcoming the ringing of the telephone, a knock at the door, the arrival of the mail. And he began to accept more invitations for morning appearances—school groups, garden clubs, civic organizations.

Face it, he missed her. Missed her moving about, her domestic routine, her company at lunch. Especially missed the morning sex.

He missed, in short, what she had been. The molecular structure of their marriage had shifted. She had moved on somewhere beyond him, had broken free from the orbit of their lives. And there was now an extra dimension of time and space he had to reach across to touch her. He realized that the first time he phoned her pager.

"What's wrong?" she asked when she rang back.

"Nothing's wrong. I'm just trying to find the electric bill. I think they made a mistake on the meter reading and I want to call about it."

There was a long pause. "I'm with a client, Will," she said.

"Sorry to interrupt," he said. "Do you know where the bill is?"

"It's in my briefcase," she said. "I've already called the power company. They explained that they don't read the meter every month. They estimate. And then when they do read it, they adjust the bill." She sounded like a schoolmarm, explaining to a kindergartner the necessity of flossing.

He felt a flash of irritation. "Well. Go back to your clients. Sorry to have bothered you."

She hung up without saying goodbye. He did not page her again, even when her mother called in tears from Greensboro one morning to report that the family's ancient Irish setter, Archimedes, had passed away. He left a note for Clarice on the kitchen counter. When he got back to the Weather Center that night after a PTA speech, there was a message.

"Why didn't you call me?" she demanded when he phoned.

"I thought you didn't want to be interrupted when you're working."

"Well my God, Will. If it's something important . . ."

"The goddamn dog died, Clarice."

"You don't have to curse." He could hear the woundedness in her voice. She might cry.

"I'm sorry. I'm sorry about Archimedes."

"I loved that old dog."

"And I love you."

Again she hung up without saying goodbye.

Will wrote it off to her prickliness. She had always been a little prickly, and now that she had staked out this piece of territory quite apart from him — apart from *them* — she seemed both self-conscious about it and determined to defend it. And there was an element of fairness here, too. Payback for all those evenings he hadn't been home. Odd hours and life with a celebrity. Payback.

———

"YOU'RE NOT FUNNY ANYMORE," Clarice said to him one Sunday afternoon. They lay naked abed in the calm after sex, warm and drowsy from the familiar coupling, pleasure patterns worn into their bodies by time, like pebbles smoothed by rushing water. At the exquisite moment, as always, they seemed both joined and entirely separate, diving in tandem into a warm, bubbling spring, rising to look into each other's eyes with the old astonishment. Even after all this time, there was astonishment, which was the way it had all begun.

"What," he said now. "Am I supposed to make orgasm jokes?"

"You used to do those imitations," she said. "You were really funny. You used to make me laugh so hard I had to jump up from bed and run to the bathroom. Winston Churchill getting his rocks off, that sort of thing."

"In the course of human affairs," Will began with a Churchill growl . . .

"You used to do Mister Rogers at the dinner table and Palmer would almost topple out of his chair."

"It's a wonderful day in the neighborhood . . ."

"You don't do that sort of thing anymore."

"Well, Palmer's gone and we're both so busy."

"I miss that."

"So do I."

But what to do about it, he wondered?

He admitted to himself that he had become, over the years of their relationship, a less spontaneous person. Marriage and career and all sorts of responsibility would do that to you. "You project too much," Clarice had said to him once. "Why can't you just take things one step at a time?"

"I'm a forecaster," he had told her. "I look into the future so people can plan ahead."

And sure, it carried over into other aspects of his life. He found himself mentally projecting, for instance, the whole sequence of a vacation: the route they would follow, the places they would see, the people they might meet. He would order up a routing map from Triple-A, even if he was familiar with the roads, because Triple-A would warn him about construction, detours, new points of interest and the like. He didn't like surprises.

"Why not just set off across country?" Clarice would ask.

"Because," he would answer, "you never know what's out there."

Now, that didn't mean he was averse to seeing new places. When Palmer was twelve, they had flown to Argentina and spent a week on a cattle ranch in the pampas. Clarice had read about it in a magazine and she wanted to book everything herself. She spoke fairly good pidgin Spanish and would have considered the planning to be as much of an adventure as the trip itself. Fly to Buenos Aires, rent a car, get a map, strike out toward the pampas. But Will considered a week on an Argentine cattle ranch, surrounded by whooping gauchos, to be adventure enough. Let a travel agent arrange everything, he insisted. Sure enough, they had three flat tires between the airport and the ranch. But they were all repaired by the jocular driver who owned the car and who had been lined up in advance.

Sometimes, his penchant for planning and organizing paid an unexpected dividend, as it had one morning when Palmer was maybe five or six. Will was up early, getting a start on preparations for a summer trip to the Nags Head beach house. Palmer heard Will rustling about downstairs and came down to help. Will fixed him a cup of coffee—mostly milk, actually—but Palmer fairly glowed with the novelty of it, being up and about when it was still dark outside, drinking a grown-up cup of coffee. They had carried their own suitcases to the car and stowed them away in the trunk, leaving room for Clarice's things, and then had gone to wake her. It was barely light. She rose and joined them in the kitchen where Will and Palmer fixed toast and scrambled eggs while she sipped coffee at the breakfast table and watched them, amused. They had been on the road by seven, beating the rush hour traffic out of Raleigh. It had been a good morning.

But no, there hadn't been anything like that in a good while. And maybe Will wasn't as funny and spontaneous as he used to be. But why would Clarice say something about it now, just when they had finished making love?

From the very beginning, their sex life had been spontaneous, frequent, and inventive. Clarice was a willing experimenter, even an instigator of new acts, positions, locations. They balled lustily and Will found himself in a perpetual state of delighted astonishment at what they did and where they did it.

When Palmer was five, he had tubes implanted in his ears to relieve pressure and improve hearing. He developed a low-grade fever and was kept in the hospital for several days. Clarice slept on a cot in his room. Will visited every morning and on his dinner break at night. One evening, as he was preparing to leave, he kissed her at the door, just a peck on the lips. Then she touched his cheek — just the slightest touch, but it was enough. It was a private room with its own bath. They closed the bathroom door, and with Will seated on the commode and Clarice astride him, they thrashed against each other feverishly. Near orgasm, they heard the outer door to the room open. A nurse: "Mrs. Baggett . . ." They froze, both suspended in that most exquisite of moments. "I'll be out in a moment," Clarice managed in a strangled voice. Then they heard the door close again. Will returned to Channel Seven that evening with the intense smell of her permeating his brain like nerve gas.

Okay, so their sex life was not as spontaneous, frequent, or inventive as it had once been. After this long, whose was? And with Clarice working days and Will working nights, they were sometimes like ships passing in a fog. But when they did make love, there was still that old thing. The astonishment.

———

"YOU LIKE PEOPLE in the abstract," she said.

They were in the kitchen, Clarice at the breakfast table with the *News and Observer* spread out in front of her, engrossed in the classifieds. She rarely bought anything listed in the classifieds, but she never missed a day perusing them. There was a story behind every item, she said. It was interesting to imagine. The classifieds didn't interest Will at all. He had quite enough to do without poking about in other people's lives or wondering about the things that fell out of their closets. It all reeked of self-absorbed history. Greensboro kind of stuff.

He was at the coffeemaker. He had gotten up early this morning so they could have coffee together before she dashed off to sell real estate and he puttered. She was already dressed for the day, in a smart navy blue suit and a red-and-yellow figured silk scarf tied nattily about her neck. She looked smashing. He was still in robe and slippers.

"What do you mean, I like people in the abtract?"

"All that handshaking and baby-kissing you do, working the malls, Rotary Club picnics—you really hold people at arm's length."

"I think that's a little unfair," he said. "I like people."

"In the abstract."

He poured her coffee, added cream and sugar, brought both cups to the breakfast table.

"It works both ways," he said. "Celebrity sets you apart. People can't see past the guy on television. Take Chuck Durkin. They've been living next door for . . . what, fifteen years? We've had dinner back and forth . . . what, fifty times?"

"Not that many."

"And when we're together, Chuck can't ever talk about anything but the TV station. 'What are Jim and Binky really like? Have you ever met any of the Weather Channel people? Gee, those network news guys are a bunch of liberals, don't you think?'"

"If you weren't a celebrity, would you still hold people at arm's length?"

"I don't," he insisted, his voice rising just a bit. "I don't hold *you* at arm's length." He reached to touch her just behind her left ear, the place that made her shiver when he kissed it in bed. "We could . . . ," he started.

"I've got to meet a client in a half-hour. Some people from Massachusetts."

"Oh. Well, Massachusetts . . ."

"You're wrapped up in yourself," she said.

"My God, Clarice. This is getting a little vicious here."

"I didn't mean to be vicious," she said. "I was just making an observation."

"Well, it's unfair." He was, truly, stung. He got up from the table with his cup of coffee and went upstairs. He heard her car start up and back out of the driveway a few minutes later.

Unfair, he thought. Then he remembered something Glenda Turnipseed had said to him long years ago. "There's something missing with you," Glenda had said. And he had been baffled then, as he was now. For God's sake, what was he, some sort of emotional cripple? Had something of himself gone down at sea with that planeload of people? And then had the odd circumstance of his upbringing left him without some essential instincts that other, more normal people used to transact human commerce? If so, then why had he done so well since he had put all of the business of his upbringing behind him? Why did so many people like him so much? Why did they honk their horns? *Yo, Will!* Well, it was because they thought he was a regular guy. No, he didn't like people in the abstract, and he didn't hold people at arm's length. Clarice was wrong about that. Hell, Will Baggett was Raleigh's most popular TV weatherman. It just didn't compute.

———

WILL'S FINEST HOUR CAME in early September of 1996 when Hurricane Fran hit Raleigh, barreling up from the coast and still packing winds up to a hundred miles an hour when it plowed into the city. Raleigh was a mess—several thousand downed trees, smashed homes, littered and flooded streets, an almost total power blackout. Will sent Clarice toward Greensboro as it became clear the storm would target Raleigh. She picked up Palmer at Duke on the way. They stayed in Greensboro while Will slept on a cot at Channel Seven (which was powered by a huge emergency generator) and stayed on the air almost constantly. There weren't many people watching at first, but as lights and TV sets flickered on again, there was Will, anchoring the station's coverage of the aftermath and cleanup. When the city had returned to something akin to normality, the City Council passed a resolution declaring "Will Baggett Day" in honor of his efforts to keep people calm and informed. "I just don't know what we'd have done without you," the mayor said at the City Hall ceremony where they presented Will with a framed copy of the citation. Clarice and Palmer weren't there. Palmer was busy with classes and Clarice had clients.

Clarice had a lot of clients. "It takes more than a hurricane to stop Raleigh," Fincher Snively said to Will at the company picnic. A poll of readers of a major financial magazine had named it the best place to live in the United States. And Clarice Baggett was riding the wave. Her finest hour, too.

———

IT SEEMED TO WILL, in the twenty-fourth year of his marriage, that he and Clarice had reached a sort of equilibrium in their lives. They each had something, and they both still had each other. He had done with his life what he set out to do, what he needed to do. And Clarice was doing what she set out to do. They had endured and persevered, accommodated differences, made a life together *in spite of.* A long and mostly happy life. Things had turned out just fine.

And if he had fallen short, had erred in any way in his relationship with his wife and his son, he would make it up to them along the way. They had plenty of time for that. All the time in the world.

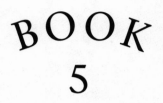
BOOK
5

18 | "You've got a visitor," the deputy said as he unlocked Will's cell door. He led Will to a room partitioned into small booths, thick glass separating the free from the incarcerated. Will slid into a chair. There was a vented hole in the glass through which they could talk. The deputy parked himself in a chair across the room behind Palmer and took a magazine out of his pocket.

Morris had been his first visitor, and now Palmer was his second, a week into his thirty-day sentence in the Wake County Jail. It was the first time he had talked to Palmer since the night, two weeks ago, in Chapel Hill. Palmer had tried reaching him by phone through Morris's office, but Will hadn't returned the call. He thought a little time and distance was called for—for both their sakes.

They looked each other over for a moment. Palmer was freshly scrubbed and nicely dressed in chinos and a baby-blue oxford cloth shirt, buttoned-down and economical in movement, nothing like the wretch Will had found in Chapel Hill. But he was nervous—eyes darting, hands busy with the two paperback books he was holding. Will gave him what he hoped was a reassuring smile.

Palmer held up the books. "Brought you something to read." He nodded at the deputy. "He said they'd have to check 'em before they gave 'em to you."

"Standard procedure," Will said.

They were both novels—one by Chekov, one by Danielle Steel.

"I don't know what kind of stuff you like," Palmer said. "I read the Chekov in a lit class last year. I picked up the other one at the drugstore."

"They're fine," Will said. "I'm probably somewhere between the two."

Palmer studied the covers of the books as if seeing them for the first time, then put them aside. "Are you okay?"

"Fine."

"You're growing a beard."

"I wasn't sure they'd let me, but as it turns out, there aren't a lot of unreasonable rules here. It's sort of like kindergarten. As long as you raise your hand to go to the bathroom and don't break in line, they don't hassle you."

The levity was lost on Palmer. "It looks, you look . . . different," he said.

Will scratched his chin. "I'm getting used to it. Doesn't itch as much as it did at first. And I've lost some weight. Food's okay, but I thought I needed to drop a few pounds. I was getting a little thick in the middle."

"Yeah. I mean, you were all right. Maybe a little thick. In the middle. Not much."

"Uh-huh."

"And you're wearing glasses."

Will slipped off the glasses and looked at them. "Contacts are too much trouble in here."

"I don't remember you wearing glasses."

"It's been a long time." It had, in fact, been in New Bern, back when he was just getting started. When Channel Seven hired him, Old Man Simpson insisted he switch to contacts. "Glasses don't look good on somebody who's appearing on TV," Old Man Simpson had said. "They create a subtle barrier between you and the viewer. Folks want you to look them in the eye. Straight in the eye." Well, now he didn't have to look anybody straight in the eye, and nobody expected him to. If you were looking for a benefit to being a convicted felon, maybe that was it.

"Are you going incognito?" Palmer asked.

Will laughed. "Oh, everybody knows me in here." Later, now . . . well, that was a different matter. He might, indeed, go incognito. Keep the beard and the glasses. Disappear without going anywhere.

Palmer dropped his eyes, stared blankly at a spot on the counter in front of him, and took a deep, ragged breath. "This is pretty god-damn awkward," he said softly. "This . . ." his hand fluttered, indicating jail, personal situation, life in general, ". . . is one screwed-up mess."

Will leaned back in his chair and folded his arms over his chest, waiting.

"I'm sorry," Palmer whispered. Will couldn't really hear him through the vented hole in the glass, but he could see his lips forming the unmistakable words, could see the glisten of tears in his eyes. Still, he waited.

Palmer glanced over at the deputy, then he leaned close to the hole in the glass. "I oughta go over there and tell him."

Will unfolded his arms and leaned close. Their faces were only inches apart. "But of course you won't. That would ruin everything, Palmer."

"But doesn't it . . . for you . . ." His voice trailed off.

Will gave him a wan smile. "It is one more shovelful of manure added to the pile, but the pile was already getting pretty big."

"Don't you *care* anymore?"

Will didn't answer that. He wasn't sure what the answer would be.

"Why did you do it?" Palmer asked.

"I'm pondering that and a lot of other things. You have a lot of time for pondering in a place like this. I think the best thing for me to do is keep pondering for now, and then after I get out of here we can talk about what I've figured out. If anything."

Palmer shook his head and then stared at the counter again.

"Did you go see the dean?" Will asked.

Palmer looked up, relieved to change the subject, at least a little. "Yeah."

"And?"

"He said it has to go to the admissions committee."

"Did he seem sympathetic?"

"I guess. He was pretty pissed off at first."

"But he didn't say no."

"No."

"When do you think you'll hear?"

"He didn't say."

Palmer studied his hands. He had slim fingers. His nails were trimmed. As far as physical appearance was concerned, things seemed to be pretty much reversed here — Will with his orange jail jumpsuit and scraggly beginnings of a beard and his thick-rimmed eyeglasses.

"How's your mother?" Will asked.

A pained look crossed Palmer's face, replaced almost immediately by a flash of anger.

Will waited for him. "We really ought to talk about it, don't you think?"

"What's to talk about? You guys . . ."

"I hope we can work things out. But whether we do or not, I don't want you to feel like you're caught in the middle. It has nothing to do with you."

"Bullshit!" Palmer barked. The deputy looked up sharply from his magazine. "I know how it is when parents split. They always run around telling the kid it's not about him. Well, what the hell, isn't the kid part of the family? And if you're gonna split up the family, isn't that about the kid? And even if I am twenty-three years old . . ."

Will nodded. "You're still our kid."

"Mom said the same goddamn thing. 'It's not about you, honey . . .'" His voice mocked her bitterly. "Well, to hell with that."

The deputy stood. "Is there a problem over here?" he asked.

Palmer blanched, then turned to him. "No sir. Sorry."

Will waved his hand to indicate things were okay. The deputy sat back down and re-opened his magazine.

"Palmer," Will said quietly, "It *is* about you, but it *isn't* your fault. It's your mother's idea, and it may be all *my* fault, but she won't talk to me about it. And I'm not asking you to tell me anything she's said. I don't want you in the middle." He took a deep breath. "This is all, as you say, a mess."

"A screwed-up mess," Palmer said.

"But remember this. You've got a bit of a mess of your own. And I assume you haven't told your mother about that."

Palmer shrugged.

"Well, don't. Hope it works out."

"And all the other?"

It was Will's turn to shrug.

Palmer pushed his chair back from the counter. "I guess I better go," he said. But he didn't get up, not yet.

Will leaned close to the hole in the glass again, his lips almost touching the metal vent. "Did it embarrass you, coming here?"

"Yeah, I guess. I mean, your father in jail?"

"Especially me."

"Yeah."

"Well, it's not the first time I've embarrassed you," Will said.

Palmer pulled the chair back close to the counter.

"Remember the seventh grade?" Will asked. "I came to your school as the Weather Wizard. You got sick. You asked me not to ever do that again."

"Well," Palmer said, "when you're in the seventh grade you just want to be . . ."

"A regular guy."

Palmer grimaced.

"And having your father up there in front of all of your friends wearing some goofy costume . . ."

"Not just that," Palmer said with a shake of his head. "Being on

TV every night. Everybody knowing who you are . . . were. People pointing in the hall. 'That's the weather guy's kid.' "

"Embarrassing."

Palmer made a face. "It's not like I was ashamed of you or anything."

Will smiled. "Even in the Weather Wizard costume?"

"Well, yeah. But most of the time, just . . ."

"Embarrassed."

Palmer nodded mutely.

"You realize," Will said, "that this is really the first time we've talked about any of this. In fact, this—and over in Chapel Hill the other night—is the first time in a long time we've talked about anything much."

Palmer's face clouded. "Are you doing this because you think you owe me something?"

"Like I said, I'm pondering all that."

"Well," Palmer said, "don't."

Then he got up and left.

———

WILL HAD ONLY ONE other visitor during his incarceration. Mr. Dinkins showed up one afternoon during the third week. He looked rather spiffy in a dark suit and tie and held himself carefully erect—nothing like the shambling old man who had puttered around the halls of Channel Seven all those years. He was carrying a hat, an old-fashioned snap-brim, which he placed on the counter in front of him.

"Barfield Simpson died a couple of nights ago," Dinkins said. "Didn't know if you'd read it in the paper, but I thought I'd come by. Just been to the funeral. There was a big crowd."

"I don't usually read the paper," Will said. "I'm sorry to hear it. He was a good man, Mister Dinkins. One of the best I've ever known. Like a father to me. I hope it wasn't bad at the end."

Dinkins shook his head. "He thought a lot of you, Will."

"Did he know about all this?"

"No," Dinkins said. "Over the last few weeks, he didn't know much of anything. Right after you saw him the last time, he went downhill pretty fast."

"I'm glad. I mean . . ."

"I know what you mean." Dinkins picked up the hat, and Will thought he was about to go. But he looked it over carefully, turned it 180 degrees, examined it closely, and put it back down on the counter. "Even if he had heard about it, he wouldn't have believed it. I don't."

Will was careful not to say anything, not to move a muscle.

"You're a good man, Will."

"I appreciate that." Then, "Mister Dinkins, what is your first name?"

"Abner."

"I'm sorry I never asked before."

"Well, it's Abner. Don't even have a middle name. Just Abner Dinkins, plain and simple."

"Now that Mister Simpson is gone, I guess you'll be getting along to Alaska," Will said.

Dinkins smiled. "No, I've pretty much rid myself of that idea. Alaska's too cold for an old man's bones. And the distances are too far. Alaska? That's something for a young man. Now you, Will, you could handle Alaska. You're young enough. Maybe you should think about someplace like Alaska. A fresh start, you know."

Will returned the smile. "I guess it's worth considering. Among other things."

"Any idea what you'll do now?"

"Not a clue," Will said. "I've got another week in here with nothing to do but figure out what matters and what doesn't."

Dinkins picked up the hat and stood. "One thing, Will."

"What's that, Mister . . . Abner?"

"You're still vertical. Remember that."

"That's what my cousin said. His name is Wingfoot Baggett. He's had some hard knocks, but when I asked him how he was making out, he said, 'I'm still vertical, Wilbur.'"

"Is that what your family calls you? Wilbur?"

"Yeah. I didn't become Will until I got to college. Told everybody my name was Will Baggett. Not Wilbur."

"A makeover," Dinkins said with a smile.

———

What matters and what doesn't? he thought when he was back in his cell. All of it mattered, of course, if you put it on the plane of the entirely personal—the coming-apart of things he had cherished, things he thought were safe and inviolate. Job, marriage, self-respect. All gone and replaced by smashed hope and riven opportunity and public humiliation and lost love and plain old bad luck. If you had carefully arranged a life that you thought mattered and it suddenly and without warning came crashing down around your ears, then that had to count for something. Prayers of intercession should be offered, the veil of the temple should be rent. Instead, life had gone on, even—miraculously—his own. And perhaps that meant that in the larger scheme of things, it really didn't matter much at all.

He suspected that the quite public Will Baggett saga was by now pretty much relegated to water cooler conversation, on a par with scandal in the White House or a rock music star with an incurable disease. He imagined that he had become mostly a curiosity to most of the world outside the Wake County Jail. The truth was that his own personal loss didn't really matter very much to most people, who went on with their lives as if he existed only as a picture on the front page of the paper.

Okay, a good bit of it he had done to himself. Stepped off the cliff with his eyes wide open. Maybe he could have convinced Judge Broderick Nettles that the packet that fell out of his pocket in the courtroom was not his at all, that they should go in search of one Palmer Baggett, now cooling his heels over in Chapel Hill and trying to figure out how to get his ass out of a very tight sling. Maybe. And if he did convince the judge of that and it was Palmer lying here on this bunk instead of Will, then Will could, as he had vowed to Wingfoot, get his life back. Channel Thirty-two. Or maybe another television market entirely. Get out of Raleigh and leave the mess of his marriage and his son behind. Start over. Sacramento or Houston. Cedar Rapids or Providence. The world was always in need of a good weatherman.

But hell . . . he couldn't do that, not really. There was such a thing as a man's responsibilities. For all of the glorious public celebrity he had so carefully crafted for himself through dint of sheer will and work, he was at bottom still just a man—a common, ordinary, everyday man—who had to wipe his butt and account for himself to himself.

That had been a sobering thing to face—the idea that he was, at rock bottom, just like everybody else. He might have been on TV and he might have been a little cuter than most folks because of it, but he was really just like everybody else. He had faced it, and that might have been the toughest thing of all.

So, faced with an awful choice, he had stepped willingly off the cliff because it just seemed the only possible thing to do at the time. *Okay, Will—choose. Your own ass or your son's.* He might not have been the best father who ever came down the pike, but by God, he had helped bring Palmer Baggett into the world and had changed his diapers and provided for him as best he could and he wasn't going to cut and run now when it came down to this one awful choice.

Will, you are a noble sonofabitch. Take a victory lap.

Still, any sense of ennoblement he might feel was greatly undercut by the other half of the equation. In being noble he had screwed himself royally. He was a mess, bruised and battered, victimized, stripped of dignity and visible means of support.

However, as Abner Dinkins had said, he was still, in the figurative sense of the word, vertical. An upright vessel, emptied of its contents. Lying here on his bunk in this barred and windowless place, he felt the thought of it begin to calm him. He felt something drain away and recognized it as both anger and fear, something he had been holding onto fiercely since they had locked him away. He had told himself over and over during the past three weeks in this place that he was not angry, not fearful. But he was. He was pissed, and he was scared to death. But now, he felt himself letting go of that, at least a good deal of it. His breath became shallow, just enough to sustain vital signs. Stillness descended, drawing a curtain against the jail noises.

He waited for a long time. And finally, it came down to this: *On the surface, everything is gone; but if everything is gone, anything is possible.*

19 | THERE WERE NO REPORTERS PRESENT when Will emerged from the Wake County Jail on a mid-morning in early June. He was old news.

It was raining. He had watched the weather on Channel Seven the evening before, along with his fellow inmates, and had seen how a front had stalled across the southeastern and mid-Atlantic states. An Interstate 85 front, Brent the weathercaster had called it. In winter, it would have meant the clash of northern cold and southern moisture that inevitably signaled snow. Now, it was just lingering rain.

Will thought that Brent still looked like he was only a couple of years out of junior high school, but he had turned his boyishness into an advantage, settling into a peppy, cheerful style that might one day, if he stuck around long enough and matured a little, make him Raleigh's most popular TV weatherman. Or, Brent might be in Chicago or Miami a year from now, trading on his youth and good looks to land a big major-market salary, one day speaking of Raleigh as the way station where an odd thing happened to the Number One Guy and he got his big chance. Ask him ten years from now who that Number One Guy was, and what odd thing had happened to him, and Brent probably wouldn't be able to remember.

No reporters, just Wingfoot and Morris waiting for Will — Morris under an umbrella, Wingfoot under a rain-soaked floppy hat and a soiled gray poncho.

"You look like a Confederate deserter," Will said to Wingfoot.

"Thanks. I like your beard," Wingfoot said to Will.

Morris tried to offer Will space under his umbrella, but he backed away and stood in the drizzle with Wingfoot. He turned his face skyward and let the rain patter against his face and dribble through his beard, listening to the wetness squishing under the tires of passing cars on Salisbury Street.

The rain felt good. So did the beard. It was soft and fine and it had just, in the past week, gotten long enough to require trimming. It was dark brown, like his hair, but there were flecks of gray, too. It had become a topic of conversation among the deputies and other inmates, and the more lush it grew, the more he seemed to be accepted as something other than the former TV star who had fallen upon hard times. The jail was a much less daunting place than he remembered from his first brief incarceration. The deputies had been mostly pleasant. Will got no special privileges, but he was quietly shielded from the jail's roughest element. The food was decent, if uninspired. He got regular exercise and had lost fifteen pounds. Other than the three visitors — Morris, Palmer and Dinkins — he had been left alone by the outside world. That suited him. Anyway, most people he knew would have found it incredibly awkward, like a visitation at a funeral home. Never exactly the right thing to say. *Does it hurt? Is there anything I can get you?*

Cookies? Magazines? A hacksaw? No need to put people through that.

Morris spoke up. "I've got some papers . . ."

Morris was in a new uniform today, or at least an old one recycled—dark blue pinstripe suit, ecru shirt, muted red tie with tiny blue dots, matching handkerchief peeking from his coat pocket. He had new glasses, a pair of wire-rims that made him look faintly like some musician from Will's memory (John Lennon, he finally decided) and a new haircut, pulled back severely from his forehead and plastered, wet-look, close to his skull. Morris had a major new client, a large and prestigious advertising agency.

"You're looking especially spiffy today, Morris," Will said.

Morris gave a tiny bow. "Packaging," he said. "All the world is packaging."

"Do you agree with that, Wingfoot?" Will asked.

"Absolutely," Wingfoot said. "I've been buying sterile poo-poo for my nursery."

"What?"

"I get it from the sewage treatment plant in Wilmington. They take sewage and run it through some kind of process and dry it and put it in nice-looking bags. It does wonders for plants and it doesn't even smell like shit."

"But it is still shit," Will said.

"Like the man said, everything is packaging."

———

DURING WILL'S JAIL TIME, Morris and Clarice's lawyer had been negotiating a separation agreement. The estranged couple must, under North Carolina law, remain scrupulously apart for twelve months before a divorce could be finalized. A lot of things could transpire in twelve months, Will thought, and so he intended to make no fuss over the temporary division of assets. In the Danielle Steel novel Palmer had brought him in jail, the heroine came to her senses at the end and ran away with the man of her destiny. Perhaps, when Clarice came to her senses, she would do the same.

"Whatever she wants," Will had said to Morris. "Give her anything she wants."

But he wasn't quite prepared for what Morris handed him a few minutes later in the quiet of his office. Will read it thoroughly while Wingfoot stood next to the window, gazing out at the passing foot traffic on the Fayetteville Street Mall. He was still wearing the floppy hat, but had hung the poncho on a hook at the front door. Will, sitting on the leather couch, finished his reading just as Morris returned from an errand elsewhere in the office. Morris raised an inquiring eyebrow.

"Where am I going to live?" Will asked. The agreement called for Clarice to occupy the house.

"You'll have to find a place," Morris said. "Maybe the YMCA for starters?"

"You could go live with Min," Wingfoot said, his back still to them. "You could work on the family history. Or you could stay with me."

"Afraid not," Morris said. "Terms of his probation say he has to reside in Wake County. Weekly check-ins with the probation officer."

Wingfoot turned from the window. "So he's stuck here?"

"Pretty much," Morris said. "Unless the probation officer gives him special permission for an out-of-county visit."

Wingfoot shrugged and turned back to the window.

"And what am I going to live on?" Will asked.

The agreement called for their joint assets to be frozen until such time as the divorce was finalized, and then "equitably divided between the respective parties."

"You've got your severance money from Channel Seven."

"Fifty thousand dollars," Will said. "I guess that will hold me for a while. After that, there's always armed robbery."

Morris picked up a file folder from his desk and leafed through it. "Well, not quite fifty thousand. There's fifteen percent for the bail bondsman. For starters."

"I thought you said ten percent."

"He went up on his prices."

Will did some quick arithmetic. "Seventy-five hundred."

"Then there's my fee," Morris said without a flinch. Morris had not the slightest hesitation when it came to talking money. He would tell you right up front that he was good and he was expensive and if you wanted a cut-rate deal you should go find one of the polyester-clad crowd at criminal court. He read from the file now. "April eighteen, long-distance telephone conference with Mister Baggett. April nineteen, prepare brief for initial court appearance on traffic charge."

Will's face was beginning to itch under his beard. "What brief? We went to court and sat on our butts all day and then the goddamn cop didn't even show up and . . ."

"April twenty-one, court appearance, seven hours . . ."

"Awright, awright." Will waved him to silence.

Morris gave him a close look. "And then there are your expenses."

"*My* expenses?"

"Motel room, meals, transportation, incidentals. I handled all that."

"Transportation?"

"Sixty-five dollars for a taxicab to Snively and Ellis Realty. Remember? Also, there were several times when I toted you around in my own car."

"You're charging me for that?"

Morris smiled and held out his hands. "A man's got to make a living."

"Packaging is expensive," Wingfoot said over his shoulder.

Morris ignored Wingfoot. "And you'll be getting another bill for my more recent services. The separation agreement."

"What services? It looks like Clarice's lawyer did all the work."

Morris's gaze was unflinching. "You don't have to accept it as is, you know. We can make a counterproposal. Re-open the negotiations."

"How much of a bill?" Will asked. "For your services?"

Morris waved the file. "I'd say it'll come to another twenty-five hundred or so. Unless we re-negotiate."

"Okay," Will said wearily. "How much does that leave? Out of fifty thousand dollars?"

Morris plucked a check from the file and handed it to Will. The check came to a grand total of eighteen thousand, two hundred fifty-six dollars and thirty-four cents. Will stared at it for a while, then carefully folded it into thirds and tucked it into his shirt pocket. He picked up the separation agreement, studied it again, then looked up at Morris. "I'll need to borrow your pen."

It was a very nice pen, a Mont Blanc, burgundy with gold fili-gree. It looked new (perhaps a gift from his new ad agency clients), but then with a Mont Blanc, it was hard to tell. A Mont Blanc could look new for a long time. "Remember," Morris said as he handed the pen over, "you'll need to put aside some of that for taxes."

———

HE TREATED WINGFOOT to lunch at McDonald's. Wingfoot had a fish sandwich and a medium soft drink. Will opted for the six-piece Chicken McNuggets and water. They split a large order of fries. When their order was ready, Wingfoot tried to pay. Will wouldn't hear of it. "This is a celebration," Will said. "On me."

"What are we celebrating?"

"I'll think of something."

They occupied a booth at the side of the dining area. Through the plate-glass window Will could see that the rain had stopped for the moment, but the sky was still gray-clotted. It would start again before long. As Brent the weathercaster had said, the front would linger, maybe for a couple of days. There was nothing to push it out of the way. "Try to remember how this feels," Brent had said cheer-ily to the faux-whining of Jim and Binky, the news anchors, "in August when we've got one of those big Bermuda highs hanging around and it's as dry as dust and hot enough to fry an egg on the pavement." In Will's day, he would have announced the beginning of a Mold and Mildew Festival. But it was no longer Will's day.

They ate in silence and watched the McDonald's lunch crowd ebbing and flowing outside. A long line of cars snaked around the back toward the drive-in window.

"How about an apple pie for dessert," Will offered.

"No thanks," Wingfoot said.

"Look, I'm not destitute. I can afford an apple pie."

Wingfoot popped the last of the french fries in his mouth and chewed thoughtfully. "What are you going to do with yourself, Wilbur?"

"Go incognito. Seek anonymity."

"The beard helps. And the glasses."

McDonald's had been a test. Will had looked the clerks and the other customers straight in the eye, and as far as he could tell, not a solitary soul had recognized him. It was a good sign. Incognito.

"You're virtually broke, homeless, and without visible means of support," Wingfoot said. "Some places I know, you could be picked up on vagrancy charges."

Will finished his Chicken McNuggets and drained his cup of water, then gathered up their debris and took it to a nearby waste receptacle.

"So, what *are* you going to do with yourself?" Wingfoot asked when Will returned to the booth.

"As far as a job?"

"Well, that's part of it, maybe not even the main part. But yes, for starters, a job."

"I'll have to find something. I'm just not sure what. I have a criminal record. Hell, I can't even vote. Lots of businesses don't want to hire someone with a criminal record. At the jail, they posted notices of people who would, but they were all things like cooks and car-wash attendants."

"Nothing wrong with cooking or washing cars."

"Except that I don't know how. Cook? I can't boil water."

"Auto mechanic?"

"I don't know a spark plug from an air filter."

"Ditchdigger?"

"Now there's a possibility." He tapped the pocket where the check rested. "I could purchase a shovel."

Wingfoot stared at the table and traced a small circle with his forefinger. Then he looked up again at Will. "What skills *do* you have, Wilbur?"

"Most of my adult life, I've done the weather on TV," Will said. "I was pretty damn good at it. I was the most popular TV weatherman in Raleigh. You ask what skills do I have? TV weather skills. Unfortunately, Wingfoot, there ain't no market anywhere for my particular weather skills—now, or anytime in the future."

"Is there *anything* else you know how to do?"

Will thought for a moment. "Mow grass."

Wingfoot's eyebrows went up.

"I meant it as a joke," Will said.

Wingfoot leaned back and stared at him. Then his eyes seemed to sort of glaze over and he looked away, out the window where the rain had started again. After a moment he said, "Min wants you. I'm obligated to tell you that. She said, and I quote, 'Tell Wilbur he needs to come home.'"

"You heard what Morris said. I can't leave Wake County without special permission as long as I'm on probation."

"After that, then."

"You think I should go?"

"I promised Min I wouldn't have an opinion," Wingfoot said, poker-faced.

"You think I shouldn't go."

"As I said . . ."

Will thought about the deteriorating old house with its expanse of heart pine floor and its hulking dark furniture and its high windows looking out toward the Cape Fear River. Then he thought about the boxes and stacks of family detritus Min had lugged down from the attic on his most recent visit, about Wingfoot and Billy coming to get him. A rescue, they called it. He might have gotten out just in the nick of time.

Wingfoot might have been thinking the same thing. He said,

"Remember sitting out front of my trailer the day after your guest appearance with the band?"

"Yeah."

"You said you were going to Raleigh and get your life back."

"So?"

"Get it back."

"It's gone, Wingfoot."

Wingfoot gave an impatient toss of his head. "I said *life,* Wilbur. I didn't say baggage. Think outside the box. Act on impulse."

"I don't have any impulses," Will said. "I barely have a pulse. I'm sort of numb." He thought about it. "Act on impulse."

"It may be your last chance."

They sat for a while longer in silence. The rain started up again outside. A truck passing on the street made a rooster-tail of water as it passed through a puddle, splashing the statue of Ronald McDonald near the curb.

"How's Peachy?" Will asked.

Wingfoot's face clouded. "Fine, I guess."

"What . . ."

"She's in Nashville."

"Really?"

"A record producer showed up at Baggett's Place about a month ago, listened to the band, and told Peachy she needed to be in Nashville. Wanted her to cut a demo, and then he was gonna take it around to the record companies. Capitol, RCA, those folks."

"And?"

"She left a couple of days later."

"Well damn, that's great, Wingfoot." Will pictured Peachy unfolding from her Spitfire in front of one of the big record company offices. Executives gawking, rushing out to meet her.

Is this the right place?

Yes ma'am. It sure is.

"Well, how's she doing?"

"Haven't talked to her since she got there."

"Why?"

"I told her when she left, don't think about me. Don't write, don't call. Just sing and kick ass. All she needs is a little break, Wilbur. She could hit it pretty big."

"And you're just gonna let her? A magnificent woman like that and you sent her off to the bright lights and the big city with the risk you might lose her?"

"It's her life."

"Shit!" Will said, a little louder than he intended. A woman in the next booth gave him a frown. He raised his hand in apology, then leaned across the table toward Wingfoot. "It's your life, too. That woman's in love with you. You're in love with her. Here you are telling me to act on impulse. Well, cousin, you need to get on your horsey and ride like hell to Nashville, Tennessee, and wrap your arms around her so tight she'll never get away."

Wingfoot stared at the table, then finally looked up at Will. "I did that one time with something I wanted so bad I would have killed for it. It near about killed me when I lost it. And I ain't gonna make that mistake again. You ought not to want something so bad that it near about kills you to lose it. You of all people oughta know that, Wilbur."

"You're a goddamn fool," Will said softly. Then, "Maybe I am, too."

There was just the slightest twitch at the corner of Wingfoot's mouth. But he didn't say anything.

"I have to go to the bathroom," Will said after a moment.

When he returned, Wingfoot had disappeared. There was a slip of paper on the table with a handwritten address on it.

———

IT WAS A TWO-STORY gray frame house with a wide front porch, nestled behind two large silver-leaf maples that shaded a patch of anemic fescue grass in need of trimming. The house was in Boylan Heights, a once-grand but somewhat faded older neighborhood only a mile or so from Will's own. Former neighborhood, he kept telling himself. He didn't live there anymore.

He knocked, peering through the screen door into the gloom of the front hall. He listened for sounds from inside, heard none. He looked about the porch. To his left was a collection of white wicker furniture with colorful floral-pattern cushions—love seat, straight chair, rocker, occasional tables. The space to his right was filled with potted plants, arrayed on two long benches, and ferns hung from the ceiling above the banister.

"You're Wingfoot's cousin," said the voice at the door.

She was short, stocky, broad-faced, white-haired, ample-bosomed. She pushed open the screen and stepped onto the porch.

"Will Baggett," he said.

She offered a hand. "Dahlia Spence."

"Dahlia. Like the flower?"

"Yes."

"You know Wingfoot?"

"I order plants from him. Over the Internet."

Not long ago, Will might have been surprised to find that Wingfoot's nursery was selling on-line. Or that Wingfoot even had a nursery. But nothing about Wingfoot surprised him much now. No telling what there was yet to find.

"You've come about the apartment," she said.

Will showed her the slip of paper Wingfoot had left in the booth. "He gave me your address." He was, in fact, just following what he took to be Wingfoot's instructions—an address, nothing more. Wingfoot hadn't said anything about an apartment. Will had gotten quite used to following instructions in jail. It was easy, not having to make up your own mind about anything. Just do what the people tell you, follow the rules, hunker down. Watch whatever the other guys are watching on TV. He had seen a nasty fight between two inmates over *Jeopardy* versus *Entertainment Tonight*. Deputies had clobbered both of them.

"Well, let's not rush things," Dahlia Spence said.

Will smiled. "I've got plenty of time."

"So I understand."

He waited in the wicker rocking chair while she disappeared

inside, returning after several minutes with a large tray laden with tea pitcher, ice-filled glasses, cloth napkins, plate of oatmeal raisin cookies, and crystal dish of lemon slices. He rose quickly, swung open the screen door, and reached for the tray. "I've got it," she said. "Just hold the door." It was quite a load, but she handled it deftly. She poured tea with a steady hand from the cut-glass pitcher into the tall, thick glasses and handed one to him. He squeezed a slice of lemon into the glass.

"Sugar?" he inquired.

"I don't keep it in the house."

"Oh."

"I'm eighty-four and take no medication."

"I'm forty-eight and take Zocor," Will said. "For my cholesterol."

"Well, there you have it. With a cholesterol problem, you don't need sugar."

"I don't really have a cholesterol problem. The Zocor . . ."

"You should solve the problem with diet and exercise."

"It could be hereditary. But I'm not sure about that." Did Uncle French have a cholesterol problem? Did Tyler? No way of knowing. If Will's problem was inherited, he thought, it was just about the only thing they had left him.

She took a large sip of her tea, gazing at him over the top of the glass as she drank. Then she set her glass down on the tray. She had quick, lively eyes that took all of him in and made him feel as if he were being sized up for tailoring. But it wasn't an unkindly scrutiny. "Ernest had high blood pressure."

"Beg pardon?"

"My late husband."

"Oh."

She turned and called out toward the screen door, "Ethel . . ."

He expected a housekeeper, but instead a dog, a Dalmatian, peered out from behind the screen. Mrs. Spence rose and opened the door. "Come and meet Mister Baggett," she said. The Dalmatian stopped at Will's knee, cocked its head and waited to be petted.

"This is Ethel." Will administered a behind-the-ears scratching. Then Ethel backed away and sat on her haunches next to Mrs. Spence's chair.

"Do you like dogs?" she asked.

"I honestly can't say if I do or don't. I've never had one. My aunt had a dog, but an alligator ate it, and that may have deterred me from wanting one myself."

"You've grown a beard," Mrs. Spence said.

"Yes."

"You don't think it fools anybody, do you?"

"Actually, it does. It worked pretty well at McDonald's," he said with a smile.

"And that's another reason you've got high cholesterol," she said. "Ernest liked fast food, too. He would sneak around and eat hamburgers and french fries and Little Debbie snacks. He thought I didn't know, but I can smell a french fry a mile away, and I used to find Little Debbie wrappers crammed in the back of his nightstand drawer. It certainly wasn't good for his blood pressure."

"Mr. Spence . . . a heart attack?"

"Goodness, no. He fell off a fire truck. He was a member of the Raleigh Fire Department. Two days before retirement, he was on the way to a fire, hanging on the back of the truck. At his age, he could have gone to the fire in the chief's car, but he always insisted on riding the truck. Anyway, as it rounded a corner, a gust of wind caught his helmet and when he grabbed for it, he fell off the truck."

"I'm terribly sorry."

"And was hit by a car."

"It was . . ."

"Thirty years ago. The fire department gave me his Dalmatian as a memento of his service."

Will gave Ethel a close look. "She doesn't look that old."

"Oh, she's not," Mrs. Spence said. "She's descended from the original."

"Ah, yes."

"Wingfoot tells me I'm something of an original myself," Mrs. Spence said with a bright laugh.

"I'll bet he's right."

She took another sip of tea and held the glass in her lap. "My family didn't want me to marry Ernest. They go back a good ways in Raleigh. At one time, had some money. Still have the name."

"Old Raleigh."

"Yes. So they didn't like my marrying a fireman. Said he wasn't good enough. But I did anyway. Ernest was a good fireman and a good husband."

"No regrets."

"No," she said firmly, "except that I wish he had ridden in the chief's car."

Mrs. Spence held out the cookie plate. "Homemade," she said, "with artificial sweetener." They had a nice taste, but they tended to crumble when you took a bite. Lack of sugar, he imagined. A small chunk fell from Will's cookie to the floor. Ethel eyed it, then looked up at Mrs. Spence. She nodded, and Ethel scooped it up with a sweep of her tongue and went back to her haunches.

"An obedient dog," Will said.

"Better than most people."

They sipped their tea and munched on cookies and talked on at some length about nothing in particular. Dahlia Spence seemed to be in no hurry, and Will had nothing pressing on his agenda either. Eventually, though, he came to what he felt was a necessary point: "Mrs. Spence, I must tell you that I've lost my job and I've just been released from jail," he said. "My wife and I are separated."

"Oh, I know all about that."

"The newspaper . . ."

"Most of it. Wingfoot told me about your wife. I don't believe that part has been in the paper."

". . . and television."

"I don't have a set. Never watch. This is only the second time I've ever laid eyes on you."

"The other?"

"You spoke to the Raleigh Coalition of Garden Clubs last year. I was sitting next to Pinky Perlin, and while you were speaking, I leaned over to Pinky and said, 'Pinky, who is that man?' And Pinky said, 'He's the weatherman on Channel Seven.' You were quite witty. You told some jokes about the weather."

"I'm glad you enjoyed it."

"And when you were through, I leaned over to Pinky and I said, 'Pinky, that was a waste of time. I thought we were going to hear something useful.'"

"Sorry to disappoint," Will said. "Are you a gardener?"

"I putter."

It was a good deal more than puttering. When she led him through the rear of the house and out into the back yard, after they had finished their tea and cookies, he was quite taken aback. It was all lush green and vivid color—banks of shrubs and beds of annuals and perennials, interspersed with flagstone walkways, all leading to a central patch of Bermuda grass on which sat a couple of weathered cedar love seats and a birdbath—all of it surrounded by a chest-high brick wall and sheltered by low-growing trees. Bird feeders and birdhouses hung from branches and perched atop posts and poles. Birds swooped and darted, filling the space with their chatter and twittering. Will stopped in his tracks. It was a riot of color and noise and heady smells, a sensual overload, and it almost took his breath.

Dahlia Spence marched on ahead of him and he caught up as she started up the narrow stairs that climbed the outside of the garage. She trudged smartly upward, leaning her bosom into the effort. Will was breathing hard by the time they reached the top. He might have lost weight in jail, but he was still badly out of shape. He would start walking, he thought. This was a nice neighborhood with sidewalks.

The apartment—two rooms, actually—was spare but neat, equipped with odds and ends of sturdy old furniture. A small bedroom with a double bed, night table and chest of drawers. Off the bedroom, a tiny bath with a shower. A larger room with a modest kitchenette at one end and a seating area at the other. The kitchenette had an ancient electric stove, a small refrigerator, forties-era metal cabinets, similar to the ones they had found in the LeGrand kitchen when he and Clarice bought the house, and a Formica-topped table with two chrome-and-vinyl chairs. The cabinets were equipped with an assortment of odds-and-ends of dishes, pots and pans, silverware. The seating area consisted of a sofa covered in some sort of shiny green textured fabric, an overstuffed chair with a reading lamp beside it, and a large, faded fake-Oriental rug. The window next to the chair, bordered by tied-back curtains made of the same fabric as the sofa covering, looked out over the back yard. Pine floors, except for a stretch of linoleum in the kitchenette. There were a few nondescript framed prints on the walls — still lifes, pastoral scenes. And hanging next to the door, a calendar: 1952. The top sheet was February.

"Take your time," she said. "Would you feel more comfortable if I left you alone for a while?"

"Oh," he said, "no need." She sat at the kitchen table while he wandered about, poking into corners, opening drawers. There was something almost familiar about the place. It took a moment, but on his second circuit through the rooms, he realized what it was. It reminded him in an odd way of Baggett House. The furniture wasn't as grand or massive, but it was all solid wood, and just old enough to be a poor cousin. And like Baggett House, this place seemed plucked out of time. He stood at the window, gazing over the back yard, watching a bluejay bullying at a sunflower feeder.

He thought about Min. *Come home,* she had messaged him via Wingfoot. That was an option, of course, at least when he was done with his probation and could go about when and where he wished. But Baggett House wasn't home, hadn't been for a long time. Maybe never was, not really.

But no sense chewing over all that now, he thought. Now was June and the time and space and possibility that stretched between now and fall was meantime. The question was, what would he do in the meantime? And how would it affect everything?

He turned to Dahlia Spence. "I suppose I'm something of a refugee."

"You should aspire to be a pilgrim," she said.

"Oh?"

"A refugee is fleeing something. A pilgrim is going toward something."

"I see. Yes. A pilgrim. I'll work on that." He looked about the room again. "I like the apartment, Mrs. Spence." He looked again out the window. "And it has a nice view of the back yard. I can imagine quiet evenings here. Contemplating my pilgrimage."

"You can change anything you like except the calendar," Dahlia Spence said.

He turned to her, eyebrows questioning.

"This was my son's place when he was growing up. He was killed in Korea."

"February of 1952."

"Yes."

"I'm sorry."

She ran her hand idly over the tabletop. "I've never rented it out before. Until last week, it had been locked for forty-eight years."

"Why now?" he asked.

"I decided to deal with it. I'm eighty-four. I didn't want to arrive at ninety-four having never come to grips. It came to me in the middle of the night. I woke up thinking that I've kept too many things closed up in here all these years. And that wasn't really fair to Roscoe. Or me. So I got up from the bed and came out here and opened up the place and started cleaning." She slapped her hand smartly on the table for emphasis.

"Are you sure . . ."

"Yes. It needs living in. I need a real live person out here." She waved her hand. "Oh, I won't bother you, Mister Baggett. I won't expect you to be Roscoe. I've taken all his things to the house. If there's a ghost, he's in there with me now. You may come and go as you please. All I ask is that you keep the place tidy and behave your-self."

"How much?"

"Two hundred a month."

"That's awfully cheap. You could probably get double that."

"It's not air-conditioned."

"Still . . ."

"It's not the money," she said firmly. "You can move in whenever you like."

"I've got some odds and ends out in the car," he said. "Clothes and stuff. But I'll have to pick up some sheets and towels."

She headed for the door. "You can borrow from me. Sleep here tonight."

"I can't pay you until I set up a checking account. I'll do that tomorrow."

"Whenever," she said. She stopped at the door. "Wingfoot tells me you have a son, Mister Baggett."

"Yes."

"You and he are close?"

Will hesitated for just the tiniest moment, long enough for Dahlia Spence to say, "My Ernest and Roscoe were close. They did things together, but it was more than that. They genuinely liked each other. When Roscoe was killed, Ernest had no regrets, not about their relationship. There was grief enough in losing him without saying, 'I should have . . .'"

"He's in medical school," Will called as she went out the door and down the stairs.

———

HE PULLED HIS CAR INTO the driveway and parked next to the garage steps. Mrs. Spence's gray Oldsmobile occupied the only garage bay. She drove it seldom, she had said—mostly to the grocery store, the hairdresser's, or garden club meetings. It was a 1979 model and had lasted because she had it serviced regularly and kept it out of the weather. Will's car would have to remain outside.

No problem, he said. It had been parked at the rear of Morris's driveway while he had served his time. It was in need of a good scrubbing, but he would get to that. It would give him something to do.

He carried his things up the stairs—several boxes of clothing, toiletries, odds and ends of personal items—all of it packed by Clarice while he was in jail and left for him, along with the car, at Morris's. The clothing was entirely casual attire. He had seen no use for suits and sport coats and dress slacks. He wasn't anticipating any kind of white collar employment. Jeans, chinos, loafers, knit shirts, sneakers would do just fine. It all fit neatly in the drawers of the dresser and the tiny bedroom closet. Afterward, he sat in the over-stuffed chair next to the window overlooking the back yard and watched the birds, thinking how simplified life had become in his new state of affairs, how little *stuff* he needed to get by. There was a great deal more back at the house, but he couldn't think of a thing that was essential.

He had thought at one point of asking for the computer, but then thought better of it. He decided he had spent far too much time on the computer on those long mornings when the house was quiet and Clarice was away making a career in real estate. He had checked weather-related sites on the Internet (to be better prepared by the time he reached Channel Seven in the afternoon), dabbled a bit in the stock market, and e-mailed. But now he had no need for detailed weather information, his stock holdings were—what was the word in the separation agreement? . . . frozen—and there was not a soul he wanted to e-mail.

Mrs. Spence was back just after six, bringing linens and inviting him to supper. They dined on pork chops, rice and broccoli at the dining room table while Ethel watched from the kitchen nearby. There was homemade lime sherbet for dessert—made, she assured him, with artificial sweetener. After the meal she served decaffeinated coffee on the front porch. The midday rain, despite what Brent had predicted on Channel Seven last night, had given way to a pleasantly clear afternoon and evening.

"This is very nice of you," Will said. "A delicious meal and much better company than I've had recently."

"I can imagine."

"Miss Manners could have a field day at the Wake County Jail."

Mrs. Spence just smiled.

"Are you sure you're okay renting to a man with a criminal record?"

"Wingfoot says you're harmless. He says you're a bit of a tight-ass, but nothing to be afraid of."

"About what you read in the paper . . . I don't smoke pot."

"It's probably not good for a man with high cholesterol."

They sipped their coffee and contemplated the evening. Will looked out across the lawn. It could use some work. The grass was patchy under the maples, spiked with crabgrass out where the sunlight hit it. Such a lovely garden, such a scruffy lawn. Given the choice himself, he would have had it the other way, especially since the lawn was here in front of the house where the rest of the world could see it. "Who takes care of your lawn?" he asked.

"Why, I do."

"Ummmm."

"More coffee?"

"No thank you. Would you mind if I give it a little attention? I don't have one of my own now."

"Be my guest," said Mrs. Spence. "The lawnmower is in the garage."

He set his coffee cup down on the table between them and rose. "I think I'll give it a quick trim."

"Right now?"

The mower was an ancient engine-less machine with two wheels and a cylindrical set of blades. It took a fairly strenuous push to get it into motion. He manhandled it around the corner of the house to the front lawn. Mrs. Spence was gathering up coffeepot and cups on the front porch. "You actually push this thing yourself?"

"Of course," she said as she disappeared into the house. "It keeps me fit."

"I'll bet."

He started at the sidewalk and worked his way toward the house. The blades weren't very sharp and he had to retrace his steps, going over each strip twice. But he soon began to get into a rhythm. The whirling blades made a pleasant clatter, snippets of grass flew in the mower's wake and gave off a familiar sweet freshly cut smell. It had been a while since he had smelled freshly cut grass. There was something comforting about it. He trudged back and forth, leaning into it, working up a bit of a sweat. The air cooled, the sky purpled above the rooftops across the street, lights began to come on in the houses.

This was, he imagined, much what the neighborhood might have been like in 1952 when an off-duty Raleigh fireman pushed a clattering mower back and forth across this stretch of grass — thinking perhaps of a son off at war. It would have been a pleasant, comfortable place to come home to. It seemed still to be. There were tricycles and basketball hoops in driveways along the street. Boylan Heights was enjoying something of a revival these days — young people moving in, fixing up the old homes — New Raleigh infiltrating the havens of the Old. And then there were a few, like Dahlia Spence, holding on to something. A history — some good, some not so good. But a history, nonetheless. It would be, Will thought, a comfortable place to spend his meantime.

It was almost dark when he finished and put the mower away in the garage. He made a mental note to pick up a can of 3-In-One oil and a file from the hardware store tomorrow. The mower was okay. It just needed a little maintenance. He liked the way it sounded and felt. Solid. Dependable. Uncomplicated.

Upstairs in the apartment he showered and put on pajamas and slippers. He turned on the radio and listened to the news from the public station in Chapel Hill. Then he turned off the radio and the lights and sat in the dark letting the night close in around him. He tried not to think of anything in particular, and he pretty much succeeded. A good while passed, and then he got up and went to bed.

He slept soundly and awakened early. There was just the faintest light outside, the first twittering of the stirring birds in the trees of Dahlia Spence's garden. He looked at his wristwatch on the bedside table: 5:48. He had become accustomed over the past month to waking early, or at least to being awakened. Deputies marched along the hallways of the Wake County Jail every morning at six announcing that it was a glorious new day and the inmates, if they were to take full advantage of its opportunities, must arise from their fart sacks. After years of working at Channel Seven until nearly midnight and then sleeping until eight, it was a novel thing to Will. A sea change in habit, to which he had adapted more easily than he had expected. And now, free from confinement and regimentation, he thought that he would keep the habit. There was now the added pleasure of bird sounds and of early sunlight.

But there was something else here, something nagging at the back of his mind, an itch of an idea that he couldn't quite make out. Something that had come to him in the night while he slept. A dream? Perhaps. But what had he dreamed? He couldn't quite make it out at first. It seemed hidden behind a curtain, waiting for some signal to reveal itself. He got out of bed and went to the open window overlooking Dahlia Spence's back-yard garden. He stood there, trying to look obliquely away from the thing instead of straight at it. He waited for several minutes while the new light got stronger and objects in the yard came slowly into focus—birdbath, love seat, plants and grass. Grass. He remembered.

It wasn't a dream at all, not in the sense of a dream in which images drifted in a netherland between pseudofact and fantasy. It was, instead, a vivid and lucid re-creation of a specific moment from his past. A summer day in Dysart, North Carolina. He was mowing Buster Dysart's lawn. There was a sense of exquisite pain about it, of something lost. But, too, and this surprised him utterly, there was a sense of something worth seeking, worth finding again. It had something to do with grass, but it was more than that. Still, it started with grass.

He turned from the window and padded to the bathroom and stared at himself in the mirror above the lavatory. His eyebrows went up and a tiny smile tugged at the corners of his mouth and he said softly to himself, "Well, I'll be damned."

———

HE SPENT THE DAY, a Friday, making domestic arrangements. Using the check Morris had given him, he opened two bank accounts: one for personal use, one for his new business. He put in an order for telephone service. He had the oil changed in his car. He shopped for toiletries and a few grocery items: mostly canned and frozen goods; milk, orange juice and shredded wheat for breakfast.

He bought a cookbook that advertised, on its cover, that it was for people who hate to cook. It wasn't that he hated it, but that he was ignorant and thus inept about what went on in a kitchen. Put him at the grill on the back deck with a nice sirloin and he could do just fine. Now, though, he had no back deck or grill and—given the size of his bank account—he didn't expect to eat a lot of sirloin, not anytime soon. Maybe later when his new business got off the ground.

His business. He was still astonished both by the idea and by the way it had come to him. Where *had* it come from? Maybe something Wingfoot had said while they were eating lunch at McDonald's. Or Mrs. Spence's lawn, the clattering old push mower, the smell and feel of freshly cut grass. Or his real-as-life dream. All of the above. Whatever, the seed had sprouted as he slept, and now it was emerging as the day went on as a full-grown thing, leafy and multibranched. He didn't even need to focus on it. Details appeared unbidden at odd moments. He could see in his mind a bookkeeping ledger in which he would tote up accounts—income for this, outgo for that—in neat columns. Figures that represented specific, concrete acts. He could see himself doing exactly what his idea called for him to do. It not only made perfectly good sense, it was right.

So Will spent a busy Friday, occupied with mundane details of establishing some mode of living while the plan took shape virtually on its own, a self-propelled idea. He was the empty, upright vessel, being filled with this thing that—if not a way of getting his life back, as he had originally intended—was a way of beginning to make a new one.

As night came he sat in the chair by the window and put the idea into words on a legal pad. It was so fully formed that what he wrote needed almost no editing or rearranging. When he finished he looked it over carefully. And then at the bottom he added a name. A partner.

———

HE ARRIVED AT PALMER's Chapel Hill bungalow at midmorning on Saturday to find Palmer emerging from his BMW, two plastic grocery bags in hand. Palmer stood at the open door of the car as Will pulled into the driveway behind him and got out.

"Hi," Will said.

Palmer eyed him warily. "You're out."

"No, I escaped. There's a posse out looking for me, but I thought, hell, Chapel Hill? A posse would never think of Chapel Hill."

"Your beard's grown out a lot," Palmer said.

Will ran his fingers through his beard. "Another reason the posse won't catch me." He reached for one of the grocery bags. "Let me help you with those." He followed Palmer into the house. "I've been doing some grocery shopping on my own. Winn-Dixie had a special on frozen dinners. Yesterday, I had mesquite chicken with English peas. Oh, and a cookie. It was part of the dinner. I don't have a microwave, so I had to cook it in the regular oven. But they tell you on the back just how to do it. Anybody who can read directions can heat up a frozen dinner."

He stood in the kitchen doorway while Palmer put away the groceries: a six-pack of beer, a large bag of pretzels, granola bars, a carton of orange juice, several cans of chunky soup. Palmer crumpled the plastic grocery bags and dropped them into a flip-top trash can.

"You know, you really ought to save those. If you'll put your trash in those smaller bags and tie up the top, it's easier to handle. And when the garbage truck comes around . . . you do have curbside pickup, don't you? Amazing, that big mechanical arm on the truck that reaches out and picks up the whole roll-out garbage container and dumps it in the top. Just like pouring soup from a can into a pot. But if the trash inside the roll-out thing is loose, sometimes it just scatters all over the place, especially if there's any wind. If it's in the small grocery bags, you don't have that problem."

Palmer stood there open-mouthed, staring at him. Then he walked past Will into the living room and on out the front door. He sat down on the front steps. Will followed and sat down beside him.

"What do you want?" Palmer asked softly after a moment.

"Just checking in."

"Aren't you violating your probation by being out of Wake County?"

"Well, I haven't had an official visit with my probation officer yet. That's Monday. So . . . well, yes, you're right."

"You could get arrested again if the cops caught you over here."

"And the judge would stick my shiny pink ass right back in jail."

Palmer propped his elbows on his knees and massaged his temples with his thumbs. Will thought he seemed to be pretty much his old self: hair freshly cut, face shaved, attire—khakis, Docksiders (no socks), knit shirt clean and wrinkle-free. And there was no smell of marijuana in the house. Palmer would be wanting to return to his former life, now that Will had cleaned up his mess.

Palmer caught Will looking him over. "I met with the committee," he said.

"And?"

"They're letting me back in. On probation."

"Like me. Probation."

"Yeah."

"Congratulations."

"Yeah."

"Nobody knows but the people at the medical school?"

"No."

"Your mother? Sidney and Consuela?"

"Like you told me. I lied like a dog. Only I didn't have to lie, just keep my mouth shut. I guess in the strictest sense, keeping your mouth shut amounts to a kind of lie. But . . ."

"So," Will said, "you got away with it."

Palmer gave him a sharp look, but didn't say anything. He went back to massaging his temples.

"Now that that's settled, have you given any thought to what you're gonna do this summer?"

"Well," Palmer said hopefully, "I thought I'd do some reading, get ahead on stuff for the fall. Maybe some time at the beach."

"Sounds like fun. But what if you got a fantastic offer?"

Palmer's thumbs froze.

"I have a business proposition," Will said.

"What kind of business?"

Will sketched out the plan in the air with his hands. "I've got it all worked out. A truck with a small trailer to hold the equipment. You see 'em all the time tooling around Raleigh. The trailer is a little low, flat-bodied job with wire mesh on the sides and a ramp in the rear that folds down so you can roll the equipment out. The bed of the truck holds the small stuff."

Palmer's mouth worked silently for a moment before anything came out. "What small stuff?"

"Gas cans, leaf blower, toolbox, spare parts. Small stuff. The only thing I don't have is a name."

"Oh, shit," Palmer said in a voice so low that Will could barely hear him.

"No, I don't think so," Will said. "I don't think it would do for a convicted felon to be driving around town with a sign on the side of his truck that reads Oh Shit. A sure way to get in trouble again. I had thought about Mowers 'R' Us. Or Two Guys and a Rake."

"Two guys."

"Me and you. You and me. Frick and Frack. Father and Son."

Palmer shook his head slowly.

Will nodded his head slowly. There was a rhythm to it, even though their heads were going in opposite directions.

"Let me get this straight," Palmer said. "You're going to start a lawn care business? Mow lawns for a *living*?"

"I've got to support myself. It's something I know how to do."

"Well, I don't."

"Ah, there's nothing to it. Just keep going in a straight line, remember to turn at the end of each row. And as you say, you've got the summer . . ."

They sat there for a moment before Palmer finally said, "What are you up to?"

"Like I said, just a business proposition. Take it or leave it."

Palmer stood with a jerk. "You think you've got my ass in a sling because . . ." He waved his arms, taking in Chapel Hill, medical school, the Greensboro Palmers, Clarice, marijuana, all of it. He bounded off the steps into the yard and stood there several feet away, glaring. "You think I'm going to push a fucking lawn mower around Raleigh all summer because you've got my ass in a sling."

Will felt a little twitch of anger at the back of his neck, just below the hairline. He smiled and it went away. "Aren't you glad we're having this talk, son? I mean . . ." he spread his hands, ". . . all these years we've hardly had anything to say to each other. And here we are having a frank discussion about the future course of our lives, yours and mine, at least over the next three months. I say *bully for us!*" He punched the air with his fist like a quarterback completing a sixty-yard touchdown pass.

Palmer's face flushed, his fists clenched. "Okay. That was a helluva thing, what you did. But you did it on your own. I didn't beg you to bail me out."

"I can't force you to do anything," Will said. "You're a grown man. Making your own grown-up decisions. The master of your fate, the captain of your soul. And now, by the grace of God and the dean's committee, once again a medical student, a disciple of Hippocrates, a healer in training. Therefore, I can certainly understand why you don't want to push a fucking lawn mower around Raleigh all summer. Yadda, yadda, yadda." Then he got up and went into the house.

The telephone number at his former home had been changed. No surprise there. Clarice had sent adamant instructions through Morris: Will was not to attempt to communicate with her in any way. If he did, she would get a restraining order, and that would just mean more legal trouble for Will. But she had taken no chances. She had changed the number.

It was Saturday morning. She wouldn't be at home anyway. One of Raleigh's best and most successful real estate agents would be out there hustling houses on a day when prospective buyers were out there looking.

"May I ask who's calling?" the woman at Snively and Ellis Realty inquired.

"It's her husband and it's urgent and it's about our son," he said.

He could hear some kind of saw in the background when she answered her cell phone, a high-pitched whine that dropped a bit in pitch as it cut through a board. He had come to know the sound well in the days that he had been at home with the Christian Renovators while they demolished the rear of the house. Clarice was obviously at a construction site, one of those new subdivisions.

"What's the matter?" she asked, a rush of panic in her voice. "Is he hurt? Where is he?"

"He's fine. A little distracted, I think. He's been studying so hard."

Will looked up to see Palmer in the bedroom doorway. He stopped there, but his hand came up, reaching out toward the telephone receiver, as if he might levitate it out of Will's grasp from several yards away. He was shaking his head. *Don't do that,* his eyes pleaded.

"Just a moment," Will said to the phone. He cupped his hand over the mouthpiece and waited. Palmer's shoulders sagged.

"I wanted to tell you about some plans we've made for the summer."

"We?"

"Palmer and me."

"He told me he was going to be doing research in Chapel Hill."

"It seems he's changed his mind."

Palmer disappeared from the doorway.

"To what?" Clarice asked.

"He and I are starting a lawn service."

There was a long pause. The saw whined and the engine of some fairly hefty machine started up in the background. "Is he there with you?" Clarice asked.

"Not at the moment," Will said. In the living room, the television came on. The tinny sound of explosions, pulsating music, frantic voices. A kids' show.

"Tell him to call me," Clarice ordered.

"I will. I'm sure it will be soon." He paused. "Just one other thing, Clarice. Are you handling celibacy any better than I am? Or are you not handling it at all?"

Click.

In the living room, Palmer was on the sofa, hunched forward toward the television set, staring blankly at the screen. He didn't look up.

"We'll have a good summer," Will said. "Father and son bonding. Lawn mowing, after all, is a guy thing."

"Blackmail," Palmer said bitterly, biting off the word.

"Why, Palmer . . . did you think I was about to rat on you?"

Palmer shook his head in disgust.

Will started for the front door. "By the way," he said, "you don't have to push."

Palmer looked up then. "What?"

"You don't think we're going to run a professional lawn service with a rinky-dink push mower with a twenty-one-inch cut and a two-horsepower Briggs and Stratton engine, do you? Son, we're talking self-propelled. Big-ass mowers with a little platform on the rear that you stand up on and ride like a Roman chariot. They're magnificent machines, son. Magnificent machines."

20 | WILL HAD CRUISED THE STRIP of automobile dealerships on Capital Boulevard on Sunday afternoon, stopping to check the used-truck sections, and he had spotted what he thought was a likely candidate. He and Palmer were in the lot now at nine-thirty on Monday morning, giving it a once-over. Or at least Will was. Palmer didn't seem much interested.

It was a 1991 medium-green Ford F-250 pickup with 107,852 miles on it. Automatic transmission, air-conditioning, AM/FM tape player, 8-cylinder 5.0 liter engine, power steering. It had a large metal tool chest that took up almost a third of the open bed in the rear, the kind he had seen on trucks driven by carpenters and plumbers and the like. It was a useful-looking truck, nothing fancy, in good shape inside and out except for a minor crease on the left corner of the rear bumper. Splashed in big white letters and numbers across the passenger side of the windshield: LOW MILEAGE GREAT BUY $7,495.

Palmer gave it a sour glance, hands jammed glumly in the pockets of his khakis, his shoulders semi-hunched against the morning, as if he were leaning into a stiff wind. There was, in fact, a bit of a breeze that flapped the plastic pennants hanging above the used-truck section, but not enough of a wind to hunch your shoulders against.

"It's already got a trailer hitch," Will said.

Palmer shrugged.

"And I guess the engine's big enough to pull a trailer load of equipment."

Another shrug.

"What do you think?" Will asked.

"Dad, I don't know a damn thing about trucks. I drive a BMW."

"Is your car a stick shift?" When Palmer had arrived home with the BMW a year ago, they had gone for a ride, he and Clarice, she sitting in the passenger bucket seat, he in the back. But he could not remember whether the transmission was manual or automatic. It was the only time he had been in the car.

"Stick shift," Palmer said.

"Well, the truck will be easier to drive. It's automatic. We'll have to get used to pulling a trailer, though."

Palmer grunted.

A salesman had spotted them and came loping across the lot now, calling out, "Hep' ya'll?"

"My son and I are in the market for a truck," Will said. "We're going into the lawn care business."

The salesman, a stocky silver-haired man, gripped the tailgate of the truck reassuringly. "Well, this 'un will do the job for you. Plenty of engine, low mileage, body's in good shape."

"Low mileage? The odometer says more than a hundred thousand."

"Truck like this," the salesman said, patting the hood, "well maintained, that's hardly any mileage at all."

Will pointed out the crease in the rear bumper.

"You could probably get 'er straightened out for a coupla hundred dollars," the salesman said, "but ain't hurtin' anything."

"Gas mileage?"

"You gonna be pulling a trailer?"

"Yes."

" 'Bout twelve, thirteen in town."

"That's not much," Will said.

"Well," the salesman drawled, "I can sell you a truck that'll get better gas mileage. But if you're gonna be pulling a trailer, you need something with some heft to it. A little dinky-ass truck? You'll have transmission problems by the end of the summer."

Will pointed to the windshield. "Is that your best price?"

"That's our no-haggle price. Wanna drive 'er?"

"Sure," Will said. "I guess I'd better."

While the salesman went back to the showroom for the keys,

Will walked slowly around the truck and gave it what he hoped was a careful inspection. He opened the driver-side door and slipped in under the wheel. Cloth seats, rubber mats on the floor. No cracks in the vinyl of the dashboard. He found the hood lever and pulled it, then got out and opened the hood and peered in at the engine. He wasn't quite sure what he was looking for, but it seemed reasonably clean. He closed the hood. Palmer was standing several yards away, back turned to Will and the truck, hands still in his pockets, watching the traffic moving by on Capital.

"Green," Will said.

Palmer looked back at Will, just a turn of his head.

"Good color for a lawn service truck," Will said.

Palmer turned back to the traffic.

The salesman returned with the keys and handed them to Will. "Take your time," he said.

Will offered the keys to Palmer. "Want to drive?"

"No," Palmer said, and got in on the passenger side.

Will started the truck and listened for a moment to the idling engine. It was . . . well, idling. Nothing seemed amiss. Just as he was about to back out of the parking place, Palmer rolled down the window on his side and asked the salesman, "What if the transmission falls out next week?"

"Thirty-day dealer warranty," the salesman said. "Anything happens, you bring 'er back and we'll fix it."

Will drove along Capital Boulevard for several blocks, heading toward downtown.

Palmer turned on the radio and flipped through the pre-sets—a couple of country stations, an oldies, public radio in Chapel Hill. He re-set all of them with pop and rock stations, working intently at it. Will cast sidelong glances at him, and suddenly he had a strong urge to touch Palmer—anything, just the barest brush of his arm would do. But instinct told Will that trying too hard—a touch or the wrong word—might well spoil things. Palmer seemed like a skittish colt, ready to bolt if spooked. And if he did, if he just said, "To hell with it," what would Will do? Not a damn thing. He would let Palmer go because that would be the only possible thing. But he wanted desperately for that not to happen because he didn't want to blow this one. He had blown some other things. Not this one.

Instead he said, "That was a good point, about the transmission. I wouldn't have thought about it."

Palmer finished fiddling with the radio, left it on a station that was playing a rap song with lyrics that Will couldn't understand, and sat back in the seat, body turned slightly away.

"The radio . . . is it pretty good?" Will asked.

"Okay," Palmer said. "You didn't expect mega-bass in a ten-year-old truck, did you?"

"I guess not."

"Are you gonna buy it?"

"I think so. Seems okay to me."

"Is it a good price?"

"I guess."

"Drive by the house," Palmer said. "I'll find out." Will gave him a puzzled look. "I'll look it up on the Internet."

He let Palmer out in front of the house on LeGrand. "I'll park down the street," Will said. "I'm not supposed to be here."

Palmer said, "She's really pissed at you, you know that."

Will made a face. "When somebody asks for a divorce after twenty-five years . . ."

"I don't blame her," Palmer said.

Will didn't want to get into all that just now. They would eventually, he supposed, have to thrash it out. But there was enough on the plate right now without it.

He parked a half-block from the house. He waited ten minutes, twenty. He rummaged through the glove compartment of the truck — registration, some old state safety inspection reports, an owner's manual. *Safety tip: headlights should always be on when windshield wipers are on. Many states require this.* He tried the windshield wipers, emergency flasher signal and dome light. Everything worked except the dome light. A bulb, he thought. He would ask about it when they returned to the dealership.

He saw movement out of the corner of his eye and looked up to see Phyllis Durkin jogging by on the sidewalk next to the truck, clad in shorts and T-shirt, arms pumping. Phyllis had gotten into fitness about the time she had gotten into religion. The Lord's temple and all that. She occasionally rose early enough to jog with Clarice. She had great legs. Not as good as Clarice's, but great, nonetheless. She listened to Bible study tapes as she jogged. She had her headphones on now. Phyllis glanced at the truck as she passed, then stopped several yards down the sidewalk and looked back at it. Will started to wave, but he saw that she was really staring hard, brow creased, and realized after a moment that she didn't recognize him and that she thought he looked suspicious. A Neighborhood Watch kind of stare. He could see her making mental notes: bearded middle-aged man in green Ford pickup truck. He thought for a moment she might retrace her steps and look at the tag, but she didn't. She turned away and went on, glancing back a couple of times over her shoulder. He hoped Palmer would get back before she called the cops.

Amazing. His next-door neighbor for all these years and she had no idea who he was. Neither did anyone else, apparently. A couple of times in the days since his release from jail, he had noticed a turn of head at the sound of his voice. But the voice and the appearance didn't connect. He had disappeared into the crowd, into the mass of ordinary humanity, right here in the middle of Raleigh, where he had, just a month ago, been the most recognizable face and voice in town. As he had intended. There were moments when he missed his former persona, but he was finding a freedom in ordinariness that he had only guessed at. People treated you differently if you were ordinary. As Phyllis Durkin had done.

Palmer was back, carrying a plastic grocery bag. "Too much," he said as he slid in on the passenger side.

"Too much what?"

He produced a piece of paper from his pants pocket, unfolded it and handed it to Will. A computer printout. "This Internet site tells you how much used vehicles are worth." He showed Will the results of his search: a Ford F-250 truck of this vintage, condition and mileage, equipped as this one was, had a trade-in value of $5,500 and a retail value of $7,305. Retail was what you could expect to pay on a dealer's lot. A fraternity brother, Palmer explained, had showed him the Web site. That made sense. Palmer wasn't a used-vehicle kind of fellow. More the new-BMW type. "You sure you want a truck this old? With this much mileage on it?" he asked.

"It's what I can afford. And it seems to run okay."

"Then offer seven thousand."

"The salesman said it was a no-haggle price."

"Are you gonna just take his word for it?"

"I've never haggled over a vehicle before."

"Neither have I. I've never *bought* a vehicle before. But one of these days, I probably will. And I'll haggle."

"Does your mother haggle?"

"You ought to see her at the flea market."

"What's in the grocery bag?" Will asked.

"The name of your lawn service."

"Our lawn service."

He opened the bag and pulled out a baseball cap. It was the one Clarice and Palmer had given Will for Father's Day years ago. Gold letters stitched across the front: CAPTAIN SATURDAY.

Will put it on. "What do you think?"

"I think you look like a dork." He took the cap off Will's head and bent the bill double, forming a sharp crease down the middle. He handed it back to Will, who put it back on. "Better."

"Can I pass as a lawn care professional?"

Palmer stared at him for a long moment. "I don't want you to think I'm getting into this."

"You mean *into* as, like, you know, getting *with* it?"

"Yeah."

"Why did you bring me the cap, Palmer?"

He shrugged. "I guess it was being in the house, just by myself. Neither you or Mom there. It's been a while since I've been there by myself. I don't, you know, like, live there anymore."

"Neither do I."

"That's just what I thought. I thought, 'The poor sonofabitch doesn't live here anymore.'"

"I'll take whatever I can get," Will said. "Pity will do just fine."

"Dad . . ."

"Yes?"

"I'm pissed, too. At both of you."

Then he turned his head away and stared out the window at the sidewalk.

Will started the truck and headed down LeGrand. When he passed the Durkin house, he saw Phyllis looking out her living room window. He waved. She didn't.

They went back to the dealership and made the offer, then settled on a price of seventy-one hundred. So much for no-haggle. The salesman even threw in a full tank of gas. When they sat down in the dealership office to fill out the paperwork, the salesman finally recognized him. "Will Baggett!" His eyes brightened, and then he remembered. "You . . . ah . . ."

You could almost see the newsreel playing in his head—headlines, pictures, dramatic music, Paul Harvey: *And in Raleigh, North Carolina, a television legend meets a fateful end . . .*

"Yeah," the salesman said. "The beard, the glasses . . . sure fooled me. You don't look like yourself."

"He's not himself," Palmer said.

The salesman gave them both an odd look.

Will said, "Don't worry, I'm paying cash."

Actually, a check drawn on his new bank account. The business account. It was a temporary check, one of a small book of them he had picked up at the bank en route to the dealership this morning. The permanent printed ones would arrive later in the mail. The account was set up in the name of Baggett Lawn Service. He reminded himself to go by the bank when they finished here and change the name. The salesman looked at the check for a long moment. Will thought he was about to say, "I'm sure it's all right."

But instead he disappeared for a few minutes through a door marked BUSINESS OFFICE and returned apologetic.

"No problem," Will said. "You can never tell about people these days."

Ford F-250 truck: $7,385 including tax, tag and title.

The consummation of the truck deal—including a visit to the bank and a trip to the state Department of Motor Vehicles for registration and a temporary tag—took the rest of Monday.

On Tuesday Will and Palmer shopped for a mower, their most basic piece of equipment, settling on a massive big-tired yellow machine called a Hy-Ryder. They had done research at McDonald's, where a couple of the already-established lawn services regularly took their lunch breaks, parking their trucks and trailers in the supermarket lot next door. Will, accustomed to the faithful purring Honda which he had followed about his yard for several growing seasons, was impressed by the size and bulk of the professional mowers with their five-gallon gasoline tanks and muscular engines and huge cutting decks. They reminded him in a way of military vehicles—self-propelled howitzers and tank-killers, grease-stained and battle-scarred. One trailer held a Hy-Ryder. While Palmer got Big Macs and fries from McDonald's, Will climbed onto the trailer and stood on the rear platform of the mower, gripping the handlebars, imagining the machine propelling him briskly across a vast expanse of ragged green lawn, leaving a pristinely clipped work of art in his wake. It felt right—solid, trustworthy, efficient. A sticker, peeling from the side of the mower deck, told where it had been purchased. They took their lunch to a picnic table in Pullen Park, then went to the dealership and, after a lengthy discourse with a salesman, purchased a Hy-Ryder Model XG-70 with three forward gears and two reverse, a twenty-horsepower engine and a forty-eight-inch cut. They also bought a new self-propelled Honda for trim work.

Two mowers: $5,398.

On Wednesday morning they acquired a used flatbed trailer through a classified advertisement in the *News and Observer.* Using the measurements of the two mowers, they determined that they would fit nicely onto the trailer and still leave plenty of room for smaller equipment.

Used trailer: $750.

On Wednesday afternoon they towed the trailer to a welding shop to add sturdy metal sides and a fold-down rear ramp and, at Palmer's suggestion, a metal enclosure at the front end of the trailer to hold the smaller equipment and protect it from bad weather, road dust, theft, et cetera.

Welding: $390.

Thursday morning, while the trailer was being outfitted, they returned to the lawn equipment dealership and purchased a string trimmer, a backpack leaf blower, and a shrubbery clipper, all gasoline-powered.

Assorted power equipment: $1,825.

On Thursday morning, they ordered two plastic signs with magnetic backing to place on the doors of the truck. Then they spent a couple of hours at Home Depot, where they bought two five-gallon plastic gasoline containers, tie-down straps, assorted hand tools (wrenches, screwdrivers, pliers), grease-cutting hand soap, a length of rope, a roll of duct tape, a can of WD-40 ("You never can tell when you'll need rope or duct tape or WD-40," Will told Palmer), a case of thirty-weight motor oil for the mowers and another of two-cycle oil mixture for the hand-held equipment, a large thermos jug for ice water, and a first aid kit.

Magnetic signs, Home Depot purchases: $461.

They stood at the rear of the pickup outside Home Depot after loading their purchases into the tool chest. "Uniforms," Will said. "I thought maybe green. To match the truck."

"Hell no," Palmer said. "I ain't wearing no goddamn uniform."

"Son, that's not like you—using improper English."

"I'm doing it for emphasis."

"Oh."

"You can tell Mom and Daddy Sid and Mama Consuela and the dean and anybody else what this is all about. You can gather a crowd on the capitol steps and sell popcorn and inform the world. But I ain't wearing no goddamn uniform."

Since Monday morning, Palmer's mood had ranged from mild interest to outright disdain, even occasional flashes of righteous anger, with a great deal of determined sullenness in between. Will had managed, for the most part, to ignore it. At least, Palmer had not out-and-out refused anything. Until now. "Just trying to be helpful," Will said. "Didn't want you to get your good clothes all messed up. Grease and grass stains and stuff."

"I'll mow buck naked if I have to, but I ain't . . ."

". . . wearing no goddamned uniform."

"Bet your sweet ass."

"Do you mind if I do?"

"Look like a goober if you want to," Palmer sniffed.

"Okay. No uniforms. For now."

On Friday morning they picked up the trailer from the welding shop. The welder had done a nice job. The sides and fold-up rear ramp were of a thick wire-mesh material—sturdy enough to protect the equipment without adding a great deal of weight. The metal enclosure for the smaller gear was of similar construction, with a solid aluminum top much like the tool chest on the pickup. Both ramp and enclosure had hasps for padlocks. The welder had even fashioned a couple of triangular metal chocks to go under the rear wheels of the big mower to keep it from rolling about in transit.

They attached the trailer to the truck, connected the lighting harness to give them brake- and taillights and turn signals, and then drove slowly away toward the lawn equipment store with Will at the wheel. He thought it handled just fine. You could tell there was something back there—it had a feel and noises of its own—and you had to be careful turning corners to give it plenty of room, but if you were careful and didn't get in a hurry, you'd probably do okay.

The equipment fit perfectly—big and small mowers at the rear, tied down with the straps they had bought at Home Depot, the string trimmer and other smaller equipment stowed neatly in the metal enclosure along with the gasoline containers. Everything else went into the tool chest on the truck.

Will stood back, admiring truck and trailer and equipment, then walked all the way around the rig, admiring it some more. It was all of a piece. It fit. It looked right. They had scrimped on nothing, buying only first-rate stuff that was unlikely to break down, become balky, cause bothersome and irritating problems.

Will harbored a natural suspicion of machines—going back, he thought, to that wretched excuse for a lawn mower he had pushed through the clotted Bermuda grass of Dysart in his twelfth summer. Now he had an entire truck and trailer rig *full* of machines, and the sight of it all, this collection of engines and carburetors and wheels and blades and gears and belts and other assorted moving parts, made him just a bit queasy.

Will pulled a small notebook out of a rear pants pocket and totaled the figures of the purchases he had made over the past five days: $16,209. He had bought so well that he was now virtually broke. There was a little money in his personal bank account, but the business account was all but bone dry. The goddamn stuff *better* work.

He turned to Palmer, who was sprawled on a bench in front of the lawn equipment store—legs splayed, arms folded across his chest, eyes closed. "What do you think?" Will asked.

Palmer opened his eyes and grunted.

Will indicated the rig. "It appears we're combat ready."

"May I go now?" Palmer asked. "I'm spending the weekend in Greensboro."

"Not yet. We've got to try all this stuff out."

Palmer's face twisted into a disgusted snarl. "Where?"

———

THEY TRIED THREE OF THE corporate headquarters in Research Triangle Park before they finally found one that would let them mow the sweeping expanse of grass that surrounded it. *We don't want money, we just need to test some equipment. Pay your regular guys.* Palmer sat glowering in the truck, looking each time Will returned as if he might bolt, flag down a cop, and yell that he was being held captive by a madman. He didn't, but he said to Will after the third stop, "You're a fucking lunatic, you know that?" Will made what he hoped was a reasonable imitation of a lunatic — mouth twisted, eyes rolled, guttural sounds — and drove on.

The building manager at the pharmaceutical company headquarters, though as taken aback as the ones at the first three buildings, at least had a sense of humor. When Will explained what they were about, he shrugged and said, "Be my guest. Just be careful around the azalea beds."

It took them the rest of the afternoon. The parking lot began to empty just after five, everybody heading home for the weekend, joining the flood of cars backing up along Cornwallis Road. Will rode the big mower, feeling a bit like General Patton driving hard to rescue the Bloody Bastards of Bastogne. It sang and vibrated underneath him with a deep bass voice that pulsated through his limbs, surrounding him with the smell of grass and the tang of the engine settling itself into a groove. It was a bit scary at first, so much machinery, so much power. But by the time he had ridden it for a half-hour, learning how to maneuver, shift gears, handle the throttle, he began to feel somewhat more comfortable. The thing was, he realized, to let the machine do the work. Just ride and guide.

Then he turned it over to Palmer, who was by now fairly seething with anger, his motions jerky and impatient while Will showed him the controls and gave him a few pointers. He barreled off across the lawn — back rigid, eyes flashing — while Will started the Honda and cut close around the flower and shrub beds. He used the string trimmer around the trees and then powered up the blower and scoured the sidewalks and driveway of grass clippings.

He finished and was stowing away the blower in the trailer's locker when Palmer eased the big mower up to the ramp at the rear and cut the engine back to idle. His clothes — knit shirt and khakis — were sweat soaked. His hair was plastered to his head.

But the anger seemed to have leaked out of him. Will tossed him a towel. He wiped his face. "You want to put it on the trailer?" Palmer asked.

"Go ahead. Looks like you're doing okay."

Palmer shifted the mower into forward gear and gave it a little gas. There was a fleeting look of panic as it clattered up onto the ramp, but then he eased it onto the trailer bed and brought it to a stop beside the Honda. He cut the engine and climbed down, lifting the ramp and securing it in place. "I've never done anything like that," he said, staring wide-eyed at the mower. There was something almost like awe in his voice. He was trying to keep it out of there, but it sneaked through anyway.

"Well," Will said, "it all works."

"Yeah."

"I guess we'll get started for real on Monday."

Palmer looked over at him now. "Do you have any customers?"

"I'm still working on that one," Will said.

———

MORRIS DELESSEPS, elegantly informal in khaki walking shorts and purple polished-cotton short-sleeved pullover, was hovering over a succulent-looking hunk of pork tenderloin on his patio cooker when Will pulled down the driveway and eased to a stop on the parking pad at the rear of the house. Morris stared, barbecue fork hovering in midair, mouth slightly open. Will got out of the truck and walked over to the grill.

"All right," Morris said. "What?"

"I hijacked a shipment of lawn equipment."

Morris kept peering at the truck and trailer. Enroute, Will had picked up the magnetic signs and had attached them to the truck's doors: CAPTAIN SATURDAY'S LAWN SERVICE / 338-2506.

"Who is Captain Saturday?"

Will thumbed his chest.

Morris put a few hickory chips on the cooker's charcoal fire and closed the lid. Smoke drifted through vents on the sides and top. He went into the house and came back with two bottled beers. They sat. Morris had nice teak patio furniture. Expensive stuff. The beer was a European brand with a rich, full taste.

"You're my first customer," Will said.

"I already have a lawn service."

"But I'm going to tend your lawn for free. Well, almost."

"Almost what?"

"I'm going to park here at night."

"The hell you say."

Morris got up and walked over to the parking area and made a circle of the truck and trailer, carrying his beer bottle, taking an occasional swig. He returned and sat down again. He hiked one leg over the other, showing lean calf. Morris was, in most of his personifications, a trim and well-proportioned man. He had at one point several years ago developed a comfortable paunch to go along with one of his rumpled, tweedy, pipe-smoking phases, but once that was over he joined a downtown health club and took two-hour midday breaks to work out on Nautilus machines and slam himself around a racquetball court. Morris referred to the game as squash. He had a lean jaw and a flat belly. He wore clothes well. Now, Will felt grubby in his presence—clad in old jeans, dirty jogging shoes and a T-shirt that had SWIFT CREEK ELEMENTARY SCHOOL lettered on the front, a gift from one of his Weather Wizard appearances. He could smell his own sweat, faintly rank but honest.

"That's quite a get-up," Morris said, indicating the truck and trailer.

Will took a pull on his beer and eyed Morris across the rounded end of the bottle.

"I'm really quite astonished," Morris said.

"As my able and distinguished attorney says, I've got to make a living."

"It's not quite what I had imagined. Where did you come up with the idea?"

"My cousin Wingfoot, actually. At least, he planted the seed of the idea. Palmer and I . . ."

Morris's eyebrows shot up. "Palmer?"

"My business partner. For the summer. He's taking a break from academic rigor."

"What does Palmer think about"—he waved at the rig—"all this?"

"He says I'm not myself."

"And does . . ."

"Yes, Clarice knows. I've talked with her."

Morris made a soft buzzing sound, something like a fluorescent light that needs a new ballast.

Morris rose and tended the grill. The pork tenderloin was bubbling and aromatic, its juices wafting on the smoke from the hickory chips. Will was hungry, but he wouldn't stay for dinner if asked, not that Morris had given any indication of asking. Perhaps company was coming. Neighbors.

It was a tony North Raleigh neighborhood, a fashionable address. Morris had lived all over town at one time or another—even, at one point, on the fringe of a low-income area on the east side, during a particularly liberal period when he was doing a lot of pro bono legal work and serving on the boards of several fashionable charities. But now he was here with the rich folks. Spacious homes on spacious lots, not a thing in the area under a half-million. The developer had hauled in thirty-foot maples and river birch and oaks and had created the illusion of longevity on a hundred acres that had been mostly pasture land only five years before. Snively and Ellis had been the exclusive sales agent for the development and Clarice had sold several lots and homes, including the one Morris and his present wife, Sylvia, were living in. She had probably made enough on commissions here alone to pay for the addition on the rear of the house on LeGrand.

Back when the development was just getting started, she had mentioned in passing the possibility of their buying a lot and eventually building. But Will had discouraged it. He liked the house on LeGrand just fine. A reversal of roles. She was the one who insisted on an Old Raleigh address at the beginning. But over the years he had become more Old Raleigh than she, while she was now out making a lot of money from the New Raleigh crowd. He wondered how long she would keep the house on LeGrand, once the divorce was finalized (if indeed it was). She would get the house, he had no doubt of that. The woman always got the house, didn't she?

"So you've talked to Clarice," Morris said.

Will glanced at his watch. "Is your meter running?"

"No. I'm off duty."

"Yes. I called Clarice to tell her that Palmer was going to be working with me this summer. And I asked her if she was screwing Fincher Snively—well, not in so many words. She hung up."

"Goddamn," Morris sighed.

"Is she screwing Fincher?"

"I don't have the slightest idea. I don't have any contact at all with Clarice except through her attorney, who is as mean as a shithouse rat and would have my ass if I contacted her client directly. I am your attorney. And as *your* attorney, I will advise you again not to have any contact with Clarice. None, Will." He jabbed the air with the beer bottle. "None."

"Thank you," Will said.

They sipped on their beer. The back door opened and Sylvia leaned out. She was a busty redhead, an aerobics instructor at a health spa, with a big, throaty laugh and a tinge of country-girl coarseness. She held her liquor well and enjoyed ribald humor. Morris had married her during his buckskin-and-cowboy-boot phase. Now that he was affecting dark pinstripe and Gucci, Will wondered if Sylvia would last. "Morris honey, why is the lawn service here on . . ." Then she spotted Will. She stared.

"Hi, Sylvia. That's my truck and stuff. I'm going to be parking it here."

"Oh," she said. "I didn't recognize you. You look so different."

"I've lost some weight. That could be it."

"Probably."

"My son says I'm incognito."

"Yes, you are." Then, to Morris, "Which wine?"

"There's a new case of some rather good Beaujolais. Might go well with the pork."

Sylvia glanced at her watch. "The Thaggards will be here in thirty minutes," she said to Morris. Then she gave Will a tiny wave and closed the door.

"So Wingfoot gave you the idea," Morris said to Will.

"Not in so many words, but that's where it came from. He gave me the idea and then he disappeared, and I didn't even know it was an idea until I was dreaming and . . ." His voice trailed off. "Anyway, I worked out the rest myself."

"Wingfoot, as I remember you telling me, has a habit of disappearing."

"Yes."

"Are you thinking about disappearing?"

"Why should I disappear?"

"Might be easier on everyone concerned," Morris said.

"But I'd be a fugitive from justice," Will protested.

"Yes, there is that."

Will said, "When I was visiting with Wingfoot over in Pender County a few weeks ago, after I lost my job and banged up my knee, I told him that I was going back to Raleigh and get my life back. And Wingfoot told me an interesting thing. He said that everybody has two lives—the one he lives and the one he *might* live. I don't remember his exact words, but that's the gist of it."

A sweep of Morris's hand took in Will, his disguise, his truck and trailer full of lawn care equipment. "And is this your other life?"

"I don't know yet," Will said. "First things first. Figure out how to make a living, then make a life. I'm open to possibilities. It's sort of like bungee jumping, I imagine. I might crash to earth, or not. Right now I'm in free fall."

"A little scary?" Morris asked.

"Sure. No idea how it'll all turn out. Maybe when you die, whatever shape you're in at the exact moment you draw your last breath . . . well, that's how it turned out. Meanwhile, I guess I'm reinventing myself. But then, you of all people should know about that."

Morris frowned and cocked his head to one side. "How do you mean?"

"You reinvent yourself about every six months or so, Morris. You've been doing it as long as I've known you."

Morris seemed amused. "Would you call it reinvention or transformation?"

"What would you call it?" Will asked.

"A little of both, I suppose."

"Why do you do it?"

"I get bored," Morris said.

"Well, at least I've got a better reason."

"What's that?"

"I don't have any choice. And on the other hand, I have every choice in the world."

"And is that, to use your word, 'better'?"

Will finished his beer, placed the empty bottle on the teak table at his elbow, and rose to go. "Well, different. I shouldn't judge."

Morris stood and walked with him to the driveway. "As long as I've known you," he said, "you've been a pretty earnest guy. Almost painfully so. And a little naïve. Over the years you've undergone a transformation of your own. Will Baggett, TV star. But it appears to me you're still at heart an earnest guy. And still a little naïve."

"I suppose. You were always a great deal more worldly-wise than me, Morris. Better able to see those things."

He laid a fraternal hand on Will's shoulder. "You've fucked some things up, Will."

You asshole, Will thought, but he resisted the urge to lash out. "Sorry I can't stay for dinner," he said. "But I've got Salisbury steak and mashed potatoes waiting at home. Some other time."

"You're a piece of work, Will," Morris said with an even smile. "You were just kidding about your rig."

"Partly," Will said. "I'm taking the truck. Try to keep the neighborhood kids off my trailer, okay?"

21 | It was Dahlia Spence who found their first real customer. In fact, three of them.

Will had outlined his venture as they sat in his kitchen having Sunday breakfast, to which he had invited her on a spur-of-the-moment whim Saturday evening while they stood talking in the back yard. He prepared coffee, eggs, bacon and English muffins and managed to bring the whole business off in more-or-less-edible order by the time she arrived promptly at eight, already dressed in a bright print dress, hat and gloves for church services.

"So you've bought a lawn mower," she said over a second cup of coffee.

He smiled, thinking of the hulking machine that sat on the trailer in Morris's driveway. Was it making Morris a little crazy? He hoped so. "Yes ma'am, I certainly have bought a lawn mower."

"You could have borrowed mine," she said. "It's a perfectly good mower. I thought you did a right nice job with it on my yard."

"I appreciate the offer, but I thought I probably ought to have my own equipment."

Dahlia nodded appreciatively. "I admire your entrepreneurial spirit. Have you been mulling over the idea of a lawn service for some time?"

"No ma'am," Will said. "It just came to me all of a sudden. An impulse, I guess you'd call it. Wingfoot said I should act on impulse."

He was sitting in his easy chair by the open window late that afternoon, reading over the manuals that had come with his power equipment and listening to the birds chatter in the back yard, when Dahlia's voice floated up to him. "Mister Baggett . . ."

He looked out to see her standing at the top of her back steps. "I have something for you."

What she had was three addresses. She had been on the telephone all afternoon, contacting members of her garden club. Did anyone need a lawn service? Well, she knew of a good one. "But," Will mildly protested, "you don't know whether I'm any good or not. What if I embarrass you by destroying somebody's azalea bed or scalping a lawn?"

Dahlia gave him a slightly disgusted look. "Anybody can mow grass and stay out of the azaleas," she said. "You seem like a nice man, Mr. Baggett, but I get the impression that you're a trifle tenuous at times."

"I guess I'm just trying to feel my way these days. I've been a little off balance."

"Don't pussyfoot through this life," she commanded. "Go boldly. Occasionally, go impulsively."

"As Wingfoot said."

"Wingfoot is partly full of bull-hockey, but once in a while he says something worth remembering."

Will accepted the piece of scented notepaper on which she had carefully written the names and addresses of his first customers. He gave her a little salute. "I'm grateful," he said. "And henceforth, Mrs. Spence, I shall, as you say, go boldly."

———

HE WAS UP ON Monday morning at five, feeling fit and fresh. He pushed back the furniture in his apartment and did some calisthenics: deep knee bends, side-straddle hops, trunk twisters, jogging in place. Being up, being vigorous this time of the day reminded him of college, the semester he had had an early-morning radio job. The guy who had the early shift before him got fired because he was chronically late to work. Will had no problem. He liked emerging from his apartment as the very first hint of light began to pale the sky above the trees across the street. He had felt lively and quick, at the very edge of something. It wasn't the job. It was being up early, getting a good start, getting ahead of things. Here now, thumping about in his apartment, he remembered how it felt way back yonder before he had acquired the habit of late-sleeping. Again, he felt lively, if not quite as quick as he had been at twenty-one.

Exercises finished, Will showered and dressed in old jeans and T-shirt and new work boots he had purchased at Wal-Mart. He drank three cups of coffee while he sat in the chair next to the window, glancing over the equipment manuals again. Then at six forty-five he fitted his Captain Saturday cap on his head and stepped out into the morning.

———

PALMER WAS LATE. They had agreed to meet at McDonald's at seven, have breakfast, and get on with the day's work. But by seven-thirty, there was no sign of him. Will waited outside in the truck, then finally went in, ordered two Egg McMuffins, hash browns and orange juice, and sat down at a table to eat. By seven forty-five he was finished. Still no sign of Palmer. Will began to fret. Had he had car trouble? An accident? He had gone to Greensboro for the weekend and they hadn't spoken since Friday evening. Palmer had Will's new phone number, but there had been no call before he left the apartment. Will sat for a while longer, but he hated to take up a table with the breakfast crowd bustling in and out, so he gathered up his trash and put it in the trash bin and went back to the truck.

He sat there for several minutes, worry vying with irritation. Was this going to be a constant hassle all summer, Palmer late and grumpy and unreliable?

To distract himself, he reached into his shirt pocket and pulled out the sheet of notepaper with his first three customers' addresses written on it. They were scattered all over town—one in a neigh-borhood not far from Channel Seven, another just north of down-town, the third on Highway 64 past the Beltline. By the time he went to Morris's house and picked up his trailer and got to the first location, it would be nine-thirty. If Palmer showed up right now. He craned his neck, looking down the street for some sign of the BMW. Nothing. He tucked the paper back in his pocket and sat drumming his fingers on the steering wheel.

A lawn care rig pulled into the parking lot and joined the line of vehicles snaking toward the drive-in window. It was a boxy late-model Volvo truck with a large rear platform that held two big mowers and assorted other equipment and gear. Two young guys were inside. A neatly lettered sign on the side of the cab read BUDDY'S LAWN SERVICE.

Will started going over in his mind how these guys would handle a lawn: one on a big mower, another edging and trimming, unless of course it was a really big stretch of grass and then they had the two big mowers that they probably handled as deftly as race car drivers on a road track. Zip, zip. Make quick work of the lawn, blow off the driveway and sidewalk, park the mowers back on the truck, collect the money, and then . . .

Collect the money? Collect how much money?

Will realized he hadn't given a thought to what he would charge, how much he *needed* to charge to make a profit. Ask too much and you wouldn't get the business. Don't ask enough and you'd be run-ning in the red. But how much? There were all sorts of rigs like this running around Wake County, maybe hundreds of them, all vying for customers. And what did he have? Sixteen thousand dollars worth of brand-new equipment, the names of three members of Dahlia Spence's garden club, and not the foggiest idea of what he should charge to mow their lawns.

And what else?

Insurance. What if his mower hit a rock and it smashed into the windshield of some guy's Cadillac sitting in his driveway? What if a blade came off and decapitated some little old lady? What if Will himself were injured? His medical insurance had evaporated with his dismissal from Channel Seven. And insurance aside, these were big, powerful, potentially dangerous machines that he and his son were about to embark upon. His son. What if Palmer were maimed and unable to become the doctor he aspired to be? Will felt a sudden rush of nauseous panic. This truck he was sitting in and the equipment out there on the trailer in Morris's driveway represented virtually all of his spendable resources. And more than that, his possibility.

Will scrambled out of his pickup and loped across the parking lot to the drive-in lane. "Hi," he said as he reached the Volvo. "Which one of you fellows is Buddy?"

The two guys grinned at each other. They were in their late teens or early twenties, he guessed. They wore khaki uniform shirts with BUDDY'S LAWN SERVICE stenciled over the pocket. "Buddy's the big man," the driver said. "We're just the hired help. Summer job." He reached out the window and tapped the fender of the truck where it said UNIT 7 in small black letters.

"How many units are there?" Will asked.

"Eleven," the driver said.

Good grief. A lawn care conglomerate, probably with its own maintenance facility and a huge customer base and a computer system and insurance and all of the other things that Will Baggett didn't know diddly about. He was penny-ante, small potatoes, a tenant farmer in the presence of an agribusiness giant.

"I was thinking about getting into the business myself," Will said. The truck inched forward in the drive-in line, and Will walked along with it.

"Yeah?" the driver said, "well you probably oughta wait until next year."

"Why's that?"

"Most lawns are under contract by now."

"Contract?"

"Buddy's got about four hundred customers. Me and Duck"—
he nodded at his co-worker—"hit about forty a week. They pay a
flat fee every month, twelve months a year. That way it don't cost
'em an arm and a leg when the grass is growing, and Buddy's got
income when it ain't."

"How much do you charge?"

"Depends on the size of the lawn." He turned to Duck. "No
harm in giving the man a price sheet, y'think?"

"Naw," Duck said, and fished in the glove compartment for a
piece of paper he handed out the window to Will.

"Thanks," Will said.

"Good luck," the driver said as he pulled away.

Will returned to his own truck and sat staring at the price
sheet. Buddy's Lawn Service, with its fleet of Volvos and its
phalanx of equipment, offered a vast array of services. Buddy
would not only see to the grooming of your lawn, he would
aerate, fertilize, de-thatch, treat for lawn disease and weeds, prune
your shrubs and trim your trees. Basic services were contracted.
The rest was extra. The words and numbers marching down the
page told the story of a lean, professional, highly efficient and obviously profitable operation. In short, Buddy knew what the hell he
was doing.

What have I been thinking? He, Will Baggett of the well-planned
and well-ordered life; he of the detailed thinking-ahead, whether it
be a trip to the Argentine pampas or a weathercast. What the hell
was going on here? His thinking about all this had gotten to a certain point and simply stopped. He had left an enormous amount to
chance, to fate, to possibility. Why? Had his troubles short-circuited
something in his brain?

It occurred to him, out of the blue, that this sounded like something Tyler Baggett would have done back there in his golf-
hustling days. Get up the game, then figure out how to win the
money. *My God.*

"Act on impulse," Wingfoot had said. "Go boldly," Dahlia

Spence had advised. Well, he had. Was he headed boldly for disaster? Could he get his money back?

"Dad . . ."

He stared out the window at Palmer. "I don't know a fart from a hurricane where it comes to running a lawn service," he blurted. Then, "Where the hell have you been?"

Palmer's jaw tightened and he turned away with a jerk and started across the lot toward McDonald's.

"Where are you going?" Will called after him.

"To get some breakfast," Palmer threw over his shoulder.

Will caught him before he reached the door. "You're an hour late," he said. "Get whatever you're gonna get and let's go."

Palmer whirled on him. "No, I'm not gonna get anything to go. I'm gonna sit down like a civilized person and eat breakfast."

Will pulled the piece of notepaper from his pocket. "We've got customers waiting."

"Look," Palmer said, backing away, "I drove all the way over here from Greensboro this morning."

Greensboro. It set off a little explosion in the back of Will's brain. "Why didn't you drive back to Chapel Hill last night?"

"Because it was after seven when Daddy Sid and I got back from the club, and by the time I took a shower . . . they said just spend the night. So I did."

The club.

Palmer started again toward the restaurant door.

"Well," Will snapped, "I sure wouldn't want you to do anything to upset the Greensboro folks."

Palmer stopped in his tracks and stood there for a moment before he turned slowly back to Will. There was a strange look on his face. "Mom's right," he said. "You can't stand 'em."

"Not true," Will said. "I've been married to 'em for twenty-five years. And I wasn't the one who called it quits."

"You can't stand the fact that I spend time in Greensboro, that Daddy Sid pays for my education, that . . ."

"I'm not going to stand here in the parking lot of McDonald's and discuss my in-laws. Go get your breakfast and let's get moving."

"No, goddammit! Let's have it out, right here in the parking lot at McDonald's."

"All right," Will barked. "Shoot."

"You're a snob, you know that, Dad?"

"Me? *I'm* a snob?"

"A reverse snob."

"And what in the hell does that mean?"

Palmer jerked an arm in the general direction of Brunswick County. "Your crazy family . . . you've got a chip on your shoulder because they're a bunch of weirdos."

"Is that what your mother said?"

"You're jealous," Palmer spat the word, "because Daddy Sid and Mama Consuela are regular people."

"Regular? Hah! The only thing regular about them is their bowel movements. Their bowels wouldn't dare be anything *but* regular."

They were fairly shouting at each other now, standing perhaps ten feet apart, the air between them crackling. Several people exited the McDonald's, stopped and stared. A van rolled between Will and Palmer, headed for the drive-in lane, and stopped, momentarily blocking Will's view. The scrawny man wearing the Durham Bulls baseball cap sitting in the passenger seat leaned out the window. "Hey, didn't you used to be Will Baggett?" Will stared at him. He looked vaguely familiar. Then he saw the sign on the side of the van: CHRISTIAN RENOVATORS. "Go tear up somebody's house!" he bellowed.

"Kiss my ass," the guy fired back. The van jerked ahead, once again revealing Palmer — glowering, fists clenched.

"You've been over there in Greensboro all weekend getting your head filled with crap," Will said. "I'll bet they told you not to mow lawns."

"As a matter of fact, they said it's nuts. I could get hurt."

"And you might get your hands dirty."

"Yeah. I might."

"Well, to hell with it. Get in your car and go on back to Greensboro and spend the summer whacking around the golf course and lunching on petit fours. I don't give a shit, Palmer."

Palmer's mouth curled in a snarl. "And if I do, you'll tell. Right?"

"Why do you think that?"

"Because you think I owe you."

"Maybe."

"Well, you owe me, too."

"Maybe."

Palmer slashed the air with his hand. "So, we're even."

Will threw up his hands. "Okay, I tried."

"Damn!" Palmer yelped. "What did you think you were gonna do, Dad? Tie me to the back of a lawn mower all summer, captive audience, and we'd become good old buddies? Grease under our fingernails? Sweat in our eyes? Go drink a beer after work and have some laughs and make up for all the time you weren't around? Well, to hell with that! Go ahead and tell. I don't give a shit. They probably wouldn't believe you anyway."

A crowd had gathered at the door of McDonald's, muttering and pointing. Inside, diners were staring out the window.

Palmer turned to the crowd. "You know who that is?" he yelled, pointing at Will. "That's Will Baggett. The TV star. Go on over and meet him. Get his autograph. He really loves his fans. Hell, you people know him a lot better than I do."

Will felt a blow, a palpable fist, hammering the pit of his stomach. He staggered backward, raising his hands, then turned and scrambled toward the truck. Palmer's voice flailed at his back but he couldn't hear the words any longer, just a terrible noise blasting away at his brain, like someone cranking up a chain saw next to his ear. He flung open the truck door and threw himself inside and sat there gripping the steering wheel, knuckles white, heart racing, stomach lurching. After a moment, he looked back toward the McDonald's. Palmer was gone. And then Will got a glimpse of his car, tearing out of the parking lot, disappearing into the morning traffic. Several people from the crowd outside McDonald's were headed across the lot toward him. Will fumbled in his pocket for the keys, started the engine, backed out of his parking space, and fled.

————

HE WENT THROUGH THE DAY in a fog, numb and shaken. He sat for a long time in the truck in Morris's driveway, then finally climbed out and hitched up the trailer. He pulled the list out of his pocket and stared at it, uncomprehending, until the names and addresses finally came into focus. *Move,* he told himself. *Move or give up.*

It took him all day to do the three lawns. The customers Dahlia Spence had lined up were all, like Dahlia, elderly widows with older homes on fairly small lots. But he was slow, still unfamiliar with the equipment, and he took his time, concentrating on the work. At the end of the first stop he consulted the price sheet from Buddy's Lawn Service and charged thirty-five dollars, undercutting Buddy's price by ten. He did the same for the others. He worked on through midday, applying sunscreen to his arms and the back of his neck, taking frequent drinks from the water cooler he had brought along. There was an apple and some snack crackers in the glove compartment of the truck, but he wasn't hungry. At the third stop, the woman brought him a glass of lemonade while he worked, and when he finished, he carried several boxes of junk from her garage to the curb for the trash collectors to pick up the next morning.

It was after five-thirty when he left the trailer again at Morris's house. No one was at home, but a neighbor walking his dog gave Will an odd look.

When he returned to his apartment, Dahlia's Oldsmobile was gone from the garage. He took a shower, changed clothes, and then went to sit quietly on the love seat in the garden. He still wasn't hungry. There was a great empty void somewhere down near his stomach, but it had nothing to do with food.

Whatever anger he might have felt there in the parking lot at McDonald's this morning was replaced by the inescapable conclusion that Palmer was right. Will had counted on the summer as a time to re-connect, reconcile, forge a bond that had slipped loose in the blur of the past ten or twelve years when Palmer had grown up and Will had grown . . . well, what? Busy. Distracted. Perhaps even a little obsessed. He had, face it, conceded Palmer to all of them — partly because he was too busy and distracted and obsessed and partly because he just didn't know what to do with Palmer, how to find some common ground. He just didn't know how to be a father. Maybe it was because his own father hadn't really been much of a father. No role model there. But that was no excuse. He had blown it. He had let other things get in the way of fatherhood.

Will had imagined a time somewhere in the depths of the summer, probably when neither really expected it, when they would have a quiet man-to-man talk, get a lot of things out in the open, say what needed to be said on both sides. They would be doing something mundane, maybe changing the oil on the mowers, and something offhand would be said by one or the other and that would start it.

There would be, of course, the undercurrent of the magnificent thing Will had done on his son's behalf. Noble Will, throwing himself in front of the speeding bullet, giving up all. Palmer would be riven with remorse and gratitude. He would welcome that opening, that moment in which they could reconcile.

Instead, they had had a vicious shouting match in the parking lot of McDonald's and they had both said some nasty things and it had blown sky-high. And Palmer had said, "We're even."

Would he have told? Having once made the decision to help Palmer cover his ass, having told him to lie like a dog, of course he wouldn't have told. Well, Palmer was smart and clever and could figure out all that and had called his hand. So, it was over, and just a big fine mess in the process. Will Baggett had lost the two people he should have clung to most fiercely. His wife wanted a divorce and his son said they were even. So now he felt utterly alone, as alone as he had been when they brought the news to Baggett House that his parents were gone for good.

He hadn't thought much about losing his parents for a long, long time. For years, he had made a habit of not doing so. Nothing to be gained by dwelling on that. Go on and make a life. Be somebody. Get off probation. But now the old bleak aloneness, the feeling of being on the outside of things, came back — and with it, a parade of the other lost pieces of his life. It hadn't been a perfect life, but it had been pretty damn good. And now all he had left was a trailer full of lawn mowers.

———

AND THUS IT WAS THAT the knock on his door at five o'clock on Tuesday morning surprised him. A man as alone as he did not expect company.

But what utterly astonished him was to open the door and find Palmer standing there. Palmer didn't say anything. He wrinkled his nose and pulled at his earlobe, but he didn't say anything. He didn't have the look of a person who was bringing bad news, but he did look like he hadn't had much sleep.

"I'll make coffee," Will said.

"Mom said I was acting like an ungrateful little shit," Palmer said.

"She used that word?"

"Yeah."

Palmer sipped his coffee. He sat deep in the chair by the window. Will had pulled over a chair from the kitchen table. He waited. He was very still, very careful not to say or do anything that might disturb the delicate thing that hung between them just now.

"I told her what happened," Palmer said. "All of it." He paused, choosing words. "I didn't intend to. But we got in an argument. I'm not sure how it came out, but once it started, I couldn't stop."

"All of it?"

"Yeah."

"And what . . . how did your mother react?"

"She started crying."

"Oh."

"And then she was pissed."

"Who is she pissed at, Palmer?"

"Both of us."

Palmer finished his coffee and Will got up and fixed them another cup. Black for him, cream and sugar for Palmer.

"Did your mother elaborate on why she's pissed at both of us?"

"She said we've both made an incredible mess of things."

"Well," Will admitted, "I suppose that's the gospel truth."

Palmer made a face. "Me, especially."

Will couldn't help but smile. "I think we're running about neck and neck on that score."

"Except that my mess can be fixed. Yours can't."

"Well"—Will spread his hands—"there's fixing and then there's fixing. I can't put everything back like it used to be, but I'm trying to cobble something together here."

Palmer put down his coffee cup, got up and walked to the window. He leaned on the sill and looked out into the early morning darkness. There was nothing to see, not right now. And not much to hear except for the faint rustle of traffic a few blocks away on Wade Avenue. The early risers.

"I'm sorry," Will said softly.

Palmer turned back from the window and looked at him for a moment. He nodded. "Me too."

"You're right about one thing. We're even."

"Well, that's what I said to Mom, and she said it's better for a relationship when you owe each other something. That way, you keep trying."

He sat for a moment, letting the words tumble around in his head. *Well, maybe that's what happened with Clarice and me, at least some of it. We broke even and there wasn't anything left to try for. No sense of obligation. And without an obligation . . .*

"So," Palmer went on, "she said we ought to figure out something we owe each other."

"How do you want to go about that?" Will asked.

Palmer shrugged. "I guess we should spend some time together."

"When?"

"I've got a few weeks this summer. How about you?"

"Well, I have to make a living."

"Yeah. That's what I was thinking, too."

Will shook his head. "Palmer, I don't want you to do this . . . if it's, like, a threat. Coercion. Not on my part or your mom's. I hope she didn't lead you to believe . . ."

"That she's gonna spill the beans about my mess?" Palmer smiled. "No, I don't think so."

Will tried to picture Sidney and Consuela Palmer having an accident in their pants. No, Clarice wouldn't do that. What she *might* do, though—in Will's case, not her parents'—that was something else. She had fought for Will Baggett once a long time ago. In a way, she had done that again just now with Palmer. Maybe it was a stretch to think of it that way, but Will would settle for a stretch. There might be something beyond all this as far as Clarice was concerned. Or maybe not. That, too, was a very delicate thing.

"What do you think we ought to owe each other?" Will asked.

"Well, we could start with breakfast."

"McDonald's?"

"No," Palmer said, "I don't want to go back to McDonald's."

———

THEY ATE AT A WAFFLE HOUSE, and after breakfast they left Palmer's BMW on the curb at the house on LeGrand. Clarice's car was still in the driveway, and Will took a close look at the house to see if she might be peering out the window, but he got no glimpse of her.

They took the truck to Morris's, where they hitched up the trailerful of equipment. Morris, unlike Clarice, was very much in evidence. He emerged in jogging suit and bedroom slippers, hair still wet from his shower. "Will," he said, "this can't go on. The neighbors are complaining. It violates the restrictive covenants."

"Against what?" Will asked as he and Palmer swung the trailer around to the hitch on the truck.

"Commercial vehicles."

Will straightened. "That sounds awfully picky," he said. "What if you owned a plumbing company and had a truck with deLesseps Plumbing on the side?"

"I couldn't park it in my driveway," Morris said firmly. "Plumbers don't live in this neighborhood, or at least if they do, they don't bring their trucks home."

"It is an upscale place," Will agreed.

"And you can't leave your"—a wave of his hand—"stuff here anymore."

"Then you don't get free lawn care," Will said.

Morris's voice rose a little. "I never asked for free lawn care. I told you, I've already got a lawn care service. They do perfectly good work."

Will considered. "On second thought, I think we will give you free lawn care because you are a splendid fellow and a longtime friend and confidant. We'll mow your grass right now and we'll return on a weekly basis, taking care to park our"—a wave of his hand—"*stuff* on the street and be here and gone in the wink of an eye."

Morris flapped his arms in frustration and retreated to the house. Will turned back to his work.

Palmer was watching him. "He's a little stuffy, isn't he?"

"Let's get busy," Will said. "We're lowering property values."

They were pulling away from Morris's house when Will said, "There's just one problem here. We don't have any more customers."

Palmer said, "Drive by Mom's office."

"Oh no," Will said. "The last time I was over there, I came pretty close to getting myself arrested."

"This time, you stay in the truck. Mom's got something for us."

He parked across the street in front of the Kinko's, taking up several spaces in the lot of the strip shopping center and getting some dirty looks from the people in a florist shop. Palmer was back in five minutes with a computer printout. "Names and addresses of everybody who's bought residential property in Wake County in the past month," Palmer said. "Mom figures that at least some of 'em need a lawn service."

"Mom figures . . ."

Palmer shook his head. "Don't read too much into this, Dad."

"I'll try not to," Will said.

There was also a solid lead, a nursing home owned by a woman whose cousin was another agent at Snively and Ellis. It was set well back off the street on a wide expanse of lawn with more grass along both sides and a paved parking lot in back. The owner told them she had fired her lawn service the week before because one of their mowers leaked oil on the front sidewalk. "I'm picky about the way this place looks," she said. "If the sidewalk is a mess, people wonder if the inside is, too. You aren't going to put your Aunt Sally in a place where you think she might get bed sores."

"Our mowers don't leak," Will said. "They're brand new."

"How much?" the owner asked, gazing out across the lawn.

"Two-fifty a month," Palmer spoke up before Will could answer. "Twelve-month contract. Guaranteed, no leaks."

"Don't you think that's a little steep?" Will asked when she had gone back inside and they were unloading mowers from the trailer.

"Hey," Palmer said, "I'm gonna be a doctor. Think of this job as elective surgery, like a face-lift or a tummy tuck. Charge what the market will bear. The little old ladies? That's HMO work."

It took them a couple of hours to finish the nursing home and then they started knocking on doors in a subdivision out past the Beltline off Six Forks Road. There were several addresses on the list that Clarice had given Palmer, and of the people they found at home, two of them said yes, they did indeed need a lawn service. They stopped at several other homes where the grass was long and ragged, and lined up one of them, too. By the shank of the afternoon, Captain Saturday's Lawn Service had seven customers and had barely scratched the surface of Clarice's list.

"Do you think we should split up?" Palmer asked as they sat in the truck beside a convenience store, drinking sodas and eating snack crackers. It had been a good day, Will thought. They were slow, feeling their way with the machinery and each other. They took turns running the big mower. All of the equipment worked fine. The weather was warm, but not hot. They had gotten along. They were tiptoeing around each other, being excessively polite. But it was a start.

"What do you mean, split up?"

"One of us mow grass, the other look for customers."

"We could do that. Which would you want to do?"

"You're better with the equipment," Palmer said. "And since you're incognito, your former notoriety isn't doing you any good."

They watched as a van from a day care center pulled up to the gasoline pumps in front of the store. It was packed with kids and it rocked slightly from side to side as the kids inside bounced and tusseled. The driver, a plump woman with close-cropped hair, looked weary and harried as she climbed out and began pumping gas. She ignored the kids — probably, Will thought, happy to get away from them for even a few minutes. She had the same kind of look as the women who used to bring packs of Cub Scouts to tour Channel Seven.

Palmer was watching the van, too. "I wonder what that woman would think if I pulled her over here and introduced her to you. She wouldn't believe it. The TV guy. Mowing lawns."

"The doctor-in-waiting, trimming shrubbery."

"It's not the same," Palmer said. "Lots of people do something like this — mow lawns, drive a truck, camp counselor — *before* they go on to something bigger. One guy in my med school class spent two years in the Army. He carried a rifle. Went to Kosovo. He says somebody took a shot at him one time. All the time he was studying for the M-CAT, getting ready to go to med school. Some day he'll be a doctor and he'll look back and say, 'I was in the Army and I went to Kosovo and got shot at.' But you . . ."

"One day I'll look back and say I used to be a TV guy."

"Yeah. You've got it reversed."

"Well, circumstance . . ."

"I used to get really pissed at you," Palmer said flatly.

"Are you still pissed, Palmer?"

Palmer thought about that for a moment. "Yeah. Some. But I'm trying to get over it. It doesn't do any good to stay pissed."

"I wasn't there when you were growing up."

"Well, you were . . . but . . ."

"I was gone a lot, especially at night. And I was wrapped up in my own thing."

"Being the TV guy."

"Yes.

"And it wasn't just the TV thing," Palmer said, "it was the goody-ass thing."

"Goody-ass?"

"Always worrying about what other people would think. Protecting your image. Raleigh's most popular TV weatherman. Did you ever get really tired of that?"

"I always figured it was just part of the job. Went with the territory."

"Don't shit me, Dad. You really got off on it, didn't you."

All right, let's be honest here. "Yeah," Will said. "I really did."

"Will Baggett, TV guy."

"Uh-huh."

"There's a billboard over near Chapel Hill that still had your picture on it last week," Palmer said. "You and those other people on Channel Seven. Four of you, lined up like crows on a wire."

"Smiling."

"Of course. But they papered over it a couple of days ago."

"The new Channel Seven anchor team."

"No, Pepsi."

They both laughed. It felt strange to Will to laugh with his son, and he could tell that Palmer felt the same. But they laughed anyway. It was okay.

They finished their sodas and crackers and Will collected the plastic bottles and wrappers and took them to a trash can beside one of the gas pumps. The day care van driver was just finishing. She hung up the nozzle and started past him toward the convenience store. "Hi," Will said. "Know anybody who needs a lawn service?"

She stopped, gave him an odd look. Her mouth opened, closed again. Then, "Are you . . . ?"

"No," Will said. "I'm just a lawn mowing guy."

Back in the truck, he was about to crank up when Palmer said, "Where did you get this lunatic idea?"

"I told you. Wingfoot."

"Is that all? Wingfoot said you oughta mow grass, so you went out and bought all this stuff?" He waved at the trailerful of equipment behind them. "That's a helluva stretch."

"Well," Will said, "I've been in the business before."

"You have?"

Will told him about Dysart, the summer of his twelfth year, the heat and the insects and the dying lawn mower and that sonofabitch Buster Dysart.

"And after an experience like that . . ."

Will smiled. "Well, this time I ain't pushing no piece of junk. And, this is sort of life or death." He paused, remembering. "Come to think of it, that thing back there in Dysart seemed a little like life or death, too."

And then he found himself telling about Tyler and Rosanna, Tyler being gone for long periods and Rosanna holding things together while they waited, and Wilbur mowing grass to make a little extra money.

Palmer stared, brow knitted in fascination. "I've never heard any of this. Why haven't you told me?"

"I haven't really given much thought to them for a long time."

"My other grandparents," Palmer said. "Most kids have two sets."

"Yeah, I guess so."

"Mom told me one time that they were killed in a plane crash when you were a teenager."

"Thirteen."

"And that's about all I know."

"Well, you've got two living grandparents in Greensboro. I guess they've more than taken up the slack."

Palmer shifted in his seat to face Will. "That bothers you."

Uh-oh. Back in that minefield . . .

"All right," Palmer said. "Save that for later. Tell me about your parents."

"I just did."

"More."

Will shrugged. "They've been gone a long time, Palmer. I don't remember much."

"Bullshit," Palmer said simply. "You were thirteen."

Will sat there for a moment staring out the window. The day care van pulled away. One of the kids in the back was mooning the world, the round pink globes of his butt hiked up over the rear seat. Kids.

"My father was a golf hustler," he said. "He made his living gambling on golf games. He would leave wherever we were living at the time and be gone for weeks—traveling all over the south and east, getting up a game here and there, winning more than losing. He would come home with a wad of bills in his pocket, driving a real nice car, and we'd take trips and spend it all and then he'd take off again."

"No kidding," Palmer said slowly. "He was good?"

"Could have been a successful pro, I think. In fact, he was thinking about doing that when he and Mom and Uncle French and Aunt Margaret took off. They were going to Augusta to the Masters."

Palmer hesitated for a long moment, then asked softly, "Did you miss him?"

Will started to answer, but his voice caught in his throat and he realized that he was suddenly, astonishingly, on the verge of tears. *Did I miss him? Do I still?* He looked quickly away, fighting to bring it under control.

Palmer touched his arm. "Dad. I'm sorry."

"It's okay," he managed to say.

They sat there for a minute or so and then Palmer said, "I think I'll take a bathroom break," and he was out of the truck and gone, giving Will some time and space to compose himself.

When he returned and climbed in, Will said, "We'll have to talk about all that sometime. When I figure out how."

Palmer looked him straight in the eye. "It's about us, too."

"Yeah, I guess so. It's about us. It's all connected."

"Well, I want to know."

———

THEY DROVE BACK TO LeGrand to pick up Palmer's car. It was after six o'clock. Clarice wasn't home yet.

"Are you gonna stay over here?" Will asked. "Maybe you should. I don't think you got much sleep last night. Long way back to Chapel Hill."

Palmer climbed out of the truck. "I like having my own place," he said. "I'm all grown up now, Dad." He closed the door and started away, then turned back. "Morris called you Wilbur," he said through the open window.

"That was my name until I got to Chapel Hill. Then I told everybody I wanted to be Will."

Palmer cocked his head to one side. "Do you mind if I call you Wilbur?"

Will thought about it for a moment. "No," Will said, "I don't mind. In fact, I think that might be just fine."

———

THEY CAME TO HIM as he sat alone in the dark. After all this time. He had been afraid of them, he supposed—of what they might say about Min's banishment and his own acquiescent betrayal. Afraid that they would be angry and vengeful, that they would haunt his wakings and his sleepings, pointing accusatory fingers. But it was not so. They were vivid but gentle spirits.

Rosanna with her marvelous hair, long and straight and fine, cascading mane-like down her back. He could feel the strands of it in his hands, wet from washing, as she bent over the bathroom tub. And the feeling of having lived in a protective backwater that she provided for him, even — especially — when things were tight. *Something will turn up. Trust me.* He did. And something always turned up, until there at the last.

And Tyler, swinging into the yard at Baggett House behind the wheel of that wonderfully long, gleaming Cadillac convertible, arriving just in the nick of time. *You thought I forgot!* Strong arms around him, a cocoon in which he might rest for a while until it was time to fly free.

Perhaps most wondrous of all, the realization that it was his own son who had summoned them. He had been afraid to miss them for a great long while, but what Palmer had said — no, what he had not said — had made it suddenly all right. *It's okay to miss them. I would miss them if I were you.* Perhaps Palmer knew all too well. But they had set about remedying that, father and son, and maybe that had opened this other door.

There was another realization now on the heels of the first: that he might have gained something from them, that even though they were long lost, there were remnants of what and who they had been that were useful to him in his present dire circumstances, when he had been brought crashing down as they had been thirty-five years ago.

Small but sturdy and resilient Rosanna. Just do what needs to be done. Something will turn up.

Tyler, that maddeningly intriguing mixture of free spirit and orneriness. Get up a game and let's see what happens.

They were his history, and Uncle French was right about that — you could make use of your history or not. But first, you had to acknowledge it.

He had kept Tyler and Rosanna locked in an out-of-the-way closet of his past for a long time. But now, here they were, just when he needed them most.

22 | HE SOLD HIS CAR. He didn't need it anymore, not with the truck, and he did need the money.

Palmer had suggested the classified ads in the *News and Observer,* had even helped him word the advertisement: *FOR SALE: 1991 Buick LeSabre, clean, runs good, new tires. $5,200 OBO.*

"What's OBO?" he asked.

"Or best offer."

"You know a lot about the classifieds."

"From Mom."

"Shouldn't it say, 'good mechanical condition'?" Will suggested.

" 'Runs good' sounds more down-to-earth," Palmer said. "Guy's looking in the paper for a used car for his teenaged daughter. He sees Buick LeSabre and he thinks, 'Old Man's Car.' "

"I beg your pardon."

"Face it, Dad, a Buick LeSabre is a good car, but it's not rad."

"Rad?"

"It's a phrase. You know, like, what was it your generation used to say? 'Cool'?"

"I get the picture. I'm not completely old-fashioned."

"But you're not rad."

"I guess not."

"So anyway, the guy sees Buick LeSabre and he thinks some old geezer's been driving it around town at twenty miles an hour and leaving his blinker on for eighty-three blocks. But then he sees 'runs good' and he thinks, 'Well, maybe this is, like, your average dude who knows something about cars and has taken good care of it. Buick LeSabre's a good car and this one runs good. Might be just the thing for my teenaged daughter.' "

Palmer was constantly surprising him like that. There was a savvy down-to-earthness, an almost street-smartness about him that didn't fit the picture of the buttoned-down oxford cloth-chino–Bass

Weejun young man Will had thought him to be. This was a young man with texture, a young man who could smoke pot and nearly flunk out of medical school. There was a sort of duplicitousness in the way he presented one image to his grandparents and his mother, and yet had this other side that was rough-woven, like a reversible jacket. Like the jacket Will had been wearing in court that afternoon. It was troublesome, Will thought, but also intriguing. Layers there that Will had never imagined, nooks and crannies of Palmer's personality that made him infinitely more interesting. It was almost like discovering a child from a long-ago, forgotten liaison who showed up suddenly one night on the front porch. And intriguing to wonder where the rough-woven side came from. It sounded a little like . . . *good God* . . . Tyler Baggett. He laughed at the thought.

Palmer had also proved more adept with the machinery than Will. He handled the big mower easily, and when something broke, he was more likely to figure out what was wrong. He had even spent an evening on the floor of Will's living room taking apart a carburetor, studying the diagram that came with the owner's manual, finding and extracting the piece of trash that had caused the mower to run roughly.

"Gesundheit!" he cried, using a very bad fake-German accent, "ve haf located the appendix! Ve take out the appendix und leaf the bowels for another adventure."

"You're going to make a wonderful surgeon," Will said.

So Will had the classified advertisement published in the *News and Observer* exactly the way Palmer had suggested. A man who worked on the assembly line at a manufacturing plant in Fuquay-Varina bought the LeSabre, not for his teenaged daughter, but for his elderly mother. He drove to Raleigh one night after work and took the car for a test drive. "Runs good," he said to Will when he returned, and he wrote Will a check for five thousand dollars after they haggled a bit.

"I should pay you a commission," Will said to Palmer.

"Keep it," Palmer said. "A few years from now when you need your appendix removed, I'll charge double."

THEY WERE ON the Beltline. It was a mistake. It was the shortest route to their next customer and they thought the traffic wouldn't be too bad this time of day, midmorning, but there had been a wreck at the Western Boulevard exit and traffic was backed up, two lanes of parked vehicles trying to go south, but nothing moving at all, not for the past fifteen minutes. Palmer was driving, or would have been had there been any driving to do.

They had heard about the wreck on the radio—an eighteen-wheel flatbed loaded with lumber. It would take a while to get things cleaned up and get traffic moving again.

Palmer was flipping through the stations now. He was grumpy and nettlesome. Raleigh was gripped in a July heat wave and the air-conditioning on the truck was spasmodic. There was no time to take it back to the dealership for service, not with thirty customers lined up waiting to have their lawns mowed. The radio was all about the heat wave and the traffic tie-up, and neither one made Palmer very happy. He punched the buttons on the radio. "You keep changing the settings, Wilbur," he complained. "Every time I get in here, you've changed the settings. You add the public station in Chapel Hill and that stupid hillbilly stuff and take out Big Rock 97."

"It's a test of will," Will said. "No pun intended."

Palmer made a face and punched the buttons some more . . .

. . . *with an expected high today of 95* . . .

. . . *on the Channel Seven Noon Report, details on the wreck that has snarled traffic* . . .

. . . *"I can see that mournful teardrop . . ."*

. . . *for the best deals in Raleigh on* . . .

"Hey!" Will yelped, startling Palmer. He pushed Palmer's hand away from the radio and punched the button for the country station again.

". . . you look like you been had by a woman that's mean and bad . . ."

"You really like that stuff, don't you," Palmer said, disgusted.

"Shut up."

"*. . . but let me tell you this before you start . . .*"

"Look," Palmer snapped, "if you think I'm going to sit here with sweat running down the crack of my butt and traffic backed up to East Jesus and listen to some redneck woman . . ."

"She's not a redneck. She's from Pender County. Well, actually from Greenwood, South Carolina. She was Miss Greater Greenwood."

"My God," Palmer shook his head. "Are you a member of some fan club?"

"I know her," Will said.

"*. . . but I ain't baby-sittin' no broken heart.*"

"You mean you really, like, *know* her?"

"She's Cousin Wingfoot's girlfriend."

While Palmer stared, mouth slightly open, Will told him as much as he knew about Peachy Delchamps, what he recalled from an acquaintance that had lasted less than twenty-four hours, some of which remained fairly murky in his memory. He told how Wingfoot and Sheriff Billy had fairly kidnapped him and taken him off to the wilds of Pender County and thence to a night of revelry. "I got up on the stage and played the tambourine with Peachy's band," he said. "And I am told that at one point toward the end of the evening, I rendered a tambourine solo."

"You're kidding me," Palmer said with both wonder and skepticism.

"I am telling you what I remember and what was recounted to me later. I fell in with what Cousin Wingfoot described as the trashy side of the Baggetts and apparently acted accordingly."

"You actually got drunk?"

"That's what they tell me. Drunk and rowdy."

"I didn't know you had it in you."

"Neither did I."

"God*damn.* "

"But I have been on the straight and narrow ever since."

Palmer indicated the radio. "And what about this woman?"

"Off to Nashville where she has, apparently, made a recording."

"And she's Wingfoot's girlfriend."

"Well, used to be. Still should be. Wingfoot's a damn fool, but then he's been knocked about, too." Will told him about West Point, the years of aimlessness, then the life Wingfoot had carved for himself out of the piney woods of Pender County with Peachy, the woman he had let get away. "It appears we Baggett men are unlucky in love," he said.

Palmer just grunted.

"So what do you think of Peachy's singing?" Will asked.

Palmer made a face. "It's country music. But she's got an interesting voice. Like she might be, you know, kinda . . ."

"Yes," Will smiled. "I got the impression that she is just that. A handful."

"Is Wingfoot in love with her?"

"Yeah. And she's in love with him."

"Then why didn't he go to Nashville with her?"

"He wanted her to see what she could do without any entanglements."

Palmer drummed his fingers on the steering wheel for a moment and looked out the windshield at the traffic. There wasn't much you could see. A big Office Depot delivery truck was right in front of them, blocking their view. They were pretty well stuck here for a while, it seemed to Will. There wasn't another exit before Western Boulevard.

"He's stupid," Palmer said after a moment. "If he loves her, he ought to be with her. He ought to go fight for her." Then he turned and looked hard at Will. But he didn't say anything else.

———

HE CALLED BAGGETT'S PLACE from his apartment that night. "I heard Peachy's song on the radio," he said to Cousin Norville. They both had to shout over the noise—booming music, what sounded like a big crowd of very rowdy people, and somewhere near the bar, a woman with a braying laugh.

"Yeah," Norville shouted back, "it's already up to number fifteen."

"What?"

"On the country music charts. Number fifteen and climbing."

"I know you're real proud of her."

"Real what?"

"Proud!"

"Oh, hell yeah. Got her start right here. If Peachy hadn'ta been singing the night that record producer came in, she'd still be growing azaleas."

"How's Wingfoot?" Will asked.

There was a pause. "Wingfoot's a damn fool," Norville said.

"I said the same thing about him just a few hours ago. I was thinking maybe I should talk to him."

"Ain't no use talking to Wingfoot. He's not only a damn fool, he's a stubborn damn fool. I don't know where he gets that from. Ain't none of the rest of us Baggetts that way." Norville laughed, enjoying the joke.

"Well, I just wanted to get word to Peachy that I heard her song on the radio," Will said. "If you talk to her . . ."

"Then call her."

"You mean, like, *call* her?"

"Sure. Pick up the phone and dial the number. Just like you did with me. Hold on a minute. I got the number here someplace." He put the phone down again for a moment. "Okay. Area code 615, that's Nashville, 555-9482. Got it?"

"Yes."

"When you coming back to see us, Wilbur?"

"I'm not supposed to leave Wake County right now," Will said. "I guess you heard about my trouble."

Norville laughed. "That's what you get for associating with the trashy Baggetts. We must be a bad influence on you, Wilbur."

"No, I got in this all by myself."

"Well, you come on over when you get the chance. Last time, I think you had a pretty good time."

"That's what I'm told," Will said. "That's what I'm told."

*   *   *

It was after eleven when Peachy called him back. She was in Newton, Kansas, she said, spending the night at a motel along Interstate 135 after a performance in Wichita. Tomorrow night, Denver. She was the warm-up act for Dwight Yoakam. Will had heard of Dwight Yoakam, hadn't he? Well yes, he had. Dwight Yoakam had a part in a movie Will had seen a few years ago about a man who cut off another man's head with a sling blade. He had taken Clarice to see the movie, and about a half-hour into it, a man seated just behind them had leaned over and asked Will to autograph his popcorn box. Clarice hadn't been very happy about that. In fact, he remembered now, it had been the last time they had gone out to a movie together. But the movie had been pretty good. Dwight Yoakam played a bad guy and in the end, he got his head chopped off, too.

"That's pretty big stuff isn't it?" he asked now, "warming up for Dwight Yoakam?"

"I just have to pinch myself," Peachy said.

Will could hear a lot of the subtle things in her voice, the kind of nubby texture that made her sound so good on the radio. He had never paid a lot of attention to things like that, he thought, had never really listened hard to what a singer sounded like. But he remembered Peachy's voice like it was yesterday, leaning into the microphone on the little stage at Baggett's Place, the way she wrapped her voice around a song and made something more than just words and music. Some important people in Nashville must like it a lot, too.

"I heard your song on the radio today," Will said. "You really sound good. Cousin Norville said it's already up to number fifteen."

"We just got the advances from next week's *Billboard*," said Peachy. "It'll be number twelve."

"That's great. Congratulations. I went by a music store this evening and tried to get a copy, but they didn't have it."

"It's just a single," she said. "I'll have a whole CD out real soon. We laid some tracks last week. Dwight even wrote a song for me."

"I'm glad things are going so well for you."

"And how about you, Wilbur?"

"I guess you heard about my trouble."

"Yeah. You must love that boy a lot."

"We've started a lawn service. He's helping me this summer before he goes back to medical school."

There was a long pause, then Peachy said softly, "You oughta be with the one you love."

"Yes you should," Will said emphatically. And then he was a little surprised at himself, saying something just that way to Peachy Delchamps. The way he said it made it sound like advice, and he didn't need to be giving advice to an up-and-coming country music star, a woman he barely knew, really. But then he wondered to himself, *Just who am I giving advice to?* "You oughta be with the one you love," Will went on. "It sounds like a line from a song."

"It is. I just wrote it about an hour ago."

"For the CD?"

"No. For Wingfoot."

"Are you going to call him on the telephone and sing it to him?"

Another long pause. "I hadn't thought about doing that."

"I'm not trying to give you any advice," Will said. "I mean, it's your business."

"I tell you, Wilbur, I've been wrestling with this thing."

"You and Wingfoot."

"He wants to give me plenty of room. Nothing to tie me down, nothing to take my mind off of business. But"—there was just the tiniest break in her voice—"I do miss that sonofabitch."

"Have you told him so?"

"I haven't talked to him in several weeks."

"Then do," Will said, abandoning reticence. "Call him right now. Sing to him."

"You think?"

"Damn straight."

"Just call him and sing to him?"

"Do it, Peachy."

"You oughta be with the one you love," Peachy sang. It had a nice,

sweet melody to it. If you listened to the whole thing, he thought, it might make you cry.

"He's a stubborn sonofabitch," Peachy said.

"That's what Norville told me a little while ago. But it runs in the family. Sometimes we Baggetts just have to be jerked up by the scruff of the neck to get us headed in a different direction."

"You know, Wilbur," Peachy said, "for a fellow who's been through what you've been through, you sound okay. More than okay, in fact."

"I'm vertical, Peachy. Getting along. One day at a time, you know."

"That's good," she said. "Look, the next time I'm going to the studio to cut some tracks, you want to come play tambourine?"

Will laughed. "I think I'll retire while I'm ahead."

After she had hung up, Will put the phone down and sat by the open window listening to the sounds in Dahlia's Spence's back yard, smelling the green lushness that drifted in on the warm night air. He thought of Peachy Delchamps, calling long-distance from Newton, Kansas, and singing to Wingfoot Baggett over there in the wilds of Pender County. *You oughta be with the one you love.* If that didn't do the trick, she should give up on his sorry ass.

23 | Sunday night. He heard footsteps on the outside stairs, a knock at the door. He rose from his chair by the window and put aside the copy of *Professional Lawn Care Monthly* he was reading and went to the door. He flipped on the outside light and opened the door to find the very last person on earth he expected to be there at nine o'clock on a July night: Sidney Palmer. He was clad in navy blazer and light gray slacks and open-necked dress shirt.

Will stood there for a moment, unable to form words. It was Sidney who finally spoke. "I've come about Palmer," he said.

My God . . . he's told.

"Palmer wants to know when you're going to get your wife back," Sidney said.

Did he say life? No, wife.

"Come in," Will croaked.

Sidney sat in the chair by the window, looking about the room.

"I'd offer you a drink, but all I've got is beer," Will said, as much for just something to say as anything.

"A beer would be fine," Sidney said.

"It's cheap beer. Old Milwaukee."

"Cheap beer is fine," Sidney said.

Will went to the refrigerator. "A glass?"

"No. Just the can. The can will do just fine."

Will brought the beers and pulled up a chair and they sipped on their beers and studied each other. It was, Will thought, only the second time he had ever been one-on-one with the man.

"Are you doing okay, Will?" Sidney asked finally.

Will hesitated, then took a deep breath. *What the hell.* "I've been screwed over pretty royally," he said. "I've lost my wife and my job and I have a criminal record. But I'm still vertical, Sidney, and I'm mowing lawns like a sonofabitch." He expected Sidney to flinch at such, but he just nodded and took a sip of his beer.

"So Palmer wants to know when I'm going to get my wife back," Will said.

"Yes."

"And he deputized you to drive all the way over here from Greensboro and tell me that? On a Sunday night? We'll be mowing lawns together tomorrow. He could have told me himself."

"He says you won't talk about it."

"I don't want Palmer caught in the middle."

"He is, Will. He's had some, well, pretty heated arguments with his mother. And he doesn't feel like he can broach the subject with you. He's trying not to take sides, but . . . yes, he's caught squarely in the middle." Sidney cradled the beer can in both hands. They were rather large hands, Will noticed for the first time. Over the years, he realized, he had paid little attention to Sidney Palmer the physical person. He had always looked at Sidney sort of obliquely. And now here they were, just the two of them, without much to look at except each other. "He's torn up about it," Sidney went on. "He's upset with both of you, you and Clarice. And he doesn't know what to do. But he didn't ask me to come over here tonight. That was my idea."

"Wow," Will said. "He doesn't mind telling me how Clarice is pissed off at me. And at him. And now it appears he's pissed off at Clarice and me. So it appears, Sidney, that I'm the only person in our little triangle who's not pissed off. I'm just trying to make a living. I don't have time to be pissed off."

Sidney made a face. "Well, you *sound* like a man who is, as you say, pissed off." It took an effort for Sidney to use the word, Will thought. But give him credit, he handled it okay. "And," he added, "I can't say that I blame you."

"So you've come over here to tell me it's my job to get my wife back. I wonder if maybe that might depend just a smidgin on my wife."

"Of course."

"Then why doesn't she talk to me? She's sent word by *her* lawyer," he let the word drip with sarcasm, "to *my* lawyer that I'm not to have any communication with her. Upon pain of legal action. And for a guy who's on probation for a criminal offense, Sidney, that just puts my butt in one helluva sling when it comes to, as you and Palmer say, getting my wife back."

"I can see that."

"I take it you've broached the subject with her."

"I have. Her mother and I both have."

"And?"

"Clarice has had a headstrong streak since she was a small child," Sidney said with a shake of his head. "When she gets stubborn about something . . ."

"As she did when she decided to marry me."

"Yes."

Will polished off his beer and stood. "Look, Sidney, Clarice and I had what I thought was a pretty darn good marriage. Twenty-five years' worth. And then all of a sudden, when I'm flat on my ass, she changes the locks on the house and sends word *by my attorney* that she's fed up with me and doesn't want me to communicate with her in any way, shape, form, or fashion. And you want *me* . . ."

"To make an effort, Will. Take the first step. Break the impasse."

"For Palmer's sake."

"If nothing else."

"Do you want another beer?"

"I've got to drive back to Greensboro."

"What the hell, Sidney. Have another beer. Sleep on the couch if you want."

Sidney stared up at him. He offered up his can. "I'll have another beer."

Will fetched them from the refrigerator. By the time he returned, Sidney had taken off his blazer and draped it over an arm of the chair.

"Let's talk," Sidney said.

Will lifted his beer can in toast. "Shoot."

"You've always resented us."

"And why not? You didn't want your daughter to marry me. Shabby old Will Baggett, son of a golf hustler. Clarice called me on the phone, after that wonderful lunch at the country club, and said, 'I can't marry you.' I didn't measure up, Sidney. I never have. And now she's finally done what you wanted her to do in the first place. Got rid of me."

Sidney's eyes dropped and he looked down at his beer can for a moment. "Will," he said quietly, "I want you to be fair about this. No, Consuela and I didn't want Clarice to marry you. We thought there was a lot of baggage. But when she chose, we said okay, if that's what Clarice wants, that's fine. We accepted you. We tried to make you feel at home with us. I offered you a place in the family business. But"—he waved the beer can, being careful not to spill anything—"you've always had a chip on your shoulder, Will. And I don't think it's just about what we advised Clarice there in the beginning."

"What, then?"

"You think we're snobs."

"Yes I do."

Sidney shrugged. "We're comfortable with who we are, Will. Are you?"

Will looked away, felt the anger rising in him. It took a good while to get it enough under control so that he could speak without smashing his beer can into Sidney Palmer's patrician face. "I used to be," he said finally.

"I think being comfortable with who you are has almost nothing to do with what you have, the material things, where you live, the country club you belong to, the friends you hobnob with. It's about being honest with yourself." Sidney took another pull on the beer can, then set it down on the table next to the window. He stood. "Your son thinks you're a lot more honest with yourself than you used to be. He's rediscovered you, Will, and I think you've rediscovered him. I think you've been honest with him about how things might have gone awry with the two of you in the past. And now, maybe you can do the same thing with Clarice."

Will stared at the floor. "Go crawling back."

"No. Just be honest."

"All my fault, Sidney."

"Of course not."

He looked up now. "There's somebody else. Did you know that?"

A look of pain crossed Sidney's face. "Try," Sidney said softly. "For Palmer's sake."

Something lurched in Will and he felt foolish and inadequate in the presence of the man's naked asking and in the knowledge of his own long-smoldering resentment.

"I'd do anything for that boy," Sidney said. He hesitated, glancing away for an instant, then added, "As you have." And then picked up his coat and turned abruptly toward the door.

He was on the landing outside by the time Will recovered himself enough to catch up with him.

"What has Palmer told you?" he demanded.

"Palmer hasn't told me anything. But it doesn't take a genius to see what's going on here." He started to say something else, then shrugged and started down the stairs. Will thought he looked a tad wobbly.

"Are you okay to drive?"

"I think so."

"Sidney . . ."

He stopped, looked back up.

"Did you get me that job at Channel Seven?"

"Of course not."

"But you made a phone call. Barfield Simpson said you called, and that's why he took a look at me."

"When did he tell you that?" Sidney asked.

"The last time I saw him."

"Well, he didn't remember it the way it happened. I called, yes, but it was well after you applied. Right after we had lunch at Carolina Country Club and you said you wanted to stay in TV. Barfield cut me off before I could get started. He said he'd already decided to hire you because you had talent and ambition, and he told me to keep my goddamn nose out of the television business."

———

THE NEXT MORNING, as they ate a hearty breakfast at Shoney's— eggs, hash browns, sausage, plump biscuits—Will said, "Your grandfather came to see me last night."

Palmer pursed his lips. "I know."

"Have you told him anything about . . . all the other?"

"No." Palmer chewed on his upper lip for a moment. "But I'm going to have to. It's the only honest thing to do."

"That sounds like something he said last night. About being honest."

"We've always been honest with each other," Palmer said. "I've always thought I could tell him anything and he would tell me exactly what he thought." He ducked his head. "It's been terrible, Dad, keeping that from him."

Will could see then how it must be, or at least had been all these years, between his son and his father-in-law—a relationship that went far beyond an indoctrination into the cloistered world of upper-Greensboro society and Palmer family legacy. They had shared things. It was genuine. Will felt, and struggled to control, a pang of the old familiar envy. Enough of that. Envy might have been one of his biggest sins.

"You could have said what your grandfather said. About your mother."

"Would it have had the same impact?"

"No. It was . . . I've never had a conversation like that with him before. Nothing even remotely close."

Palmer picked up a biscuit from his plate, held it with the fingers of both hands, studied it for a moment. "Well, what are you gonna do, Dad?"

"I don't know."

Palmer threw the biscuit at him. "Well, do *something,* even if it's wrong."

———

BUT WHAT? And how? And to what end?

He had had a glimmer of hope a month ago, when Palmer had come to him in the pre-dawn darkness. Clarice had dressed Palmer down and called him an ungrateful little shit and had sent him to make amends. She had said that Will and Palmer needed to owe each other something.

So what about Will and Clarice? Could they find something to owe each other, some toting of accounts that would give each and both an opening to raise something from the ashes? He took what Clarice had told Palmer to mean that there might be an opening there. And then the next day she had done a quite concrete thing, the list of potential customers. Will had felt a rush of hope.

A week after that, he had seen her for the first time since she looked out at him from the front window of Fincher and Snively and told him by telephone to go away and leave her alone. He picked Palmer up each morning at the house on LeGrand, where he left his BMW for the day, and took him back each evening. She was in the front yard late one afternoon watering the shrubbery. She had redone the shrubbery beds to suit her. They were larger now, irregular in shape, filled with new plants—acuba, nandinas, dwarf hollies, some things he didn't recognize. Clarice had her back turned to the street, concentrating on her watering. She must have heard the truck door slam when Palmer got out, but she gave no indication. Will watched her back for a moment, thinking he might catch her eye, that a look might pass between them and that he could tell if there was anything there, anything at all. But she didn't turn around, even when Palmer joined her at the edge of the shrubbery bed, and he finally drove away.

Since then, nothing. And now, in the absence of a sign—something more than Palmer's hope and Sidney's asking—he was at a loss.

But more than *what?* or *how?* was *why?*

There was Palmer, of course—a good reason, but good enough? Easy for Palmer to want his parents back together, but then Palmer wasn't the one who had to transact the messy business, and whether it worked or not, he would go on about his life. Palmer might suspect how the marriage had come unglued, but he didn't know everything—how the ground had cracked and the crack had widened so slowly but inexorably that neither of them had really seen how it was growing until it was suddenly a Grand Canyon of a thing. But when she had seen it, she had rejected him so suddenly and utterly that it had riven him with pain and humiliation. Hell yes, he was pissed off. And he would have to get control of that before he could even think of *doing* something, even if it was wrong.

So, for a good number of days, he did nothing. And he and Palmer didn't talk about it. They just mowed grass.

———

THE AIR CONDITIONER BROKE. It was a small window unit that he had installed in the bedroom of the apartment, a used one that he had found in the classified section of the *News and Observer.* Will came home one evening about seven to find it blowing tepid air, the apartment stifling. He opened all the windows and borrowed a fan from Dahlia, but even by ten the place was still unbearable.

So he went for a walk.

Lights were still on in most of the houses along Dahlia's street and its surrounding neighborhood, a warm glow across lawns and sidewalks. Through windows that weren't shade-drawn he could see an occasional person moving about, the dancing colors of a television set. In his years at Channel Seven he had often wondered, as he drove back to the station at midevening, what people did with their nights, how they transacted the ordinary commerce of their private lives—homework, sex, talk, fights, the drone of conversation competing with the music from a kid's stereo, sitcoms, telemarketers. Of course there were other people like him who worked odd hours, who drove the streets at midevening and midnight, who lived slightly out-of-sync with the rest of the world. And there were a fair number who boarded planes at the Raleigh-Durham airport on Monday morning and didn't return until Friday night. They, too, no doubt felt out-of-sync. But most people, he thought, created an existence out of the quite ordinary. He had occasionally wondered what it would be like to be ordinary, to be one of those people on the other side of the lighted windows. But then, there had been no use dwelling on things like that. He hadn't been ordinary for a great long while.

But he was, even now, he thought to himself as he walked, anything but ordinary. He was an oddity, a man with a career gone suddenly and spectacularly belly-up, a failed ex-celebrity taking refuge behind a beard and glasses, and—most oddly, to his mind—a man alone. All of that separated him from those ordinary people muddling by in their ordinary lives, as much as his past celebrity had. He just couldn't seem to get past those lighted windows, no matter what.

He walked for a long time, block after block stretching out until, he realized, he was in his old neighborhood and wondered how and why he had got there.

It was almost eleven when he turned onto LeGrand. He passed his house with only a glance, brief enough to see that Clarice's car—and only hers—was in the driveway and that a lamp was on in the upstairs bedroom window, slivers of yellow through the plantation shutters Clarice had recently installed. Will had always insisted on blinds that would keep out the early sun so he could get a full night's sleep. But Clarice rose early and went forth into the real estate world. Plantation shutters would suit her just fine.

He continued down the block to the intersection with Barden. He stood for a while on the corner, started several times to cross the street, but then finally turned back and retraced his steps. He was on his fourth pass of the house when he saw the light in the upstairs window go off. He hesitated for a moment, then turned down the driveway and started toward the back yard.

The smell and sound of it almost overpowered him — the gurgle and splash of the fountain, the sweet aroma of flowering things. Clarice had left the fountain undisturbed, but in the soft light of a half-moon he could see that she had expanded and rearranged the flower beds. And she had ripped out all of the liriope that had made such a neat green border for the old beds.

She had hated the liriope, the way it ran its tendrils underground and popped up in the middle of the bed, choking out the flowers she had planted. They had argued about the liriope when he had first sprigged it years ago. He wanted neatness and order, some definition to the yard where the beds bordered his turf. One morning not long after the sprigging was done, he had come down to breakfast to find Palmer — perhaps three or four at the time — standing on a chair, gazing enraptured out the kitchen window. Will stood just behind and followed his gaze. A rabbit was nibbling on the tender liriope shoots, jaws working, great brown eyes darting furtively, ears alert.

He had opened his mouth to bellow when Clarice barked, "Will!" And he turned to see lightning bolts in her eyes. *Say a word and you die.*

Palmer looked up at Will. "Dad. See the bunny?"

"Yes, son. I see the bunny."

"He's having breakfast."

So now Palmer was grown and the liriope was gone and the rabbit had no doubt long passed on to wherever good rabbits went. And Clarice had remade the back yard in her own image, unfettered by his obtuseness. With the beds expanded, there was considerably less grass. And she had planted a fair-sized tree of some kind — apple or pear? — next to the goldfish pond. It would eventually shade the small slate patio and the two Adirondack chairs she had added.

And what was that over there beyond the goldfish pond? A bird feeder, for God's sake, a metal contraption with a cantilevered perch, the kind that was supposed to be squirrel-proof. Even in the palest of light he could see that the grass underneath it was already becoming ragged and broken. He knew from experience how it happened. Birds perched on the feeder and pecked busily through the sunflower seeds, tossing three aside for every one they ate. They worked furiously with their beaks, extracting the meat and then dropping the shells, which clotted the turf and smothered the grass. And then chipmunks burrowed busily from below to feed on the uneaten seeds the birds had discarded. Before long, the ground beneath the feeder would look like the mostly bald pate of a man who had undergone a disastrous attempt at hair transplant. But Clarice wouldn't mind. She liked birds and flowering things.

He wandered about the yard, examining all the changes she had made, and then he took a seat in one of the Adirondack chairs. It faced the rear of the house, dark now. But with the half-moon there was enough light to see that the Christian Renovators had finished their work. What had been the breakfast room and kitchen now extended a good ten feet beyond the original. Wide steps led from the yard to a new and larger deck. The rear of the addition was a double glass door and a row of tall windows—a different style from those on the rest of the house, but complementary. If he remembered the plans correctly, the kitchen was much bigger and included a more spacious breakfast nook and small seating area. There would be gleaming appliances, new cabinets and countertops, tile splashbacks, all of it color-coordinated in deep reds and off-whites.

The addition was well and admirably done. The Christian Renovators had cleaned up nicely after themselves. What was left of the back yard was both compact and transformed. A cozier place. A few short months ago it would have made him uncomfortable—cramped and riot with green, growing things. But now, after mornings and evenings by the open window overlooking Dahlia Spence's back yard, his perception had changed. This place was no longer his own, not in fact nor in feel. But it occurred to him that he could, if given the chance, be at peace with it.

A light came on in the kitchen. He froze, heart in his throat. He felt suddenly like a sneak thief, a Peeping Tom, a trespasser. Light splayed across the back yard. He would be clearly visible from the house if Clarice glanced out the window as she moved across the kitchen. But she didn't. She went instead to the counter and busied herself, and he realized after a moment that she was making a cup of tea, no doubt the herbal kind she liked, boiling a cup of water in the microwave, steeping the tea bag in a tall mug. The mug would be her favorite, of course, one that Palmer had given her for a birthday years before with WORLD'S GREATEST MOM imprinted on it. She was wearing a robe he hadn't seen before—dark blue with white piping around the lapels and sleeves. A good color. Clarice had always looked good in dark blue.

She came now to the breakfast table and sat, presenting her profile to the window. She cradled the mug in her slender fingers and brought it to her lips. He could almost feel the warmth of it. In the summer months, she liked to keep the house just barely above what would be uncomfortably cool at night. It was always something of a shock to him, coming in after midnight from Raleigh's muggy warmth. He shivered as he undressed and occasionally he complained, but to no avail. The house was hers and Palmer's during the evenings while he was away at work, and after Palmer had gone off to college, it was just hers. So she kept the thermostat turned down and warmed her hands with a ritual cup of herbal tea just before she went to bed. He would find the cup in the sink when he came home. Always there, just the one cup and still-soggy tea bag. Everything else in the kitchen would be neatly put away in cabinets, cupboard, refrigerator, dishwasher. And Clarice would be burrowed down in the bed like a small animal, sheet and light blanket pulled up to her chin against the chill.

She drank again from the mug, and then she set it aside and spread open a newspaper on the breakfast table. She bent over it, hair falling about her face, studying it intently. The classified ads, of course—people's lives represented by the things they sought to buy and sell, the services they offered or needed, the personal messages they broadcast hopefully to a nameless and faceless world.

He was struck suddenly by a sense of remorse so profound that he half-rose in the Adirondack chair. He reached to her with everything in his being. He hung there in mid-reach, levitating, fingers stretching. But then he settled back with a slump as if a great icy hand had shoved him in the chest. He knew, as certainly as he had ever known anything, that he could not reach her.

This is what I lost. This, not all the other. And I went about losing it for a long time before it was suddenly gone.

He sat there for a long time watching her until she closed the newspaper, rose and took the cup to the sink. She turned to the doorway, her hand on the light switch, then hesitated for a moment and stared at the windows that looked out over the back yard. Did she sense his presence out here, could she feel the exquisite vibrations of his pain? He felt a sound rise in his throat, then catch and die as she flipped off the light, plunging the kitchen and breakfast room into darkness. Here in the back yard his eyes adjusted slowly to the return of moonlight. Just enough light to see the outline of the house that held the thing he had squandered. After a while he rose and, though his heart could barely stand the strain of movement, went slowly into the night.

———

SEVERAL DAYS LATER, he spied her car in the parking lot of a wine shop. It was, unmistakably, hers—Duke decal on the rear window, R for realtor sticker on the bumper.

It was a Saturday afternoon. Palmer had gone to Hickory to see what of his relationship with Anna he could rescue. He had bumped into her in a supermarket in Chapel Hill. They had talked. She was wary, but she hadn't objected when he asked if he could visit on the weekend. Palmer didn't reveal much, but he sounded hopeful.

Will was by himself in the truck, headed back to the apartment after visiting Abner Dinkins, who was recovering from triple bypass surgery. He had taken a day off from work to be at the hospital for the operation. Dinkins had at first said he wouldn't go through with the operation. Just let nature take its course, as Barfield Simpson had done. "The hell you say," Will had said. "I don't know anybody else who plays cribbage." Dinkins had taught him the game and they played one night a week at Dinkins's home or Will's apartment. A couple of times, when they met at Will's, Dahlia Spence had joined them. "It's nice that you have your evenings to do things like this," Dinkins had said the last time they played, the evening before the bypass operation.

It was Clarice's car, all right. It was parked in the small lot just to the right of the wine shop. As Will's truck drew even with the shop he saw the two of them through the big front window—Clarice and Fincher Snively. They were in earnest conversation over a bottle of wine, which Fincher held up to the light. He said something, turning to smile at her. She laughed.

Will jammed on the brakes and made an abrupt turn into the parking lot, drawing an angry bleat of horn from the station wagon just behind him. He passed Clarice's car and kept going to the rear of the parking area, wheeled into an open space, and killed the engine.

He sat there for a minute or so, wondering what the hell he was up to. He seemed to be on some kind of autopilot. He might get out of the truck and go into the wine shop and break a bottle of Beaujolais over Fincher Snively's head. What was it Palmer had said just a few days ago about Wingfoot and Peachy? "If he loves her, he ought to fight for her." *But how? How do you engage the enemy when the true enemy is you? And why, when the battle is long over?* Fight for her? Easy for Palmer to say. He hoped Palmer had better prospects in Hickory.

So instead of fighting, he might walk into the wine shop and buy a bottle of Beaujolais himself and pay for it at the counter and never give the slightest hint that he had seen Clarice and Fincher, just let them stare at him while he paid for his purchase and walked out and got back in his truck and left. Or he might do absolutely nothing. What he really should do, of course, was just leave, and do it as unobtrusively as possible so that neither of them saw him and there was no possibility of an awkward moment. That's what he *should* do.

He got out of the truck and walked over to Clarice's car. Her keys were in the ignition, all of them—car, house, business, along with a tiny red Swiss Army knife Palmer had given her for Christmas several years ago—all of it on an ASK A REALTOR key ring. One bad habit she hadn't broken. She might have got rid of him, but she still left her keys in the car.

———

HE WAS SITTING IN Clarice's den, watching a baseball game on television and drinking a beer, when he heard the doorbell ring. He let it ring a couple more times. Maddox was pitching for the Braves. He had his fastball working well and his slider was downright wicked. It was just the fifth inning, but he had already struck out nine. He smoked another one past a Dodger batter, retiring the side. Will heaved himself off the couch and headed for the front hall. But he didn't open the door, not yet.

"Who's there?" he asked.

From the other side: "You know damned well who it is, Wilbur. Let me in."

"Don't you have your keys?"

"Open the door!" she commanded.

He opened the door. She stood there on the stoop, eyes flashing. "I could have you arrested for automobile theft."

"The phone"—he pointed—"is back there in the kitchen. By the way, nice job on the kitchen. I really like the new cabinets and countertops."

He looked out at the driveway where Fincher Snively's Jaguar was idling behind Clarice's car. Fincher peered through the windshield. Will leaned out the door and waved to him. Fincher kept peering. Clarice finally waved him away and he put the Jag into gear and backed out into LeGrand. Clarice glared at Will for another moment, then pushed impatiently past him into the house. Will closed the door.

She turned on him. "You know that I've reported my car stolen."

"No," he said, "I didn't know that. Have they put out an all-points bulletin?"

She gave a little aggravated sound and headed for the kitchen. He went back to the den, picked up his beer bottle, and sat down on the couch. The Braves were at bat, nobody out and Chipper Jones on second. A double? Or a single and a stolen base? Chipper could run pretty well, at least for a white man. It might well be a stolen base.

She stood in the doorway. "You don't watch baseball and you don't drink beer."

He held up his beer bottle. "I am a changed man, Clarice. With my altered circumstances, I've discovered the joys of idleness and dissipation. I've even learned to play cribbage. It is, by the way, pretty good beer. I tend toward the cheap stuff myself. But I see that someone has introduced you to the joys of a nice import. Next thing you know you'll be driving a Saab. Like Morris." He could have said "Jaguar," he thought. Like Fincher, he thought. But he didn't.

She shook her head, then turned off the television set with an angry punch of finger and flounced down in a chair, well away from him. He finished the beer and set the bottle on the coffee table, being careful to wipe the bottom on his pants leg to make sure there was no moisture to make a ring. It was a nice new mahogany coffee table, a low, squarish thing with an open shelf underneath for books and magazines. It matched the nice new end tables and the nice mahogany cabinet of the big new television set. The sofa and chairs, upholstered in a rich nubby-weave red plaid, had mahogany trim. The old den furnishings had been oak. He had liked oak, solid and reassuring. But Clarice was more a mahogany sort of person and she had finally got her way about the den.

There was a soft, comfortable, Saturday afternoon silence about the house. If you listened carefully you could hear the soft *whoosh* of the air-conditioning, the faint drone of a lawn mower over on the next block, the muted splash of the fountain out in the back yard.

"That was a ridiculous thing you did," Clarice said. She sat primly in the chair, knees close together, hands clasped in front of her. She was wearing a smart khaki skirt and a loose-fitting cotton shirt, a paisley sort of thing. Her face was flushed, the color high in her cheeks. God, she looked smashing.

"You realize—no, of course you don't realize—that you made a mess of the company picnic."

"And how did I do that?"

"That's why Fincher and I were in the wine shop. Buying wine for the picnic. Then we walk out and find that the god-damn-car-is-gone," she strung out the words. "Oh," she went on with a wave of her hand, "we went ahead with the picnic. But Fincher and I were an hour late because the police had to come and take a report. And it just cast a pall over everything. My car stolen." She paused, her lips pressed together in a grim line.

Will waited. She would reveal all. She would tell him everything in great detail. And he would listen, nodding to show that he not only heard, but understood. It came to him, how calmly he would be able to sit here and do that, because it was not something, in his earlier life, that he had had time or patience to do. Nor had he understood that such a thing needed to be done. Clarice would begin to talk, to unravel a scenario of one sort or another in fine detail and with frequent digression, and Will would feel himself getting itchy and short of breath, almost a panic kind of thing, and he would *say something.* Then Clarice would stop abruptly and stare at him with a surprised expression as if to say, *Why did you say that?* It didn't matter what he had said, only that he had said *something* in an effort to bring some kind of closure to whatever she was rambling on about.

It had dawned on him once, a few years ago, that she didn't want closure, or an answer, or even a response. She just wanted him to sit there and keep his mouth shut and let her verbally work out whatever it was she was trying to work out, as if the mere matter of words would give shape and meaning to it. The more words, the more definite the shape. He had tried then to be more responsive. Or, more to the point, less responsive. But that was about the time that Palmer had gone off to Duke and Clarice had got busy with the real estate thing. He had been more willing to listen just at the time she had become less talkative. They had missed connections on that one. Now, sitting here in the expanded and redecorated den, surrounded by all this new mahogany and upholstery, he had all the time in the world.

But she surprised him. "I don't want to talk about that. I'm too upset."

Will stood, fished in his pocket for the set of keys, laid them gently on the mahogany coffee table, and sat back down. She stared at the keys, then ran her fingers through her hair. It fell down around her face. It made his heart ache.

"You've been acting ridiculous for a couple of months now." Her voice trailed off and she looked away, out the window toward the back yard. "What's gotten into you?" she asked softly.

It was a long time before he responded. What indeed? Two months in which something—God, fate, the Great Kahuna, sheer blind bad luck—had grabbed him by his ankles and held him upside down while blood rushed to his brain and all manner of flotsam and jetsam and things he thought were irreplaceable fell out of his pockets. Vertical, but upside-down vertical, struggling to get upright again.

"I'm trying to get a grip," he said finally. And that, by golly, was the simple truth.

A long silence. She still wasn't looking at him. "Palmer told me everything," she said.

"I know."

She chewed on her lower lip. He thought she was about to say something sympathetic, but she surprised him again. She turned back to him with a jerk and said, "What did you think? That going to jail would remedy"—a sharp sweep of her hand took in the house, themselves—"all of this? Were you trying to be a hero, Will? A martyr? Looking for sympathy? Or maybe it was like committing suicide. *After I'm gone, they'll be sorry they were so mean.*"

Will shrugged. "I just thought it was the right thing to do. Under the circumstances. No hidden agenda, Clarice."

She turned away again, giving him her profile. He couldn't fathom what she was thinking, not even a hint of it. For the longest kind of time, since their beginning, he had been able to read her, or so he thought. Her face had said everything, hadn't it? Well, come to think of it, no. He had misread, especially there toward the last. Misread and just plain missed.

She stood abruptly. "I don't know why you did it, or why you stole my automobile. Right now, I want you to go."

"I hoped we could talk, Clarice. I've been trying to talk to you since . . ."

"That day you acted like a goddamn fool right in front of my office," she flashed.

"Yes."

She looked down at him. Something tugged at the corners of her mouth, but nothing came out.

Will spread his hands. "Please . . . ," he said quietly.

She sat back down. Now it was her turn to wait.

Will looked her straight in the eye. "I've been coming over here at night." Her eyes narrowed, but she didn't say anything. "Sitting out there in the back yard. Watching you through the window. Thinking. Trying to figure out how and why I screwed up so royally. Trying to come up with some excuses, I suppose. Thinking, 'If I could just talk to Clarice, I could explain how things came to pass, how I toted a lot of baggage around with me and how I let the wrong things get in the way.' But then it came to me that excuses and explanations are lame and late and maybe even irrelevant." He looked down at his feet, then back up at her. Her gaze hadn't left him. "So I stole your keys and came over here and waited for you to come home so I could just say I'm sorry. That's all. I owe you that. And you don't owe me a damn thing. So I guess now that I've said it, we're even again."

Their eyes broke and they both looked away. They both waited.

He could have said more. He could have invoked the name of Sidney Palmer, could have told her about that Sunday night visit. He could have mentioned Palmer, too. *Do* something, *even if it's wrong*. But he didn't, because this wasn't about Sidney and Palmer. It was just about the two of them. After a while, it was obvious she wasn't ready to say anything—maybe not ever, but for sure, not just yet. And he had said quite enough.

He got up and saw himself to the front door. He stepped outside into Saturday afternoon and was just about to close the door behind him when he looked back into the house and saw her standing down at the end of the hallway, framed in the doorway to the den, looking at him. "You wouldn't want to give me a ride to the wine shop, would you?" he asked. "My truck is there."

She didn't say anything for a long time. Then, "When you were out there on the lawn . . ."

". . . at your office. Holding up that sign and stopping traffic and making a ruckus and a fool of myself."

"Yes."

"What about it?"

"I could have had you arrested then."

"You could, indeed. I would have been in deep shit. Why didn't you?"

"I thought, 'He came to fight for me.'"

"Yes. That's exactly why I was there, Clarice."

She hesitated for a moment. Then, was there just the tiniest trace of a smile? "I liked that," she said.

"Then why . . ."

"Because it wasn't enough. And too late."

"Yeah," he said. "I guess so."

"But I'm glad you tried."

"And now?"

"Go get your truck," she said. "It's not too far. The walk will do you good."

He closed the door behind him.

———————

ON SUNDAY NIGHT, he watched enough of the late news on Channel Seven to know that showers were probable tomorrow afternoon. He called Palmer. "I'd like to get an early start in the morning," he said. "If we get way behind on Monday, we're behind all week."

"Wilbur, you are taking this lawn care business entirely too seriously," Palmer said. There was no irritation in it.

"How did Hickory go?"

"Okay."

"Just okay?"

"Are you going to ask me if we made out on the couch?"

"I didn't mean to pry. Just showing fatherly interest."

"Well, I'm on probation," Palmer said. "She thinks maybe I've gotten my act together, but she's not absolutely sure. She was pretty interested when I told her what I'd been doing all summer. She said maybe it had given me a little character."

"Probation," Will said. "It's a start."

He hesitated, thinking maybe Palmer had talked with Clarice since he had gotten back from Hickory, and that if he had, maybe she had told him what had happened Saturday afternoon, at least enough to let Palmer know that he had done *something,* even if it was wrong. Was it? Wrong? Hard to tell.

But Palmer said nothing.

"Seven?" Will offered.

"That's pretty early, Wilbur."

"International House of Pancakes?"

"Seven-fifteen."

He was brushing his teeth before bed when the phone rang.

"All right. Seven-twenty."

"That beard and the glasses are really ridiculous looking," Clarice said. "And you've lost a lot of weight. You really don't look like yourself."

"I'm not myself," he said.

"That was a terrible thing you did yesterday."

"Terrible?"

"Well, not very nice."

"Target of opportunity."

There was a long silence. Music in the background, the public radio station from Chapel Hill. He guessed she was in the bedroom. They had one of those fancy radios that the manufacturer said sounded like a concert hall. He had given it to her as an anniversary present several years ago when they first came out and they had put it on the dresser across the room from their bed and turned it up quite loud when they made love. Beethoven and ecstasy. He stirred, mildly stimulated, at the memory of one time when "Bolero" had been playing. It had been magnificent. It was always good, but with "Bolero". . .

"I just wanted to say," she said, "that I think that was an incredible thing you did."

"Which one?"

"For Palmer."

"Oh."

"And I shouldn't have questioned your motives."

"Only natural, I suppose. I questioned them myself at one point, after I had done it. But when I did it, I just did it."

"That's not like you, Will. Just doing something. You always thought things through."

"One of my most maddening characteristics."

"Yes."

Another pause. He heard her breathing, very light, almost not there at all. "Are you okay?" she asked.

"Yes," he said quickly. "I'm making it."

"If there's anything you need . . ."

He thought about that for a moment. All the things he might need, or at least want. The list was surprisingly short. A little grace, perhaps? We could all use a little grace.

". . . I mean, from the house. Clothes, books, things like that?"

"I don't need anything from the house," he said. "Nothing from the house."

"Well . . ." The way she said it made it sound as if she were ready to hang up.

"What I needed was to say what I said yesterday."

The silence this time seemed to go on forever. Finally she said, "I have . . . an entanglement."

"Interesting way to put it, Clarice. What I can't figure out is, was it cause or effect. I mean . . . what? . . . Did you just stick around until you got a better offer?"

"No, Will. I stuck around until I couldn't stand it anymore."

"It was that bad?" he asked.

"Not . . . bad. I just . . . got weary. Nothing was going to change."

"Except you. You moved on. And I'm not talking about your entanglement, or criticizing you for moving on. But you did change. You found your own pair of britches."

"That's an interesting way of putting it."

"So, you moved on, and you have an entanglement, whether one has anything to do with the other or not. But it's an interesting word, Clarice. Entanglement. An entanglement, I would think, has to go somewhere. One direction or the other."

There was a tiny sound on the other end of the phone, something so brief and small he couldn't tell whether it came from the radio or from Clarice. He waited for something else, some clue, but there was nothing. "Well," he said, "thanks for calling. I've got to get an early start tomorrow. Customers waiting. Palmer and I are having a good summer. Staying busy. Making a living. Catching up on some things."

"I know," she said.

"About the beard and the glasses . . ."

"Yes?"

"I don't need 'em anymore. But I think I'll keep 'em, just for the hell of it. No particular reason. Just for the hell of it."

After he hung up, he sat in the chair by the open window in his boxer shorts. It was too hot to sleep in anything more. He might even take the shorts off and lie atop the sheets and let the small oscillating fan stir the air across his body through the night.

Tomorrow, he would remove the air-conditioning unit from the bedroom window and take it to a repair shop. Rain would cool things off around Raleigh, at least for a day or so, and perhaps the repair shop could get the unit back to him before the weather steamed up again. A little thing like air-conditioning could mean a lot. And he didn't think he'd be taking any more long walks in the middle of the night.

Across the yard, the light was still on in Dahlia Spence's bedroom. She was staying up later than usual these days—engrossed, she said, in a book about a man with a crippling mental illness who had helped to write the *Oxford English Dictionary*. She was reading it aloud to Ethel, her Dalmatian. It was an astonishing story, Dahlia said, astonishing that a keen intellect could co-exist with fevered madness, how one part of the brain could fight so hard to maintain some kind of coherence when all else was chaos and torment. Dahlia thought the madman was brave in his struggle for sanity against such overwhelming odds. "Sometimes," she said, "you just have to grab one small thing and hang on to it for dear life." Maybe, Will thought now, the madman was just trying to be ordinary. Not sane, just ordinary. Or maybe the two things were one and the same.

Mowing grass, as Will was doing, that was pretty ordinary, part of that basic thing that was his life, his existence. He was as dependent on grass as a cow. He had finally, he thought, become ordinary—and in this, even more ordinary than usual. He had learned that many of the lawn care services operating around Raleigh were owned by firefighters who used the businesses to supplement income on their off-duty days. That was an extraordinary thing, being a firefighter. You might be a hero, or you might fall off the back of a speeding truck, as Dahlia Spence's late husband, Ernest, had done. But Wilbur Baggett had no such other existence. He was just an ordinary mower of grass, with miles of green stretching both before and behind him. Mundane, pedestrian, as ordinary as an old bedroom slipper.

If somebody had told him back during his former extraordinary life that he would be existing as he did now, it would have cleaved him with a deep, gnawing sense of loss and yearning. But now it didn't, at least not for those things that he now saw as trappings, fringe benefit, decoration. He did yearn, oh yes indeed he did yearn, for the thing he had lost that was the only thing truly worth yearning for. He ached with the yearning of it, and of the tiny, fragile flame of hope that he now cupped in his hands, protecting from the elements. He had done something. And if it had been the wrong thing, why had she called? And what now?

But then . . . *what if she were to say, "Come home?" What would I make of all the rest of it? Who would I be? Not what, but who?* He might, he suspected, just continue to be ordinary. Like an old bedroom slipper. And that might be the most extraordinary thing of all.

———

DAHLIA SPENCE HAD GIVEN OVER the bay of her garage to his trailer when he had been banished from Morris's driveway. She parked her Oldsmobile now on the gravel next to the house. The garage was a great improvement, once he got the hang of backing the trailer down the driveway and into the bay where it was protected from the elements. He had set up a small maintenance shop against the rear wall—nothing fancy, just some hand tools hanging from pegboard above a workbench he had cobbled together out of two-by-fours and plywood. He had mounted a vise and a grinder on the workbench and he could sharpen mower blades, change oil, wash air filters, replace worn cables, reload string trimmer spools, and the like. He was in the garage on this rainy Monday afternoon, working on his equipment.

"Well, you got me into this goddamned mess," Wingfoot said from the doorway.

Will turned to him with a plastic bottle of thirty-weight motor oil in his hand. "I'm right in the middle of this," Will said, pointing to an old kitchen chair propped against a side wall. "Sit down and be quiet. If you distract me, I'll forget that I've drained all the oil out of my Hy-Ryder and when I crank it up in the morning the engine will seize up and I'll have to have it rebuilt."

"That's a helluva mower," Wingfoot said. "Do you stand on the little platform in the back? Like a Roman chariot? Wilbur Baggett, the Ben Hur of Raleigh lawn care."

"I said, sit down and be quiet."

Wingfoot sat, tilting back against the garage wall in the chair, feet propped on the front rail. He watched in silence as Will finished changing the oil and then cleaned the air filter, washing it in detergent and water and squeezing out the water and setting the filter aside on the workbench to dry.

He turned finally to Wingfoot, who was watching him with a bemused expression. "What?" he asked.

Wingfoot lowered the chair to the ground. "You act like you know what you're doing."

Will shrugged. "What kind of mess have I gotten you into?"

Wingfoot made a face, scrunching up his lips until they almost touched his nose. "Peachy asked me to marry her. She called me in the middle of the night from someplace in Kansas a couple of weeks ago and sang to me and then asked me. She said you told her to do it."

"A couple of weeks ago."

"Yeah."

Will sat down on the back of the trailer, facing Wingfoot. "Well, what have you been doing in the meantime?"

"Pondering."

"And?"

"Well shit, Wilbur. What am I gonna say?"

"I hope you're gonna say yes."

"Why do you hope that?"

Will gave Wingfoot a long look. "How many women have you known in your life, Wingfoot?" he asked.

"Some."

"Anybody like Peachy?"

Wingfoot shook his head.

"If you had to do without her, could you?"

Wingfoot pondered on that for a moment. "I *have* done without her."

"And you have been . . ."

"Miserable."

"Then you can't do without her. She's a magnificent woman. And that has nothing to do with all that Nashville business. She was magnificent before she went to Nashville and she'll be magnificent when Nashville gets finished with her. Good God, man. When a woman writes a love song and calls you on the phone all the way from Kansas to sing it to you and then asks you to marry her . . . well, you're a fool if you can't see. And you've waited two weeks? Pondering? Be a fool in love, but don't be a fool in general."

Wingfoot gave him a wry look. "You're one to speak about fools in love, Wilbur."

That hurt, especially with what had happened over the past couple of days, but he tried to keep it to himself. "It's one thing to love somebody you can't do without, and quite another to love somebody who can do without you. I seem to fall into the latter category, to my everlasting regret."

Wingfoot stared at his hands. "Forget I said that."

He started to tell Wingfoot about Saturday, about the phone call last night, but he didn't. There was something delicate in the air, a mere breath of possibility, and he didn't want to spook whatever it was. Instead, he asked Wingfoot, "Well, what do you think you oughta do?"

Wingfoot drew in a deep sigh. "I guess I oughta say yes, huh?"

Will made a face. "You know, Wingfoot, for somebody who otherwise seems to have his shit together, who seems like he's gotten his life straightened out and overcome whatever kind of setback he had in the past, you sure are acting obtuse about this. Hell yes, you oughta say yes. Go upstairs and use my phone and keep calling all over East Jesus U.S.A. until you find her. And say yes as quick as you can before that magnificent woman changes her mind."

Wingfoot rose and departed.

He was back a half-hour later.

"You did it?" Will asked.

"Yep."

"Congratulations. Now go away and let me finish working on my equipment. Goddamn, Wingfoot. Coming over here and asking for advice to the lovelorn from somebody like me? You must be hard up."

"Yeah. And hard up for a Best Man, too."

"Well, I work cheap," Will said. "If you're asking."

"Yep."

"One other thing. Have you talked to Min about this?"

"Nope." He paused and then asked, "How do you think she'll take it?"

"She'll be just delighted, Cousin. Just delighted."

"Shit."

"Yeah. That's what I think."

24 | Two nights later, Min called. Sobbing. "I need you!"

"I'm coming," he said.

But first he called Wingfoot. "What did you say to Min?"

"I told her everything. About Peachy and the nursery and a lot of other stuff we've avoided talking about."

"What was her reaction?"

"She said, 'Well, then,' and hung up."

Will was on the banks of the Cape Fear by midnight. The house was dark, the doors locked. He went to the back yard and stood under the open second-floor window of Min's bedroom and was just about to call up to her when he stopped himself. No. She was sure to have heard his truck pulling into the yard and stopping next to her car by the back door. She knew he was out here. Well, he could be as perverse as she. He slept in the back seat of her car, which she had neglected to lock. When he woke at first light the kitchen door was standing open. He could smell bacon frying.

He climbed the steps, opened the screen door, peered in. She was at the stove, her back to him. Bacon sizzled in one skillet, scrambled eggs fluffed in another, a pot of grits bubbled next to a platter piled high with pancakes. The Mr. Coffee gurgled on the counter. He kissed her on the cheek. She didn't respond. He fetched a mug from the cabinet, poured a cup, and sat at the kitchen table sipping the hot coffee and coming fully awake, watching her broad, sturdy back. Waiting. When she finished with the bacon she took plates noisily from the cupboard, loaded them with breakfast, and brought them to the table. Enough there to feed a small army, he thought. Enough for a wedding feast. She sat across from him and they ate in silence. He ate what he could, but it made only a dent. Most mornings he had a bowl of shredded wheat and a banana for breakfast. He folded his napkin, tucked it under the edge of the plate, pushed his chair back with a scrape, and rose to get another cup of coffee.

"That's why you're so skinny," Min said when he returned to the table. "Doing menial labor and eating like a bird. You look like a scarecrow with whiskers, Wilbur. Like some near-dead refugee."

Will raised his cup to her in salute. "Okay Min, let's have it."

She speared a thick forkful of pancake and chewed for a good while, washing it down with a gulp of coffee. "I don't want to talk about it."

Will set his cup down rather forcefully on the table, sloshing a little coffee. "Well, we're gonna talk about it. I rousted my weary ass out of an easy chair last night and drove all the way down here . . ."

Min stared at her plate for a moment, then suddenly dropped her fork with a clatter and sprang to her feet. The chair went over backward and she bolted. She was out the door and headed for the stairs by the time Will could get up. He hurried after her, both of them bounding up the stairway. She was surprisingly quick for a hefty woman, and she was slamming her bedroom door behind her by the time he reached it. He banged on the door. "Min, open up!"

"Go back to Raleigh, Wilbur. Leave me alone."

Will tried the doorknob. Locked. "You said you needed me, Min. Well by God, here I am. And I ain't leaving until you tell me what it is you need. I'll stand out here in the hall until you pee in your britches if I have to."

"You don't have to cuss, Wilbur. You never used to use profanity."

"I do a lot of things I didn't used to do."

There was a long silence. He heard her footsteps, moving toward the other end of the room, over by the window. And then her voice, muffled and distant. "He's leaving me."

"He was never here," Will said.

Then the footsteps coming back, fast now, the key rattling in the lock, the door flung open. There was a wild look in her eyes, her hair a mess where she had been clutching at it. "How's she going to take care of him? She spends her time up on a stage shaking her tits and singing hillbilly songs."

"How much do you know about Peachy?" Will asked.

"Enough," she spat.

"She's an intelligent and well-educated woman. She's pretty and talented and graceful. She loves Wingfoot and he loves her."

"You're taking up for her?"

"I'm taking up for both of them. It's the best thing that ever happened to either of them. And I told Wingfoot that if he didn't grab that good woman before she gets away, he's a fool. Damn right, I'm taking up for them."

"Who do you think you are, giving advice?" Her voice lashed at him. "You can't even hold on to your wife or your job."

He fought the urge to fire back. One. Two. Three . . . "I am not the issue here, Min. You are."

"Me? I'm not the one who's running off to Nashville, Tennessee. I'm perfectly happy right here at home, right where I've always been. I don't need Nashville or Raleigh or any other place on earth." She was beginning to cry now and the harder she fought it the worse it got. "I don't need you or Wingfoot or anybody else. I never have and never will." An angry slash of her hand. "Go on back to Raleigh. Take Wingfoot and Miss Peaches Whatever-Her-Name-Is with you. The lot of you can go to hell!"

"Her name is Peachy Delchamps. She and Wingfoot are getting married right here in Baggett House two weeks from tomorrow."

"Here? No!"

"Yes. And as the mistress of Baggett House and Wingfoot's closest living relative, you are by God going to be the gracious hostess or . . ."

"What?"

"I will whip your ass."

Min's mouth dropped open. She stared at him, bug-eyed, and then she seemed to shrink from him. She didn't move a muscle, but something seemed to go out of her. "I'm not a hateful person," she said in a tiny voice.

"No," he said gently, "you are not a hateful person. You're a very giving person. You've given too much, actually. But this thing, you need to give some more."

She stumbled backward and sat down heavily on the edge of her bed, shoulders slumped, eyes downcast. "You don't know . . ."

"And neither do you," he said. "You've got blinders on, Min. Have had for thirty-five years."

She looked up sharply. "What do you mean?"

Will took a deep breath. "You got stuck at eighteen," he said. "And in a way, I got stuck at thirteen. When the plane went down, we all sort of froze. You with some warped notion of responsibility because Uncle French left you in charge. Wingfoot obsessed with West Point because Uncle French told him that's what he needed to do. And me . . ."

"What about you?"

"You stole from me, Min. You stole my parents. You wouldn't let me talk about 'em. You wouldn't let me grieve so I could work my way through it."

"So I'm to blame for all your troubles," she said bitterly.

"Oh, no. I'm entirely to blame. Back yonder at the beginning I was a coward. I should have fought you. But I just did the easy thing. I stuck 'em back in a closet where they wouldn't cause any trouble. I betrayed 'em. And then I went overboard in the opposite direction from what you did." The words were pouring out of him now, giving voice to all that had been seething in him for weeks, maybe years. He could no more have stopped them than he could have stopped life itself. "I reinvented myself," he went on. "A man with no history, no baggage to tote around. Only, the man I invented took over. Ate me alive. Became some sort of monster who was desperate to be liked, but held the people he was supposed to love at arm's length. And then when all that invented stuff went south, I was nobody. I didn't exist, Min. It's one thing not to have a history. It's a damned sight worse to cease existing."

Min's face twisted. "A man with no history. You're not a Baggett," she said. "You don't care a thing . . ."

"And you care too much. Baggett's just a name. We're people, Min. Not a name, people. We stumble and fart around and try to make our way the best way we can. Me, Wingfoot, you, everybody. We try to grab a little love and grace where we can. And I'll tell you what I've learned since I lost my wife and my job, Min. I've learned that a little love and grace is a helluva thing, and you better grab it when and where you can."

She got up from the bed now and went to the window and stood there, arms wrapped tightly around herself, back rigid.

"Min," he said, "I love you. I can't ever make up for what you sacrificed for me and Wingfoot. I can't take all that back and make it right. The only thing I can do is say what's been begging to be said for a long time. And right now I'm saying that Wingfoot and I need you again. And we're expecting you to do the right thing. If being a Baggett means so much to you, then act like one."

She was crying again, shoulders shaking. Will felt a pang of remorse. Did he have to be so brutally honest? Well, yes he did. But it was hard, so very hard, for both of them. All Min had really ever wanted, he thought, was to be needed. And there at the beginning, after the plane went down, he and Wingfoot had needed her desperately. No matter what warped sense of responsibility she had, she had come through when they needed her. And then when they didn't need her anymore they had gone off to their separate lives and left her alone here in this crumbling old house, surrounded by ancient mahogany and boxes of trivia that made up some kind of past you could try to cling to. But mostly, just alone. She had maybe clung to a slender notion over the years that Wingfoot still needed her in some vague fashion, but now that was about to be dashed, too.

They stood there for a long time, the great silence of the old house broken only by Min's soft whimpering. Finally she uncoiled her tightly wound arms and rubbed fiercely at her eyes and then turned back to him, face ravaged. She tried to speak, but the words caught in her throat. She waited, tried again. "The wedding? Here?"

"It's the only thing that will do," Will said. "We are Wingfoot's family and this is our home and he needs us."

He turned then and left. When he climbed into his truck he saw her standing at the bedroom window, watching him.

"I'll be back," he said.

————

WHEN THE GROOM ENTERED from the foyer, he was accompanied by his Best Man and the Best Man's son, who was the ring bearer. It was perhaps a trifle unusual to have a ring bearer who was twenty-three years old, but then the entire business was a trifle unusual.

The bride, for instance, as she entered from the kitchen — tall and stunning in a teal wedding gown — stopped just inside the dining room door where her Nashville band, attired in teal tuxedos with ruffled shirtsleeves, augmented by local musicians Pedro and Cisco, struck up a tune, a sweet and winsome melody. The bride sang lyrics of her own making:

> *"You gotta move heaven and earth*
> *when it gets in the way of your heart;*
> *'Cause you gotta be with the one you love."*

Several people in the audience cried. The ring bearer wiped away a tear or two, but the Best Man thought it might be partly due to his physical condition, he having spent the evening and much of the wee small hours celebrating the upcoming nuptials at Baggett's Place over in Pender County with his cousins Wingfoot and Norville and a multitude of other folk, and having arrived back at Baggett House in a state of befuddlement. Now, with about three hours of sleep and the effects of the previous night still upon him, he was shaky and weepy. A hangover could make you emotionally raw, the Best Man thought, remembering his own similar experience. But all things considered, the ring bearer was bearing up fairly well. It was, indeed, an emotional moment.

For his own part, the Best Man had stayed at Baggett House last evening and spent a quiet few hours with Cousin Min, who was still in a melancholy mood and in need of his company. It seemed to have helped her spirits. She had plied him with an enormous supper and several glasses of scuppernong wine and they had talked at length of the family, of history, of the place and its time. They had not spoken of the things that had been said two weeks before. All that had needed to be said about that had been said then. Will had felt almost light-headed since then, as if some ungainly, lead-assed bird, long nesting in his brain, had taken flight through his ears.

And Min? She sat now dry-eyed in the front row of the audience in the place of honor customarily reserved for the mother of the groom. The parents of the bride were just across the aisle from her, the mother among the weepers, the father beaming proudly. When the bride finished her song, her father rose and joined her as she and the groom and the rest of the entourage assembled at the front of the room where Sheriff Billy Hargreave stood ready to perform the ceremony.

Will felt mildly splendid in his tuxedo, which Palmer had retrieved from the house on LeGrand a couple of days before. The tuxedo fit him comfortably for the first time in several years. And for the first time in three months, he was off probation. There was no legal reason for him not to be in Brunswick County this fine August morning. He would have come anyway, as he had done two weeks before when Min had called, but there was now no need to fear the wrath of Judge Broderick Nettles of Wake County Superior Court. Judge Nettles, in fact, seemed to Will to be a figment of his distant past, as did much that had transpired in the recent few months. He had come, he thought, a long way.

The windows of the dining room were open to the midmorning and a breeze off the Cape Fear River stirred what could otherwise have been a stuffy atmosphere. The dining room table was out in the yard now under the live oak tree, laden with the wedding feast. Its twelve lyre-backed mahogany chairs formed the first row of the seating arrangement, filled in behind by folding vinyl-and-metal seats brought by Sheriff Billy from the Brunswick County Senior

Citizens Center. Min had fussed a bit about that the day before when the dining room was being set up for the ceremony. Vinyl-and-metal was tacky, she said. Inappropriate. But there hadn't been any alternative and it didn't seem to matter here on the wedding day because all of the chairs were filled with people and you could scarcely tell one chair from another. Billy had promised that the vinyl-and-metal would be gone by nightfall.

The multitude included a good-sized contingent from the Nashville music industry, including a reporter from *Country Cookin'* magazine who had arrived the afternoon before and stayed for supper and had pronounced Min's stir-fry vegetables in red-eye gravy sauce the best she had ever tasted (the recipe would appear in *Country Cookin'*s October issue); an assortment of Baggetts, friends of Baggetts, and Peachy fans from Pender County (Min was wary of them, but she had made a commendable effort to be gracious); several members of the 1993 Clemson University women's basketball team; a number of Mexican workers from Wingfoot and Peachy's nursery business (one of whom provided a muted translation of the proceedings to the others); and a good-sized representation from Greenwood, South Carolina. They filled the chairs and spilled out into the adjacent foyer and the parlor beyond and then on out the front door and into the yard where speakers had been set up to broadcast the proceedings inside.

"Well," said Sheriff Billy Hargreave to the assemblage, "here we are. I'm just here to make everything legal and proper, and there's not a lot I need to say, especially after Miss Peachy put so beautifully into song what we're all feeling today. Now, we haven't rehearsed any of this. I just told Peachy and Wingfoot to say to each other what they're feeling this morning. So," he said to the bride and groom, "if you two will join hands and gaze into each other's eyes, the rest of us will just be quiet and listen. And then I'll sort of wrap things up."

"Wingfoot Baggett," said Peachy when she had taken his hands in hers, "you are the light of my life and the crystal clear note of my symphony. There's just nobody else in the world I want to be with, now or ever. I'm glad you let me go off to Nashville and try my wings. I would have stayed here if you'd asked me to. But you didn't, and I love you for that among all the other things. But I'll tell you this, I spent a lot of lonesome nights in Nashville and out on the road. Even with all the good things going on, there was always this empty spot" — she released one hand and tapped her heart — "and I knew exactly what it was."

Peachy took up Wingfoot's hand again and looked over at Will. "Wilbur, I thank you for your telephone call." To the audience she said, "Wilbur called me one night while I was out on the road. What was that place?"

"Newton, Kansas," Will said.

"Right. I was sitting there in my motel room and feeling about as empty as you can get. And then Wilbur called to tell me he had heard my record on the radio. And to make a long story short, he told me to call Wingfoot and sing him a love song. Which I did."

She turned back to Wingfoot. "The way I sang it that night, it said that you ought to be with the one you love. But the version I sang just a minute ago said you've *got* to be with the one you love. So, like Billy says, here we are. Here I am with the one I love and now I don't have to be lonesome and empty when I'm out on the road. When I sing love songs to an audience, you'll know I'm really singing 'em just to you." She paused for a moment, then said, "I guess that does it."

Wingfoot shuffled his feet a little bit and turned loose one of Peachy's hands long enough to tug at the collar of his tuxedo shirt and clear his throat. "I can't top that," he said. He gave a jerk of his head in Will's direction. "Wilbur here told me not to be a fool in general, but that it's okay to be a fool in love. Well, I'm a fool in love. I can't write love songs and I can't sing 'em, but I'll do all those other things a fool in love is supposed to do."

There was a long silence and Sheriff Billy asked, "Is that it?"

"I guess so," Wingfoot said.

"Then you two can put your rings on."

Palmer bore the two rings, plain gold bands, on a small satin pillow which Min had retrieved from a trunk in the attic the day before. It had been used at Baggett family weddings since before the Civil War and was somewhat yellowed and musty-smelling with age, but the fabric was still in decent condition. Min and Palmer had spent a couple of hours up in the attic at midafternoon and had emerged dust-smudged and sweaty with pillow in hand. Palmer confided later to Will that he had never seen such a pile of "family shit." Min had raised the possibility of his writing a history of the Baggett family—after he finished medical school, of course. He had been noncommittal.

He offered up the rings now. Wingfoot took one and slipped it onto Peachy's finger and she reciprocated. Wingfoot held up his hand and looked at the ring closely. "Feels sort of strange," he said. "I've never worn jewelry before." He grinned. "But I think I'll get used to it pretty quickly."

"You'd better," Peachy said. And the entire multitude laughed.

Sheriff Billy pronounced them man and wife and the groom kissed the bride and then they all trooped out into the morning to enjoy the feast and the breeze blowing in off the Cape Fear River.

It was, Will thought, the best wedding he had ever attended.

Will and Palmer wandered down to the river and tossed chunks of french fries to Barney, the old alligator who lounged in the reedy shallows. Was it the original Barney or some descendant? No matter. An alligator went with the place. Will told Palmer how Barney had survived Wingfoot's attempt to dynamite him, how the entire family had been blasted from their beds in the dead of night by the explosion.

Palmer stood gazing at the water, at the gator's knobby leathered back, just barely showing above the surface. "Min told me a little more about your parents while we were up in the attic yesterday."

"Your grandparents."

"I've tried to think of them that way, but I'm not having much success. I just don't know 'em. Daddy Sid and Mama Consuela are the people I think of as grandparents." He turned and looked back at the house, the sprawling lawn party. The house looked the best it had in years. Min had consented to let Wingfoot have it painted for the occasion, and he had taken things somewhat further than that. He had had the stucco repaired, rotting wood replaced, the roof re-covered—a madhouse of activity in the two weeks since Will had last been here. It seemed to sit rather proudly now among the live oaks, presenting its best face to the Cape Fear.

"God," Palmer said. "All this history."

It surprised Will. "Interesting to hear you say that. I told your mother once a long time ago that I didn't have a history, not in the way she understood the term. She fairly reeks with it, and I don't mean that in a bad way, or critical, or anything like that. She comes from a fine family. Sid and Consuela are a little stuffy, maybe, but good people. They have a history."

Palmer waved his arm at the house. "But this is history, too. I know something about Daddy Sid's family, and they don't hold a candle to this. These people go back centuries, Wilbur. Min told me you're named for the original. Squire Wilbur. Helluva guy, the way she tells it."

"Min's always harped on all that stuff," Will said. "I guess I just tuned it out. For me, history began when I left here. But you know, I've thought about the history business a lot lately, at least my particular part of it. And you're the reason."

"Me?"

"You said something back a few weeks ago about my parents. Did I miss 'em? Well, yes, I do. I guess I always did, but I just didn't admit it. Until you said that."

Palmer started to say something, but instead he just smiled. Then he put his arm around Will's shoulder and they walked back to the house.

———

WILL WAS UP EARLY the next morning, intending to hurry on back to Raleigh where work was piling up and customers would be antsy. End of the week, grass growing. People liked to have freshly mowed lawns for the weekend. You couldn't mow every lawn on Thursday or Friday, but you did what you could. It was already Wednesday.

But at breakfast in Min's kitchen Palmer said, "No. We're not going back until this afternoon." He had been up even earlier than Will. He looked clear-eyed and fresh-faced this morning. Scrubbed and neatly dressed, but not as buttoned-down as he would have been a few months ago. Perhaps the summer had something to do with it. On the job, he had taken to wearing old T-shirts and cutoff jeans and a ratty pair of sneakers. He was browned by the sun. Some days he didn't shave. He had peroxided his hair, showing up one morning a month ago with it bleached a fine, almost-white yellow. His mother had raised hell at that, he said. He looked forward to going to Greensboro that weekend. "Mama Consuela will shit," he said. He had reported back on Monday that the Greensboro Palmers had gone to enormous lengths to avoid saying anything about his hair. As he was about to depart, he finally asked them what they thought. "It will grow out," Consuela had said. It was multihued now, darker strands growing in among the lighter. Palmer said that if he didn't make it in medical school, he would become a cartoon character like Funky Winkerbean and play air guitar. He could be, Will thought, quite astonishing. Wingfoot must have thought so too, thought enough of Palmer to take him off to a night of frivolity in Pender County, the way he had done with Will back yonder.

"We've got work," Will said, protesting around a mouthful of Min's eggs scrambled with chunks of french fries left over from yesterday's wedding reception. That had been Peachy's idea: barbecue, slaw, french fries; gallons of incredibly sweet iced tea, so thick a spoon might float in it. And for dessert, handmade and hand-scooped ice cream.

Min turned from the stove and looked at Palmer. Something passed between them, but Will had no clue.

"Why aren't we going back this morning?" Will asked. He looked again at Min, but she had given him her back.

"Because there's something we need to do here."

"What?"

"Something you should have done a long time ago." Palmer looked at his watch. "Eat up, Wilbur. It's time to go."

––––––––

IT WAS 9:45 WHEN they left the house in the truck, Palmer driving, an old manila envelope on the seat between them. Will picked up the envelope. "What's this?"

"Later," Palmer said.

It was not until they turned off Highway 133 onto the grounds of the tiny Brunswick County airport near Southport that it began to dawn on Will. Palmer stopped the truck next to the concrete ramp where several single-engine planes were parked—one of them with its doors open, the young pilot circling it, checking things out, testing the control surfaces with his hand. Palmer got out of the truck and stood with the door open, waiting. Will sat there staring at the plane, feeling something he thought might be panic rising in him. He shook his head slowly. "Palmer . . . I don't know . . ."

"It's not just for you. It's for me, too."

They took off, climbing through a thin layer of clouds that had drifted in on an ocean breeze, breaking free at five thousand feet. Palmer sat in front with the pilot, a map spread across his lap, both of them wearing headsets. Will was in the back, just behind the pilot, his ears filled with the steady drone of the engine as the pilot leaned it out and set the trim. The manila envelope was beside him on the empty seat.

Fifteen minutes into the flight, Palmer turned and looked back at him. His eyes sought out the envelope and he mouthed the word *open*. Will did, understanding that it had come from the attic, from Min, from the hidden-away part of his life.

The young man in the yellowed photograph was leaning on a golf club—a driver, from the length and shape of it—dressed in casual slacks and open-necked knit shirt, grinning out from under a snap-brim cap, one two-toned golf shoe crossed jauntily over the other ankle. He stood on a tee, a sweep of tree-lined fairway behind him, green and sand traps just visible over his shoulder. The young man looked like he owned the place. The young woman was holding on to the young man's arm with one hand. In the other, she held a fistful of cash. She was looking up at him with something between amusement and adoration. They were young and fresh and full of life. Just the two of them. Tyler and Rosanna.

The same photograph was in the newspaper clipping. GOLFER AMONG MISSING IN PLANE DISAPPEARANCE.

> *. . . massive search on land and at sea, headed by the Civil Air Patrol . . .*

Will peered out the side window of the plane. The clouds were broken now, showing patches of green and brown, a river glinting in sunlight. Palmer turned again and handed him the map. It had a plastic overlay on which he had drawn with a red grease pencil — a straight line from Southport to Lake City, then just south of Sumter, the curve beginning, becoming more and more pronounced until it was a great sweeping arc down toward Orangeburg and St. George and Monck's Corner, across the expanse of the Francis Marion National Forest, and finally crossing the coastline just below McClellanville. The red line went to the edge of the map where it was all colored blue now. ATLANTIC OCEAN, it said.

He felt the plane bank almost imperceptibly, beginning its gentle turn in clear sky. The upper reaches of Lake Marion off to the left. And then the twin ribbon of Interstate 26 headed southeast toward Charleston.

> *. . . spotted on radar by air traffic controllers in Columbia . . .*

He looked up at the ceiling of the plane, at the shiny nozzle of the air vent. His hand on the nozzle for a moment, feeling the cold metal, then turning it. A soft whoosh of air on his face. He lowered his hand to his lap, then closed his eyes. Sudden, wrenching memory of a night huddled in a corner of the tree house, wracked with shame, guilt, betrayal. A wave of nausea swept over him now. His vision swam. Then a hand on his knee. Palmer. *Are you okay?* He nodded weakly and turned away again to the window. He would turn back if he could. But he couldn't.

They flew on. Cultivated fields, pine forest, cross-hatched streets of small towns beneath them. Interstate 95 now, then again across I-26. Charleston off to their right, barely visible through the haze. The unending green of the national forest. And finally, the yawning Atlantic. Crossing a narrow strip of beach, dun-colored from this altitude. Out, out across the steel grayness and on and on until there was nothing but empty sky and empty water that had no beginning and no end. Only, there was an end somewhere. An end so alone and final that it left a great, aching hole in the ocean somewhere out here, a hole so profound that if you went forever — as far out and as far down as you could go — you would never find its bottom.

He should be overcome with emotion now, out here in this vastness, coming at long last to visit the graves of his parents. There should be hot, cleansing tears. But he felt empty, drained, casting about in search of people and things that had eluded him for a great long while.

There were no tears. Instead, there was the dawning realization that Tyler and Rosanna weren't out here, any more than if they were a pile of dust-becoming bones beneath a marble slab somewhere on land. They were the people in the picture. *You're the spitting image of your daddy,* Cousin Norville had said. But it was more than that. They were himself, part of his essence, their echoes and hauntings, and that was something he must consider carefully and at length in the days ahead. Finally, after all this time, must consider. And grieve over, if that's what it took. Grieve and celebrate. Wasn't that what you did when somebody died? Even if it took eons to do? No, Tyler and Rosanna weren't out here, and he couldn't grieve hot tears now and put them to rest. They were himself and always had been and always would be. They were himself and they were his son, sitting up there in the front seat. The living part, that was the thing—not what was lost, but what was left. It was all a man had to go on, what you had to make do with.

He looked down again at the Atlantic, at a tiny break in the gray made by the white wake of a sailboat. Even from five thousand feet you could see that it was a sleek thing in full rig. Sailing with the wind or against? He couldn't tell. Under way, that was the thing. Then he lost sight of it as the plane banked again, turning back at the point beyond which it could not safely go, heading back toward land.

He felt his son's touch, strong and steady on his shoulder. He turned from the window and looked at Palmer and smiled and took his hand and held it tightly. He did not, would not, let go until they were firmly back to earth.

Back at the house, he said to Min, "You should go."

"You're probably right," she said. "Maybe later."

"Don't wait until it's too late. I almost did."

25 | THEY WERE ON THE BELTLINE north of downtown, three lanes of brisk midafternoon traffic, headed west toward the Glenwood interchange and then to a neighborhood near Crabtree Valley Mall. The next job was a favor to Dahlia Spence—an elderly friend and fellow garden-clubber who had fallen off her riding lawn mower the week before and was limping about the house,

bruised and sore, unable to mow her lawn. The house wasn't close to anything else they had on the schedule that day and it would cost them an extra half-hour just to get there, but Will had promised that morning that they would work it in.

Palmer had groused about it. "We'll be mowing until dark. Trying to get the last pound of flesh?"

"Of course." Tomorrow, he would be alone. Tomorrow, Palmer started back to medical school. There were forty-two regular customers now, plus an occasional add-on like this one. Will wasn't sure how he'd manage by himself. At a gallop, he supposed. One thing about it, he was making a living, even after splitting everything fifty-fifty with Palmer during the summer. Palmer kept grousing about that, too. It was Will's equipment. He should get more than half the income. But Will insisted. Palmer had some money of his own in the bank now. He would still need help from Sidney and Consuela during the school year, but not as much. He seemed to take some satisfaction in that, and his grousing was half-hearted.

Cruising along at fifty-five in the left lane. Peachy on the radio:

You gotta be with the one you love . . .

It was number five on the Billboard Country Top Fifty. RCA had released it the week after the wedding. Peachy had wanted to keep the song just to herself and Wingfoot, but Wingfoot said something that sweet ought to be shared with the rest of the world. Wingfoot was becoming a regular sentimental old fart. He and Peachy had called from Jackson Hole, where they were honeymooning, and had sung the song in duet to Will. It was awful. Wingfoot couldn't sing worth a damn. Besides, Will didn't think he needed anybody to tell him he should be with the one he loved. Maybe they ought to call and sing it to Clarice.

"She is one more hunk of woman," Palmer said. He leaned against the passenger-side door, elbow propped on the window frame, fingers of the other hand tapping time on the dashboard.

Wind rushed past the open windows, rumble of traffic mingling with the music. They had never found time to get the air conditioner fixed, not the one in the truck. But then they had decided that it made no sense to ride in air-conditioning anyway when you were between jobs. It just made you feel that much hotter when you climbed out and revved up the equipment again. So with the passing of weeks they had gotten fairly used to the heat of summer. They were, Will thought, adaptable.

"Peachy could whip me in a fair fight," Will said now.

"Would you fight fair?"

"Of course not."

Palmer shook his head. "We shouldn't be talking about Mrs. Wingfoot Baggett like this. It's disrespectful."

"But she is, as you say, one more hunk of woman. I am mildly stimulated just thinking about her."

Palmer gave him an odd look. There it was again, the one unresolved matter here in the shank of the summer, hanging in the air between them. He had done what Palmer asked. He had done *something,* even if it was wrong. Apparently it was. The ball was on Clarice's side of the net and there was no hint of a return. Maybe he should tell Palmer that, tell him right now on their last day together before Palmer resumed his former life. He opened his mouth to speak, then . . .

"Whoa!" he yelped as a green Jeep Cherokee drifted into the lane just ahead of them. He mashed down on the horn with the heel of his hand and braked sharply, the equipment-laden trailer rattling in protest behind, trying to ride up on the hitch. The Cherokee kept drifting, barely missing his front bumper.

Palmer bolted upright. "She must be drunk."

Will, fighting the steering wheel, trying to keep the trailer from fish-tailing on him, got a brief glimpse of a woman behind the wheel of the Cherokee. He watched, amazed, as it kept going to the left, clear across the lane, and then smacked sideways into the concrete median with a screech of anguished metal. *Holy shit. I am seeing a wreck.* Sparks flew as the Cherokee plowed along the median, the entire left side scraping the concrete. Something flew off, bounced on the pavement, then *thumped* underneath the truck as they passed over it. The force of the impact threw the Cherokee off the concrete, back into the lane just ahead. It seemed to shudder there for a moment, then started drifting left again.

"Dad, something's wrong with her!"

Will glanced in his rearview mirror. Traffic was slowing, dodging bits of debris in the roadway. Will had the truck under control now, keeping it steady. He winced as the Cherokee bounced off the concrete again, tearing a big piece of metal from the left fender, showering the highway and the truck with glass from a shattered headlight. Will turned the steering wheel to the right, easing the truck and trailer into the center lane, out of the direct line of fire. They could see the woman clearly now, slumped forward in the shoulder harness, being slung back and forth like a rag doll as the Cherokee whacked the median again and caromed off. Her arm must be caught in the steering wheel, he thought, pulling it left.

"She's unconscious!"

Another glance at the rearview mirror. There was a lot of open road behind them, traffic in all three lanes braking, giving the disaster ahead a wide berth. Somebody would be on a cell phone, calling the cops.

Palmer pounded the dashboard. "We gotta do something!"

"Us? What?"

"I don't know! She's gonna get killed."

The Cherokee whanged against the concrete. Chunks of metal and glass flew, raining on the cab of the truck. They both ducked. The Cherokee was tearing itself apart. "We gotta get it stopped!" Palmer yelled.

"How?"

"Use the truck!"

He had an insane thought—an old Western movie where the hero stops the runaway buckboard by leaping from his speeding horse onto the backs of the terrified buckboard team. Only that was the movies, where the hero always won and got the girl and didn't run the risk of splattering himself all over the Raleigh Beltline.

The Cherokee hit the median again. Something big came loose from the front of it, got airborne and flew over the top of the Cherokee, narrowly missing the truck as it sailed past. "Do it, Wilbur!" Palmer screamed. "Goddammit, just do it!"

Awwwww God! He stepped on the gas and closed the distance to the Cherokee, giving it plenty of room to the right. It hit the barrier again, careened off, then smacked it again. Something banged off the side of the truck cab not far from his head. He steered with his right hand and used the left to frantically roll up the window. Just in time. Another piece of debris hit the glass, leaving a nasty crack from top to bottom.

They were parallel with the Cherokee now. Heart in his throat, blood pounding in his ears, breath coming in gasps. "Hold on!" he yelled. Palmer grabbed the door handle with one hand and gripped the edge of the seat with the other. Will gave it a little more gas, pulling the truck a couple of yards ahead of the Cherokee. Then he gritted his teeth and turned the steering wheel sharply to the left. A horrible explosion of grinding metal as the Cherokee hit the truck just behind the cab. The impact almost tore the wheel from his hands. He fought frantically to hold on, pulling hard left, forcing the Cherokee into the barrier, trapping it between the truck and the concrete, the two vehicles locked in a death grip. The side window shattered, glass peppered his face. Then a powerful blow to his head as it smacked against the door frame. Glasses flying, blood in his eyes. Palmer screaming. He manhandled the steering wheel, using the weight of the truck and the trailer full of equipment to battle the Cherokee. His foot found the brake and he jammed down hard. Smell of burning rubber from the squawling tires, everything coming unhinged. In the rearview mirror he saw something big and yellow launched from the trailer—the Hy-Ryder. Then the trailer itself, the left side rising up in the air, toppling to the right, another terrible screech of metal as the trailer floundered on its right side onto the highway, spilling equipment and gas cans, trying to tear loose from the truck. A sudden eruption of flame back somewhere behind. He couldn't see now, but he stood on the brake, willing the careening mass of blasted, agonized metal to a grinding stop. Smoke. Fire. Stench of disaster. And then he blacked out.

———

HE DIDN'T REMEMBER sitting up on the stretcher, didn't remember talking to the firefighters or the paramedic who was trying to get him to lie back down, but there he was on the front page of the Raleigh *News and Observer,* looking like a survivor of a terrorist bombing—singed hair and beard, face blackened and blood-streaked. He stared for a long time at the photo, and at the one next to it, an old picture of him standing in front of the weather map at Channel Seven. They didn't look at all like the same person. But then, he thought, they weren't. The guy at the weather map was a figment of somebody's imagination. A made-up thing, like a cowboy hero rescuing a pretty girl from a runaway buckboard.

"You look like hell," Palmer said. He sat on the edge of Will's hospital bed. There was a strip of white bandage high on Palmer's forehead. Five stitches to close the cut made by a piece of flying glass. But otherwise, he was unhurt.

"I *feel* like hell." He would have nodded, but it still made him a little woozy to move his head. Concussion. Compound fracture of his left arm just below the elbow. Enough bumps and bruises to make him feel ancient and used up. The young woman in the Cherokee had come out of it best of all. Not a scratch on her, even after all that hurtling and smashing and coming-apart. A month pregnant, and no damage there, either. Probably what caused her to black out, the doctor had told the *News and Observer.*

Will had a sudden rush of panic. "The customers . . ."

"Buddy's Lawn Service," Palmer said. "I gave 'em the list. They'll take care of everybody and send you half the money." Palmer took the paper from him and turned to an inside page where there were more photos and sidebar articles. He folded it so Will could hold it in one hand and read:

> . . . *owner Buddy Slayton said his company would also provide Baggett with equipment while he replaces his own, all of which was destroyed in the wreck. "This guy's a credit to lawn care professionals everywhere," Slayton said.*

Palmer took the paper from him and put it on a table next to the window. There was a big stack of get-well cards there and some flowers sent by the young woman who had interviewed him for Dan Rather's newscast. There had been a lot of other flowers, but at his insistence, they had sent most of them on to a nursing home recommended by Dahlia Spence.

"My dad the hero," Palmer said drily.

"It was your idea," Will said.

"That's what you kept yelling at the scene. 'It was his goddamned idea.' Like I was insane or something."

"I would have cut and run."

"But what are you gonna do with your son sitting there beside you yelling, *'Do it!'*?"

"Yeah."

Palmer headed for the door. "Get some sleep."

"Where are you going?"

"To be a doctor."

"Next time, maybe *you* can sew me up."

Palmer stopped in the open doorway. "A helluvan end to the summer." He smiled, mostly to himself. "A helluva summer." He hesitated for a moment and then he said, "I told Daddy Sid and Mama Consuela. About medical school and everything."

"Everything?"

He nodded. "It just seemed like the right thing to do."

"What did they say?"

Palmer smiled again. "They just went right on with their dinner."

———

"IT WILL BE," Morris deLesseps said, the "damndest press conference in the history of Raleigh." He sat in a chair next to Will's bed, one trim leg hiked over the other. He was wearing jeans, scuffed work boots, and a short-sleeved denim shirt, open a few buttons from the top, revealing chest hair. A hard hat, the kind construction workers wore, was on the floor beside him. He was, he had explained, doing all the legal work for a developer who was adding a couple of hundred acres' worth of apartments and homes to North Raleigh's sprawl. Spending a lot of time on the job site, he said. Fascinated by heavy equipment, he said. They had even let him drive a bulldozer.

"The mayor will present you with a framed resolution passed by the City Council, commending you for your act of bravery," Morris said, "and he'll announce that you've been nominated for a Carnegie hero's medal."

Morris went on to say that the governor would also attend and present Will with a full pardon, expunging from his record any mention of past misdeeds. Along with the pardon, he would receive from the governor the Order of the Long Leaf Pine, North Carolina's highest award for distinguished citizenship.

The Raleigh Chamber of Commerce, in conjunction with the Raleigh Professional Lawn Care Association, would present him with the keys to a new Ford truck to replace the one that had been totaled in the wreck.

And the Raleigh Coalition of Garden Clubs would make him an honorary member. Will could see the fine hand of Dahlia Spence in that.

"But here's the kicker," Morris said. "The deal to sell Channel Seven has fallen through."

"What? I thought the FCC had approved it."

"They did. But Spectrum, it turns out, is in deep financial doo-doo. Debt overload, maybe some hanky-panky with the books. The chairman of the board has resigned. Auditors are crawling all over the place. So they've pulled the plug on the Channel Seven purchase."

"Ox in the ditch," Will offered, trying for something that would go along with Morris's construction persona.

"Yeah. Well, they had to pay a million dollars to get out of the deal, so now Roger Simpson's still got his TV station. He's decided he likes being the boss, so he's going to keep it. And . . ." he paused for effect, ". . . he wants you back."

Will felt his mouth drop open, but nothing came out.

"Name your price. An ironclad lifetime contract."

"Why?" Will managed.

"They're in deep doo-doo, too. They came in second in the ratings in July. Place is in chaos. And here you are, a front-page gen-you-wine gold-plated hero. Prophet with honor in your own country. Savior of Channel Seven. As I said, name your price. They'd like to announce at the press conference that you'll be back."

"I don't know what to say."

"Will," Morris said, "it's time for you to return to reality."

"Which is?"

"You're gonna get it all back, old son. The fickle finger of fate has turned. It's no longer pointing at Will Baggett."

"Get it all back, huh?"

"Fame and fortune, old son. They've already ordered billboards."

"Well," Will said, "I'll be damned."

———

WINGFOOT AND PEACHY CAME the next day, back now from Jackson Hole and catching a plane in Raleigh for Nashville. Peachy's song was number one in *Billboard*. Will winced when she gave him a hearty hug. But it felt good. It had been a while since a woman had hugged him.

He told them about the press conference. The pardon. Channel Seven.

"Have you said yes?" Wingfoot asked.

"I told Morris I'd think about it."

"Well, think about this, too. We need somebody to run the nursery."

"But I can't speak Spanish," Will said.

"You could learn," Peachy put in. "You didn't know anything about running a lawn service three months ago, but you've learned. And Cisco is making some headway in English."

"You could live with Min and commute," Wingfoot said. "She told me to tell you she'd love to have you. For sure while you mend, and for as long as you want to stay afterward."

He tried to picture himself back on the banks of the Cape Fear, for good this time—letting the evenings settle gently around him after a long day among the rows of growing plants, watching the tugs and barges pass on the river, leaving wakes that lapped gently against the marshes where old Barney snoozed. Just sit and feel the quickening breeze off the ocean that would soothe the afternoon's heat, and then eventually a thundershower to chase him inside. Easy to stay a night and a morrow and beyond, to sleep among the massive mahogany pieces upstairs and let time spin out on its own and carry him along like the Cape Fear current, down to the sea and out where creatures large and small swam among the graves of the missing. Souls of seamen—shipwrecked on treacherous shoals, foundered in raging seas, torpedoed by German U-boats. Four people in an airplane. All resting quietly, lost to the living, who—by bits and pieces—had to seek them out, wherever and whoever they were, and then go about reclaiming them. It was, he thought, a sort of deep sea diving.

"Why me?" he asked.

"Because you're ready to start growing things. Some folks make things grow and some folks cut things down, and I think you've progressed to the point that you can be a grower, not a cutter."

"It's a nice offer," Will said.

"You can buy into the business."

"That would be good."

"So?"

"I'll think about it."

———

HE LAY AWAKE IN the after-midnight darkness pondering it all. A nurse came in and gave him a pain pill, and he thought he might sleep after that. But all it did was muddle his mind. So about four o'clock he got up and somehow managed to pull on clothes over his broken arm and aching body. He opened the door and peered into the hallway. He could hear a mutter of voices down at the nurse's station, but there was nobody in sight. He closed the door behind him and headed for the elevator.

Downstairs, a woman in a nurse's uniform was getting out of a cab. He took it and went to an all-night coffee shop on Hillsborough Street, thinly populated with bleary-eyed college students who gave him odd looks. His clothes were the ones he had been wearing in the truck on the Beltline. He felt his face. A couple of days of stubble, bandage covering stitches on his chin.

Coffee helped. He drank three cups, then paid and went outside and stood on the sidewalk in the cool air. Summer nearly gone, fall a few weeks away. And then the rest of his life, whatever he chose to do with it. An occasional car passed, but the street was mostly quiet. There was just the faintest hint of approaching dawn over downtown to the east, down where they would be setting up in a couple of days in the state capitol rotunda for the press conference to welcome him back to . . . what was it Morris had called it? Reality?

He looked up, seeing the dim outline of stratocumulus clouds beyond the glare of the street lamps. The untrained observer might see stratocumulus and think rain was on the way. But a weatherman knew better. Not much moisture there. Probably clearing by midmorning. A good day. For whatever.

He felt clearheaded now. Not very quick at all, but very much alive. It came to him then, the thing he had been gnawing at since Morris had showed up, and then Wingfoot and Peachy. Worrying it like a dog with a bone. And now it came to him, what he should do with the next few minutes of his life.

He started walking. Maybe some other stuff would come to him. It did.

By the time he had gone the first block, limping along and feeling ancient, he had decided that he didn't want to be Raleigh's Most Popular Weatherman anymore. And as much as he felt drawn to the Cape Fear and Pender County, to riverbank and fields of growing things, he knew that wasn't the right thing either. Easy, but not right.

He stopped, full of the knowledge of it. There was a pay phone across the street.

"Up early," he said when Palmer answered.

"Yeah. Studying gross anatomy."

"There's nothing gross about anatomy," Will said. "The human body is a beautiful thing."

Palmer laughed. "Not the way I get to see the human body." It was a good, easy laugh.

"Have you named your cadaver?"

"Mabel. About forty-five years old, five-three, just over a hundred pounds. Died of asphyxiation. May have been a house fire, but no tissue damage."

"Wonder what her history is."

"They don't tell you that."

"Everybody's got a history."

"Well," Palmer said, "I guess Mabel's history just belongs to Mabel."

"It'll have to do, I suppose."

"How are you feeling?" Palmer asked.

"My physical condition?"

"Not really."

"I'm okay," Will said. "Maybe even better than okay. I've been meaning to ask you, have you seen my Captain Saturday cap?"

"Not since the wreck. Probably got messed up and thrown away. Why?"

"Well, I guess I need a new one."

A long silence. "Really?"

"Yeah. I've thought about it."

Palmer said, "Well, I'm glad. It's something you're good at."

"I guess so."

"And . . . what else? What about the other?"

———

THE EARLY LIGHT WAS much stronger by the time he reached LeGrand, a couple of blocks from the pay phone. The first rays of sun were dappling the tops of the oaks along the street. He stopped on the sidewalk and looked at the house. A light was on back in the kitchen, another peeping through the plantation shutters in the upstairs bedroom. Plantation shutters looked nice, he decided. They would do just fine.

He knocked on the door.